A West Line Ranch Novel

Western Heat

Also by Caroline Richardson

Out of His League

A West Line Ranch Novel

Western Heat

Caroline Richardson

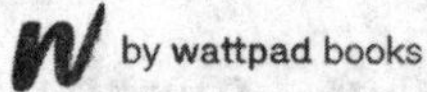

An imprint of Wattpad WEBTOON Book Group

Published in Canada by Wattpad WEBTOON Book Group, a division of Wattpad WEBTOON Studios, Inc.

36 Wellington Street E., Suite 200, Toronto, ON M5E 1C7 Canada

www.wattpad.com

First W by Wattpad Books edition: January 2026

ISBN 978-1-99834-137-5 (Trade Paper original)
ISBN 978-1-99834-138-2 (eBook edition)

Library and Archives Canada Cataloguing in Publication information is available upon request.

Printed and bound in Canada

1 3 5 7 9 10 8 6 4 2

Cover illustration by Art of Nora
Cover design by Monique Narboneta Zosa
Typesetting by Delaney Anderson

For Royce.

I found home in the least expected place when I met you.

AUTHOR'S NOTE

Dear Readers,

Western Heat is a contemporary romance that features characters who experience several heavy topics that some may find uncomfortable to read.

Themes of grief, parental abandonment, and childhood trauma are present, as well as mentions of drug and alcohol addiction. There are also some scenes that involve fist fighting, injury, and violence, as well as consensual, descriptive sex. It is my hope that I have portrayed the characters experiencing these themes in a realistic and positive way.

Your mental health is important. Please reach out on my social media @carolinerichardsonauthor if you have any questions or wish to learn more about any of the situations and themes within this book.

CHAPTER ONE

The big black car drove up the lane toward the barn, pulling up just short of the doors. Dust swirled, coating the shiny paint with a fine film of good country dirt.

Liz leaned against the door frame, arms crossed, a frown on her face. The only time black cars like this showed up was when something bad was coming. The past few weeks had been nothing but bad, so her radar was up. She straightened and steeled herself to deal with whoever it was that had arrived.

The driver-side door opened and her stepfather's attorney poked his salt-and-pepper head out, expensive sunglasses winking in the early afternoon sun.

"Hello, there!" he shouted as he waved, a big, lawyer-sized grin on his face. Liz's insides clenched. It wasn't that Frank was a terrible person; he was nice enough. It just meant dealing with more of the shit left behind when Brett West had keeled over three weeks ago, dead as a doornail, leaving the entire ranch, and her family, in the lurch.

"Frank! What brings you out this way?" she asked, being as friendly as possible and walking toward the car, wiping her hands down her jeans.

Frank grabbed her hand and shook it vigorously as he lifted his sunglasses.

"Elizabeth, my girl! I'm here with some paperwork for your mom, Tanner, and Brady to sign. Going to finally read this dang will too. They about?"

Liz nodded and pointed back at the cattle operation barns. "I'll walk you over to the boys. Good drive from the city?"

Frank nodded and hefted his briefcase, smiling again, a flash of perfect white teeth punctuating the moment as he slammed the car door. Liz wondered why he couldn't have couriered the paperwork, but then she didn't pretend to understand how legal stuff worked. Plus, you had to be in person to read a will, didn't you?

They walked in silence, Liz's well-worn work boots a contrast to Frank's shiny dress shoes. They were expensive leather; she could at least tell that. They'd buried Brett in his best boots, a beautifully tooled pair of Boulets that he hadn't been able to wear for years because his gout made wearing them painful. She hoped, wherever he was, that he was enjoying the fact that he'd gotten to wear them one more time.

Tanner was coming around the corner of the barn when they walked up, and he stopped, his frown mirroring Liz's.

"Frank! What brings you out this way?"

Frank chuckled and stepped forward, shaking Tanner's hand. Tanner's eyes narrowed, and he shared a look with Liz. Obviously he was also feeling apprehensive about an unexpected visit from his dad's lawyer.

"I have some papers for you to sign, son, and I need to chat with you, Peony, and Brady. I also have the will ready to read."

Tanner nodded and gestured to the office off one side of the large cattle barn. Liz turned to go. This was none of her business; she wasn't blood family. She had things to do.

"Liz, wait. You're part of this family too."

She turned. Tanner was beckoning her with an outstretched hand, waiting for her to follow them. She sighed and followed him reluctantly. Damn it, he was right. Her mother might need her.

Tanner jabbed angrily at his phone with one finger as they entered the office, and a few minutes later her mother poked her head in the door.

"Frank! What brings you out this way?" she said as she sat in one of the beat-up old chairs by Brady's desk, shooing a cat from it with little kissy noises. The cat scurried out the door toward the main barn, hissing. Liz wished she could do the same thing, hightailing it out instead of clamping down on the uneasy feeling something bad was about to happen.

Frank chuckled again and threw up his hands, his grin wider, the humor in him bubbling out. "If Brady asks me the same thing, I may just lose my mind."

Liz smiled despite her sour mood. Family thought alike, it seemed.

"Now, Frank, don't you dare. I need that mind to deal with the mess my husband went and put us in," Peony chided, her own large smile mirroring his. Liz watched her mother delicately cross her legs, wincing slightly at the pain, and she gave her a concerned look, to which her mother made a sourpuss face back.

"Frank! What brings you out—" Brady said, then stopped as everyone else broke into laughter.

Frank threw up his arms, and Brady looked around in confusion, but let it go as Frank pulled his briefcase over and opened it, signaling it was time for business.

"Okay. I have some standard forms for the old man's personal bank accounts, that kind of stuff," Frank said as he passed a sheaf of documents to Peony. She glanced at them quickly then handed them to Tanner, who then proceeded to read them over carefully.

"Says here to transfer all remaining personal balances to the working accounts on the ranch, then close them. Can he do that?

What about Peony?" Tanner asked abruptly, looking up sharply from the papers. "Doesn't she get to have a livable income?"

"Now, hang on, Tanner. I'm sure that's not the case," Peony said, while Brady peeked over Tanner's shoulder. Tanner pointing out the line to him, and Brady sucked in a breath.

"All of it?" he murmured, eyes swiveling to his stepmother.

Frank folded his hands, and Liz's guts clenched. Here it was. The real reason he'd driven out with the documents and the will on the same day, instead of sending them by fax or email. She knew it. Bad was happening.

"Jesus, Frank. What is it?" Peony said quickly. "I know that look. Something's up. Enough with the paperwork and will reading. Why are you really here?"

Frank gazed around the room and nodded. "Okay, okay. Now that the death certificate is stamped, I can let you in on Brett's final wishes. He asked me not to until it was time."

"Time for what?" Tanner asked, setting the papers down and folding his arms, his eyes snapping fire. He was close to popping, his famous temper simmering near the surface, his jaw so tight he could probably pulverize diamonds between his teeth.

"Well, I don't know how much you know. But I was able to contact Jake," Frank said, frowning. "He's due here this afternoon, and then I can read your father's will."

"Who the hell is Jake?" Brady asked, coming around to perch on the desk, his own arms folded in mirror of his brother's.

"So you don't know. Shit," Frank muttered, and ran a hand down his face. He glanced at Liz's mother, who looked guilty and averted her eyes, hunching with the stress of that statement.

"Know what?" Tanner growled through his teeth, standing up and balling his fists. Brady put a hand on his shoulder, then shook his head when Tanner looked back at him. Seeing Peony's hands move to her chest, Liz went to her mother's side.

"Mom?" she murmured, but her mother wouldn't look up. Her mother knew who Jake was. That much was certain.

"He's their older half brother. Your, uh, step–half brother, I suppose," Peony said quietly, gesturing over at Tanner and Brady. "Heather's son."

Tanner sat back on the desk with a *thunk*, and Brady went a little wide-eyed and ran a hand over his head, his hair flopping through his fingers.

"Wasn't she Dad's girlfriend when he took over the ranch?" Tanner said into the awkward silence. "I heard him mention her once to someone, but he never talked about her."

Peony looked up at Tanner. "Yes, that's the one."

Tanner snorted and looked away, his lips a thin line of frustration.

A new brother? Liz didn't know much about Brett's personal life—let alone any other kids—before Tanner and Brady's mom Veronica, other than rumor and gossip. If Brett had secrets, obviously he'd never shared them with either of his sons, and neither had Veronica. Liz turned to Frank, who was waiting quietly, eyes darting between everyone in the room, obviously uncomfortable as the family grappled with the news.

"What brother? They don't have another brother, so you'd better explain this one more time, in detail," Liz said for them, after absorbing for a moment the shock of what her mother had just revealed, which had obviously left the West brothers speechless.

Which, honestly, was a first.

CHAPTER TWO

Jake hung the gas nozzle back on the pump, and the machine spit out his receipt, the buzzing abrupt and irritating.

He snatched it and folded himself back into his rental car, his dress shirt already sticking to his arms due to the oppressive heat. He still had a few miles to go, and he'd gotten away from the airport later than he'd wanted. The line to grab his rental car had taken over an hour, the gas pumps here pumped fuel like it was molasses, and of course, the air conditioning in the car they gave him wasn't working worth a damn.

As he pulled out of the gas station, he reflected that he wasn't in New York anymore and needed to stop being such an asshole. Out here, life was slower. People had a different pace. He lifted his shoulders and let them drop, pushing out some deep breaths and trying his best to inject calm into the stress that had crept in only two days before.

Two days ago, he'd found out his father had died. A father he didn't remember, but who had requested he be at the reading of his will. A lawyer from Calgary had called Jake, and now here he was, driving out to West Line Ranch, a place he and his mother had apparently left when he was three, and a place he knew nothing about.

The radio was pure static so he switched it off, preferring to think in the relative calm of wind noise from the open windows. He was headed southwest, according to his phone's GPS. Into prairie, crops, cows, and country people.

Which was the exact opposite of his life, all the way across the damned continent in New York City.

Three weeks ago, he had been sitting in his restaurant in a swanky part of Greenpoint, signing paperwork to close its sale to the Urban Lumberjack Entertainment Group.

Shitty as it was, he was relieved to be signing it. Brooklyn was changing. Classical French cuisine was just not bringing people in the door anymore. Patronage was down, and there were nights he'd had to send waitstaff home early. It made it hard to keep people, and sometimes he'd been the one serving tables, instead of barking orders in the kitchen.

People these days wanted to drink everything out of thrifted crystal and eat strange concoctions off plates shaped like old tractor seats or barn boards. He was so done with hipster bullshit and the trend toward obtuse, weird food.

Just as he had crossed the *T* on the last signature, the restaurant door had swung open and his ex-wife, Ashley had waltzed in. Perfect timing, as always. Like a frigging TV show.

The law clerk had gathered her papers and run out of there. After seeing the look on Ashley's face, Jake would have, too, if he could've. But she had a big envelope in her hands, which meant she needed something from him.

She had flourished the divorce settlement papers, and he had endorsed them with the same efficiency he'd just applied to the sale papers, his mind numb from the sheer impact of what he was signing away in the mere space of five minutes. She'd left, papers in hand, without saying more than a dozen words to him, and he'd helped himself to a few shots of the best scotch behind the bar before he'd closed up the last five years of his life for good. The sun through the big, retractable windows cast a sad, spiky pattern on the far wall from the chairs upended on the tables, and he'd had one last look at it before locking the doors.

On impulse, he'd taken the bottle home, along with his favorite expensive crystal tumbler from behind the bar. They wouldn't miss it, and if they did? Screw them.

He'd dragged his ass home to Gordon's apartment, where he was staying while he looked for a new condo. He hadn't yet found one he liked since selling the place he and Ashley had shared for their year-and-a-half-long marriage. He finished the scotch sitting on the Natuzzi leather couch, staring out the huge windows that had the best evening view of Manhattan, and feeling miserable about his entire life.

In the blink of an eye, he was no longer a restaurateur, was officially divorced and living with his former sous-chef, and was shit-faced by himself.

Rock fucking bottom.

He'd been propped up on that same couch scanning real estate listings when he'd gotten the call from the lawyer in Calgary. He was in a giant rut, spinning his wheels, so when he was told the plane ticket was paid for already, he figured it couldn't hurt to get away. Go out, have the will read, say his condolences, and then come back and figure shit out with a bit of fresh air in his system.

He had to. The money from the sale of the restaurant and condo was decent, but he didn't want to fritter it away. He needed work. He needed to keep his reputation as a top chef in one of the busiest cities in the world intact to prove he still had it before the next guy came along and eclipsed him. The perpetual reinvention was exhausting, but it was what you did as a restauranteur.

He couldn't do that sulking on his friend's couch, feeling sorry for himself. As much as he and Gordon got along, and Gordon was always there for him, Jake would wear out his welcome eventually. Finding a new place to live was also a top priority.

Jake scanned the horizon out the windshield, letting the open space and the blue skies settle him further.

Cows dotted a field off to his right, and he wondered what was in store for him. Apparently, Brett had a big ranch just outside of Brightside that did well, with cattle, horses, and crops, now run by his sons. So, he had half brothers. The lawyer was hazy on details, but it didn't really matter.

Brett West was no more his father than a stranger on the street, so "brothers" was a stretch too. From what his mother had always told him, she'd left that "shitty backwater" when Jake was still a toddler, hightailed it back to the US, and given him a real life. When he was a kid, he'd often wondered why she hadn't left him behind, even secretly wishing she had when times had been tough.

Jake shook his head, not wanting to relive all the upheaval that growing up with his mother had involved, and forced himself to focus on the here and now. The welcome sign for Brightside loomed ahead.

He turned left into the outskirts of town, and the map app on his phone announced that in another five miles he would be at his destination. A curl of apprehension wound through his stomach. What would he say to these people, who probably didn't want him there? He'd never been a part of their lives. He wasn't looking forward to any of this. But maybe they would be nice, decent country folk and it wouldn't be a shit show.

A line of tall pine trees came up on his left, and he turned into a driveway. A big, carved wooden sign with a bright blue painted *W* and a wavy line under it, followed by the words WEST AND SONS underneath greeted him. Petunias and geraniums burst out of the flower boxes below it in a riot of reds and whites. The grass was partially cooked from the summer sun, but the fence line was straight as an arrow, heading up the driveway toward what appeared to be a cluster of houses. He could just see another driveway farther down, and barns.

He took a deep breath. Well, here went nothing.

Liz was sitting on the front step of her house when she saw a black Toyota hatchback drive in and stop beside Brady's rig, parking sideways in front of the main house. She shaded her eyes with her hand. That must be the long-lost brother.

For the second time that day a black car driving in was bringing bad with it. Well, hopefully not too bad, she amended. Couldn't be much to worry about in the long run. He certainly had no claim on this place, and the boys would never put up with an uptight, citified asshole staking a claim even if he tried.

She stood and walked over, ready to face the reason her family was yet again in upheaval. Might as well be friendly.

Yet again.

When the tall, dark-haired man unfolded out of the tiny car, she stopped, wondering if she was seeing double, or at the very least a mirage in the heat.

The wave in his hair, the way he stood, and the set of his jaw were unmistakable. That was Brett West's son, to the letter. He and Tanner could be twins.

Her mother, standing at the top of the steps of the front veranda of the main house, gasped and put her hand to her mouth.

"My god, you look just like him," Peony declared, and carefully moved down to him.

"Ma'am," was the response from the stranger, a polite smile forming as he reached her. He held out a hand, which she gratefully took, to help her down the last step.

Liz reached them and really looked at him for the first time.

Intelligent, warm brown eyes stared back, and she blinked in surprise. Brett had been a good-looking man in his youth; she'd seen the pictures. Tanner and Brady were good-looking guys, too, but this one . . . well, he had been given the West genes in spades.

He was fucking gorgeous.

Like the models in the watch ads from the back of the fashion magazines her mother always bought. She found herself staring like a heifer would look at a fresh alfalfa bale, and backed up a step to gain her bearings.

"You must be Jake West," she decided to say, to break the tension, and offered her hand. "I'm Liz Baker, and this is my mother, Peony."

The man blinked again, meeting her eyes, and took her hand. At least he had a firm grip. Liz's first impressions of a man were always based on how he shook hands, how he treated animals, and how he walked. This one had already ticked two of the boxes.

"Yes. Jake West." He rushed the words out awkwardly, and made that face people do when they offer sympathy. "I'm so sorry to hear about your, I mean our, father passing away. I just found out two days ago."

"Ohhh, no. He's not my father. My mother married Brett when I was a kid. I'm not a West," Liz blurted, determined to make that perfectly clear.

A silent *O* shaped his mouth, and he quirked an eyebrow. Her face flushed and she looked away, clearing her throat, embarrassed. *Awkward.*

Her mother let out a small sound and took his hand in both of hers, squeezing it, and smiling. "Oh, bless you, young man. Yes, yes, we're aware this must be a bit of a strange situation for you."

"You could say that," he said, another smile cutting the hard planes of his face. In that instant, he looked every bit a West. This was going to shock the hell out of her brothers.

"Please, come up out of the heat. I have some tea on, I hear you Americans like sweetened cold tea on hot days?" her mother added, and tugged on his hand.

A masculine chuckle escaped him as her mother went back up the steps with more energy than she'd exhibited since the day her husband had died. Liz let out a big breath, following them. Too late, she averted her eyes after taking in Jake's very well-toned backside, clad in perfectly fitting jeans.

He was fit. From what Frank had said earlier, he was a chef. She had expected plump, or odd, like those chefs she saw on TV all the time, but this man looked like he could vault onto a horse and be at home. Damn.

They entered the cool of the house, her mother chirping on, asking him about his flight and the drive, his short answers reverberating back. His voice was deep, just like her brothers', but had an American lilt to it, like the cops in movies. Frank had said Jake was from New York City, so that was probably why.

They made their way to the main living room, and Liz slipped off to the kitchen. She heard her mother tell Jake to make himself at home, that she'd be back in a moment.

Peony bustled into the room, and they looked at one another, both of them raising their eyebrows at once.

"Holy hell, Mom."

"Don't we know it," her mother replied as she hefted the tray of iced tea and drinking glasses. "I don't think there's any doubt he's Brett's. Go get the boys and Frank."

CHAPTER THREE

Jake studied the pictures along the fireplace mantle, waiting for Peony to come back. He flexed his hand, still feeling tense, but remembering Liz's firm grip as they shook hands. Her eyes were a unique shade of blue, reminding him of sapphires, and her voice was sexy and firm, like a smooth, aged whiskey. His head had emptied of any sort of intelligent, witty response when she'd spoken.

Why he'd had that response, he wasn't sure, because now was definitely not the time to be even contemplating anything to do with attraction to another person. She wasn't posh or polished in any way either, was completely unlike the type of woman he was normally intrigued by. But there it was. He ran a hand down his face and chalked it up to a long drive and a strange situation.

Pictures of his father and a myriad of horses were the focus in many of the frames. A wedding shot of Peony and Brett was there too, with a much younger Liz with piled-up hair, wearing some lace concoction, standing in front of them.

Another picture off to the other side was of a beautiful, auburn-haired woman sitting on a log with two teenaged boys, all of them in very nicely knitted sweaters, the fall leaves surrounding them. They must be his brothers, he thought. He picked up the picture beside it, with just the mom sitting on the log, looking back and forth between the two pictures. He didn't recognize himself in either boy.

"Her name was Veronica. She was my mother," a voice said from behind him.

Jake looked up and put the picture back quickly before doing a double take. Standing in the door was a more weathered version of himself, tall, dark haired and dark eyed, dressed in worn-out jeans and a dark-blue flannel shirt, holding a brimmed hat in his hands.

"Jake West," Jake said, walking toward the man, hand outstretched.

"I know who you are," he snapped, not taking Jake's hand. Jake dropped it, sensing the uncomfortable atmosphere that had entered the room with the other man.

They eyed one another, neither of them moving, and Jake knew he had been measured and found wanting. This guy was the real deal, and right now, he probably resented the hell out of Jake for even existing. Jake had faced down restaurant critics who had been less intimidating.

"Tanner West!" Peony admonished the man as she returned, carrying a tray with a pitcher and stacked glasses. "I know you're upset, but don't you be rude to our guest."

Tanner's flinty gaze turned from Jake and softened slightly. "Sorry. I'm on edge. We didn't kn—"

"You must be Jake!"

Jake turned to see another man bound into the living room, a smile on his face. He was a bit shorter than Tanner and had auburn hair, like his mother in the photo. "I'm Brady, the baby."

Jake smiled and shook his hand. "Nice to meet you." It was an honest statement. At least one of these men wasn't being an asshole. He was thankful for that.

"Frank's taking a quick phone call," Brady said as he flopped onto a chair and put his hat on his knee. Peony handed him a glass of tea, and he poured it down his throat in one smooth motion. Jake put his hands in his pockets. He felt like an interloper. This family was obviously close, had lived here their whole life. He was . . .

Well, he didn't belong here. At all. Peony handed him a glass of tea, and he nodded in appreciation.

"Thank you."

"So, Jake. Frank tells me you're a chef in New York City?" Peony said, sitting on the sofa and balancing her own glass, her eyes focused in on him. He nodded as he took a sip of his tea.

"Yes. Just sold my restaurant in Greenpoint."

"Oh, is that a nice area?" she asked politely. "Whereabouts is that in the city?"

"Brooklyn."

Silence followed. Neither of the other two men had said another word, but they were watching him like hawks. He shifted on his feet and wondered where in hell the lawyer and Liz had gone. Anything to break up the tension in the room.

"How long have you lived there?" Peony continued, her eyes flitting to his brothers. She was uncomfortable, too, but trying her best to be a good hostess. The strangeness of his presence intensified.

"Most of my life. My mother and I moved back there when I was three, I think? We lived in Washington Heights for a while and moved to Brooklyn when I was a teen."

"Yes, I think I remember Heather," Peony said quietly. "Red hair, snapping green eyes, voice like cracked glass?"

"That would be her," he said, surprised. "How did you know her?"

"I grew up in Brightside. Your mother was quite a newsmaker back in the day," Peony said, a hint of humor in her voice as she winked.

Before Jake could ask Peony to explain, Tanner let out a frustrated-sounding growl and peered out the closest window, flicking the curtain back with an irritated gesture. Jake got the distinct impression from the way Tanner was fussing that he didn't take kindly to waiting, or imposition of any kind.

"Where the hell is Frank?" Tanner added, pacing to the front hallway. Jake watched his newfound brother's jaw flex, noticing the similarity to himself. He was brought right back to earth about why he was here, and how much of a shock it was for everyone concerned.

"Mrs. West," Jake started, but Peony waved her hand, and he stopped.

"Call me Peony, please, my dear. You're family now."

Another angry sigh from Tanner threw doubt on that, but Jake let it slide and smiled at the woman. He noticed the exhaustion on her face, the slight tremor.

"Truthfully, this is a shock to me." He moved over and sat on a large ottoman beside her. Peony reached out, patted his leg, and shook her head.

"I know," she said quietly, then leaned in. "Brett told me about you, about a year ago. I didn't believe him at first. But—"

She stopped and pursed her lips together, looking down at her hands and taking a breath. When she looked up, Jake blinked. Gone was the humor, replaced by something he couldn't place. Grief? Maybe regret? It was hard to tell, but it was obviously sad.

"He never once told either of those boys. They found out about you today."

Brady, who'd been listening in, nodded.

"I gotta say, you're quite a surprise, New York. Dad never once spoke about you or Heather. So . . . yeah."

"I didn't know about you either," Jake said honestly, looking over at the younger man, raising an eyebrow at Brady's automatic assignment of a nickname. "I don't remember my father, and my mother never talked about him other than to say . . . well, let's not go there right now."

Brady looked up then and levered himself out of the chair. Jake stood as the clomp of boots on the floor signaled more people were joining them. An older man, whom he assumed was the lawyer, came in, with Liz behind him. Liz was attempting to hide her tension, the work gloves in her hand clenched in a death grip the only giveaway. He watched her eyes flit over her brothers before she made her way to her mother, gently sitting down beside her. She was protective of them. For good reason, right now.

"Ah, Jake. You made it," Frank said, and stepped quickly to him, pumping his hand as they shook. "Good flight?"

"Yes, thanks," he replied, and Frank smiled.

"Good, good. I won't take up much more of your time. Let's get to it, shall we?"

Everyone but Tanner settled in chairs and on the sofa. Liz was holding her mother's hand, Brady sank back into his armchair, and Frank sat down on another tall-backed chair, setting his briefcase on the coffee table in front of him.

Tanner leaned on the fireplace, arms folded, eyes glittering with animosity. Jake pulled up another chair from the side of the room for himself and sat, holding his glass of tea in his hands for something to do with them. He sensed the awkward, strange tension again. It was as if he was watching a movie unfold around him, was a mere spectator.

"Okay. Brett, in confidence, contacted me about a year ago to give me his will and set up all his funeral costs."

Jake glanced at Peony, who had closed her eyes, and his heart lurched for her. She must have gone through hell with all this. All of them, really, but it seemed to have taken a toll on her. He looked back as Frank cleared his throat.

"Brett had cancer. He didn't want to burden any of you with it, so he asked me not to say anything. We talked about this already, but Jake here, he's not aware of many details."

"Get to it, Frank. We've got a ranch to run," Tanner said, and shifted his stance at the fireplace. "You can fill him in after."

Frank nodded. "Fine, fine. So, Brett also asked me to reach out to Jake, but only after he had passed away. He was firm on that part, so I didn't question why. I honestly thought he'd told you boys, and Liz here, about him, but I guess not, and now here we are."

An irritated noise from Tanner made them all look his way, but with one shoulder leaned on the fireplace and his arms crossed tightly, it was obvious he was frustrated at the entire situation when he looked away from them to glare into the hearth. Frank pulled out a thick envelope and continued.

"I was instructed to only read the will once Jake was back on West Line Ranch soil. So, thank you, Jake for making the trip on such short notice for the sake of a formality."

Jake nodded silently, noting the raised eyebrows on Brady, who shifted uncomfortably in his chair. It was a long way to come for a formality, even if Jake hadn't minded. Plus, he'd had two days to get used to knowing he had brothers, and what was happening. They'd had an hour, tops.

Jake watched as Frank broke the seal on the envelope, looking around at each of the other people in the room as he did. It must be a thing in Canada that wills were sealed, not that he'd ever been at a will reading before. He waited, the uncomfortable anticipation sneaking up his back and roiling his stomach.

He wasn't entitled to one thing here, and he didn't want to take anything away from anyone else. He'd already resolved that if he was left money or some sort of belongings, he would give it back. He'd never known his father, and his father had never tried to find him or his mother. Even during the lean years, when they had little to no money, his father had never been there. When Jake was younger, that had hurt. But he'd long ago given up the bitterness that came with the hurt, mostly so he could move on and make something for himself. It was what it was. So, in that vein, he'd also given up any right to have a piece of what his father had left behind.

"All right. I was instructed that another firm other than mine had vetted the legality of this will, and, as executor, I was not to open the envelope until now. I followed the instructions, but last week I did contact my colleague who worked on the file, and he verified for me that this is all aboveboard. So, let me scan this quickly, folks, before I read it out, so I can explain it if you have questions."

Nods all around, and Jake watched Frank settle his glasses on his nose, scanning the document quickly, his hands moving down the page. But then Frank stopped, his face blanching, and he took his glasses off again, rubbing his eyes.

"Holy shit, Brett," he muttered, and looked up, directly at Tanner, who was now watching the lawyer with the same scrutiny he had offered Jake earlier.

"Frank . . ." Tanner stated ominously.

"I'm so sorry, Tanner. So truly sorry," Frank said, laying the papers down on top of his briefcase.

Brady shot to his feet just as Peony breathed in, one hand settling on her chest. Liz turned to her mother, then swiveled to Tanner, then looked at Jake. He caught the concern and worry in her eyes, the stiffness she was holding in. You could slice the stress in the room with a knife.

"Tell us," Peony said quietly, steel in her voice even as her hand shook. "What has that fool old man has gone and done, Frank?"

Frank cleared his throat twice before he could speak. He looked directly at Peony and placed both hands flat on the papers. They were shaking slightly.

"He's left the entire operation to Jake."

CHAPTER FOUR

The room erupted, everyone talking at once. Tanner snatched the papers before Frank could get a word in edgewise.

Liz couldn't believe it. The old coot had fucked them over. Well, not them. Tanner and Brady. It was their ranch—they deserved it—but now it belonged to a complete and utter stranger who shared some of their DNA.

"What in the absolute hell?" Brady muttered, launching himself over to Tanner, who was furiously scanning the will, his eyes snapping. Liz stayed put, a death grip on her mother's hand. Her mother was several shades paler than normal.

"Peony. Please, have something to drink."

Liz looked over to see Jake at her mother's side, offering her a full glass of tea. Peony opened her eyes and nodded, taking the tea and sipping it carefully. Liz looked incredulously at the man. After what Frank had just said, Jake was offering her mother tea instead of being steaming mad like everyone else?

"What in the absolute hell?" she echoed Brady, and Jake looked over at her, confusion in his eyes. She sensed a great deal of worry coming off him. Or maybe it was shock.

They were all in shock.

"We'll get this sorted out. There must be some mistake," Jake said, and got up from her mother's side and walked over to Tanner and Brady. "May I?"

Tanner thrust the papers at him and strode out of the room without another word. The front door slamming made her mother jump. Frank was rubbing his eyes again, obviously realizing this was now much more of a legal headache than it had been five minutes before.

Jake smoothed the papers out carefully, then, with a quick glance at Brady, looked the document over.

Liz watched his eyes go back and forth, then looking up and catching her eyes again. They shared a momentary acknowledgment of something, and she looked away, feeling the contact was too personal right at that moment.

"Frank, this is bullshit. I don't want a ranch. It belongs to these people."

His words flooded Liz with relief. They didn't know Jake from a hole in the ground. If the will said he got it all, and he was a greedy asshole, he might just take it. But maybe he wasn't. She wished he'd been able to say that before Tanner had stormed out. It might have helped.

But it was still fact that Brett had, in one fell swoop, doomed the ranch, and likely this wasn't going to be something you fixed with a phone call and the assurances of the sole inheritor that he didn't want it.

"I know, son. But there are goddamned clauses in the damned thing. If you try to give it back to Tanner, Brady, or Peony, the entire operation goes on the market for a charity, for a buck. He was pretty clear."

"Is this even legal?" Brady asked, looking up at Frank. "I mean, real estate law, next of kin, and all that. Plus, Jake's not even Canadian!"

"Actually, I am," Jake muttered. "I was born right here in Brightside, and I still carry dual citizenship. I kept it to make travel easier."

"Fuck," Brady muttered, and turned away, obviously upset.

"It is legal, Brady. Brett has every right to disperse his assets to whomever he wants no matter who is the next of kin," Frank interjected. "Now, I'm going to look into some things, so nobody panic. For now, we have to assume that this place will run as normal. Brady, you may want to go find your brother before he beats something to a pulp and hurts himself."

Brady nodded and left the room, the front door slamming for the second time in as many minutes.

Liz felt the loss for her stepbrothers. All the time and work and sweat they had poured into this place beside their father, and it had been taken away with the stroke of a pen. Salt in the wound from his death. A spit in their face from the grave. Why? What had they done to make him so angry? What in god's name would have made Brett snub the only sons he'd raised and who'd dedicated their lives to this place?

Liz stood up and motioned to Jake to give her the papers. He did without a word, an apologetic look in his eyes, and she again was taken aback at him and the situation. He was much more even-keeled right at this moment than his brothers were.

She looked over the tight, spiky scrawl that was Brett's signature, and scanned the first page. Just like Frank had said, he'd left the entire place to Jake. Lock, stock, and frickin' barrel. He was to be the sole owner and was required to live there and to operate the ranch. If he tried to sell it, live off property, or revert ownership to either of his half brothers, the executor was to immediately put the ranch on the market for a dollar.

Not one mention of her in any of the confusing language, which, for a moment, irked her, but she let it go. She wasn't a West. Brett would often remind her of that when they argued about some decision she'd made in the stables without his approval.

She scanned farther, but there was no mention of anything for her mother either. There had to be something for her in here. Money, some way to live.

"Frank, my mother isn't mentioned," she said, flipping the pages.

"No, she isn't," Jake replied. "At all."

Frank motioned for her to give him the will, and he took his time to read through it while they waited. Her mother had leaned back on the couch, her eyes closed again.

"Mom?" Liz asked. "You okay?"

"I'll be fine, dear. Just letting it all sink in. This has become quite an eventful day."

Liz swallowed the lump forming in her throat and looked out the window at the far side of the room. This place was her mother's home, *her* home, and her job. What was going to happen now?

Frank shuffled some additional papers in the sheaf from the envelope. He sighed and opened his briefcase.

"Okay. There's a copy of the deed in here, as well as some inheritance-law paperwork. I have to draw up further papers and talk to our real estate lawyer about this."

"What happens if I take ownership for one year, enough to thwart the inheritance taxes, and then sell? There's nothing in there about doing that," Jake said quickly. "And when I do put it up for sale, they buy it back for that dollar. Or I could sell it to Liz now, she's not related to me, my brothers, or Brett by blood, it would be aboveboard, too, yeah?"

"That is an avenue I will pursue, yes, but let's not be hasty, there might be another way around all this. It also says here the buyers, should you decide to sell, must be a registered animal charity, which, well, Liz isn't."

"Easy enough to set up," Jake snapped back, seemingly grasping at straws, thinking out loud.

"What in hell was he thinking?" Liz blurted, more to herself, but

Frank answered with a sound that was half exasperation and half annoyance.

"I don't know, my dear. He never once clued me in to what he was thinking. I kind of feel—"

"Cheated," Jake finished for him, and the two nodded at one another. Everyone was silent for a moment, the only sound the ticking clock on the far wall. Cheated? This was beyond that.

"Yes. Okay. Jake, you need to move here ASAP to meet conditions of the will. Until we get this sorted out, stick close," Frank finally said, as he gathered everything up.

"Frank, how can I—" Jake started, then stopped. He looked frustrated. She watched him thinking, looking for the words, the furrow in his brow identical to Tanner's. The enormity of how many lives had just been completely screwed over hit her, and the anxious lump in her stomach turned into tears behind her eyes. She needed to leave, right now. It was too much, and it was overwhelming her.

She took one more look at her mother, who nodded silently, and then stormed out of the room, taking her turn to slam the front door.

* * *

Liz found Tanner exactly where she expected, sitting in the big loft above the stable, legs dangling out the elevator chute door. Brady was nowhere to be seen, but she figured he had his head underneath the hood of one of the farm trucks. Tanner sulked when he was mad, and Brady tinkered. Liz normally just doubled down on the job, but right now, she didn't want to get on a horse. Her patience was so thin she'd do more harm than good.

"Tan," she said quietly, and he turned at her voice. She could see he'd been crying, which was unusual for him. He was the most stoic, uptight man she'd ever met, next to Brett. This was big, though. This was his life. Tears were justified.

"Hey," he said, wiping at his face and scooting over for her, attempting to hide the emotion he'd obviously been unable to cope with but didn't want to share. She lowered herself down beside him, and they sat shoulder to shoulder and looked out over the back pasture. Horses lazily cropped at grass or stood in the shade, tails flicking, not a care in the world. A serene, never-changing view, and Liz felt at odds with that, because it had changed, irrevocably.

"What did we do?" Tanner said suddenly. "What would make Dad do that? Did we upset him, or—"

"I have no idea," Liz said quietly. "I wish I did."

"Not like I can ask him, can I?" Tanner replied, irritated. "Jesus, Lizzie. How in the hell am I supposed to make this work?"

She couldn't answer him right away and squeezed his arm, letting the silence envelope them once again. The dust motes floating through the air and the fresh, fragrant hay stacked to the rafters were soothing to her nerves.

What did you say? What could you say about what had just happened? She picked at her fingers, looking over at Tanner, whose face was reverting to an unreadable mask. Tanner always bottled shit up, which made it ten times worse when it overflowed. He had an explosive temper, and it meant that in the past, he and Brett had raised quite a ruckus arguing over ranch matters.

"If it helps, your long-lost brother is no more on board with this idea than you," she offered finally. "He and Frank are looking into loopholes right now."

Tanner, all thirty years old of rough, tough ranch foreman, took on the face of a petulant child, and spat, "I don't want that asshole here. He's no brother of mine."

"Tan," Liz warned. "He's a West, even you have to see that. And it isn't his fault that your dad decided to be a jackass. He's gotta be here, or we lose the place. You saw the will."

"Fuck!" Tanner spat, and turned to her, his ire up again. "It's bullshit. What the hell is he going to do, huh? Take over my job?"

"Hey, I doubt that! He'll likely have to sign some paperwork and he'll, I don't know, live here in the guest room until we can get it signed back over to you and Brady. It's not impossible, Tan. Just a bump. You believe that, right?"

Tanner stood with a jerk and dusted off his jeans. He stopped, let out a tired, creaky groan, and held out a hand, pulling Liz up. "I'm sorry, Lizzie. I can't take it out on you, that's not fair. I'm being stubborn and I'm not dealing, which I should be."

"Fair? Fuck fair, Tan. You've got a right to be mad."

Tanner turned, his hat in his hand. She touched him on the shoulder, and he stopped, and then she did what she'd done for him every time he'd gotten into a scrap with his father, or another boy at school, or something had rubbed him the wrong way. She grabbed him before he could protest and hugged him around the waist. He was her brother—maybe not by blood, but it mattered that he was her chosen family.

Tanner hated hugs, but from her he'd take one, in private, and not for long. He hugged her back, squeezing her just a little, then let her go.

"I have no idea what the fuck to do," he muttered.

"We'll figure this out. Frank's a good lawyer."

"I sure hope so," was the response as he slid down the access ladder opposite the hay chute to the stable aisle, striding away as soon as his boots hit concrete. Liz stood in the loft a moment more, then threw the night hay down. Might as well get back to work. Horses didn't care who ran the joint, as long as they got fed.

CHAPTER FIVE

"It's fine, Peony. Really."

Jake looked into the comfortable guest room, the en suite door peeking out from along the far wall. It would more than do. It wasn't a cold couch that doubled as a bed in someone else's apartment. He wanted to lie down in the massive queen-sized bed right then, but other matters were more important.

"Well, I'm sure your home in New York is much nicer," Peony replied, and shook her head ruefully. "I bet it has big windows and a huge kitchen overlooking the river."

Jake chuckled. "It did. I had to give it up not too long ago."

Peony made a noise and gestured into the bedroom. "Well, this is yours while you're here," she said wearily. Jake looked sharply at her.

"You should be resting."

"No time. Need to get dinner on. We gave the cook the evening off, so someone needs to feed everyone," she replied and shuffled toward the main area of the house. He saw the funny gait, the tremble, and reached her side in two steps, hand on her elbow.

She looked up into his face and patted his hand on her arm. "It's okay. Just my arthritis kicking up. Stress does that. I'll be fine."

Jake nodded but steered Peony around, back down the hallway. A need to take care of her overwhelmed him, just like it used to when his mother would come home drunk—or worse, high. He realized there must be something inherently broken in him to be comparing those terrible nights to this, but he let it pass so he could focus on making sure this woman took the time to rest. Today had been a huge shock. For everyone.

"You do remember I can cook, yeah? Go rest, have a hot bath, or sleep. Let me make dinner for everyone."

Peony stopped and looked up at him. She smiled, the same smile her daughter might have, he suddenly thought.

"You are a West, my dear. I can see it in everything. The way you walk, talk—" She stopped, and he urged her forward, shoring her up with an arm around her waist. She leaned into him with a sigh.

"I never knew my father," he said quietly. "Sometimes I used to wonder if I was like him. My mother never even had a photo of him, and he certainly wasn't her favorite person."

"You are," Peony said. "Tanner's like him too. Likely want a DNA sample from you for all of this."

"Already ordered the kit while Frank and I finished up. Least I can do," Jake said, pushing open the door that Peony pointed to. He ushered her into her room and set her on the edge of the big master bed. The suite was huge; Gordon's whole apartment was smaller. The entire house was a sprawling maze of wealth, and it hit him that he didn't remember one bit of it.

"Thank you, Jake. I mean it," Peony said as she shifted into her bed, and he pulled up the covers. She lay back and he turned to go, but she stopped him, her hand on his arm.

"Follow the hallway back and then turn right toward the big dining room, kitchen is back behind that."

Jake nodded and left her to her nap, closing the door softly—there had been enough doors slamming for one day. He made his way back to the main living room, then through an enormous dining room with a butler pantry, to the kitchen just as Peony had said. He stopped short, taking in the expensive stone countertops, massive gas cooktop, big double-door commercial fridge. A chef's dream kitchen was staring back at him, gleaming in the late afternoon light.

He leaned on the island and looked around, processing the past couple of hours. In one fell swoop, he had been tied to this place until their lawyer could figure out a way to break it. He didn't have time to sit on his ass out in the middle of nowhere; he needed to be back in the city, getting on with his own life. But here he was. A few days of clothing wasn't going to cut it—he could be here a month or more, so he fished his phone out of his pocket and called Gordon.

"Hey, man, how's the middle of nowhere?" Gordon said as soon as he answered. Jake's shoulders lowered as he leaned on the counter, happy to be talking to someone familiar.

"A lot of cows," Jake replied. "How you doing without me to harass you?"

"Aww, you know I miss your sweet face first thing in the morning, Grumpy."

Jake chuckled. "'Grumpy'?"

"Hah. Whatever. I secured that gig at The Grill, you know they brought on a new head chef. She was looking for some deep experience, so I'm the new pantry chef. Not exactly what I wanted, but it's a foot in the door."

"Hey, that's great!" Jake said, a pinch of excitement reverberating in his stomach. The Grill. It was a great place, one he'd tried to get into once, but they were interested in European fusion cuisine rather than Jake's specialty at the time. Gordon could helm the place easily, if he wanted. Jake sobered. Time to get to the point of his call.

"Listen, I have a situation."

"When don't you?" Gordon teased back.

"Hah, funny. I need you to ship me my clothing and stuff. I might be here a while."

Gordon *hmm*ed and Jake heard paper shuffling on the other end of the call. "Okay. Spill, what's the situation?"

"Well, my dad, he.... Well, he willed me the entire ranch. I have to stay while the family's lawyer finds a way out of it."

Gordon let out a whistle. "Wow, that's a situation for sure. You'll need all your shit, then, huh? I can do that. Are you okay? Do you need me to come out there?"

"Nah, I'm good. I don't know how long I'll be here, maybe a week, maybe a month or more. I'll find a spot to settle in, and the main house here has a really nice kitchen. Could be worse. Plus, I might learn a thing or two about my dad. I have half brothers, two of 'em, can you believe it?"

"Instant family, man. That'll be new for you. I can send you some audio from Fifth Avenue at rush hour, too, if you want. The lack of sirens and horns is going to drive you nuts," Gordon said, and then *ahh*ed under his breath as more paper sounds made it through the phone. "Here it is, I knew I wrote down the address where you were going. I can send all of it there?"

"Yeah. If anything important comes in the mail, can you forward it as well?"

"Yep. But when the executive chef invitation for The Odeon arrives in our mailbox, can I pretend to be you?" Gordon said.

"Not on your life, but if it does, I'm bringing you with me," Jake replied.

Gordon let out a laugh. "Hah, like you have a choice. Anyway, I'll get it all out to you, no worries. You sure you want all of it?"

"Yeah, gonna need to think practical if I'm here for a while. Thanks, man, I owe you. Let me know what to send you for it."

"Yes, Chef," Gordon said. "Take it easy, might find you like the peace and quiet compared to this madhouse, get your head on straight while you figure out where your next restaurant's going to be."

"Not likely," Jake said, looking around. The lack of city lights and people was going to make him jumpy. But right now, he didn't have a choice.

"All right. Gotta move, my first shift starts in two hours. Cheers, man!" Gordon said, and ended the call.

With that taken care of, Jake's brain slowed down, focusing on the immediate problem of his presence at this ranch. Frank had left him with strict instructions to not go too far away, the complexity of the will not making it a simple retraction or a refusal on his part. As complicated as it was, Jake was intrigued by the process, looking forward to sinking his teeth into the problem. Gordon had alluded to maybe using it as a chance to really get his act together. Couch surfing and licking his wounded pride was going nowhere fast.

As he stared at the kitchen, the thought ping-ponged around his head that he no more belonged on a ranch in the middle of nowhere than his half brothers could live in the city. The sheer audacity of his late father's idea made him wonder what he'd been like as a man. Had he been he a vindictive asshole? Mentally unstable? It seemed impossible to reconcile the idea of a man who had successfully run this ranch with the one who, in some strange fit, had willed that ranch to someone he'd never known and didn't want.

One who had been married to the kind woman Jake had just helped into bed.

"Well, okay, West. If you have to stay for a bit, you need to get your shit together," he said, and straightened up, turning on the lights over the island and sink.

"You think?" came a terse reply, and he turned to see Tanner stomp in, phone in his hand, hat still on his head.

Jake and he eyed each other for a moment. Jake felt a small pang of regret he'd never gotten to know him. It would have been nice to have family growing up. Maybe, under different circumstances, they could have been friends.

"Where's Peony?"

"I sent her to rest," Jake said, the moment gone, moving around to the far side of the kitchen, opening drawers, looking for towels and aprons. "She was exhausted."

He watched his brother look away and swallow, the anger and resentment rippling off his body. Jake felt his own temper rise, and clamped down on it. He knew that if he didn't, they might be nose to nose in a moment, screaming their fool heads off. His temper had gotten the better of him at times, and his team had witnessed it in spectacular fashion when a dinner rush was failing.

"I don't want you in the house," Tanner spat at him. "You don't belong here."

"Right," Jake replied, readying for the assault, yanking out the first apron he could find in the drawer. "You read that damned document. I have to stay here or this whole place goes to Tree Huggers for Hippos."

He caught the hint of a smirk from Tanner at the attempted levity, then it was gone, and the angry face was back. Tanner swiped his hat off and shifted his stance a couple of times. He was no stranger to arguing, Jake could see. This guy had a temper just like him. *Marvelous.*

"I don't care at this point. You—"

Jake waved a hand, cutting Tanner off. "I get that you don't want me here. I get that this is a huge slap in your face. Same here, pal. Apparently, our father decided to be an asshole before he died. Not my problem if your pretty pink panties are in a bunch about it. But for now, you get to have me here so I can help your lawyer get this monkey off my back. Then I'll be gone."

Jake's blood was hurtling through his veins now, and he glared at

Tanner. That was a speech. He'd tried to keep his mouth shut, but it hadn't worked.

Tanner was glaring back, jaw working, "Fine. But stay out of the barns. You'll just get hurt."

"Seriously, cowboy? What do you take me for?"

"And stay away from Liz," Tanner added, jabbing a finger at him. "Don't get any ideas. I saw how you looked at her."

Looked at her? This guy had a serious fucking control problem. Jake raised an eyebrow as he tied on the frilly pink apron. Tanner had barely had time to see the two of them in the same room before he'd stomped off. But, Jake realized, what he'd seen of Liz, he'd liked. Maybe it had shown? He'd have to be more careful.

"Looked at her? Shit, I've barely even been introduced to her. What the fuck is your problem?"

"You are, City Boy."

"May I remind you that I am older than you, *little brother*? I would also prefer if you used my name," Jake snapped, goading Tanner on for some ridiculous reason.

"Oh, for fuck's sake—" Tanner started, but Jake stalked around to him, standing a foot away from him, folding his arms. They went toe-to-toe, egos snapping like a rubber band between them.

Jake's knuckles cracked in the fists he was making, and he clamped his teeth down. He desperately wanted to put this pompous, high and mighty asshole in his place. His temper won, but he didn't want to hit the man. At least, not yet.

"You really don't like not being the boss, do you?" he added, before he could stop himself.

Tanner growled, poking Jake's chest with his finger and looking him straight in the eye. "You, asswipe, are not anyone's boss here. I call the shots, and I say what and when. This is my ranch."

So that was how it was going to be. Animosity and a pissing contest.

But the reality of Tanner's statement put ice in his blood. It really was their ranch, and Jake had no business dictating anything. He was getting bent out of shape for no reason, other than the guy had tried to push him around and called him on looking at Liz. Which he had.

"Look, Tanner, let's just—" Jake said, forcing himself to back away, changing his tone to try and make amends. Tanner gave him one final, seething glare, which stopped him mid-sentence, before spinning on his heel and leaving. Which was exactly what he would've done, if he'd been in Tanner's shoes.

"This is going to be a fucking party," Jake muttered into the empty kitchen, and turned to the fridge to see what he was working with.

* * *

Jake lifted the pan off the stove and tossed the sautéing onions. It felt good to be cooking, and he hummed as he set it back down on low heat to simmer, peeking in the oven at the roast marked *Thursday* he'd found in the fridge. So, it was Tuesday; they'd deal. He couldn't resist when he'd seen the red, marbled meat. The quality of the roast was exceptional. Fresh rosemary from the garden he'd spied out back was peeking out around it, along with some savory and thyme. Garlic cloves stuffed into the folds were turning golden brown.

Heaven.

The whole kitchen smelled like roasting meat, caramelizing onions, and herbs, and it was calming his nerves after the bombshell of a day. He'd discovered, as he explored the cupboards, that this kitchen was stocked with anything he could possibly want. Seriously, there was an entire pot drawer with top-line pans, double ovens, and a spice rack that rivaled his own, although most of the selections—except for the usual oregano and Montreal steak rub—were unopened.

"Well, making yourself useful, New York?" Brady said as he stepped into the kitchen from the back porch.

Jake smiled at the nickname Brady had given him, like an automatic acceptance compared to Tanner's, which was meant as an insult. Jake resolved that he wasn't going to let Tanner get to him. If his half brother wanted to be a jerk, let him. He'd just stick to the oasis this kitchen provided, when he could.

"Peony said the cook had the night off. She was exhausted, there was no way I was letting her put dinner on the table for all of us when she could barely stand."

"I appreciate that," Brady said, as he wearily eased onto one of the stools at the island. "She's been through a lot."

Jake nodded in agreement and, after checking the vegetables one more time, leaned on the counter opposite his younger half brother. Brady looked more like his mother, and for Jake, that was a relief at the present. Arguing with Tanner had been like yelling at himself in a mirror.

"So, where is your mother in all this? Tanner said her name was—"

"Veronica. Yeah. She died a long time ago. She had bad kidneys," Brady said, looking down at his hands.

"I'm sorry," Jake replied quietly. "That must've been tough."

"This will be tougher," Brady said. "Dad dying sucked because we didn't have time to say goodbye. Now, to lose the ranch too—"

"You're not losing it," Jake interjected, and Brady nodded tiredly, acknowledging him, then leaned on his arms and gave Jake a serious look.

"I—damn, you likely have family and a job back in New York. It's as much a shitstorm for you as us, and I just realized it now."

"Not as many ties as you'd think," Jake admitted, waving his hands and giving his brother a serious look back. "I'll deal okay. Survived worse."

"Fair enough," Brady muttered, and they stared at one another again, awkward silence between them. "Still, I want to apologize."

"This is one strange, messed up situation. No need to be sorry," Jake blurted, wanting to fill the air with something. He liked Brady, and he relaxed as they spoke.

"Doesn't look like you'll have much trouble. It smells great in here," Brady admitted, and stood up, stepping around the kitchen to look in the saucepan. "I cook from time to time, but—"

"But what?" Jake said, glad to find something to talk about with his brother. It would be nice to not feel at odds with the entire family, and it brightened his mood.

"Oh, it isn't anything like this. Not like you can, I'm sure. I can make pasta, barbeque, that sort of thing," Brady said, backing away, hands in his pockets. Jake shook his head and laughed, stirring the onions once more then turning off the heat to the element.

"Nonsense. I'm sure it's fine. Cooking isn't some nebulous art form, it's more science, really. Following the rules, breaking a few to see what happens, playing with flavors. It all boils down to the basics, no pun intended."

Jake sensed that Brady was happy to change the subject.

"The difference, if you want to compare it to science, is that I barely passed grade twelve chemistry, and you've got a PhD. But thanks for the vote of confidence." Brady was grinning at him, and Jake was thankful he seemed to be easier going than Tanner.

Brady sighed, plopping his hat back on his head. "I have to go see what help Liz needs. Trevor had to leave to go get his kid from camp."

"Dinner will be on in less than an hour," Jake said as he turned back to the stove. Brady nodded silently and left out the back door. The kitchen was quiet once again, and Jake's shoulders lowered. At least one brother wasn't ready to murder him. He'd take it.

CHAPTER SIX

The aroma of cooking beef made Liz's stomach rumble, and she levered her boots off inside the back mud porch quickly. Her mother must be putting a spread on for their guest, hence the delicious smell coming out of the kitchen.

She stepped through the door and stopped short. Jake had his shirtsleeves rolled up to his elbows, her mother's peony flower-print apron, which Liz had bought for her at that expensive kitchen store two years ago, expertly snugged high on his waist. His face was flushed from standing over the steam on the stove. Music from his cell phone, which was sitting in a small metal bowl, was playing in the background.

Jazz? That was a first in this house.

He was humming along, the muscles in his forearms flexing as he lifted a pan and expertly poured gravy through a strainer. She leaned against the door frame and ogled him, fully aware she was staring at a very fine specimen of the male species. This was straight out of a fantasy, the way he exuded sexy, competent man. No one could look that good cooking unless it was Hollywood, could they?

She sighed, aware she was objectifying him again, like she had when he'd showed up this afternoon. She would hate it if someone did that to her. She cleared her throat to let him know she was there, and to stow those thoughts.

She steeled herself to make conversation, and put on a smile as best she could. If he was going to stay then she needed to get to know him. She didn't fully trust him yet—who would, really—but in this situation, they had to figure out how to coexist until Frank could work his magic.

Jake looked up at her, finally noticing her presence. He smiled back and gestured to her.

"I have to tell you, wherever your cook gets their beef, it is fantastic quality."

"It's ours. We only ever eat our own beef," she replied, walking in and leaning on the island, looking over the spread. "Where's my mom?"

Jake turned back from putting the pot on the stove and wiped his hands on the apron. He pointed to the bedrooms and grimaced a bit, maybe in apology? She looked sharply at him.

"I sent her to lie down after Frank left. She was exhausted. She could barely stand."

Guilt washed over Liz for having left her mother when she'd stormed out. She should have stayed and made sure Peony was okay. She let her emotions get the better of her, again. *Damn it.*

"Shit. Thanks for that. I suppose we need to talk about all . . . well, today," she replied cautiously. "What are your plans? Do you need to run into town for anything?"

Jake shrugged and picked up three plates already mounded with food. Liz picked up the other two. She followed him over to the large table, noticing it was set as if for a holiday meal, with the nice napkins, the good stuff from the side hutch, and matching water glasses. He'd even found wine glasses. When was the last time they had sat down to a meal like this? Christmas? Easter? Her mother would be so pleased.

They set the plates down and looked at one another across the table. The early evening light cast shadows across his face, giving him a dark and dangerous feel. She watched him eyeing the table, straightening a fork, the precision exactly what she might expect from someone who ran high-end restaurants. Again, she found it appealing, and her stomach tightened. He wasn't rough and tough, weathered from being outside all day. He was different, which was likely why she was examining him like a potential project horse. She stopped herself, blinking at the comparison. She had to stop doing that.

"There are candles in that big hutch over there," she offered, pointing. "Maybe they would be nice."

"Trying not to come on too strong, here. I'm expecting Tanner to take one look and attempt to deck me for overstepping. I already feel like I have," he said, rubbing the back of his neck, his frustration showing.

Liz frowned. Obviously he and Tanner had chatted. "He's already come in and yelled at you, hasn't he?"

"Something like that," he muttered, and straightened the fork again.

Liz *hmm*ed, uncomfortable. Jake had gone to the effort of cooking their meal, a complete and utter unknown in their house. Right. Jake wasn't far off the mark with his comment. Tanner would find this an affront and maybe attempt to turf him out of the house. She needed to show some appreciation and make up for the lack of it elsewhere.

"It's really nice," she said, changing the subject, looking at the dishes, the steaming plates of food, the wine sitting out, decanted. "You didn't have to."

"It helped me relax. I cook, it's what I do, and this kitchen beckoned—" He stopped and turned to her, clearing his throat. "I needed to do something with myself. This afternoon was stressful."

She nodded, agreeing with him, knowing that the reason for

that stress had been thrust on *all* of them, and each had their own demons to wrestle. She couldn't, by any means, understand what he must be thinking, being dragged all the way out here and having complete strangers you shared DNA with now beholden to you for something you neither wanted nor needed. He likely had a family back in New York. Work. Girlfriend, maybe? A quick thought of *I hope not* flitted through her brain, and she wrinkled her nose at the ridiculous notion. His face fell when she did, and she pasted a smile back awkwardly.

"Well, I'll go get Mom. The boys should be in soon. I'll text them both that dinner is on the table," she said quickly, before her thoughts could get away from her, and turned toward the master bedroom.

She sent both Tanner and Brady a text while she walked through the house, then quietly opened the door to her mother's room. Peony was sitting in her favorite wing-backed reading chair, a blanket over her knees, her latest dog-eared romance novel open.

Her mother borrowed all her books from friends, and they had this sharing circle of smutty, bodice-ripping novels. Liz never understood why they loved the stories so much. Life wasn't happily ever after. Relationships weren't like the ones in those stories. At least, not in her world they weren't.

"What's this one about?" she asked, perching on the windowsill as Peony looked up, smiling tiredly at her daughter.

"Oh, this one is set in Scotland. Time-traveling laird kidnaps a pretty girl, takes her back in time, forces her to marry him."

"That sounds terrible!" Liz said, shaking her head. "How is that romantic? Sexual assault, here we come!"

"Well, she does kick him in the privates when he tells her he has to bed her for it to be legitimate, if that helps." Peony chuckled and closed the book, setting it on the teak table beside her chair. Liz stood and helped her mother up, watching her wince as she got to her feet.

"Bad today?" she asked, as Peony stretched and let out a small bleat of pain.

"Last few days have been worse, yes. Jake insisted he cook, and I didn't have the energy to say no, and honestly? A real New York chef cooking in my house? I shouldn't say no. I'm famished," her mother said quickly, changing the subject.

Liz walked out with her mother, and noticed that Jake had taken her suggestion—several candles now sat on the table. He looked sheepishly at her, and she winked, hoping to indicate it was okay, which made him quirk a very handsome half smile. This silent communication was interesting, acting like they'd known each other longer than half a day, but it was comfortable. Normally men in this part of the world were verbal, and blunt. Jake felt refined, domesticated. Gentler. More observant.

She caught him flexing his hands and that was familiar, too, but in a recognizable way. Tanner and Brady both did that when they were trying to keep calm.

She would likely see the other boot drop when Tanner and Jake had to interact. There had to be some sort of flaw. Her mother fussed over how nice everything looked, and Jake shepherded her to her seat at the head of the table, offering her wine, asking her if there was anything she needed.

Jake liked taking care of people. It was evident in the kindness he showed to her mother. Liz wondered if that translated into other things, and stopped herself again. She had to quit overanalyzing his every move. Hard not to, really, but it was judgy and not a part of herself she liked.

Brady came in and sat across from Liz, looking over the food with a huge smile, his eyes sparkling with amusement.

"Wow, New York, you put on a nice spread!"

"Thanks. Your brother coming?" Jake replied calmly, sitting down beside Liz. He smelled like spices and the melon-scented dish soap her mother kept at the sink. It was nice, and her stomach did a little flip.

"Tanner went into town. Said he needed to order some supplies. He won't be in for dinner."

Liz slid a frustrated glance to Tanner's place, the steaming plate of perfectly presented food absent its owner. She knew Tanner could be a jerk, and they would weather the initial storm. Of the two brothers, he had been closer to Brett, and this kick in the gut was a lot to take on, as she had witnessed in the hayloft.

She caught Brady's eye, and his face said everything he hadn't spoken. Tanner wasn't going to come in to eat because Tanner was sulking.

Jake rose to clear the place but then stopped as Brady lifted Tanner's plate over to his place and wiggled his eyebrows.

"More for me. Doesn't know what he's missin'," Brady drawled, and dug in.

* * *

Liz loaded the last plate into the dishwasher and straightened her back with a small pop. Ever since that damned filly had thrown her last month, her lower back screamed at her if she did too much. She needed to go see a doctor, but it took time away from here, which had been in short supply since Brett had died.

Conversation flowed in from the dining room, short bursts of laughter from Brady, deeper ones from Jake. Over the course of dinner she had watched Brady happily getting to know his brother. It was a chance to have a new sibling for both of her brothers, so she was glad it was him bridging the gap. Brady accepted people easily, which she treasured about him.

She felt a hand on her shoulder, and her mother set some glasses on the counter for her.

"He's nice," Liz said quietly. "But I expected—"

"Someone less like Brett or Tanner?" her mother replied. "He's got a temper. I can see it in him. He's a passionate man. But, yes, he's nice. City-bred manners."

Liz snorted in laughter and held a hand up to her mouth. "City-bred? Seriously, Mom."

"It's true! These men from the city, they have class, and style, and graces. They need them to swim in the shark-infested waters of the social circles. Out here, a man can be genuinely blunt in his dealings. But in a big place like New York City, well, it is eat or be eaten."

Liz looked at her mother and quirked an eyebrow. "You have got to stop watching so much television."

Her mother waved her hands at her, and they both laughed. She looked more relaxed, and a good meal, plus some rest, had brought color back to her face. Liz wondered if the company also had something to do with it.

"So what happens now?" Liz asked, leaning on the counter, her mother taking over putting the glasses in the top rack. She could just see Brady, leaning back in his chair, talking about god knew what, his cheeks pink from the strong red wine Jake had somehow dug up from their small wine rack at the back of the kitchen. Brady looked happier than she'd seen him since Brett had died, which was strange, since today had been something that would make any rancher slink away with his tail between his legs. The will had left them nothing. Yet he seemed relieved, almost celebratory. Maybe he was just drunk and letting the reality they faced fade away for a while.

"We let Frank do what he has to do. And hopefully, while Jake is here, he can cook for us. I can't say I would mind," her mother quipped, patting her stomach. "Rosy may be quite put out tomorrow."

"But what about you, Mom? How are you going to live? He didn't even leave you a working checking account."

Peony, her stalwart, no-nonsense mother, turned to her daughter with one of those looks that said she was trying very hard to be strong and would not be putting up with any nonsense from anyone while she figured shit out.

Liz'd seen it before, had known it since she was a young girl, watching her mother hold it all in when they were living out of their car, moving from place to place. The grit she pulled from deep inside herself. Liz hated that her mother felt the need to gather herself up now, after all that had happened. She should be given time to grieve, rather than plan for what-ifs.

Liz let out a sigh. "Mom, don't look at me like that. You married that man and put up with him for years, took on raising those boys who weren't yours. He left you zilch. I mean, you know the boys won't let you starve, but it isn't fair and—"

"Don't." Her mother interrupted. "I have my own accounts, and some savings safely tucked away, and my old age pension helps. It isn't much, but it'll be fine."

"Fine? Define that for me, because I don't think this is fine. We can ask Jake to make sure Brett's personal accounts are reverted or—" Liz said, her emotions getting the better of her. She winced as she realized she sounded kind of whiny.

"I'll be fine, and it will all work out. Jake's a good man, and when he and Frank sort it out, we'll figure out what to do. Brady has already insisted they'll look at giving me cash out of the ranch revenue if push comes to shove, which is ridiculous."

"Well, good, but—"

Her mother cut her off again, shaking her finger in her daughter's direction. "But nothing, Elizabeth Jaqueline Baker. Honestly, Brett West didn't owe me a red cent. I wasn't expecting anything out of the deal."

"The deal? What are you talking about? You married him. You were in love. It wasn't a business transaction."

Her mother straightened, a sad look flitting across her face, and she reached for the pile of cutlery to add to the load.

Brett had been a hard man to love, even if he was certainly a charmer of the ladies, and from all the stories Liz had heard, he had been quite popular with the women of Brightside in his day. But Liz knew the truth of it, the two sides of him. Once you got to know Brett, it became very apparent he never truly let anyone into his heart. He was hard, and thought only with his head, for the good of the ranch. The rumors swirled about a woman he'd loved once—which she realized now was maybe Jake's mother—who'd hightailed it away from the ranch because he'd cheated on her. From what Liz was told, he married the "other woman" quickly, and that woman was Veronica.

Veronica had been the outgoing, social partner he'd needed when he was expanding the ranch, and had given him two sons to carry on the name before she'd died.

But Liz's mother? It had surprised everyone when Brett and Peony announced their engagement not long after Veronica passed away. Peony had been their housekeeper, lived in the small bunkhouse that Liz now occupied by herself, and no one had even known they were an item.

Her mother had been labeled a gold digger. People wondered if it was just about the sex, or if Brett had cheated on Veronica with her, continuing the wicked pattern. Liz had taken a lot of snide remarks at school about it—finding out more about her stepfather than she cared to know in the process—before the wedding.

In the end, as much as people gossiped and judged in small-town circles, they also eventually accepted. Her mother became the second official Mrs. West, and people moved on.

"Oh, honey, it wasn't that kind of marriage. It was strictly an arrangement between us, a companionship, if you want to call it something more palatable. I was lonely, and it was what we both wanted at the time. I thought you knew that."

Liz stared open-mouthed as her mother placed the last fork onto the dish rack, closed the door, and pushed the button. *What? How was she supposed to answer that?*

"But . . . you—" Liz said, trying to come up with something to say.

The dishwasher *whoosh*ed to life, and her mother pasted her stern smile back into place.

"But nothing. I don't regret marrying Brett, not for one second. He took care of us when we needed it most, and I was there for him when he needed me. We were good for one another while it lasted. So, whatever happens now, we deal with it, okay?"

With that, her mother squeezed Liz's arm and walked back into the dining room. Liz listened to the swish of the water for a few moments more.

Now it was her turn to be speechless. It had been a day of stunning announcements.

CHAPTER SEVEN

The sun streamed in through the window of the guest bedroom and Jake, still not used to the schedule on the ranch, groaned and rolled over, burying his face into his pillow to block the light.

It didn't help, so he blearily poked at his phone. Nine o'clock. He blinked and sat up, willing his eyes to open and his body to work.

The ranch started to get moving around six. Which meant he needed to completely rework his internal clock from years of sleeping the morning away, having been up the night before in the restaurant. The last time he'd woken up before dawn was when he'd opened a small seafood spot and had to be all the way up to Fulton Fish Market early to get the freshest catch. Even then, that had sucked.

Jake had never been a morning person, which was in stark contrast to everyone else who existed out here. The hurt caused by changing around his habits this time was going to be lovely and require vats of coffee.

He mentally counted. It was day three of his enforced stay, and boredom was threatening. He needed to figure out something to do other than make-busy work in the kitchen, even though that was helping to fill the time.

Frank hadn't gotten back to them about much yet. He said it would be a couple of weeks before he could put together a concrete plan and to sit tight. *Sit tight and do what, exactly?*

The first step, proving he was indeed Jake West, had arrived yesterday morning via courier. Peony had provided a small sample of Brett's gray hair from a hairbrush, tucking it into the sample bag with tweezers, her entire body quiet and withdrawn. He'd wondered if she'd cleared out any of his things yet, and took a breath to ask, but she'd walked away into the house somewhere, and he left her alone. It had obviously been hard for her to do that.

Tanner and he had done the spit/swab routine over the sink during lunch, and Brady did a swab for fun as well, even though it wasn't really necessary. Tanner had barked that he would take the samples back into town when he went into the bank, before storming out. Tanner didn't waste time, and Jake rarely saw him in the house during the day. Mind you, he hadn't sought him out either. Peace was important as he got his footing at the ranch.

Jake had stayed away from the barns as promised. Instead, he'd gone for a walk through the gardens with Peony to get a sense of what herbs and vegetables she was growing, and in the past two days, had cooked up a storm, laying in some freezer slow-cooker meals that Peony had requested for both her and Liz. Spending time in the kitchen chopping and prepping with her had been enjoyable. It reminded him of his mother's more sober moments, when they would cook together in the restaurants she worked in, stirring the soup, laughing, and carrying on.

He'd cherished those times with his mother, because they never lasted.

After a quick shower, he pulled on his last clean T-shirt and jeans, and padded down the hall to the kitchen, relishing the feel of the soft carpet on his bare feet. Peony was there, humming a tune, while their cook looked through some books and wrote on a small pad of paper.

He'd met Rosy yesterday, and played as nicely as possible. It was her kitchen, and once they had established that, she was politely friendly. He had acted as sous-chef for dinner as she cooked, trying very hard to defer to her since she was their employed cook.

Jake realized quite quickly her lexicon was limited, as were her time management skills in the kitchen. It was a wonder she could get a meal out in time, and when they first got started, he had to bite his tongue to keep from barking her an order, or correcting her technique, or coming along behind her to add more salt on something, turn heat up or down.

He had to consciously remind himself this was not a restaurant and she was not one of his staff. He was so far away from that reality right now, the loud chaos of the kitchens with metal hitting metal, shouts of *Behind you!* and *On deck!*, the slam of the low-boy fridge doors echoing off the ovens. Just a well-stocked ranch-house kitchen with a personal chef who would not last one night in one of his restaurants.

The sounds that were fuel to creating and cooking, the soundtrack to his success and his passion were missing, and he bit back the growing frustration at being stuck at this ranch over the course of dinner prep.

It wasn't about the dinner prep. When he sat later, in the dark, looking out the window, the real reason was clear as the moon staring back at him.

He was missing the cacophony of home, the busy nights, the promise of a good time no matter where you headed out. He was missing the rush of having a purpose, a business, and a crew of his own. The quiet, homebound nature of this forced vacation would be a lesson in patience, whether it was in the kitchen or when he was bereft of things to do other than cook, jog, doomscroll on his phone, or sleep.

"Good morning," he said as cheerfully as possible, and both women looked up. Rosy went still, a veneered smile appearing. Definitely not as friendly as yesterday, and he stepped back. She was tense.

"Good morning, Mr. West," she said, and gathered up her books, scooting into the dining room as quickly as she could. He watched her go, puzzled, and looked over at Peony, who was rubbing her eyes tiredly.

"Have I offended Rosy?" he asked, moving into the now emptier kitchen to grab a mug before tipping some coffee into it. The aroma was ungodly good. At least Rosy had good taste in ingredients.

"She googled you last night. She didn't realize you were Cordon Bleu trained and had cooked with Michelin-starred chefs. I think that may have intimidated her."

"Ah. I'm sorry, should I go talk to her?" he asked, a sinking feeling in his stomach. He didn't want to cause strife, but here he was, putting in wedges. All because of who he was.

"No, no, don't you worry about it," Peony replied tiredly, and then brightened. "Oh! The courier in town called. Apparently there's furniture, some suitcases, and a bunch of boxes in town for you to pick up."

"Furniture?" Jake asked. "Can't they bring it here?"

"That was what they said." Peony shrugged. "Apparently, the office doesn't have a van big enough, which is really odd, since Tessa bought that decked-out Ford not too long ago," she said with a hint of humor in her voice. "I'll see if Brady can spare Bobby today to take you in with the livestock trailer."

Could Gordon have boxed up his storage locker as well? He'd been expecting his personal stuff from the apartment, maybe some of the cookbooks he kept with him, and likely his personal kitchen equipment. Gordon was fussy about his knives and whisks, and Jake knew that his own stuff had cluttered the small Brooklyn apartment's kitchen.

Jake preferred German stainless-steel knives that had longevity in a busy kitchen, whereas Gordon thought Aogami Japanese knives could hold an edge better. In a pinch, he'd settle for Damascus steel, which Jake thought were pretty but much harder to keep sharp. They'd had many a spirited argument over drinks, each hoping to sway their friend to their own perceived "dark side." No one ever budged, but that wasn't the point.

He opened his phone and shot off a quick text to thank him, asking what he'd sent. Gordon shot back a single thumbs-up and *Everything, like you asked, genius*, which gave Jake another shot of homesickness. They had worked together for years and were good friends. He missed Gordon's jokes and ribbing.

Rosy had crept back into the kitchen and was talking to Peony quietly. Jake picked up a few words of "What if I don't make it right?" and his temper flared. One thing he hated was meekness in people, especially kitchen staff. He expected his staff to follow orders, but also to question him and suggest things. A good kitchen ran better if the entire staff was on the same page. Rosy wasn't an employee, but he wanted to work with her, and this was not the way to start out right.

"Rosy," he snapped, wincing as both women jumped at his tone. He let out a breath before saying the next bit as kindly as possible. "Please, if you're having doubts about me being in your kitchen, talk to me about them. I don't want to step on your toes."

Rosy blushed a shade of red he'd only seen on lobsters fresh from the boil pot and blinked. Well, now.

"Oh. Mr. West. I'm so sorry. I'm—" She fiddled with the edges of her sleeves.

"Worried? Don't be. If you want, let me show you a few things," he offered, gesturing to the kitchen. "I'm happy to."

She nodded, flitting glances between Peony, her boss, and him, the interloper.

"This evening at dinner, let's roast that massive chicken you picked up. I'll teach you my dry-rub recipe, and show you how to make a wicked mushroom steel-cut oats risotto to go with it. I saw some in the pantry that will do nicely."

After she'd agreed and practically run from the kitchen, he let out a chuckle as Peony looked exasperatingly at him.

"You just about scared her out of her skin, barking her name like that."

"The kitchen sergeant in me came out," he apologized. "I'll try to be gentler with her. She's a bit of a mouse."

"I think you startled both of us because it sounded just like Brett. He would storm into this kitchen and shout *ROSY!* just like you did, and then ask her what was for dinner."

Jake slugged back the last of his coffee to ward off the pit in his stomach that statement had produced. That he was so like a man he knew nothing about, whom these people knew so intimately, made him edgy.

"I'll be more careful," he said, setting his mug in the sink, restlessness taking hold. "I think I'll go for a run."

Peony waved him off, and he shoved himself into his Tracksmith shorts and tank top as quickly as possible, found his earbuds and his running shoes, and set off down the lane. He spied Brady driving a tractor toward the main barns, along a side road with some sort of machinery off the back, the row of tines shaking as he bumped along. He waved and Brady waved back, a big smile on his face.

He figured he could run up the road to the turnoff from town. It was three miles or so. A good distance to start, since he had been off a few days. He thanked himself for having the foresight to bring workout clothes just in case wherever he stayed had a gym.

Well, this wasn't a gym, but it would do.

He set off down the road, the sun warm on his face, the air so different from the city it took him no time to feel the difference. It was fresh, almost sweet, and he took in a huge lungful as he adjusted his stride to his workout playlist. He could get used to this kind of running. The river pathways this was not. No garbage, no smog, no dodging people walking their fluffy dogs with enormous whipped cream–topped coffees in their hands.

He had run to the turnoff and was starting back when wheels crunched on the gravel behind him. He turned, and Tanner's dark-blue Ford F-250 drove up and slowed down beside him on the wrong side of the road, the diesel engine rumbling. It was a huge truck, the wide side mirrors the same height as his head, and Jake moved over farther on the sloped shoulder.

"You lost, City Boy?" Tanner said out the window as he kept pace with Jake. Jake pulled his earbuds out and stopped, hands on his hips, looking back at Tanner, who seemed amused as he braked the truck, a toothpick wiggling around the corner of his mouth, his eyes obscured by aviator sunglasses.

"No. Out for a run."

"On purpose?" Tanner quipped back, looking in the rearview and then back out, not directly at Jake.

"Yeah. On purpose. Us soft, citified guys need to. We don't throw cows around for a living."

Tanner grunted and tapped the door. "Get in, I need to talk to you."

Jake hesitated. He didn't want to get in the truck. He would rather run another seven miles in the worst heat possible with no water than ride with his brother, but he sensed that this was important.

"Just get in," Tanner muttered. "It's about the bank."

Jake walked around the back of the truck, then hopped in the passenger side. He buckled in, noticing that Tanner had not, and felt once again like an outsider. Tanner hadn't moved the truck yet. He was just staring out the front windshield, the whites of his knuckles showing as he twisted his hands on the steering wheel.

"Okay, so the bank," Jake said. Might as well get this over with, because Tanner looked like he was going to rip his head off at any moment.

"Can you shoot a gun?" Tanner suddenly asked.

"Um. No, can't say I've ever had the need to," Jake replied, mystified.

"You ever helped on a farm with cattle? Driven a tractor?"

"No. Um—" Jake replied again, but was cut off by another deadpan question.

"What about ride? Ever been on a horse?"

"That I have, but it's been a while. Dated a girl who owned a jumper stable. She let me ride now and again."

A snort came from Tanner. Obviously that didn't count.

Jake stared over at his brother. "What does this have to do with banking?"

A sigh came from the other man, and his jaw jumped as he spit the toothpick out the open window. He finally looked over at Jake, and Jake felt the scrutiny of his penetrating gaze even through his sunglasses.

"What in god's name would you know about ranching, then," Tanner muttered more to himself, and pulled the truck back onto the road. "Turns out, now that you 'own' West Line, you have full signing and financial authority over the runnin' of it. Everything. Frank had to file the inheritance stuff, and the bank had to be notified to transfer all the accounts."

"Shit." Jake covered his mouth with his hand, rubbing his jaw in frustration. "That was fast."

"I can't even take out a twenty to buy a lug nut for a tire without your say so, right now."

Jake's mind ran over how he used to delegate purchasing in his restaurants. But banking in Canada was probably vastly different from in the US. Maybe he could set Tanner up with signing authority, and it would be fine. He was still foreman, after all, wasn't he?

They pulled into the barnyard and Tanner hopped out, standing with the door open. Jake did the same and came around to his side.

"What do I have to do to give you back that signing authority?"

he asked bluntly. He had gotten the sense over the past couple of days that Tanner was not frivolous with his words. Blunt worked best. Jake sort of admired that, if not for the fact that it made his brother come across like a class A jerk.

"You'll have to go into the bank and set it up. I reverted to an employee on the ranch, not a partner like I was under Dad. Same for Brady. Liz and Harry will need new purchase cards. Not sure what Peony will need for the house, Dad kept that separate."

They stood in silence a moment, Jake searching for words, Tanner stubbing his toe in the gravel on the driveway, filling a tiny pothole with stones. He didn't hear Liz come up until she was standing beside him.

"You two having a staring contest?" she asked, and Jake jumped.

"No, just discussing ranch business. Apparently, I have to go straighten the bank out, because I can't shoot a gun or drive a tractor."

Liz gave him a strange look and then turned to Tanner, who'd made a face when Jake had spoken. She walked up to him and looked him right in the face, which surprised Jake. She obviously wasn't afraid of his temper.

"Tan. What's going on with the bank?"

"Inheritance papers state he has ownership of everything, including the accounts," Tanner replied, and slammed his truck door. "I can't sign payroll for next week unless we get this shit figured out."

Liz swore under her breath. Jake realized he needed to step up, because Tanner being a jerk aside, payroll was one thing you didn't mess with.

"I'll deal with the bank so I can sign payroll, with your help. I'm no stranger to business books."

Tanner looked up at him. His shoulders dropped a little and he nodded. "Go get changed out of those ridiculous shorts and come back here to the office when you're done. I'll show you what we do so you'll know what to discuss with the bank."

CHAPTER EIGHT

Liz looked between the two men, Tanner striding away to the barns and Jake turning toward the house.

Well, now. It was one thing to have Jake own the place silently for the moment, but to have the accounts and responsibility for pay taken from Tanner? Ouch.

Liz fell into step beside Jake, watching him fiddle with his phone and earbuds, serious thoughts clouding his face.

"How's it going?" she asked, to break the mood that had settled over him, and he looked over at her, then back at the path ahead of them.

"Well, apparently all my stuff arrived in town, and I have to go get it, Rosy is deathly afraid of me, your brother thinks I'm useless, I have the finances of this place to get sorted out, and I am going stir-crazy with no coffee shops and people."

"So, it's goin' well, then," she drawled, wanting to pull him out of the spiral he seemed to be sinking into.

He laughed, and she liked the crinkles that appeared at the corner of his eyes, the way he relaxed his shoulders. She laughed, too, and he stopped on the path, turning to her.

"Yeah, pity party of one over here. I'm just not quite sure what to make of all this yet. I'm worried, tired, restless, and I don't do well without the city noise. It's so quiet here, sleeping is—"

"You'll get used to it. Weaning season is soon. Trust me, you'll wish for the quiet of the city after two days of cows bawling."

"You don't say," he replied, raising an eyebrow. "Noisy, huh?"

"Oh god, yes. It took me a couple of seasons to really get used to it when Mom and I first got here. You don't remember any of this, at all?" she asked, suddenly wanting to know. He had a tie to here, and she wanted him to remember it, make some good memories, so that maybe he would visit once they got it all sorted out and he went back to his life.

"No. My first memories are of concrete, the local park with the broken seesaw, and our third-floor walk-up apartment," he replied.

He certainly was interesting, his life so different from theirs, growing up in a place she couldn't even imagine, or want to be in. But he seemed to be adaptable, and she hoped it meant he would like it here. It had hit her last night, listening to him talk to Brady and her mother, that she was warming to the idea of him being here for the near future. He was fun, easy to talk to, which was reminding her how much she enjoyed talking that wasn't just pleasantries. She wanted to discuss things. Debate, or if not that, at least feel like the conversation was worth something.

Brady really seemed to like him, her mother was looking brighter since he had arrived, and the food was certainly better too. Rosy was a good cook, but her food was bland and carb heavy. She cooked to Brett's tastes, which had been simple.

Liz also decided she liked looking at Jake. He was easy to watch, fluid and controlled with his movements, both in the kitchen and walking beside her now. There was a power and stillness in him that a lot of men hadn't harnessed at his age that was really sexy. Whether it was to control himself, or was just his way, she didn't know yet.

"I was three when Mom left here with me. I saw a picture of me once, I think it was winter, and I was standing on the front veranda of the house here, I assume. I'm in some terrible one-piece toddler snowsuit, with a massive beanie on, clutching a bear. It's the only picture of me that mom took before we were in New York."

"Toque," she said, grateful for the small admission of his past from him. His voice was light, so she went with it.

"What?" he asked.

"Toque. If you're going to live in Canada for a while, you need to learn the terminology. What you folks call a beanie, up here us locals call it a toque."

"Ridiculous," he muttered, humor in his voice, and they continued walking. "Anyway, no, I have no memory of this place, and my mother would never talk about it other than to tell me it was hell on earth."

"Is it?" Liz asked, immediately regretting asking such a personal question. She wanted him to say no. She wanted him to say he really liked it here.

"I'll get back to you on that," he replied. "But I can say I'm enjoying the fresh air."

"Well—" she said, and they both stopped in the middle of the driveway at the main house. Liz looked down at her feet, and Jake cleared his throat.

"Yeah. I think I shouldn't keep Tanner waiting, should I?"

"Okay, then. Good talking to you Jake," she said. He turned, walking backward, and waved at her, a smile on his face that made her stop short. He was completely disarming when he was happy, and her heart skipped a beat. It didn't hurt that all his muscles were popping out from his run, and his hair was falling over one eye. He combed it back as she pulled her lower lip into her teeth. Men around here did not look like that. Mind you, men around here wouldn't be caught dead in shorts that showed off their perfectly toned thighs like that either.

"Hey. Why don't you and I go into town to get my things later today? You have time?"

"Okay," she said quickly, a funny feeling of elation hitting her square in the stomach. "I'll hook up my two-horse trailer and come get you. Around one?"

"It's a date," he replied, spun, and jogged the rest of the way up the driveway to the house.

Liz let out a breath and looked up to the sky, willing her heart to stop flailing against her chest. *A date.*

"Well, you wanted to get to know him, girl. Here you go," she said to herself, and made her way back to the stable.

* * *

Liz honked the horn outside the office, and when no one appeared, killed the engine to the truck and hopped out. They must be ears-deep in the books. She'd said one o'clock, and it was around a quarter past now.

West men, it seemed, were, to a one, not good at timekeeping.

Walking down the hallway between the main cattle barn and the office, she caught voices having some sort of an argument. One deep and even, and one frustrated. *Shit*. She should have known better than to leave Tanner alone with Jake. Hopefully they hadn't started throwing punches.

She poked her head into the office. Jake, in well-fitting jeans, a crisp short-sleeved polo, and his hair a complete mess, was on one side of the room looking through Brett's old ledger. Tanner was on the other, arms crossed, in a pair of oil-stained brown coveralls and beat-up muck boots.

They looked so different it took her a moment to reconcile that the two of them were in the same room. But they were, because the glares Tanner was throwing at Jake were deadly.

"Hey—" she started, but was cut off when Jake ran his finger across the ledger and shook his head.

"So Bobby makes more than Kevin, but both of them make less than Harry or Rowan? Trevor makes more than Liz—"

Tanner interrupted Jake. "Look, this isn't a fancy restaurant. These boys are hired for their know-how and their muscle. Hours are long. Bobby, he's newer than Kevin, but has a diploma from the Ag college. So, yeah, he makes more than Kev. Harry, he's our head cattleman, and Rowan is his son. They're the best when it comes to our beef lines. I trust 'em, so I pay 'em more. Liz runs the stables, and Trevor gets a cut of the lesson program fees on top of his salary."

"It's so arbitrary, I mean—" Jake said, flipping through more pages. "And how is it this isn't in accounting software?"

"Dad hated computers. We haven't switched it over yet," Tanner snapped.

"Lizzie," he muttered, glancing up at her. He looked beyond frustrated at having to explain everything to Jake, justifying what he paid the staff. Which included her.

She waved back silently and leaned against Brady's desk, waiting for Jake to notice she was there. He was so deep into that ledger, she was sure he was going to inhale the ink. He was taking a lot of interest in something he really didn't need to concern himself with.

She'd seen that book so many times, the spiky ink in whatever color pen Brett could find inching across the page, the years marked, the names scratched in over and over. They'd been on Brett for a couple of years about learning to use a computer for all of it, but he'd always refused. Old dog, new trick. Liz usually stayed up late right before tax time reading off numbers while Tanner plunked them in, single finger typing across an Excel spreadsheet. Tanner was only mildly better at using a computer than his father. It could be funny, as Tanner would get frustrated, swearing at the screen as if that would help.

Jake made a noise, pursing his lips. "These boys don't make much, comparatively. How on earth do they make ends meet?"

"Doesn't cost much to live out here. Those who live in the bunkhouse behind Liz's place, rent comes out of their pay," Tanner growled. "Enough. I'm through justifying numbers to you. The bank should have set up the paperwork for you to do when you go to town with Bobby later."

"Actually, I'm taking him in," Liz said, and Jake turned his head. Seeing her, his eyes sparkled with amusement. She shook her head at him, trying not to laugh as she realized he was maybe enjoying goading her brother over the numbers. Those two, under the hood, were two peas in a pod. Payback for Tanner insinuating Jake was useless earlier, likely.

Tanner made a frustrated noise, and Liz looked over at him.

"Tan?"

"Where's Bobby?" he snapped.

"Brady needs him this afternoon," she lied. "I gotta get some senior feed, salt blocks, and maybe that set of hoof nippers you ordered is in. Might as well get Jake's stuff while we're at it and I can drop him at the bank after. Trev is working the horses we need to today, so I have the time."

Tanner shook his head and flicked his eyes to Jake, who had shut the ledger and put it on Brett's desk. They hadn't gotten around to moving his things out of there yet, and Jake picked up a lumpy piece of iron, polished to a sheen. He turned it in his hand, studying it, then set it down. He ran his hands over the funny block-letter nameplate that was half buried under cattle magazines and pulled it out. It spelled out DAD and each blocky, carved letter was painted a garish color of blue.

"Who made this?" he asked, flourishing it. "It's cute."

"Brady did," Liz offered, when Tanner didn't answer. "Apparently got blue Tremclad all over the front porch painting in the letters. Made it in shop class."

Jake set it back down, letting out a breath and dusting his hands off. "You're ready for me?"

She nodded, noticing Tanner was studiously avoiding them, his hands working the muscles on the back of his neck as he looked over some papers on his desk. "I'll meet you in the truck, Jake. Need to talk to Tanner."

Jake ducked out without another word.

"Having fun yet?" she asked gently, as Tanner swiveled his eyes up to her.

"He was trying to make me lose my cool. I know it," he groaned, and sagged into his chair. "Why does he fucking care what I pay my men?"

"Because they're his men right now, and for once, you have a fresh set of eyes on the books. Someone who knows how to run a business." Liz chastised him.

Tanner sometimes didn't realize how much of a dog in a manger he was. Jake might be temporary, but perhaps he could inject some fresh thinking into some of the business practices Tanner was happy to keep status quo from Brett's way of doing things. How many times in the past had he and Brady complained that their father needed to modernize? Yet when push came to shove, Tanner would stick to tried and true instead of innovating. She loved him for his loyalty, but it also drove her mad when she wanted to do something new in the stables and would get turned down by both father and son. Maybe that would change now.

"He doesn't know the first thing about ranching," Tanner replied.

"Maybe, but he's managed people. Bobby deserves a raise. You won't keep him long unless you do. He'll find a big cash-crop outfit to hop to, one where he can use that brain of his for something other than sitting on a tractor and punching cattle when you're short a rider."

"Don't you start in on me too. I've had a long enough day as it is,"

Tanner said peevishly, rubbing at his eyes and groaning. "This place is out of control already."

"It's been three days, Tan," Liz snorted. "It's not. You're the one who feels adrift because you can't control absolutely everything right now."

"It's our money, Lizzie. Without it, this place don't run," he threw back at her.

"I know," she replied. "It's temporary. Jake knows how important something like payroll is."

Tanner groaned and sat up. "Yeah. All right. Pick up a roll of fence wire while you're at it. Twelve-inch fixed knot. We're low and we're due to fix the front fence on the north hayfields."

Liz nodded curtly. In-control-foreman Tanner was back, and conversation was over. She left him in the office to stew and gratefully stepped into the sunlight. Jake was slouched against her truck, hands in his jeans pockets, sunglasses on. He'd finger-combed his hair, and her mouth went dry.

Holy hell, that looked good leaning up against her truck.

"Boss man chew you out too?" he asked as she walked over.

She laughed and shook her head as she hefted herself into the truck. She grabbed her sunglasses and shoved them on, grinning as he much less gracefully flopped up into his seat and slammed his door.

"Ready, City Boy?" she joked, and turned the key.

"Don't you start in on me too," Jake groaned, but smiled when she put the truck in gear and they rolled out.

CHAPTER NINE

Jake thought Brightside looked exactly like a small town should as they parked by the post office. The entire street sundrenched, chrome on the cars beside them blindingly bright, canopies at the front of the stores faded. Jake had never seen a street wider than any avenue in New York with angled parking and old-time coin-fed meters painted a dull gray. If he suspended reality, he could be on a classic movie set, complete with a red and chrome facade on a diner, a department store with the side of the brick painted white over the old sign, and a grocer over on the corner, the front bristling with flowers and overflowing vegetable stands. A side street looked to have a salon, a bar, and a few smaller stores. He pictured classic convertibles and the cast of *Grease* sitting up on the back seats.

The only downside was that, as he scanned, there wasn't one coffee shop to be seen.

The drive in had been calming, full of small talk with Liz doling out trivia about Brightside. He wasn't paying close attention, stealing glances at her as she drove instead. When she smiled, her entire face lit up, and if something he said was funny, she'd glance at him before she laughed. He liked the confident way she relaxed behind the wheel, one hand draped on the top, the other on the gearshift. He'd felt the sway of the trailer behind them when a gust had slapped at them on the road into town, but she didn't even blink. She had expertly backed the entire thing between two vehicles as well, while Jake nervously eyeballed the mirror on the truck beside them, mere inches between them.

Chatting about the town helped alleviate the familiar ache from his childhood, the wood plaque that Brady had painted for their father on his dad's desk stuck in his mind as they left the ranch. It was moments like that that he felt as if he had missed out. That hurt of not having a dad when it mattered most. Tanner and Brady, they'd grown up with that influence, benefited from his guidance, chafed under his discipline, but ultimately, had been given the chance to know their father, and it had shaped them.

He would've given anything to have that. It wasn't as if his father had been dead. He had been here, just outside this apple-pie town, raising other sons.

Jake had been the one he didn't want.

"Earth to Jake?" Liz said as she rounded the front of the truck, flipping her keys in her hands, jingling them.

He looked back at her and his breath caught. She was smiling, one eyebrow lifted because he must have been staring off into space.

Hair escaping from her braid whipped around her face in the wind blowing down the street, and the freckles dusted across her cheeks like tiny stars were stark in the sunlight. He wondered if all of her was freckled. He cleared his throat as their eyes met, that thought much too forward to even contemplate, but it was there all the same.

When he'd asked her if she wanted to go to town with him, it was impulsive and not what he'd planned. When she'd agreed, it had given him a charge of energy.

He'd observed her laughing at something Brady had said at dinner the night before, completely unguarded, and he'd felt that interesting tightening in his stomach, signaling in no uncertain terms that he was attracted to her, and he couldn't deny it if he tried.

She wasn't snobby, but she guarded herself. Sassy comebacks and teasing woven around deeper conversation showed the spirit she had but held in. He liked talking to her; she was intelligent, took a joke, and was tough as nails when it came to keeping up with the men on the ranch. Just yesterday from the front deck of the house he'd caught her riding in the sand ring and had stopped for a moment to watch. Ramrod straight in the saddle, expertly riding a horse in a small circle, the dust from the sand swirling dramatically against the backdrop of sky, trees, and weathered board fencing. Then she slid the gray horse to a stop, pivoted, and rode the circle back the other way. Another rider and horse in the ring did the same pattern when she finished, but were not nearly as exacting.

She was good at what she did, and when he asked her about it later, her eyes had lit up and she had enthusiastically explained with big hand gestures what "reining" was.

Despite everything being so new and getting to know people he was now in effect living with, he could relax around her, be himself. He'd always buttoned himself up around new people. Mind you, most people he'd met in the past couple of years were in the restaurant business and he was normally talking business, even at social gatherings.

With her, he could just be Jake. Not Jake the successful chef or Jake the business owner.

"Is it always this windy in town?" he asked. He impulsively tucked a strand of her hair back behind her ear. She blushed the moment he did, lifting a shoulder in a half shrug, looking away from him.

"I suppose. Brightside is on a bit of a flat spot," she replied. "Never noticed before."

"Okay, well, I'll go see about my stuff. Where's the bank?" he blurted, wanting to distract himself from his invasion of her personal bubble. *Shit*. What was he thinking?

Liz pointed down the street. "It's just up there on the left, the sign with the funny lion on it. That's the bank."

"I'll head over there. Come find me when you're done at the— Wait, do you need me to give you money for the things you have to get?"

"The Co-op. No, I have some cash I pulled last week to use. It'll do until you get the accounts squared away. I'll come back and find you either here or there," she replied, pointing behind him. She walked around back, and within a few moments the trailer was off the hitch and propped up. She hopped back into her truck and rumbled around the corner with a wave out the window.

Jake shoved his hands in his pockets and watched her drive off. It caught him then how much more rugged she was than him. He wasn't used to not feeling like the capable one in charge. "Get a grip, West," he muttered under his breath, and stepped into the post office.

The amply built, beehive-haired woman behind the counter looked up as the doorbell tinkled, and he watched as her eyes went wide when she saw him. He supposed he was going to get that reaction from people who knew his father. Peony did say he looked very much like Brett. It was frustrating to hear on some level, but it also made him strangely proud. Like a part of his identity had been missing up until now.

"Can I help you?" the woman asked, putting her glasses on, the beaded chains wiggling as she settled them on the bridge of her nose and squinted.

"Yes. I'm Jake West. Apparently, you have a large number of boxes for me."

The woman put her hand on her chest and made that *tsk*ing noise all older women made when they were taking stock of you. He wasn't sure if it was a good or a bad noise, so he waited for her to finish. She went from that to pulling out a book and grabbing a pen.

"My word, you look like your daddy. But you've got your momma's cheekbones. I can see 'em," she clucked as she pointed to the line on the page where he had to sign. "I'll get Herb to pull your stuff. Liz left her rig out front, I see."

The post office lady was a hawkeye it seemed, and knew his mother. Did everyone? It bugged him suddenly, that there was a side to his mother he had never experienced, and that he couldn't even begin to know what she might have been like. Swallowing the lump in his throat, he nodded. "Thank you, ma'am. Much appreciated."

The clerk *tsk*ed some more, took a long look at him and shook her head. "You sound like Brett, too, Lord above. No woman in town is safe from you with those eyes and that smile either. Not one."

She prattled on as she opened the door behind the counter and stuck her head through. "HERB! The lost West boy's here for his stuff," she screamed, and Jake hung his head. *Right*. Small towns. Gossip. Everyone likely knew exactly who he was and what was happening.

She turned back and smiled sweetly at him. "He'll bring it 'round front if you want to open up the trailer."

"Thank you," he said, backing away from the noise as she screamed for Herb again.

He stepped into the sunshine and went to the rear of the trailer. He looked for a handle of some sort to open it, but found none. He looked at the side, then poked at the hinge pin. How in hell did you open this thing? He stood back, arms crossed, feeling like a complete idiot.

A throat cleared behind him and he turned to see an older skinny, bald man—Herb—behind him, a cart stacked with Jake's suitcases and several taped boxes.

"Ya never opened one of these things before?" he asked in a quiet, raspy voice.

"Nope." Jake shrugged and gestured at the back of the trailer, the feeling of inadequacy bubbling near the surface again.

Herb muscled past him and levered up a small handle Jake hadn't seen in the middle. With a squeal the hinges on both sides popped and the doors swung wide. Herb dusted his hands and put them on his hips, looking over at Jake.

"All good. I've got to go get the next load. Furniture too. Think you can manage this part?" Herb said, a hint of humor in his voice.

Jake grinned sheepishly and sighed. "Thank you. Yes."

It took several trolley loads and a few trips in and out carrying his oak table, chairs, recliner, bed, side tables, and some light fixtures, but the lot of it was loaded. Herb was surprisingly strong for his thin stature.

Jake flipped though the itemized receipt. Gordon had sent everything he'd brought to the apartment and what furniture he'd kept from his storage locker. He'd taken Jake literally when Jake had said "everything." What was Gordon thinking? That Jake would be here for longer? His entire life was now loaded into the back of a horse trailer. He looked in and it felt wrong, boxes stacked around the padded bars at the front, bits of hay scuffed up by their feet stuck to the side of the mattress bag crammed in on one side.

"How on earth did he ship all of this?" Jake asked, as Herb wedged the last dining chair in.

"We're the main parcel depot. FedEx comes into us as well since we have the space out back. We get lots of stuff for folks who move here and don't come in with their own moving truck."

"Ah," was all Jake could say.

Jake wanted to laugh at the situation. He'd have to ship it right back to New York when he was all done out here. This time, he'd get one of those pod shipping services, make it easy. It would show up to his new apartment and he could bribe friends with beer and pizza to move it all back in.

Jake turned and shook Herb's hand, thanking him for his help, and Herb showed him how to close the trailer doors. They stood for a moment in amiable silence, watching the traffic go past. Jake sensed Herb didn't want to go back inside.

"Sorry about your pa. He was a good man," Herb offered suddenly, and nodded. "A smart cattleman too."

"I'm glad to hear that," Jake said, strangely peevish at the statement. Yet another person who knew his father. "I never met him."

Herb looked surprised, and Jake nodded a curt goodbye and stepped off the curb, heading toward the bank. Let Herb tell post office lady that and grease the rumor mill more than it already was. It irked Jake that he was the subject of gossip. He didn't like being singled out, even though he did enjoy publicity when it came to his restaurants. This was different. Invading his private life, putting his struggles on display.

Jake lingered for a moment in front of the bank and sent money to Gordon to cover the total from the receipt, then typed a hasty message to call him when Gordon had time.

A noisy truck towing a flatbed trailer stacked high with round bales of hay rattled past, startling him, and he watched it slow down and turn the corner through town, the brake lights of the trailer covered in dust. He tucked his phone back into his pocket with a heavy sigh, turned his head to the sun, and closed his eyes, letting it warm him for a moment before he entered the bank.

New York had never felt farther away.

* * *

"So this document is for the line of credit. Sign here, and here."

Jake signed his name on the bottom where the yellow and red Sign Here stickers were, realizing he was again dealing with paperwork. First his restaurant and his divorce, three days ago all the inheritance stuff, now all this. Control over his life was tied to ink and paper for the foreseeable future.

He'd signed onto three different checking accounts, a line of credit, a credit card with secondaries for each division on the ranch, several long-term investment funds, and a very small mortgage taken out last year. All now his. He hadn't looked at them, just signed them. He could get into the books and see the amounts later.

"Okay, so how do I get signing authority for Tanner and Brady back onto the bank accounts?" he asked as the account manager he was dealing with gathered all the papers, tapping them into a pile and placing them in the fat folder he had beside him.

"Oh. Right. Tanner asked about that already. Well, they can come in with a written letter from you. Then we'll add them both as a signatory on the accounts you indicate. Shouldn't take long," he said. "They'll need employment paperwork, too, social insurance numbers, that sort of thing."

Jake grimaced at that. Employment papers. He was going to be the boss, officially. What a mess. Standing up, he gathered the thick binder of account information, temporary cards with his name on them, and statements jammed in.

"Thanks. I'll be in touch if I have any questions."

The bank manager nodded and gestured outward. "Of course. Thank you, Mr. West."

Jake spotted Liz sitting in the lobby of the bank, tapping her hat against her leg, her face giving away that she was bored and perhaps slightly annoyed to be waiting. He stopped for a moment, pretending to adjust the papers in the folder, to watch her while she couldn't see him.

Jake wondered if she ever truly relaxed. Not in a friendly way, like she did at dinner, but as a woman, putting aside the rough exterior. She was incredibly good-looking, but she hid it behind boots, jeans and denim shirts, trucker caps and cowboy hats. She was, on the surface, rough and tumble, even if the jeans hugged her curves and the buttons on her denim shirts strained across her breasts perfectly.

The idea of seeing her in a sundress and out of what appeared to be her natural element was intriguing, and he had a strange idea to ask her out to a nice dinner. If there was a nice place to go to dinner here, that was.

He chastised himself for trying to fit her into a box that likely she wouldn't even come close to fitting into. She was who she was, and he liked her the way she was, so far. He never liked it when people pigeonholed him, and here he was, trying to do the same to her.

She sighed and looked around as he stepped out from behind the wall.

"All done?"

He nodded and they walked out together into the sunshine. She'd already hooked the trailer back up, and the rig—as he had now learned to call it—was waiting for them just around the corner, parked across four spots. He leaned on the side of the truck, closing his eyes for a moment. He was tired; this was a lot to take in.

"Coffee?" Liz asked as she jingled her keys, and he opened his eyes, turning his head to her.

"God, yes," he muttered.

She smiled, and again he wondered what she would feel like slid up against him, because it softened her, and it put ideas into his head of what she'd look like when he was taking off the sundress after dinner.

CHAPTER TEN

"This is the best coffee I have had since I got here."

Liz put her mug down and shook her head. "It's just diner coffee. But, yeah, this is the best in town. We don't have a Tim Hortons in Brightside yet. One's comin', apparently, out on the highway."

"Am I able to buy beans at the local grocery store?" he asked, and drained his mug, a sigh escaping him as he did.

"What for?" she asked, curious.

"In that mess of boxes is my Breville coffee maker. My friend sent me everything, even the furniture I put into storage when I sold my condo. I think he misunderstood what I meant," he said, rubbing the back of his neck in frustration. "I just spent six hundred dollars to bring my entire life here, by express courier."

Liz blinked. That was a generous friend, because six hundred dollars was more than her grocery bill for a month.

"That is . . . wow," she said, deciding to ignore the price tag for a moment. "We can set yours up, I suppose. We have a great one in the kitchen at the big house. Mom loves it, and there's a grinder at the store."

"Mine grinds the beans fresh, does espresso, has a milk steamer and all that," he replied sheepishly. "A little fancier than your mom's carafe brewer. It's called the Oracle."

"The Oracle," Liz repeated. That sounded exactly like something a top chef would own. But if it did espresso, her mother was going to be over the moon. That old Cuisinart would be as good as gone when she found out. Her mom loved fancy coffees.

She remembered when they had done a day trip into the city and had stopped for a coffee at the café in the mall. Liz had hated hers—it tasted burnt—but her mother had been in ecstasy, her frouffy, whipped cream–covered drink wafting caramel and calories as she sipped.

"My mom will love that. Once you set it up and teach her how to use it, it won't be yours anymore," she said, chuckling.

"I like your mom. She has fire in her." Jake laughed as well. "When did she find out about her arthritis?"

Liz frowned. That word. For a long time it had dampened her mom's spirit. Thank god for Brett and his health plan, but now . . .

"About five years ago. She was in pain, had swollen joints, it would come and go. There were days she couldn't eat and the dizziness would incapacitate her. We took her into the doctor and after a whole set of tests, they told her it was rheumatoid arthritis. Nothing really you can do. She has these strong prescription painkillers, but she says they hurt her stomach, so often she just sleeps through a flare-up."

"Did you look into her diet?" Jake asked, picking up the saltshaker on the table and turning it absently.

"Not really. I mean, food is food, right?" she replied.

She watched his hands. They were strong but had none of the weathered creases and callouses most men she knew had by the time they were in their thirties. Despite the conversation topic, her mind wandered to what they would feel like running over skin, the palms smooth instead of rough. She took a sip of coffee to ward off that particular line of thought. Where had that come from?

"Well, let me dig up some info online about inflammation and trigger foods. I think if your mom adjusts her diet, she might have flare-ups less frequently. One of my patrons in my last restaurant, he had lupus, and he and I used to have long conversations about his diet and how he effectively shut the disease down by avoiding certain food. I'd make up special dishes for him to try based on that. He said it helped."

He was being way too nice. Liz narrowed her eyes. "Why?" she asked, suddenly annoyed both at herself for doubting him and because he seemed to be too good to be true. "Why are you so nice to us and helping us when—"

Jake straightened, looking her in the eye. It was one thing to be ungrateful, she realized, but another to voice it.

"Liz, I know you should resent me," he said quietly, and folded his hands in front of his mug. "You don't know me. I'm a stranger. I don't belong here, and I'll be gone when you get this all sorted out."

Liz kept her eyes on his hands, not his face, because she didn't want to see how her very personal question had affected him. "In your shoes, I would be so pissed off at everyone. I'm betting your temper can match Tanner's, and you've been so tolerant, and helpful, and really great."

She dared look up as he *hmm*ed under his breath, and set her coffee cup aside. Their eyes met again. She could see sadness in them. He had a life story she didn't know, apart from the snippets he had given out over the past couple of days. She wondered how hard it had been for him. How differently from his brothers he had grown up. She understood growing up without a dad, but he never even got a chance, leaving here when he was so young. She had a father she'd known, even if he was terrible.

"I can't be mad at anyone, really. It isn't Tanner's fault or Brady's. I can't blame your mom, or you, even. My . . . Brett's decision to mess around with the lives of his children wasn't your doing."

"But he's taken you away from your life in New York. Your family, your job—"

"Don't have either there. Not currently," he replied, interrupting her. He looked away, out the window, squinting. "I sold my restaurant, signed my divorce papers, and I don't know where my mom is right now."

"Friends?" she asked. There had to be something.

"Yeah, friends of course," he said and let out a frustrated breath. "Aside from that, not even my stuff is there now, since it's all in the back of your horse trailer. I intend to regroup once I get home." His voice was clipped and tense. *Shit.*

"So, you'll open another restaurant once you go back?" she asked, hoping to change the direction of their conversation to something he'd want to talk about.

"Don't know yet. Not as easy as you'd think."

"Oh," she said. That answer sounded like a lot of baggage, literally and figuratively.

He seemed to be a stable, intelligent guy who was nice to boot, so what was the catch? There had to be one. Guys like him always had one. Doubt crept in, the suspicious side of her nature getting the better of her. Why wasn't he fighting mad to get this situation cleared up and get himself back to his own world?

He'd said he wanted no part in the ranch, but what if he did? What if his mind changed, prizing the financial gain to be had in hanging on long enough to sell the place and get out, doing exactly what Tanner expected him to do? The terrible thought of developers carving up the land, or worse, a big operation coming in and bulldozing the century barns for a massive feedlot was horrifying to think.

"So, maybe the ranch could seed your next one? I mean, it is yours. You could sell it, once you can. Big payday in that," she blurted before she could stop herself, the words sounding much worse spoken than in her head. She put her hand over her mouth, wincing.

Jake sucked in a breath and his face went hard. She shouldn't have said that and poked the bear. Her mouth had gotten her into trouble, yet again.

"Is that what you think? That I could just up and pull it out from under Tanner and Brady? Leave you and your mother in the lurch? I've already said I won't," he snapped, and stood, signaling to the waitress for the bill.

"No, no, I—" she spoke quickly. "I—"

"Listen, Liz. I don't want to be here. As soon as we can get this fucking ridiculous will figured out, I'll be out of your hair. The West legacy is intact. I'm not that kind of man."

"Jake, please stop, just—" she pleaded, but his eyes shot angrily to her, and he flipped out an American twenty, slamming it on the table before the waitress could actually deliver the bill he'd asked for. He stormed out as she stood, hat in her hand, immediately angry at herself. He'd never once given her any inkling he would do that, and with one impulsive thought, she'd accused him of it.

"Sorry, Jenny, see you later," she mumbled.

Jenny gathered up the cash with a surprised face, her eyes following Jake. "You want change, Liz?" she asked, but Liz just kept walking and followed Jake out the door, embarrassed to her toes.

Jake was standing by the truck, his back tense, his shoulders around his ears, arms folded. Liz had the oddly timed thought that she needed to get him a hat or he was going to burn if he was going to stay out here much longer. If he did now, because of her stupidity.

"I'm sorry," she said, and he turned his head toward her. He sighed and shoved his hands in his pockets.

"Anywhere else you need to go?" he asked brusquely, and walked around to the passenger side of the truck, getting in, scowl firmly planted along with his sunglasses. So much for comfortable.

"Fuck," she whispered, and got into the truck. She wanted to apologize again, but part of her wasn't willing to put out the effort if he was going to brush her off.

* * *

Liz dropped Jake at the office so he could deliver the paperwork and talk to Tanner, telling him she'd drop the trailer with his stuff up at the house. He nodded silently and strode off, folder under his arm, shoulders still jacked up to his ears. She turned and drove over to the garage at the main house, backing the trailer up to one of the bays. She switched off the engine and sat for a moment, forehead on the steering wheel, attempting to shake off the tension. The past few days had been strange, and that drive had taken the cake. Silence all the way home, just the radio playing. He was as sensitive and hair-triggered as his brother, but instead of being able to weather it like she could with Tanner, she was hypersensitive to Jake's mood. Probably because she didn't know him.

A tap on the glass window startled her, and Brady shot a massive toothy grin at her when she shrieked.

"Brady! Fuck," she swore as she got out. "Why you gotta do that all the time?"

He laughed and stuck his tongue out at her, stepping over to the garage to raise the door. "Let's unload all his crap in here. We need the trailer tonight. He can sort it later on his own."

They silently unloaded the boxes and suitcases into the corner, Liz setting the one labeled *Oracle* by the door so it could go right into the kitchen. The table and chairs looked modern and fancy, the bed frame heavy. They muscled it all in carefully, both conscious that it was more expensive than anything they owned. Brady stood for a moment, hands on his hips, and looked at the pile.

"A lot of stuff," he mused. "He plannin' on staying?"

"His friend sent everything," Liz said, and sighed. "After I opened my stupid mouth, likely he won't stay a moment more than he has to."

Brady gave her a funny look and she waved him off.

"I put my foot in it, like I usually do," she replied, and walked out of the garage, stopping and lifting her face to the waning sun, willing her frustration to go away.

Brady stood beside her and looked over at her, his eyebrow quirked.

"What?" Liz said. "Don't look at me like that."

"You like him." His eyebrow quirked farther.

"Brady—"

"So now everything he says has to be analyzed," Brady interrupted. "Whenever you like a guy, you get suspicious of him, like you can't trust him, even though you—"

"I what?" she shot back, irritated.

"Want to."

He ducked as she punched him on the arm, his laughter bouncing off the wall of the garage. She threw her arms up in the air and let him have the last word. Brady could always read her like a book.

He was the sweetest of the three of them growing up, the one who was the conciliator. If someone was fighting, he wanted to make it better, had empathy in spades. Tanner just called a spade a spade, and didn't care who got hurt by it.

"No," she countered, and Brady waggled his finger at her.

"Don't 'no' me, Liz. They aren't all like your ex, Darren," he said, then crossed his eyes, stuck out his tongue, and pretended to shove his finger up his nose. "They aren't all selfish pricks."

"Seriously! Brady!" she implored, finally giving in and laughing at his impression. "Stop it."

He made another funny face at her and then laughed again,

turning to close the garage door with a thump. Dust swirled out behind it, and Liz wondered when they were going to get a good rain. They needed it. Hay was in but the second cut wasn't ready yet; it was the perfect time to have a good downpour.

She needed to get back to work. This diversion was making her slack off.

"I just accused him of wanting the ranch for the payday. All because he told me that he doesn't have much to go back to in New York," she blurted, pinching her lips together. Telling Brady would make her feel better, maybe.

Brady halted, all amusement gone. He put an arm around her and squeezed. "Precisely, dear sister. He might, just might, find something here worth staying for, and jeepers, that is scary stuff."

He was right. "Shit, Brady. You're the baby. Why you gotta be the smart one?"

"They say brains skip a generation," he jested, as he hopped around back and closed the trailer doors. "If that's true, I'm a freakin' genius next to my brother!"

"Which one?" Liz teased, and Brady stuck his tongue out again.

"I don't know anymore," he said and shrugged. "I like the new one. Can't say if he's ranch material yet, but us West boys can be pretty stubborn when we're given something new to chew on. Now, take me back to the barns, Jeeves, I have real work to do."

They got in, and she headed back out the laneway, the truck rocking back and forth, the squeak of the trailer loud now that it was completely empty. She leaned her arm out the window, casting her eyes over the field of corn bordering the front of the driveway, hot summer air and sunshine licking at her skin.

"Liz, don't overthink this, you've got nothing to worry about with Jake. I get a sense he's genuine," Brady said, and she looked over at him.

He was doing the same as her, leaning out the window, as always, eyes on a swivel, keeping tabs on everything.

She countered his thought in her head. This place was worth being defensive about. It was home. She hoped it kept being home. Both Tanner and Brady had reassured her that she and her mother weren't going anywhere, but the unrest of Brett's boneheaded move wasn't easy to shake. Maybe that was it. She was so worried that any sort of chink in the perceived plan set her off.

"I'm not overthinking it," she lied.

"You are. Apologize to him. This has us all thinking things that we likely wouldn't normally. He's been here less than a week, for Christ's sake. There are bound to be hiccups as we all get to know one another."

Liz let that sink in. *Yeah*. She would have to grovel. She sighed and turned the corner toward the barns. Less than a week. It had felt like longer, for some reason.

"At least Tanner hasn't killed him yet?" she offered, and Brady smirked.

CHAPTER ELEVEN

Tanner might just kill him, the way he was flipping through the agreements with a tense ferocity that made Jake think of an angry dog chewing on a bone.

"This it? He went through all of it?"

"Far as I know. Said he'd be in touch if anything else came up, and to come in with the letters as soon as possible," Jake replied. "The temp cards are for us to use until the new ones come in the mail, we need to cut up the old ones."

"Do we have to put new PINs and stuff in?"

"Yeah," Jake replied. "You can do that online. I have the logins."

Tanner swore under his breath. It was obvious he didn't like change one bit. Jake looked around at Brady's mostly unused desk, organized like he was living in the '50s with a pen in a weird marble holder—complete with ball chain—and a green blotter. Tanner's was crowded with a screwdriver, a hammer holding down an unorganized heap of paper, and an ancient dusty computer—the 1990-era tower case slightly yellowed—and a set of broken flat metal clippers with duct-taped handles balanced on top.

These guys needed some help; needed to get dragged kicking and screaming into the twenty-first century, that was for certain. Jake wondered if the computer even ran.

"All the books, where are they? I should probably look at them and get familiar with the ins and outs if I have to sign for a few days until we can square you away. Be a pain to find you every time I need to make a transaction."

Tanner glanced up and frowned. "Yeah," he muttered, and pointed at Brett's desk. "All of it's there."

Jake wandered over, cataloguing the cluttered desk. Invoices, ledgers, scattered receipts, fingerprint-smeared copies of work orders. A bank statement peeked out of a creased folder. Jake looked around.

"Where's the filing cabinet?"

Tanner pointed behind the desk at a rusty, lopsided cabinet painted the same dusty green as the wall. It had a Shur-Gain sticker on one drawer front and a 1978 calendar magnet from the local feed store on another. Detritus of a life lived, gathered over time. Jake felt strange looking at his father's things, overt hints at who the man had been. He put a hand on the top of the cabinet, and a dealership's business card with a picture of a Chevy truck from decades ago slipped off and hit the floor.

"Seriously? Have I been transported back in time? Is Jed Clampett going to arrive in a moment to tell us he found oil?" Jake muttered to himself, and yanked the first drawer open, the rails screeching.

"Look, assh—" Tanner's voice cracked. "If you don't like it, you can leave it to me, and all you have to do is sign shit. I don't need your help."

"Oh my god," Jake muttered, faced with file folders jammed every which way, years scrawled across the tops, pasted on with white labels. None of it was in order. "Did he do any of the books on a computer, or did you transfer it all for the accountant like this?"

"I have the year-end files on my computer," Tanner said tersely. "But all the current year paperwork is in that cabinet, and on the desk."

Jake desperately wanted to sit down for a moment, but he

wondered if Tanner would drag him out by his balls if he did. It was his father's chair, so sitting might be crossing yet another line. He leaned on the desk, his arms crossed, looking at it. At one point the fabric had been dark green. Now it was faded, the wood polished to a sheen by umpteen pairs of denim-sleeved coveralls. Jake ran a finger over the top of one armrest.

Tanner shook his head as he let out a frustrated growl, and Jake caught him rolling his eyes. "Sit in it or don't, I don't give a shit."

Their eyes met. "Didn't want to assume," Jake murmured.

Tanner snorted. "You're too sensitive, City Boy. It's a chair, not a shrine. Fucking thing squeaks."

Jake closed the cabinet door and straightened, restless and tense. He wanted out of this room; his father was everywhere. It was as if he needed to take the reminders in doses. Too much and it overwhelmed him.

"I should get back to the house. I promised to help Rosy. You going to join us tonight?" Jake asked, hopeful that Tanner might let the chip fall off his shoulder. He knew it was hard to ask Tanner to do that, with everything that had happened, but it hurt the others when he didn't join them. Jake could see it when they'd gotten the text back every night so far.

"Doubt it," Tanner grunted back, not looking up. Jake let it lie, and left the office, walking back out past the big cattle barn entrance and into the graveled space of the barnyard. He stopped, looking around him. One of the crew—Rowan, he thought—drove past on an ATV, and waved as he skidded around the corner, accelerating between the main cattle barn and a smaller lower barn that ran perpendicular to it. The buzz of the ATV faded, and the relative quiet returned except for the distant lowing of cattle in one direction and a whinny coming from the stable on the other side of the yard.

Jake felt out of place and alone, the big sky around him a marked difference from the glimpses he normally got between high-rises, the sounds organic with no rhythm. Instead of being able to tune them out, he heard every single bird, every single tractor as it trundled by. There was no predictability in it.

"You're being an idiot," he muttered to himself, annoyed that everywhere he went he noticed the differences, and it made his brain turn. It was exhausting.

He was just walking past the stables when a door slammed and shouting started from inside. Looking up just in time, he saw a big gray horse barreling out the door, right at him.

"Whoa, whoa!" he yelled, and waved his hands, trying to remember all the rusty horse knowledge he had. The horse stopped, snorting, the lead rope dangling from its halter, and looked curiously at him, the reason for flight forgotten. Jake walked up to the horse carefully, making soothing noises, and snagged the rope as Liz and another man ran out. Liz held a cloth to her face, blood seeping through it.

"Thanks," said the man as he reached them and took the lead from Jake. "Shithead got away from us while we were trying to give him worm medicine."

Jake nodded and caught Liz doubled over, the cloth still on her face. When she looked up, her eyes glittered like a pissed off cat, and he swept his eyes over her. She was hurt, but she was mad about it. He curbed his impulse to grab her and look her over.

"Liz?" he called over. "What happened?"

"Nobed me in by fabe," she mumbled through the cloth, and then lifted it off her nose to look at it. He could see blood was still leaking out of one nostril, but there was no telltale swelling of broken cartilage, at least not yet. He'd been in plenty of situations at the boxing gym to know what that looked like. Face protectors didn't always work when the other guy put in a good hit.

"You need to come up to the house. Get some ice on that," he said, and stepped over, touching her arm. She pulled away and glared at him. "I'b fine," she gurgled, wadding the cloth and sticking it back under her nose.

The man who had raced out with her gave her a look that was part amusement, part exasperation. "Listen to this guy. Go get ice on it. I'll finish up."

"Jake West," Jake said, and extended his hand. Might as well meet the staff while he could. From what he could remember from the books, this was likely Trevor.

"Trevor Hanes. Nice to meet you. Damned unconventional, but glad you're able to help them clear it all up," Trevor said as he switched the lead out of his right hand and shook Jake's hand.

Jake wondered how much of the story he knew, but let it pass. People who worked together often became close, like family, and this place would have that kind of loyalty. Hell, Gordon and several of the kitchen staff had known as much about his divorce as he had. They'd been his sounding board, often gathering for stiff drinks after a long shift to kvetch about life in general.

"Thanks. Yeah. I'll take Liz up and pass her off to her mother. Peony can fuss over her, make her really mad."

A sound came from Liz that indicated she'd heard him, and he turned to her. What she had said to him in the diner still twisted in his gut, and he'd been royally pissed off at her for assuming the worst of him.

But the more he'd thought about it, the more he'd realized it wasn't exactly untrue. In the dark moments that first night when he couldn't sleep for crickets and quiet, he'd thought about the what-ifs, the permanence of inheriting an entire ranch—a huge, cumbersome life change eliciting more questions about what he would do if he said fuck it and did what the damn will wanted him to do. Stay, then sell, and with his portion fund his next restaurant.

He'd dismissed it the next day, stupidity and lack of sleep making him think about things he would never willingly do to this family unless they wanted him to. But when Liz had blurted that out, it had rankled him, and he—once again—had let his temper get the better of taking the high road.

"Don't argue with me. Just come up to the house," he said, and she growled through the cloth again.

"No. I'b fine."

"No, you're not. Sweetheart, that cloth is turning more red than white. Now march," he barked, his patience wearing thin.

With one more angry glare, likely because he'd just called her sweetheart, she started off for the path to the house, and Jake waved at a laughing Trevor as he fell into step behind her. Watching her walk, one arm swinging angrily, the other held up, indignant elbow twisted, he wondered if now would be the best time to apologize for how he'd reacted to her in the diner. He paused that thought when she jerked and tripped on a tree root, swore, then immediately tripped again.

"Slow down," he said as he caught up to her, and got rewarded with another glare. "Let me see."

She took the cloth away from her face, and he lifted her chin to look at her nose a little more carefully.

"He got you good and square," he murmured, eyes flicking to hers. He wondered how much of the anger drilling out of them was at him or at the horse that had clocked her.

"Yeb," she mumbled. "Fuggink horth."

Jake couldn't help but laugh as she let out a whistling, nasally sigh. She gave him another equally killer glare as she pushed past him. As she did, she stumbled, dropping her cloth, and Jake caught her so she wouldn't fall.

"Careful," he breathed, his arms around her, her hands rising to his chest to balance herself. Surprised, she looked into his eyes, went white as a sheet, and fainted, right then and there.

He swung her legs into his arms and carried her the rest of the way to the house in a hurry. He kicked open the back screen door, which was thankfully on a pressure latch. He lurched through the kitchen to the back TV den, and carefully deposited her on the leather couch near the back of the room.

"Peony!" he bellowed out the door. "You here?"

He tucked up Liz's hands and legs as best he could. Her nose was still bleeding, and he propped her head up so she wouldn't choke. Her hair had come out of her hair tie and was everywhere, some of it caked with blood, and he smoothed it back, squatting beside her. Looking at her like this, he didn't like the way he'd felt when she'd fallen into his arms. The strength that had surged through him when he'd swung her up rattled him as well. That, he realized as he rubbed the back of his neck, was not an impartial feeling he'd had. He stuffed it away; there were more important things to think about, like whether she needed a hospital or not.

"What happened?" Peony said as she rushed into the room. "Should I call an ambulance?"

"She got whacked in the face by a horse, that's all I know," he said. "She fainted walking up here to get some ice for her nose. We should take her into emergency."

Peony made an irritated noise and swished out of the room, appearing a moment later with a tea towel, a blue ice pack, and a first-aid kit.

"She needs to get seen. If she has a concussion—" she said and stopped. "Fool girl. I bet it was that high-strung gray she regrets taking on."

Liz's eyes fluttered and she groaned, and Jake crouched down to her, holding her head still and looking into her face. "Hey," he murmured softly, pushing the hair back from her face. "Don't you dare get up."

She looked confused, saw her mom, and struggled to get up, but Jake gently pushed her down. "What did I say, hmm?"

She huffed and lay back, fingers gently probing her nose and wincing. "Shid," she muttered.

Rosy appeared with a bowl of water and set it down beside Jake. He looked at her and nodded, and she thinned her lips. "That looks like it needs seeing," Rosy said.

"I think so too. Rain check on the chicken tonight? I promise you and I will spend some time in that kitchen tomorrow."

Rosy nodded and left as quickly as she came, and Jake sighed. He'd been looking forward to breaking the ice with her, but it would have to wait.

"All right. Is there a car I can take? Her truck will bounce her right out of her head and my rental's air conditioning is shitty. Do you want to come with us too?"

"I'b nod goig doo a hozpidal. Doo far," she protested, and slowly sat up, gasping and wincing.

"Yes, you are," Peony admonished her daughter. "And, no, I'll stay here. She's in good hands with you, Jake. You can take her to the community medical center in Brightside," she added.

"No, nod there," Liz protested. "Anywhere bud there."

"Where else then, dear? It's a long drive into the city." Liz was now glaring at both her mother and Jake, but Peony stared her daughter down.

Jake smothered a laugh, got up from the floor, and leaned against the door frame to watch the showdown from a safe distance. If he hadn't been worried about Liz, the situation would be rather comical. Both mother and daughter were as stubborn as they came.

"Fine," Liz huffed a moment later, and crossed her arms, pouting as best she could as her face swelled.

Peony cleaned her up, clucking a little over her, earning further exasperated sighs and eye rolls from Liz. When she'd finished, Peony placed a piece of tape over the bridge of Liz's nose. She looked like a boxer. Her eyes were both going to be black tomorrow, to go with one hell of a headache.

"You can take Brett's Lincoln. Keys are hanging by the garage door. It's a smooth ride," Peony said as she finished and got up from the couch. She was moving better already, he thought. Stress was lessening, and she was getting sleep, he figured.

"Momb?" Liz said as she looked at her mother incredulously. "Bred's car?"

"Well, it's that or Jake's little rental, which will have you sweating in no time. Which would you prefer, darling?" Peony said crisply, folding the slightly damp, stained tea towel in her hands. Liz dropped her chin and let out another sigh.

"My chariod awaids then. Lead on, thidy boy," she mumbled, and then Jake did laugh as he headed for the garage.

CHAPTER TWELVE

"Damn it, I want to go home," Liz muttered to no one in particular. "This is stupid. I'm fine."

A raised eyebrow from Jake, who was slouched in a chair next to the examination table with his eyes closed, made her want to throw the tissue box beside her at him. She winced again as she shifted on the bed, her head throbbing. The ice had done wonders, and the saline sinus rinse had stung like a son of a bitch, but her nose was clear now. New tape across the bridge itched. All they were waiting for was a doctor to discharge her and tell her it wasn't completely broken, of which she was already aware. She'd broken her nose before, and this wasn't that.

"You aren't terribly patient for a horse trainer," Jake remarked, and she turned to him, narrowing her eyes. His tall, wide frame barely fit into the chair, and as she glared at him, she remembered what it had felt like falling into that frame.

Shit. She'd already been lightheaded. Then—

"Seriously?" she muttered. "What would you know about it?"

Jake opened his eyes at that point, the brown depths much calmer than she felt, and she looked away.

"I dated a girl who owned a jumper farm in the Hamptons. Got the basics for sitting on a horse from her."

"She used English saddles and jumped, then?" Liz asked. "Like at Spruce Meadows."

"No idea where that is, but if they do that there, then yes."

They lapsed into silence, the sounds of the clinic echoing around them. Her head throbbed as she shifted, the ache radiating outward. It was going to hurt more later, and she sighed, already feeling behind, knowing that tomorrow she would likely be relegated to work she could do from a desk instead of working all the horses they had in. Summer was busy season, and every day mattered.

"Where is that damned doctor?" she muttered, and hopped off the edge of the table, holding the side for support. Her eyes caught Jake's for a moment, and he tilted his head.

"You okay?"

"Fine," she snapped.

"You say that a lot," he replied, and sat up, quirking another eyebrow. "You don't like relying on other people, do you?"

She gave him a dirty look, then leaned against the table, examining her hands. "No."

"Me neither," he said. He was doing the same, but then looked up at her, letting out a chuckle. "I hated it when people would wade their way in and help. I didn't want it, would push them away, be a big dick."

"Look, I'm sorry about earlier today. I really am," she muttered. "My brain and my mouth don't always connect."

"Me too. All this—" He gestured around but was cut off when the door opened and a doctor poked his head in.

It was her ex, Darren. Of all the shittiest shit luck. She frowned as his face went from amiable doctor to pressed-together lips and tension. She knew he was not pleased to see her because his forehead was wrinkled in the way it did when he was frustrated by something. He stepped into the room and closed the door.

"Well, Liz, who'd you beat up now?"

"Really?" she snapped, and folded her arms on her chest. "Could you not?"

Jake was looking back and forth between them, obviously surprised at their reactions to one another.

"Darren, this is my . . . Jake West. Jake, this is Dr. Darren Hollister."

"Ah. The long-lost West brother we've all heard so much about," Darren said as he stuck out his hand, and Jake sighed, stood, and shook it. They nodded at one another the way men do when gauging if there was to be a territorial dispute or not. Darren was bristling, his shoulders up, his stance wary. Jake hadn't changed his demeanor except his eyes had taken on that piercing quality both his brothers had when they were thinking too hard.

"Dr. Hollister," Jake replied after a moment, his analysis of Darren done. He stood back, hands sliding into his jeans pockets, his body visibly relaxing when he added, "Can I take my prizefighter home?"

They both chuckled, breaking the tension as Darren motioned to Liz to sit back on the table. He took out his pocket light and turned to her. "I'll just take a peek and then you should be fine to go."

The idea of letting him touch her brought her shoulders up and she stiffened, leaning away from him. Darren sighed, Jake muffled a laugh, and she gave them both dirty looks.

"Just let me look, for god's sake," Darren muttered, and turned on the light.

"Be quick. I want to go home," she snapped back.

"So, what does the other guy look like?" Darren joked again as he tilted her chin up and shone the light up her nose, peering through the magnifier. "You're lucky, there's a cartilage crack, but it isn't bad. A good bash in the face that'll mend on its own. X-rays on your orbital socket were clean."

He shone lights at both her eyes, tilting her head left and right.

"Follow my finger," he said, and she rotated her eyes to keep track of it as he moved from left to right, up and down. He tilted her chin up again and checked her jaw with light circles, frowning as he did, his entire body inches from her.

She held her breath, barely listening to him as he murmured "okay" and "fine" under his breath. How many times in the past had he stepped close to her and tilted her chin up right before he'd kiss her? She closed her eyes, wishing for the memory to go away, the hurt throbbing just under the surface. All those times he'd been so sweet, the perfect boyfriend, but behind her back . . .

She jerked her chin out of his fingers the minute he finished, and glared at him, shoving her anger up like a shield. His forehead wrinkles deepened and he stepped back, not meeting her eye. Obviously it had affected him, too, which irked her even more, because it had been over a year now since he'd . . . since they'd split.

"I read that you had an accident at work, any specifics I can add? Were you kicked?" he asked as he looked at his clipboard again.

"Something about a horse's nose bopping her full in the face," Jake supplied when Liz didn't answer, not trusting her voice. "She fainted, but she's clearheaded, so I assume no concussion?"

"No, no concussion." Darren sighed, tapping her chart on his leg impatiently.

"If there's nothing else?" she spat back, and stood up again, anxious to get the hell out of the room.

Darren pressed his lips together into a thin line, and she waited for the profound Darren-ism that would always make her feel like the stupidest person in the world, the hayseed in a room of educated dicks. Not worthy of anyone with a brain in their head. Not worthy of him.

"She's free to go. I'd like to say she should rest for a day, but I know she won't. She never does," he replied, turning to Jake.

"Oh my god. Seriously. Standing right here, asshole. You can talk to me, not him. He isn't my keeper," Liz snapped as she gathered up her sweater, and Jake gave her a sharp look.

"Liz," Darren intoned, and gestured at her tiredly. "You never listen, so I'm hoping the new guy here will. He seems to give a crap about you, so maybe you won't push him away like you do everyone else?"

With that, he stepped out of the room, and Liz closed her eyes. *Shit*. There it was.

"So, how long did you two date?" Jake asked quietly. "That looked strained."

"We were engaged," she practically snarled, and pushed past him out the door.

* * *

"I filled up the tank on the car before we came home."

Jake found Peony in the massive living room after he'd stowed the car back in the garage. It had been interesting to drive that land yacht, the size and thrum of the motor very different from any car he'd ever driven. As he'd slid in behind the wheel, he'd caught a whiff of cigar, stale in the interior. His father, no doubt. With Liz angrily avoiding talking, both all the way there and all the way home, he'd been able to simply listen to the car, the wheels on the road, and wonder about the man who drove it.

Another dose of Brett's presence. He had so many questions echoing out into this place where he felt so foreign, and it seemed like there was no one to answer them. New places were supposed to feel strange, but not with the edges of personal history he didn't know. His entire life had been in one city, and now he was reconciling another part of it that he had absolutely no memory of. A life he'd been taken from, and been told was awful.

As he had driven home in the last of the day's light, eyes following the tar-filled cracks on the highway, he wished he could be somewhere familiar so he could process it all better. The newness of his situation at every turn was muddling it all up.

He leaned on the door frame and Peony looked up from her book, her legs curled under her on the couch, slippers forgotten on the floor. She was the picture of comfort, and it drew him in, wanting the same relaxation after a tense evening. He lowered himself into one of the chairs, and she placed her bookmark between the pages with care. Peony could be a ballbuster, he decided; everything she did was precise and careful, with complete confidence. He wondered how much of it right now was out of wanting control over their situation.

"Thank you. Before she stomped off to her house, she told me she was fine and to not bother her," she replied, and then smiled. "She's headstrong and stubborn, my girl."

"Her ex was the on-call," Jake said.

"Well, now. That can't have been fun."

"Nope," he replied. Silence enveloped them, and the clock on the mantel quietly ticked away. He could hear the birds outside, evening settling over the gardens around the house, putting the day to bed.

Jake rose to go, uncomfortable in the rural quiet of dusk. There were no car horns, no shouts, no constant hum. It had been a very long day, full of tension and frustration, and the relative silence was poking at him to move, to be busy.

"Wait a moment, Jake," Peony said, and straightened from the couch, dropping the book to the seat.

Jake tensed, and she folded her fingers and gave him a stare that promptly put his butt back in the chair. Now he knew where Liz got that steely gaze from, because it was identical to the one she'd been glaring at Darren.

"I want you to know you're welcome here. Brady mentioned to me this evening that Tanner hasn't been very receptive. I'd like to say it isn't like him, but he pushes people away when he's upset. He's incredibly protective of his family, always has been."

"I can see that," Jake said. "I don't blame him."

"When his mother died, Tanner took over this place for a time while Brett disappeared into himself. It wasn't easy for him then, and he feels a very large sense of responsibility for this ranch. I've known that boy long enough to know when he's hurting, and my guess is he's reconciling the sacrifices he made then to the outcome now."

"Sacrifices?" Jake asked.

Peony waved her hands. "Never mind that, it was a long time ago. You've got temper enough to stand up to him, so I know eventually he'll come around and stop seeing you as a threat. You should know that he's a good man, one of the best I've known. If push came to shove, he'd be there for you."

"I don't doubt it," Jake said, but Peony held up her hand.

She sighed. "That said, Tanner needs a kick in the ass and to stow his attitude so that the two of you can keep things running."

Jake doubted that a simple ass-kicking would help. He and Tanner were too much alike. Wounds like this didn't heal easily. His brother needed time.

"Also, never mind my Liz's tantrums. She's feeling a bit mixed up, is likely a sounding board for Tanner in all this, and I'm sure she's worried about what's going to happen to us. When we came here, we had nothing except the clothes on our backs, and this place gave her the world."

"This is your home and it's been theoretically taken from you," he said. "There will be worry from everyone."

"Indeed," Peony replied. "But it doesn't mean anyone gets to treat you poorly while you're our guest."

"Yes, ma'am," Jake murmured. "We've all got to get used to this situation. I'm trying to process the fact that a father I didn't know gave me this place with zero warning or—"

Peony made an irritated noise, interrupting him. She closed her eyes for a moment, drawing a big breath.

"I've known a bit more of the story, so this wild stunt Brett pulled may have been a shock, but after the fact, I should've seen it coming. Brett told me about you and your mother near a year ago, confessed the entire thing one night as we were getting ready for bed. I hadn't thought about Heather in a long time. I remembered she had a 'rich beau' that she'd brag about in town, but I had no idea who it was, nor was it important at the time. I didn't remember hearing if she'd had a baby, or that she'd left. It was so long ago."

"Thirty years, give or take a couple," Jake added.

"Surprised the heck out of me, to be honest, but life with Brett could be like that at times. I tried to take it in stride, the past is in the past, after all. But I think it was hard on him, he'd kept what happened with her bottled up like that for a very long time. He said he'd never told Veronica that Heather had a son until long after he started seeing her, and Ronnie never mentioned anything about how Heather left with you. No clue if she was part of it, or if she just kept quiet out of respect for Brett."

"I see," Jake murmured. What did you say to that? Surely someone knew about him and his mother's hasty exit. They certainly did now, and children in small towns weren't hidden easily.

"Did he know where she went? I'm sure she talked about New York all the time, she said she'd grown up there," Jake asked, curious. His mother had been a true New Yorker. He'd discovered at an early age his love for the city through her, and what the city could give him if he worked hard. It was a long time ago that he'd stopped caring about why she'd left the quieter country life. It was obvious she was most at home in the back of kitchens, with rough language, rough people, and all that the restaurant kitchen culture heralded.

At least he'd experienced that side of her, had grown up that way.

"He didn't know. Heather just up and vanished after she left him. He said the first place he checked was her parents' place just outside Calgary, but she never turned up there. She wasn't from New York City, Jake."

"She wasn't?" he asked. "I always wondered how she came to be all the way over here, but she never talked much about that, just that New York was her real home."

"She was from here. I think her parents moved from the US when she was young. They both worked in the oil industry and transferred back—I think her father was from here originally, hence family close by."

Jake's skin prickled, and he forced himself to take a breath in. His mother had gone on and on about growing up in New York. Was everything a lie? He sat back, a bit stunned at that. She had parents. He had grandparents. Here.

"Oh."

"Her parents are gone now, rest their souls. They helped Brett search for a while, but not long after she left he married Veronica, and it was unseemly for him to keep looking publicly when she had Tanner. But he did, continuing in private. Right up until not so long ago, when he found you."

Jake drew a breath in, then out. *Holy shit.*

His father had wanted him. His mother had told him time and time again that his father didn't want them, that her parents had left her high and dry and it was up to them to make it on their own.

But his father had looked. His grandparents had looked.

"He asked me not to tell the boys, and now, I wish I had. I think he was going to tell them about you, prepare them for what was coming, but—" She stopped and looked away from him again.

"But what?" Jake prodded.

"He sat on it too long and ran out of time. I think he told me because he needed to tell someone and was scared to tell anyone else. It was the culmination of a lot of years of searching, and I think that was when he got the fool notion to will the entire ranch to you. The regret of not knowing you pushed him to act rashly. Or the tumor was messing with his head."

Anxiously, Jake shifted to his feet, wanting to be anywhere but with another person as he absorbed what Peony had just told him. The urge to get into the kitchen, to do something to stop the tsunami of thoughts in his head and keep his hands busy roared into him, and he didn't want to have it turn to anger and upset her.

"I can see this is a lot to take in," Peony murmured, and put a hand on his forearm, the muscles corded as he attempted calm himself. Her hand was cool on his skin and sent prickles up his arm. "When Brett was at his limit, he looked just like you do. I'm so sorry, Jake. I truly am."

Jake covered her hand with his and took a deep, cleansing breath in through his nose, looking down and away. "I think I'm going to go make something to eat. Are you hungry?"

"No, dear, I'm fine," she replied, smiling at him knowingly. "Go cook. It will help."

He headed for the door and turned just as he reached it. Peony was staring at the fireplace mantel, lost in thought.

"Peony, thank you for telling me," he croaked, and strode away before he could let the emotion win.

CHAPTER THIRTEEN

Liz stepped in through the mudroom to go find her mother, thinking she must be in the kitchen since all the lights were blazing. She looked through the door and stopped.

The kitchen was a mess, and it was most definitely *not* her mom.

Jake finished expertly slicing what looked to be an onion, then slid it into a bowl with the edge of his knife, big shoulders moving, fluid and practiced. She stood a moment more, catching the smooth jazz flowing over the room from the tiny portable speaker now sitting above the sink, making the entire space feel classy.

Until Jake had arrived, Liz had normally avoided the expansive kitchen after dark. The countertops and shining metal appliances were cold and unwelcoming. But right now, warmth emanated, beckoning her. She noticed an expensive knife set and a laptop open with music queued.

She was drawn in, but at the same time, didn't want to disturb the scene. He was obviously in his element, and even though she liked watching him like this, just as she had that first night he'd been here, she felt like she was intruding.

So she leaned on the door frame and took him in, waiting for a moment to sneak through into the house. His shirtsleeves were rolled up tight at his elbow, and he'd tied a crisp white chef's apron high on his waist. His hair was finger-combed messy, and the serious way his eyes followed his hands was completely, utterly sexy.

Maybe she should go in and say hello. She couldn't really deny any longer that there was this attraction she felt for him that was entirely irrational; that it was right there under the surface, prodding her when she least wanted it to.

Maybe it was the painkillers she'd taken or the fact that she was deliriously overtired that dissolved her reluctance, but her stomach fluttered, and little sparks ran along her body when he bent into the fridge and pulled out more vegetables.

The last straw that drew her in to lean on the island was when he started humming to the music, deep and smooth.

His jaw flexed as he saw her, and she froze midway onto one of the island stools, caught like a deer in the headlights.

"Hey," he said and set his tools down, wiping his hands on his apron and turning to face her.

She gingerly ran her fingers down her nose, chastened now that he was looking at her. She was a mess. She'd had a shower, looked at the blossoming black eyes in the mirror, the white tape an angry stripe across her face. Reminded of Jake and the ping-pong of a day they'd had, she realized she'd lashed out once again, storming away from him the moment they'd driven into the garage. She owed him another apology, and her original intent was to find her mom to ask how in hell she should.

Well, here he is, just do it, she thought, and squared her shoulders.

"Hi," she replied. "I don't want to mess with your flow, but I—"

"How are you feeling?" he asked, interrupting her.

"I—" she started again, determined to get it out. "I'm fine. Look. I'm sorry for my mood this evening. Again."

He blinked and pulled a pepper from the bag of vegetables beside him. He paused as he picked up the knife. She could see his gears turning, and hoped he wouldn't rebuff her. It was bad enough he'd seen her storm off in a huff more than once. She hated that part of her temper. She wanted him to like her, and her behavior was not helping.

"Have you eaten?" he asked.

"No," she said. He was back to being nice, giving. Truly, she'd been an ass today.

"Come help me cook."

She eyeballed his knife, hesitant. Cook?

He beckoned her around the counter and then handed her the pepper and the knife. "Can you slice a few of these into thin strips? I'll start the tortilla."

She looked down at the pepper, the green skin shiny in the kitchen lighting. She set it on the cutting board and then tilted the massive knife in her hand, the blade polished to a sheen. For the first time in her life, she was intimidated about slicing vegetables.

"It's just a pepper, Liz. It isn't poison. You do eat vegetables from time to time, right? It isn't all beef and bread?" he said, humor evident in his voice. She looked at him, twisting her lips, and sighed.

"Ha-ha. Very funny. No, it's just I've never cut a pepper with such a massive knife. How—"

Before she could finish her sentence, he slid up behind her, grabbed her hands, and gently fixed her grip on the knife. His other hand adjusted her grip on the pepper like he'd done it a thousand times. The heat from his body instantly flooded hers and she leaned back, letting her shoulders touch his broad, firm chest. He took her cue, and pulled himself closer, their bodies touching against the counter.

Holy hell, that felt good. All thoughts of her bruised face and pride faded to nothing.

"Now, if you hold the pepper this way and slice it sideways first, you can pull out the seeds. Use the back of the knife to the front, slice down, and away," he rumbled in her ear, sending shockwaves down and through her stomach in time with the knife.

His forearms tensed as he moved her hands for her, and she followed the motion, letting him lead, her stomach fluttering again. The blade slid through the pepper with a fresh crunch, and the two sides fell away from each other. He carefully sliced one side into slivers, and she relaxed her muscles as his arms brushed hers, the movement of his body behind her rendering her breathless until he had finished.

"You teach a lot of people how to cut vegetables like this?" she asked weakly, the grip he had on her knife hand softening as he finished.

He cleared his throat and chuckled low in her ear. "A few, yes. Knife skills are one of the most important kitchen tools you can have."

She slid her hands out of his grip and peeled the seed core out of the other half of the pepper, conscious of his body still behind her He didn't move away, his hands traveling up her arms, his head dipping toward the crook of her neck, a soft, rumbling groan meeting her ear. If he kept going . . .

She turned, her back pressing into the edge of the counter. Pepper in her hand, she looked up at him with intent, the instinct to kiss him so strong she might not be able to stop if—

The heat in his eyes surprised her as he braced his hands on the counter on either side of her, caging her in. *Well, now*. That changed her thoughts on the matter completely. Her eyes darted to his lips, then back to his eyes, and another deep groan made its way from his chest. *That was incredibly hot*.

"Any other tips?" she asked, quirking an eyebrow, emboldened by how close he was and the hungry way he was taking her in. If she was going to explore this, she might as well go whole hog.

But as she leaned toward him, he cleared his throat, his hands flexing as he pulled them away. "I think you have it."

A wave of disappointment hit her as he turned to a cupboard, pulling out the flour canister. She finished cutting the pepper, then sliced another one from the bag beside her, before she spoke. That should have ended with them kissing. She wanted it to end with him kissing her, damn it.

"So, you make tortillas?" she finally said, wanting to break the awkward silence that was punctuated by the crunch of her knife and the *ting* of utensils hitting the side of his metal mixing bowl as he added various ingredients. He hummed an *uh-huh* and turned his head to her as he tipped water and lard into the mixture, not even measuring.

"Once you learn to make tortillas, you'll never, ever go back to store bought. I guarantee it. Doesn't Rosy make her own?" he said.

"No, at least I don't think so. She doesn't do much outside dinner rolls or white bread. Brett liked meat and potatoes, simple food. Well-done steak—which is a crime, by the way—veggies boiled to mush. Mom ate like he did. I sometimes wonder how she stood it, the same thing day in and day out, the lack of flavors."

His hands dipped into the bowl, his biceps straining through the fabric of his shirt as he kneaded the mixture. She decided that the way he moved could not be more of a turn-on, and picked up a piece of pepper, chewing on it as she tamped down on the arousal flaring low in her belly.

"Love will do that," he replied. "I'm sure it drove her nuts, but it was what he liked, so she compromised. She had her own things to balance it."

"I doubt it was love. I'm not sure it was that kind of marriage," she said sadly, and turned, slicing the rest of the last pepper. She pushed the slivers into a pile and set the knife down, mulling over what she'd just said. Her mother had said as much, hadn't she? Liz's heart hurt, thinking about how her mother deserved to be happy and taken care of, and how this whole situation had been the opposite.

"I don't know much about my dad . . . Brett. Your mom mentioned some stuff tonight, but other than that, he's just a person I never met."

"I can tell you a bit, if you like," she offered, and rested a hip on the counter as he rolled dough balls between his palms then set them in a perfectly straight line on a tray.

He stopped, his flour-covered fingers curling over the edge of the counter. "I don't know. I get overwhelmed by this house, his car, the office—"

His shoulders bunched up, and she stepped over to him and impulsively placed a hand on his back. His body heat tightened her and she almost pulled away, but as she stood there with him, pressing her palm into the taut muscles, his shoulders lowered. He sighed and hung his head, then ran his hand through his hair at the back of his head, leaving flour in its wake.

A realization hit her as he admitted to being overwhelmed. How could she have not thought of that? He was thrown into his father's home, with *his* family, knowing nothing of the man, and they expected . . . well, what, from him? To assimilate in three seconds flat? Brady had figured it out already, and she'd only half listened to him. She felt guilty all over again for the way she'd behaved today, and rubbed the spot between his shoulder blades, restless at the thought of not having seen his stress.

"I never even thought about how it would feel to come into his home, be surrounded by his things, and not end up a little messed up," she said.

"It hasn't been easy," he replied, his voice rough.

He turned to her, and she could see the pain in his eyes threatening to come out. She wasn't sure if it would spill like Tanner, in anger and gruffness, or like Brady, with quiet. He was so much like Tanner that she backed up a step, expecting hardness to take over, like it had in the diner. She was hoping her offer was an olive branch in their awkward back-and-forth—most of which was her fault.

It might also cool her jets, thinking of something other than him pressing her against the counter and kissing her senseless.

"I think the man is a different thing than all this," she said, gesturing around her. "I can try to tell you about who he was, not what he was, if that helps."

"I'd like that." He cracked his neck and hid the pain with what looked to be careful practice, and then smiled at her. "Would you like to learn how to press and cook tortillas? I added parmesan, they'll taste amazing."

She let out a soft breath of relief, the truce accepted. "You bet."

CHAPTER FOURTEEN

The morning sun was just warming the boards of the veranda when Jake got back from his morning run. He flopped onto one of the benches and sat, squinting at the stables, the animals moving about, the birds greeting the day with a riot of noise from the big trees around the house.

It was not nearly as irritating as it had been on day one, waking him up and disrupting his sleep cycle. Maybe he'd finally figured out his clock, because today he'd bounced up at six to get his run out of the way before it got too hot. Yesterday the sun had been a murderous bitch, so this morning had been a lot more tolerable. He compared it to the city, where he could shadow dodge during a run in the middle of the day if he wanted, even if the humidity radiating off the concrete tried to kill him.

He might like this better. The slight breeze and steam rising off the fields along the road were peaceful, the sky big and open, giving him permission to breathe deeply, take up space instead of winding around people, always an apology on the tip of his tongue if he had to wade through a crowd. It was just him and the road.

The ranch was much more restful now that he was used to it, and he relaxed into the seat, his neck and back thankfully pliant and less kinked up than they had been that first night here. The pleasant exhaustion was also likely because he had just punished himself with a hard six-mile run, in an effort to sweat out the new tension that had invaded other parts of him.

The mental image of Liz in the kitchen last night snuck back in, and he rubbed his eyes to ward it off. She had been much more approachable, and they'd put the up-and-down day behind them. Then he'd gotten close to her, her body up against him as he'd shown her how to use his nine-inch chef knife. He was instantly turned on, wanting her, which was a bad, bad idea.

He closed his eyes and sighed as he ran a hand over his sweat-plastered hair, frustrated with himself. Even with her raccoon-black eyes and tape on her nose, she looked warm and soft, and it had been damned near impossible to resist kissing her as their bodies pressed together. With the look she'd given him, she'd all but invited him to do it, as well.

But he had resisted, unsure if he should take it that far. He could sense her disappointment when he'd pulled away. Him, too, in spades.

The stories she'd told him about his dad as they'd mowed down entirely too many fajitas had been funny ones, thankfully. It had helped them both keep things platonic, even though the undercurrent of attraction was still humming. She was trying to soften the man, he assumed. He'd long gathered that his father had not been easy to work for, and he noticed that she skirted around stories of their interactions, focusing more on Brett himself. His achievements, daily life, rituals.

He appreciated that. They were anecdotal and safe. The new thoughts of the man, the stories making him more than just an idea, had rattled around in his head as he cleaned up the kitchen, and when he had finally gone to bed, he was thankful to Liz for distracting him so that he wasn't as anxious as he had been when Peony had dropped the bombshell that Brett had searched for him.

Not that kissing Liz wouldn't have done the same damned thing.

"Hey, New York. What're you doing out here?"

Jake cracked an eye to see Brady, dressed for work in grease-stained blue overalls and a hat that looked like it had been chewed on by a puppy, standing near him. He had a dinged-up metal travel mug in his hand that he slurped from, overtly eyeballing Jake and raising an eyebrow.

"Just finished my run," Jake replied, and sat up, pulling his earbuds out. He felt lazy suddenly.

"A run," Brady deadpanned. "On purpose?"

Jake snorted a laugh out. "Your brother said the same thing. Yes. A run. Gotta stay fit somehow."

He felt like he didn't have to walk on eggshells around Brady, but all the same he was cautious. He looked away, down the lane, the silence after his answer awkward. But then Brady chuckled and sat down beside him, leaning back. He rested one booted foot on his knee.

"My mom loved to sit here with her tea. She said it was the best view of the stables. She loved horses," Brady said.

Jake turned his head and looked at his brother. He was so different from Tanner that sometimes he wondered how they were related, but he supposed Brady favored his mother. The auburn hair and less angular features were part of it, but he just seemed like a happier guy.

"I just realized. You haven't been out to visit Dad's grave yet," Brady added, taking another loud slurp of his coffee.

It hadn't even occurred to Jake that there was a grave for him to visit, let alone that he'd want to. He wondered if he even wanted to open that wound further.

"I hadn't thought about it," he replied.

"Well, if you want to go, just let me know. I'll take you," Brady offered.

"I appreciate that," he said, meaning it. He had a gut feeling that he and Brady were on their way to becoming friends, and it was a relief.

"All good. Hey, on that note, why don't you come find me later, I'll take you on a tour of the place. You haven't had one yet, have you?"

"No, I haven't. But I can just go for a walk, you don't need to take time away," Jake said.

"Take you a long time to walk it." Brady laughed.

Brady seemed to think that was funny, so now he was curious. "How big is the ranch?"

"We've got a thousand acres, give or take. Half of that is under soybeans and corn at the moment, we've got two hundred acres of seeded hay and pasture fields, and we have the rest as what we call grazing land, high pasture we use in the early part of summer. The main house and stables, cattle barns are around twenty acres, and the pens at the back of the cattle barns are around fifty. Our land pushes into the foothills a bit compared to some. We log that on occasion."

A thousand acres. Crops. Logging. Feedlots. Jake wasn't sure he could even wrap his head around how big that was or what it would cost to run. He made a mental note to find the ranch on Google Maps later. "Is that a big operation, a thousand acres? How do you operate it with so few crew?"

"We hire in temporary crew for the planting, haying, the calving, and often drive cattle to the higher pasture with other outfits in the spring. It works. Feedlots make it a lot easier to spread the work too."

"A lot of overhead and training, hiring in temp workers," Jake said. He'd done that for big events and to handle the influx when he opened a new restaurant, but it was never fun to manage people you didn't know well, and always expensive.

"We get regulars every year who know the routine, which helps. Dad preferred a small crew. Said it got the job done better, and we've never known it any different," Brady replied. "I'd like to bring in someone permanently to help on the crop side eventually, and we could use a couple more full-time wranglers."

"How long had Brett owned this place?" Jake asked, gesturing around him. He was asking a million questions, but Brady didn't seem to mind.

"It's been in the West family a few generations now. Each one buying a bit more land around the original ranch. Long tradition," Brady said. "You didn't know that?"

"Nope." Not one mention of that in the documentation or from anyone, and Jake sat back, heaviness settling in his stomach. *Generational.* Not only was this family's livelihood on the line, but their legacy as well. He blew out a tense breath and looked around him again.

"Well, if you're gonna be here a while, you need to know the lay of the land. Your land, at the moment," Brady added with finality as he stood and walked to his truck, keys jingling as he waved. "See you later."

His land. No, it wasn't, even if a bunch of papers said it was. Papers he hoped they could tear up so he could go back to where he was supposed to be, which was not twiddling his thumbs sitting on a thousand acres of ranch.

Thoughts about the enormity of what now had his name attached to it made him restless, and he stood, stretching, muscles he hadn't felt in a while groaning. He looked at the little car he'd driven in, parked in front of the house, a coating of dust on it. It hadn't moved since he'd gotten here.

He needed to figure out how to get that back to Calgary. Lawyers never moved fast, and Brady was right, he probably was going to be here for a while. He toyed with the idea of asking Liz to follow him in, and then drive back with her, but that might be like throwing gas on a fire if they were in the same truck for the hour or so it took to get from there back to the ranch. Maybe, with the offer Brady had given this morning, he could ask him instead. Tanner was out of the question. They'd kill each other spending that much time together in a small space.

He walked around back to head inside, passing through the kitchen on his way to his room and a shower. Rosy was bustling about in the kitchen.

"Good morning, Rosy," he said, careful not to startle her, hoping his friendly tone was enough to keep her from scurrying away. "I thought today we could do up that chicken. I'm looking forward to sharing my rub recipe with you."

She frowned and set down the fry pan she was holding. He noticed a small jumble of things in a box and a few cookbooks stacked beside that. She took a breath, her hands fidgeting. She was nervous.

"I'm so sorry, Mr. West," she said, not meeting his eye. "I'm here for my things. I resigned this morning."

Jake's heart fell. It was because of him, and once again, here he was messing around in people's lives when they deserved better.

"I'm sorry to hear that," he offered carefully. "Is there anything I can do to convince you to stay?"

She waved her hands, and then did look at him. She wasn't angry—he could see that. She looked sad, almost wistful. "No, Mr. West. I'm afraid not. I have another job lined up that starts today."

"Ah. I see," he replied.

"It isn't because of you," she blurted, then went a bit pink. "Well, not completely. You—"

"Crowd you, intimidate you?" he answered for her. "I tend to come on too strong. I'm sorry if I stepped on your toes."

She sighed and put a few more things in the box, then stopped and leveled her gaze at him. "No, no. Not like that. I cooked for Mr. West—I mean your dad—for a long time. He liked things a certain way. When he died, cooking for just the boys, the crew, and Peony the same way felt odd. So when you came along and started making yourself at home in here, cooking far better than I ever could, I just . . . I missed him and knew it was time to move on."

That was the most she had said to him since he had arrived, and he was grateful to have her explain it to him, but the pit in his stomach stayed. People in the restaurant business came and went. How many times had he had a similar conversation with a worker in his kitchens? But for some reason, he felt the loss of this person who had been part of the West family for some time because it was more change in a place that the people who lived here shouldn't have to deal with because of him.

He wondered what his father would have done, which was an odd thought to have in the midst of this conversation. He'd never wanted to measure his actions against the man before, because there was nothing to measure it with. With Brett fleshed out more in his mind, he wondered if it was dredging up emotions he'd long buried.

"You do know I'm not staying long-term," Jake said.

Rosy nodded. "I'm aware. It's time for a change, for me, Mr. West. I'm sorry."

"I understand," he replied. "I hope your new position has as nice a kitchen as this one."

That made her smile, and she relaxed her shoulders. There were no hard feelings, he hoped.

"It doesn't but it will do fine," she replied. She added her cookbooks to the top of the box and picked it up.

As she turned, Tanner stalked in, and Jake braced for it. He looked like he always did, mad and in a hurry.

"Rosy. I have your last paycheck here. Just needs to be signed by the new boss," he snapped. "You seen him?"

Rosy turned, and Tanner looked past her to Jake, standing on the other side of the counter. He thinned his lips, scanning Jake from head to toe. Disapproval radiated out of him. Jake held his tongue and gritted his teeth to endure it. Rosy didn't need to be caught in the crosshairs aimed at him.

"Good morning," Jake said instead of what he wanted to say.

"Sign this," Tanner snapped again, striding over and planting the check in front of him. He crossed his arms and looked around the kitchen. "Do you have everything, Rosy?"

"I do," she replied stiffly. Obviously, Tanner hadn't taken the news about her leaving well.

Jake found a pen on the side table and signed the check quickly. He noticed it was made out to Rosy Morrison, and he jolted at the recognition as he held it out to her.

"Morrison?" he asked. "Are you by chance related to a Heather Morrison?"

Rosy tilted her head. "Yes. Her father was my father's oldest brother, my uncle Bob, and she was his oldest child. I don't think I ever met her, she was long gone before I was old enough to remember, anyway. Why?"

"She's my mother," he answered, the rush of acknowledgment hitting him square in the chest. Tanner took in a breath, but Jake didn't look at him. He didn't have time for his asshole attitude right now.

"Well, I'll be," she said, and set the box down. "We were told she was likely dead."

Dead. Gossip and rumor abounded in a small town, but dead?

"No, she isn't," he murmured. "She's very much alive."

Rosy made a noise in her throat that sounded like surprise. He flicked a glance over to Tanner as his brother let out an impatient huff.

Jake tilted his head as he looked back at Rosy. "She would be your cousin, so that makes me your second cousin, I think?"

Rosy let out a peal of laughter, and he wished they had known sooner. All the ice would have been broken much more quickly, and perhaps she wouldn't be leaving. Which, judging by Tanner's current attitude, he was going to blame Jake for.

"I suppose it does, Mr. West. My folks live near Whistler now, retired ski bums. I'll tell them I met you. They'll be pleased to know," she said, and stuck out her hand.

Jake took it and shook, the new information rolling around inside of him. "Call me Jake, please. Mr. West—"

"Was my father. You aren't him," Tanner growled, and turned on his heel and left abruptly, shocking both Jake and Rosy.

Rosy let go of his hand, the moment gone, and moved to collect her box again, the folded check stuffed into her pocket. Jake picked up the box for her and walked her to the door, then down the steps to her small car.

"Thank you, Jake. I am sorry we met under such circumstances. If I'd known—"

"Rosy!"

Jake turned to see Peony coming down the steps. Jake recognized the small copper saucepot set that normally hung above the island, a vibrant red bow around them.

"Don't you dare leave without saying goodbye, my dear," Peony added, and when she made it over to the car, she and Rosy hugged. Rosy's eyes were misty as Peony handed her what was obviously a parting gift.

"Mrs. West, please. You shouldn't have."

"You made the best sauces in these pots. I know how much you loved them. So I should, and I did. You've been our cook for fifteen years and we love you. Won't be the same without you," Peony replied firmly.

"I think you have it well in hand with Jake," Rosy said just as firmly, and both women broke into smiles. "But he'll need a new saucepot set."

Energy vibrated through Jake as it dawned on him. He could take over the duties Rosy had, and earn his keep while he was here. At the very least, help them interview a new cook once his departure was secured. He was familiar with the kitchen, and now, thanks to Gordon, his entire kitchen was here, including a set of small pots like the one Peony had just given away.

Jake set Rosy's box into her back seat carefully, closing the door as Peony embraced Rosy one more time.

"I'll get your phone number from your file and come visit sometime soon. It would be nice to meet more of my family," Jake said, and Rosy brightened.

"Oh, please! My father would be so happy to meet you. I think her brother is still alive, we lost touch with him when Uncle Bob passed. I can't wait to tell them about you!"

A lump formed in Jake's throat at that. All this time, there was an entire family here that his mother had just given up on, thrown away. He wondered what would make her do that, when there were obviously good people who cared for her, including her parents.

"Please tell Liz I'll miss her. Brady already said goodbye when I went over to the office this morning." Rosy was edging toward her car.

"I will," Peony assured her.

With another wave, Rosy got into her car and backed out, driving down the lane. Jake ran a hand down his face and groaned. The day was barely started and already full of drama. At this rate, who knew what would happen? Maybe he should ask Tanner to go to Calgary with him and make it an epic day of emotional volcanoes.

"I swear. This place has more twists and turns than—"

Peony gave him a funny look, and he put an arm around her as they walked back to the veranda, happy to have her there with him to keep him from losing his cool.

"Rosy is a Morrison. My second cousin."

"Perhaps that was why Brett hired her," Peony mused. "She's a cousin of your mother's, then."

"Something like that. Hopefully I can meet some of them."

They walked back into the house, and both headed to the kitchen. Jake turned on his coffee machine, and as he was packing a shot of espresso, looked at Peony. She was bringing two mugs down from the cupboard, and she *hmm*ed at him as she set them down.

"So. I think you and I need to go over what Rosy did here, and how I can pick up the slack," was all he said as she leveled her gaze at him. He wanted to be useful, and right now, this was the best way he knew how.

That earned him a laugh, and Peony clasped her hands together. "Well, yes. Let's get to it, then, shall we?"

CHAPTER FIFTEEN

Liz was filling out her training journal for the day when Tanner strode into her office, madder than a wet hen. He stood at the arena window, paced to the door, then back to the window, frowning, his jaw muscles working too hard, like he was chewing rocks.

"What's wrong now?" she asked bluntly. He looked over, grimaced at her, and flailed his hands.

"Did you know Rosy quit today?"

Liz dropped her pen to the desk tiredly. She'd never been close to Rosy, but she had been part of their lives for so long. Liz had expected this would happen eventually.

"Damn. I figured she might when Brett died but—"

"It's because of that citified shithead! He's flouncing around in the kitchen with all his spices and cookbooks and coffee machine that looks like a goddamned robot. Forced her out, damn it."

"Flouncing?" Liz remarked, stifling a laugh at Tanner's rant. "I don't think Jake can 'flounce.' He's the same size as you, you big brute."

"This isn't funny, Lizzie," Tanner snapped. "He's disrupted our whole lives."

Liz eased herself from behind her desk and walked over to Tanner, putting a hand on his arm. He was worked up, likely because Rosy leaving meant yet more of his father's old West Line Ranch was changing. Change that was eating at him, especially after the way the rug had been pulled out from under them.

"Did she say that was why she was leaving?" she asked. He shook his head and sank onto the beat-up leather couch along one wall. Normally it was covered with magazines and odd bits of tack, but in a fit of boredom this morning she had cleaned her office. Trevor had taken one look at her and told her in no way was he letting her near a horse. Grudgingly, she had agreed. She felt like shit, was sore everywhere. A day to sit might be a good thing, even if she was bored to tears. There was all the never-ending paperwork to catch up on, after all.

"Who is going to take over cooking for the hands?" he asked. "City boy? I doubt he understands how to cook for a crew of men who actually work for a living."

"Do you not think, Tanner, that a man who can run a restaurant in New York City can handle preparing lunch for a crew of ten on a daily basis? Come on."

Tanner grumbled under his breath and thunked his head on the wall behind him, rattling all the framed pictures of horses and ribbons. "I just hate that this is all fucked up because of him."

"It isn't fucked up because of him. It's fucked up because of your dad," Liz stated, frustration growing.

Tanner growled under his breath, irritated that someone was calling him on his tantrum. He was truly pissed off, and in this state, normally it was like reasoning with a bull during breeding season. She was trying her best to understand his hurt, but sometimes he drove her nuts with the walls he put up.

Liz decided to try kicking his ass instead of playing to his grumpiness. She'd had enough. He was being petulant, inventing reasons to be mad at this newfound brother, instead of the situation their father had created. He was shooting the messenger, in a way, instead of being mad at the person responsible, which was Brett.

"Let him earn his keep. He's as stuck here as we are with this situation. He's a really, really good chef. But then, you wouldn't know that, since you haven't eaten dinner with us since he got here," she said.

"You defending him?"

"Damn right I am. Take the frigging pickle out of your ass, you big shithead. He's a good man. He's tryin', for god's sake," she admonished, half shouting.

Tanner looked at her, the turmoil plain on his face. He didn't respond, but closed his eyes and let out a sigh that spoke more clearly than anything.

"You have a brother. He may not be a ranch-hardened cowboy, but he is a West, and he is trying to make sure that you and Brady can keep this damned place. Which is pretty frigging gracious considering how you've treated him," she added softly.

That earned her a petulant grunt. She refrained from calling him a Neanderthal. At least Tanner wasn't storming out, and the tic in his jaw had lessened. Maybe she was getting through to him.

"How do you think he feels, being stuck out here, surrounded by memories of a man he never knew, and from the sounds of it, was told didn't want him? He had a life he's had to suddenly leave behind, and he has no anchor. You get to stay put, keep your job, and in the bargain, gain a new sibling who wants to help around here as best he can."

Tanner waved his hands in resignation. "I get it, message received. But he's pushing his nose into things he doesn't need to. I don't have time for assholes."

"Pot, meet kettle," she snapped back, which made him avert his eyes.

"What do you want me to do? Bring him some flowers and sing 'Kum ba yah'?"

"For starters, come to dinner tonight, stop avoiding it," she snapped, and sat back down behind her desk, signaling she was finished with her lecture. She picked up her pen, and they glared at one another. He stood with a jerk and took off his cap, running his hands through his hair and looking around her office, as if hesitant to leave.

Liz twisted her lips, watching him. He had the same hair as Jake. Wavy, thick, and dark. His was lighter from being in the sun, and there was perhaps a hint of Veronica in there. An image of Jake laughing at something she'd said while he cooked last night made her blink, and she sucked in a breath to make the image leave. Damn it, that was not what she needed to be thinking about right now.

"All right. I'm sorry to unload on you," he replied after a moment. "I'm fucking exhausted with all this."

"I know. You don't have to do everything, Tan. This will work out."

He fiddled with the brim of the hat in his hands, looking down at it. His shoulders were high and tight, his jaw clenched again, and Liz, even though she'd just given him a tongue-lashing, wished she could help him process this better. The only person who could set him straight when he was this twisted up was Brett, and he was gone. She leaned on her arms.

"Tan? Maybe you should go talk to Brett," she suggested.

"Talk. To Dad," he said slowly. "Did that horse knock more than just your nose sideways? He's dead, Lizzie."

"Go talk to him anyway. It might help," she replied, hoping he would figure it out.

He gave her a strange look, threw his hands in the air, and stalked out of the office, muttering about crazy people.

Liz waited a moment, then picked up her phone and texted Brady about Rosy, and added that Tanner was brooding again. Brady texted back a bunch of silly-faced emojis, which made her smile as much as her tight, sore face would let her, and then she left it. She had shit to do, and the tension Tanner had brought into the office had made her jumpy.

She found her thoughts circling back to Jake as she tried to refocus on her paperwork. How nice it was to just have time with him last night, talking, eating some of the best chicken fajitas she'd ever had. She'd stolen the rest of the tortillas, and they were in her fridge. She'd wolfed one down with a hastily microwaved egg and a slice of processed cheese this morning for breakfast, and it had been the most delicious thing ever.

It was more than good company and food, though.

All evening, once they had mended the awkwardness of the day, he'd been relaxed, laughing, his deep masculine voice soothing and exciting all in the same breath. She'd been keyed up when she went back to her house, and had sat up for an hour, watching random TV, her body thrumming with the arousal she'd had to tamp down.

"Hey."

Speak of the sexy-as-hell devil. She looked up at Jake in the doorway, wearing jeans that rode low on his hips, a T-shirt that was molded to his chest and biceps, and a dark-blue baseball cap from which his hair curled out, just slightly. He smiled and stepped into her office as she stared at him.

"So this is where you hide all day," he said, looking around.

"Not normally. Trevor is refusing to let me work the horses," she replied, gesturing at her face and pushing back from her work. Swiveling in her chair, she threw her feet up on the desk, putting an invisible barrier between her and the entirely too sexy man invading her space.

Jake moved to the window looking into the indoor arena, and his reflection in the glass showed that he was thinking much too hard. His jaw was flexing and he pulled his hat off, tossing it on the desk with a sharp huff of breath. As he shoved his hands into his pockets, his shoulders rose, tense and tight.

A copy of his brother who had left not long before.

The windows in the arena were unboarded for summer, and the side door hadn't been closed, allowing beautiful midday sunlight to beam into the office. She liked how it added warmth to the room, and it had been nice watching the horses work in the relative shade the arena provided when it was so hot out. Right now, the sunbeams were still slightly off center, casting Jake half in shadow. It made him look mysterious, which was even sexier.

"You need something?" she asked, hoping to draw out whatever it was he was stewing on. "Normally when a West man comes into my office, it's to complain or to ask a favor. Already had one come in. He was complainin'. You?"

Jake laughed at that, his face softening, and when he turned, her heart thumped erratically in her chest. He really was gorgeous, so different from his brothers. Now that she knew his mannerisms better, she saw how unique he was, not just an older, more polished West. True, his jaw was cut like Tan's, his frame and height and some of his gestures were the same, but Tanner was all rugged, sun-weathered, stoic ranch man. Jake was dynamic, outgoing, and moved with a fluid confidence, a nuance of something she couldn't put her finger on yet.

It was a relief that he had a different presence, because otherwise her attraction would've felt utterly wrong. She'd never thought about Tanner or Brady like that. Even though they weren't her siblings, they were her chosen brothers. They'd grown up together after her mom had married Brett.

"Guilty on the latter," he said, hands in the air. "I have to return my rental. I'll need a ride home from Calgary. I'd ask Brady, but he seems to have his hands full because I can't find him. You're good to drive . . ."

He trailed off and looked at her with what she figured was hope she would say yes.

She sighed. "Mom put you up to this?"

"No, ma'am. But she's roped me into feeding the crew every day while I'm here." Jake grinned and rocked on his heels, lending him an air of mischief.

"They'll be eating better than ever," she said, a laugh bubbling out of her. "Soon start asking for fancy meals instead of the egg salad sandwiches or canned soup Rosy normally put out."

His grin widened. "I'll ease them into it. Lobster thermidor on Fridays only."

That made her laugh, and she covered her mouth before she snorted. He chuckled as well.

"Listen, I figure you might enjoy a few hours away from this place."

He wasn't wrong, and she appreciated that the olive branch had been extended both ways now. She could stop at the coffee shop and get some expensive beans for her mom to try out in Jake's fancy machine, maybe get her a few new paperbacks at the big bookstore attached to it.

"I could do tomorrow. I'm trying to get caught up on work I never find time to do today, and I'm a bit sore," she answered honestly, her fingers pinching the bridge of her nose gently. "When you have lunch for the crew squared away with Mom, we could go after."

"Fair enough," he replied cheerfully, and offered her his hand. "It's another chance at a date to make up for yesterday's crossed wires. I'll steal you away before Tanner can say no."

She kicked her feet off the desk, took his hand, and he lifted her up out of her chair instead of shaking. Her eyes flew to his face, the shock of heat that reared up between them immediate, the strength of his arm as he pulled her up sexy and masculine. His eyes were trained on hers, piercing and dark, when only a moment before they'd been soft and happy. She sucked in a breath, frozen, and then blushed scarlet with the thoughts racing through her mind. Just like last night, she wanted to step into his arms and—

What was she thinking? Liz knew she looked like a train wreck, was conscious of how black and blue her eyes were, how puffy her face was. So very, very unsexy. She glanced away to break the moment, her other hand going to touch her nose again.

His index finger crooked out and tilted her chin, forcing her to look up.

"Liz," he said, his voice husky and low. "Don't. You have nothing to be embarrassed about."

She blinked at that, biting her lip to keep a sigh at bay, and he let out a very rough groan, pulling her into him. He held her there, hands slowly moving around her waist, grip tightening slightly when their bodies met. Her hands slid to his chest, the heat through the thin T-shirt material loosening her doubts, the muscles strong and smooth under her palm. She sank her fingers in slightly, relishing in the sensation as they flexed underneath her grip. Another masculine noise rumbled out of him. *Oh, damn, that was nice.*

"Jake, what are we doing?" she whispered. "I—"

He shook his head. "I don't know. I've tried . . . fuck, Liz, I—"

She dug her fingers into his chest again, quirking an eyebrow, and at that he lowered his lips to hers, her implied permission all he needed, apparently. She responded to him with a sigh, and he groaned again, both hands moving to gently hold her face as he opened his mouth and asked for her to give in to him, let him plunder.

And plunder it was. She had never been kissed like this before. Darren had either been chaste, sweet kisses, or all thrusting tongue, and only like that when he wanted it to lead to bed. This kiss was exploring her slowly, possessive but gentle, asking her to open instead of invading her without thought.

In other words, smoking fucking hot, and her knees turned to jelly as his tongue tasted hers with a languid intensity that forced her to give in and meld herself to him. Her hands slid up his body and threaded into his hair, pulling, which drew a rough moan from him.

God, that was fucking nuclear hot. She shifted against him, hip to hip. He was as hard as a rock against her lower stomach, a clear indication he was as turned on as she was.

She wanted to strip him down and climb him like a ladder right here, right now, not caring who might walk in. Stepping back toward her desk, she pulled him with her, and sat on the edge, no longer trusting her legs to hold her up. He broke the kiss, looking into her eyes with hungry need.

"Fuck." He swore again, and nestled himself between her thighs, his obvious erection against her core. He put his forehead to hers, breathing heavily as he attempted some control, his hands roaming over her body.

"Yes, please," she murmured back, eliciting a laugh from him as she arched her back, bringing their bodies flush to one another. His eyes popped open at that, and he let out a sound that she couldn't quite decipher, his grip on her tightening again, this time on her hips, and he tilted back to look down at her, a questioning look across his face.

It was all she needed to know he was as worked up as she was, but also not sure what to do. He could be dominant, but right now he needed her to tell him it was okay. She could do that. She licked her lips and tugged him down by the collar of his T-shirt, initiating another kiss.

This is more than an olive branch, she thought as his hands moved again, traveling over her back and curving against her ass as he held her to him.

It was the whole damned tree.

CHAPTER SIXTEEN

Jake left Liz's office dazed, not quite sure what had just happened. One second they had been talking, the next he had been kissing her like his life depended on it.

She'd exploded as soon as their lips met. Soft and sensual, like he'd imagined, but with this incredible sexy confidence. The idea of what she might be like in bed was playing on a reel in his head. He shook the thoughts away as his dick nudged at the zipper on his jeans, reminding him that he'd just walked away from a done deal.

He needed a cold shower, right now.

Last night he'd fought the urge to kiss her, but just now, when their hands had met and she had given him that saucy look, he'd lost what little control he'd put in place. All his inner caution about following his attraction to her evaporated. Mind you, all the blood had drained from his head to his . . . well, yeah. And she knew it.

"Shit," he muttered to himself, running a hand through his hair. "I've opened the damned Pandora's box."

He turned left and exited into the sunshine, squinting and putting his ball cap back on his head, not really paying attention to his surroundings. He was entirely focused on controlling the urge to stride right back into her office, strip her, and fuck her senseless across her desk.

Was he ready for this? Ashley entered his head the moment he thought it, dousing some of the heat coursing through his body. Liz was the first woman he'd kissed since Ashley.

He'd never had an immediate physical response to his ex-wife like what had just happened with Liz. Ashley and he had been more of a slow burn. Friends first, they'd fallen into a mutually comforting relationship and satisfying, albeit vanilla, sex. He'd assumed it was love, and so had she—they were both looking for that next logical step to secure their lives and spend less on rent, anyway. So they'd gotten married.

Nothing he shared with Ashley had been anything as spontaneously passionate as what had just happened. He'd had heady flings with sexually uninhibited women before his marriage, which had been about the adventure and the release. But that, in there, with Liz? He had no idea what he was getting into, except that it had fried his brain like an egg in a hot skillet.

"Hey, New York. Heads up, man."

Jake looked up quickly as Brady walked around the corner of the barn on a horse and stopped short of bumping into him. He was obviously just back from a ride, the horse sweaty, Brady smiling ear to ear. Jake blinked. That was a side of his brother he hadn't accounted for.

"You ride?"

"We all do. Part of the deal, growing up here. Sometimes I like to work on things that don't have bolts and pipes." Brady chuckled and stepped down from the saddle, pulling the reins over the horse's head. He swiped his dusty straw cowboy hat off to wipe his forehead. He was in full chaps and boots, and his T-shirt was emblazoned with a faded red STAMPEDE '07, several frayed holes along the hem.

Jake suddenly felt overdressed in his Rag & Bone jeans and Burberry T-shirt.

"Trev needs the help today, with Liz being on desk duty. You're welcome to swing a leg over as well. I heard you have before?"

Jake nodded. Despite feeling out of place with his fashionable, too-clean clothes, it was a chance for another bonding moment between himself and Brady. "I did. Very different than this."

"I need to get this guy in and get his gear off. I'll see you later," Brady said amiably, and turned with the horse toward the stable, plopping his hat back on his head. "Also, if you're going to kiss Liz like that, you shouldn't do it in front of a window where other people can watch. Quite the show you two put on. Stopped us all in our tracks. Surprised you couldn't hear us cheering!"

"Yeah! Thanks!" Jake choked out, surprised. They'd been caught. Yup, today was going to be full of drama. Because if Brady knew, that meant the other, grumpier brother would, too, soon enough.

The wrinkled ledger smelled like dusty copier ink as Jake thumbed through it, standing in front of his laptop, which was balanced delicately on top of file folders stuffed to the gills with paper.

Discouraged that he couldn't make heads or tails of a few entries, he switched to looking out the cobwebbed window at one of the cattle pens, his mind tumbling everywhere but into the spreadsheet in front of him.

Several crew members were sending what looked to be smaller cows through a chute. Jake watched fascinated as a little cow was frog-marched into a small cage, bawling loudly. It settled when they lowered a U-shaped bar over its neck to keep it still. One man—Jake thought it might be Harry—removed an orange tag from its ear, shouting numbers at Tanner over the noise of the cows in the pen behind them. Another younger man he didn't recognize jabbed a big needle in a flank then turned to ready another dose from a cooler bag hung on the side of the fence while Tanner ticked off something on a clipboard with a fat marker.

It was muffled through the window, but Jake caught Tanner's deeper voice as he shouted, "A dash twenty-three dash one dash fourteen," and flipped a square yellow tag with the number on it to Harry, who caught it expertly. A second later the tag was in the cow's ear and it was released from the cage to buck forward into a pen on the other side.

Jake had no idea what they were doing, but it looked difficult and unending as they cycled through cow after cow, the men working in tandem like a well-oiled machine, dirt on their overalls and dust in the air.

"Back to work," he muttered and turned away. These records wouldn't straighten themselves out.

He'd made lunch with Peony, and she had shooed him out when he'd offered to bake pies with her. She was busily rolling out pastry when she threw a *buzz off* look at him, then smiled and patted his cheek when he'd worriedly asked her if she needed help. Her hands had trembled as they held the heavy marble rolling pin.

"I'll take my time, young man. Now scoot. I like being in here by myself sometimes, just like you."

So he'd left and come here, to the barn office, hoping it would be empty, given the weather was good and everyone would be outside doing whatever it was they were doing out there.

He needed time away from everyone and space to think about what had happened with Liz. But instead of her, thoughts of his mother and the things he'd learned about her life in opposition to what he'd understood about it were swirling. As he mulled that, the inevitable comparison to Peony invaded.

He pulled at his lip, thinking about both women as he poked numbers into his spreadsheet. Of all the people here, he'd bonded with Peony the most. Their time in the kitchen reminded him of his mom in her more sober, happy years. Simple, down-to-earth, and independent to the core, not taking shit from anyone.

The comparison ended there; they were polar opposites otherwise. Peony was strong. She had a will of steel but it was wrapped in velvet, her kindness something he never saw in his mother. His mother had unashamedly used people to get what she needed, which he had always excused as a survival instinct from being poor in New York; one he sometimes couldn't blame her for while at other times he despised her for it.

Jake had tried his best not to go down that path of hardness, hating the destruction and bitterness that came with it. Even as he got older and she would use him the same way, he would turn a blind eye. She was his mom; how could he say no? He said yes every time, until one day he couldn't anymore. He'd put her in an Uber to a rehab place up in the Hudson Valley, sending both her and his money into an unknown outcome.

That was over a year ago, and he hadn't heard a thing from her except confirmation of the transfer clearing.

Peony's shaking had brought him up short, the memory of his mom's tired, bony hands trembling uncontrollably when holding a prep knife. The images of her strung out in the back kitchen of a restaurant, barely able to prep veg, Jake stealing in to take over so she could sit and mainline coffee—or worse, gin straight out of a faceted blue bottle that flashed in the fluorescent lighting every time she tilted it up. He could still hear the slosh of the liquid in his memories sometimes, remembered furiously chopping carrots and peppers for a dinner rush, hoping not to get caught by the kitchen manager.

He'd been ten when he'd started covering for her. Kicked out of more kitchens than he could count by the time he was thirteen, he'd started working as the prepper, and his mother was the one who would steal in the back door of wherever he was working, squatting in the corner, asking for handouts.

She was no longer his burden, and to compare the vibrant Peony to her was unjustified, considering his mother had utterly failed whereas his father's widow had not. His need to help Peony was instinctual from the years of being the responsible adult to the one parent who had kept him.

Peony telling him that Brett had looked for him was throwing his resentment into a new, utterly foreign direction, and that was spurring this overanalyzing of everything that was happening now. His mother had kept him from a family that had wanted him. He hadn't felt that kind of hurt in a long time, and he wasn't sure what to do with it, thankful that the pain felt less sharp than it did as a kid. Perspective, understanding, and age would give it depth, perhaps.

"Fuck," he swore softly as the edge of the paper cut the side of his thumb, halting the tumble of thoughts. He put it into his mouth to stem the bleeding, the taste of copper sliding over his tongue. Worn out from the constant drama invading his mind, he let his eyes slide shut for just a moment.

The image of Liz backed up on the desk, rumpled, bruised, and biting her lower lip entered his brain, and he groaned as he took his thumb out and examined it.

He liked punishing himself, it seemed. That was another situation he had to figure out. Liz was not a frivolous woman, and kissing her had consequences. Including Tanner's well-aimed fist if he took it the wrong way. Well, not if. He *would* take it the wrong way.

Jake was not looking forward to that stare down.

After kissing Liz this morning, the kitchen had provided a distraction. But now, he was trying—and failing—to distract himself by attempting to make heads or tails of the accounts for the ranch. If he was here for a while before they could give it all back to Tanner and Brady, he needed to get familiar with it. One, so he could sign things with an idea of what they were, and two, so Tanner would stop rubbing it in his face that he knew absolutely nothing about running a ranch.

It couldn't be that much different from running a restaurant. Ins, outs, salary, staffing, equipment, and supplies. So far, he had input the salary for the past three years, and was now working his way through property taxes, mortgage payments, and lease fees for what looked to be fields nearby.

He flipped the page in the logbook, his own fingers touching the smudged fingerprints of his father along the edges. Scanning the list, he noticed the last mortgage payment written in was April. It was late July now. Brett had died at the beginning of July.

"Hmm."

"Hmm, what?"

Jake looked up to see Tanner standing in the doorway, coveralls streaked in god knew what, dark smudges over one cheek. He looked pissed off, which was normal, but he also looked really fucking tired. Bags under his eyes, a slump to his shoulders. If they weren't so at odds, Jake would ask him if he was okay.

All the same, Jake braced for the third degree about Liz before he answered and cleared his throat as Tanner raised an eyebrow and looked over the mess on his dad's desk, Jake standing on the far side of it.

"Just setting up some spreadsheets to get my head wrapped around your books. Noticed that Dad . . . Brett, didn't input any of the mortgage past April in the ledger. Did he do bulk entries? It's July."

"Dunno. We got monthly statements from the bank and the payments were set up to come out automatically. Should be in that mess somewhere," Tanner said, flipping his hand at the paper piles surrounding Jake on the desk.

"Okay," Jake replied hesitantly. He must have communicated something that wasn't to Tanner's liking because his brother made that irritated sound he was so good at.

Here we go, he thought, and winced when Tanner strode past him to his own desk.

"You don't have to do any of this. We can handle it. You just have to sign the checks," he said tersely as he sat down, throwing the big marker and clipboard onto his paper tray with a metallic thud.

"I need to make myself useful other than cooking," Jake said, letting out a breath. "I can get all this sorted for you guys so the paperwork to sell the ranch back to you is easy."

"Sell? It's mine. I don't need to buy anything," Tanner retorted, sitting up and glaring at Jake. Jake tilted his head back in frustration, rubbing at his eyes. He couldn't say anything to this asshole without it being taken the wrong way.

"What in the absolute fuck is wrong with you? Seriously, man. I'm trying to fucking *help* you," Jake barked, frustrated.

Tanner let out a huff of air like a bull about to charge, and then collapsed back into his chair, his hand over his face. The exhaustion bled back into his frame, and Jake studied his brother for a moment without judgment.

How could they bridge this gulf? Was it even possible?

"Look, I know this place is yours. I know this is shit. Cut me some slack, let me organize this clusterfuck for you so that when I leave, you have working books you can farm out to your accountant, at least. Or would you rather spend your days in here, attached to a computer and all this goddamned paper?" Jake snapped, moving his laptop off the stack of folders so he could shuffle through them and look for the elusive mortgage statements.

Tanner didn't respond, but then his hand dragged down his face, smearing dirt into streaks and Jake knew that look. He'd seen that look on his own face many, many times in the past. Haunted, helpless in the face of something he didn't know how to reconcile.

"Yeah. Okay. Look, I—" Tanner started.

"Hey, Mr. West? Are you done with the tagging?"

They looked up in unison as Rowan poked his head in. He looked at both of them, blinking and then directing his gaze at Tanner.

"What is it, Ro?" Tanner asked tiredly.

"That feed mixer we just set up isn't working. The corn is jamming in the intake. Do you know how to set the auger back farther?"

Tanner sighed and levered himself out of the chair, picking up a wrench from underneath a stack of unopened mail. He turned it in his hand for a moment and nodded curtly to Rowan, who tapped the door frame and left quickly.

Tanner picked up the stack of unopened mail with his free hand and carefully laid it down on his father's desk, in front of Jake.

Jake looked at him questioningly, meeting his eye for a moment before Tanner averted his. Was this some sort of weird truce gesture? Did he not know about what had happened with Liz yet? Was he giving him permission to keep going? The confusion must have been plain on his face, because Tanner scoffed at him, shaking his head.

"Bank statement's likely in that pile," Tanner blurted, poking his index finger at the envelopes, leaving brown, smudgy fingerprints.

Before Jake could say thank you, Tanner strode quickly out the door.

CHAPTER SEVENTEEN

Parked in front of the TV, Liz examined the frozen dinner rapidly cooling on her lap, and with a sigh, set it on the coffee table in front of her, her appetite gone.

She would much rather be eating at the house with everyone than here, poking at a sad excuse for food, but she also wanted to be alone. She turned the channel to the news, not paying attention, her thoughts preoccupied, her nose hurting more than she'd like to admit.

The big, fat pregnant heifer that was sitting on her conscience made her want to just take a beat and think without anyone else around as well. She needed to figure out what that damned kiss had meant.

If she got involved with Jake, would it get complicated? Would Tanner be completely pissed when he found out? Not that he could change her mind, he had no say in her damned love life, but it would just be another thing to deal with right now and she was already tired.

But no matter what, she knew she liked Jake. A lot. He was different, which was a big reason behind the physical attraction. He ticked all the boxes. Tall, gorgeous, and masculine. Plus, he could cook, had a thought in his head other than trucks or livestock, but looked every inch a cowboy once you put him in those damned jeans that fit him so very, very well.

He would be a lot of fun, and she wanted to have fun, damn it.

She pinched the bridge of her nose carefully, the tape against her fingers wrinkling, angry at herself for getting caught by that damned horse. She looked ridiculous, and he had kissed her anyway. What did that say about him? What did that mean? He seemed like a genuinely good man. Her gut told her he wouldn't take advantage of her or play her, like Darren had.

It was confusing, and she hated being confused.

Being in love, all that bullshit was supposed to be straightforward. Black and white. You either were or you weren't. Darren had muddied the waters when he'd cheated on her, and she hated that she still thought of him when it came to being with someone, making her second-guess her own decisions. It was exhausting, measuring every other man against him.

It had been over a year since she'd thrown her engagement ring at him, called him a fucking asshole, and stomped out of the clinic, every nurse and orderly standing gaping. Dramatic and stupid, she knew it would mean *I told you so* and *Don't throw away the best man you'll ever have* statements from people would come and dig into her like spurs. So she'd closed that part of herself down, clueless about how to ease the hurt of being rejected.

Darren was supposed to be a safe choice; the solid, comfortable guy. Choosing him was security for the future and protection for her heart because it was simple. Now, she wasn't sure what the future with someone else looked like, only that it felt out of reach.

A fling was not the right answer to all that baggage, not with someone as volatile as a long-lost West who was currently causing havoc in her family's life. Not by his own doing, of course, but all the same, it would be a stupid move.

But the ghosted heat of his mouth on hers whispered in her ear that she really, really wanted to.

A door slamming outside broke her train of thought, and she

abandoned all thought of her dinner congealing in the plastic tray.

Being the closest bunkhouse to the main house, she could easily hear comings and goings, and that had come from the front of the house, not the back door that everyone used. Curious, she looked through the window and saw the front door wide open, a square of light in the gathering dusk.

"Better go see if Mom needs me," she muttered to herself, and shoved her boots on to walk the few steps over. As she was going up the steps to the veranda, she heard shouting and stopped, debating about whether she should go any farther.

Shit. Tanner knew about her and Jake. What else could it be? She sighed and continued up the steps. If she needed to be there to set Tanner straight, she might as well wade in.

As she entered the hallway to the dining room, deep voices echoed from the kitchen. Tanner and Jake were shouting at one another, with a swear word or two thrown in the mix. Brady was yelling at them to stop, of course. Everyone was mad.

She startled as Tanner, with his arm across Jake's throat, burst out right in front of her, Jake hitting the wall hard enough to make all the picture frames and the sconces rattle with the impact.

A West brother earthquake.

"Tanner! Stop it!" she yelled as she rushed to their side. He turned, his eyes glittering with rage, and she stopped dead.

She hadn't seen him mad like this in a long, long time.

"Back off, Lizzie," he hissed, and turned his attention back to Jake, who, now that she looked from one brother to the other, she could see was just as angry. Liz prudently stepped back just as Jake's arm came up and broke Tanner's choke hold and pushed him back against the wall on the other side of the hallway. Jake didn't retaliate, and stepped back, breathing heavily. He looked ready to swing at Tanner, his entire body rigid.

"Back off, yourself," Jake growled at Tanner, which made Tanner step in and crowd him. You could practically see the testosterone in the room, and Liz—had this not been Tanner and the guy she was attracted to—would have found the scene amusing to watch.

"You fucking asshole. You have no business—"

"What I do on my own time is none of your damned business—"

"It is my fucking business when it's Liz, dickwad."

"Kiss my ass, cowboy."

They were yelling at one another again, noses inches apart, cords in their neck popping. They were spitting images of one another, with curled fists, set jaws, and tense shoulders, making it anyone's guess who would throw down first. Someone was definitely getting punched any minute.

"Tan, stop, let's talk about it," Brady said as he stepped between them, a hand on his brother's chest. Tanner shoved him aside, and Brady stumbled.

"Dude!" he yelped as he grabbed the door frame of the dining room. "Seriously?"

Where was her mom? Liz decided to go look for her, and as she attempted to sidle past them, ear-splitting clangs echoed through the house as Peony strode out of the kitchen, banging a pot with a metal spoon. Everyone stopped and turned to her as she planted her fists on her hips, pot and spoon firmly grasped, and gave them a look of sheer annoyance.

Her mom was livid as well. Ooh . . . the last time Liz had seen that look was when she'd gotten home from playing hooky from high school and her mom had found out. Her ear had hurt for days from where Peony had grabbed it and dragged her into the house, yelling at her the entire time. She'd been grounded for weeks.

The tension in the room was palpable, and Liz's anger bubbled out. Once more, some man was being a jerk about something that he had no business interfering in. She knew Tanner would be pissed, but this? Where did he get off, thinking he could control her choice regarding who she wanted to be with? It was her life, her decisions.

"Listen up, you Neanderthals. Take your fight outside. I will not be pleased if you wreck my house," her mom said tersely, and Liz cringed on instinct at her mother's sharp tone. "I am done with this bullshit. Figure out your differences because if you don't, so help me god—"

"We're going. My apologies, Peony," Jake growled, rubbing at his throat. He pushed Tanner away from him and stalked past Liz without even looking at her, and out the front door, clattering down the steps. Tanner, a slightly shocked look on his face, followed right after him, but not before stopping to grab at Liz's arm.

"You and I are talking after this, you hear?"

"You're not my keeper, Tan," Liz snapped, shaking his hand off. "What the fuck do you think you're doing?"

He let go of her arm and stomped out the door. Liz looked at Brady, and they both headed to the door.

"Get the first aid kit and some ice," Brady said. "One of these two idiots might need it when this is done."

Liz bristled, fed up with the whole damned thing. Both of them could go to hell.

"Yeah. They can get it themselves."

Despite her statement, she opened the front closet and found the first aid kit they kept there, setting it on the key table by the front door. They'd find it easily enough, and she should go help her mother clean up dinner, which was likely still on the table. Let them beat each other to a bloody pulp. This had nothing to do with her, even if it was about her.

Her mom was in the kitchen, picking up things off the floor. The kitchen looked like a bomb had gone off.

"They started shoving each other like stupid yearling bulls in here," her mom said, and waved a hand around. "Tanner just barged in halfway through our meal, grabbed Jake out of his chair by his shirt, and threw him through the door."

"Fucking hell," Liz muttered, looking around. Papers had slid onto the floor from the side table, the wire dish rack normally on the counter was halfway across the kitchen. Liz picked up the tea towels normally hanging on wooden pegs near the ovens and threw them toward the sink. The sprayer head was sideways, knocked off the tap and hanging listlessly.

"Care to tell me why?" her mom asked, leaning on the counter. She tapped a spatula and a butter knife against her leg.

"Um, well, it seems that someone, most likely one of the hands, saw Jake and me, um, kissing in my office today."

Her mother made a noise that usually meant she was reaching a particularly good part of one of her books and raised her eyebrows. She set the things in her hands in the sink, fixed the nozzle, and turned back to level a gaze at her daughter that made Liz bite her lip and look down at her toes.

"Land sakes, my dear, you sure do know how to stir up a hornet's nest, don't you?" was all she said.

* * *

Tanner's fist connected with Jake's jaw, and his head snapped back. *Oof. That was a good one.* He shook it off and swung back, his knuckles hitting Tanner's cheekbone and glancing off, returning the favor. They'd both gotten a few good hits in as soon as they'd steamed out the door, Jake headed for anywhere but inside the house, Tanner grabbing the back of his shirt to finish their conversation.

He hadn't swung at another man in a long time, and it felt liberating, letting out the frustration of the past week of insanity and loosening shoulders that had been tight more often than not since he'd arrived.

Tanner went at him with an uppercut but Jake dodged it, stepping away, watching his brother's fists and feet, waiting for the next move. Both of them were huffing for air now, blood dripping off split lips.

Jake's years spent working off his anger at a boxing gym in Brooklyn were paying off, it seemed. His brother could brawl, but Jake could kick his ass in the ring. Tanner needed to keep his fists up more, and he was slow to adjust his stance. He supposed cows didn't punch back that often, and Jake scoffed at his own joke, deciding not to share it with the class and further piss off the steaming madman currently trying to knock him senseless.

"Bring it, asshole!" Tanner growled, and Jake beckoned him, cracking his neck. They circled one another again, their feet scuffing in the gravel of the driveway.

Bring it? He didn't want to hurt Tanner, but the way he had strode in and jerked Jake's ass up had made Jake see red. All his anger had gone into the first punch, which had knocked Tanner's hat off and sent him flying backward. He'd stayed on his feet, though, and then they'd gotten into it.

Now it was just pride swinging his fists, because the entire thing was ridiculous. Two grown men fighting over a woman, as if they had sway over her actions. Could it get any more clichéd?

"You really need to stop trying to control everyone's life, cowboy!" Jake goaded as Tanner swung, and he ducked again. "I get that you're a control freak, but Liz is her own woman."

Tanner barreled at him and Jake grabbed him before he could push Jake over. They hit the dirt and rolled. Jake levered his body weight up but Tanner was ready for him, and he ended up sprawled in the dirt, face down, his arm twisted behind him, with Tanner's knee on his back.

"You're no smarter than a steer, City Boy," Tanner drawled, and dug his knee in, pushing all the air out of Jake's lungs. Jake twisted but to no avail; Tanner had him pinned. He stopped struggling, waiting for him to ease up.

As soon as Tanner let go of his arm, he reared up, grabbed Tanner's nearest bicep, and hefted. His brother went over his shoulder and into the dirt, and Jake threw an arm across his windpipe, just like Tanner had in the house. He leaned in, right into Tanner's face, and quirked an eyebrow.

Enough was enough. They were being immature, grade-A assholes. He was bruised and tired, and could feel his lower lip splitting farther. One of Tanner's eyes was already swelling shut.

"You're no smarter than me, then, cowboy," he drawled back, getting one final dig in. Tanner grunted and looked away, giving in. Jake let him go and stood up, dusting his hands.

"This is utterly stupid. Why the fuck are you so worked up about Liz? What is it to you that she and I—"

"Stay away from her," Tanner yelled, interrupting him, stabbing a finger at Jake as he hauled himself up from the ground. "It's bad enough you have to be here, but don't fuck around with her. You'll hurt her and no one fucks with my family, asshole."

"Says who?" Liz shouted as she strode toward them. She threw an ice pack at Tanner's feet, and stood there, hands on her hips just like her mother, glaring between the two of them. Jake slid his aching hands into his pockets, all his knuckles popping, and waited for her to continue, thankful for her intrusion.

"I am so sick and fucking tired of men telling me what I can and can't fucking do! So what if I kissed him, Tan? So what? Not your call who I decide to be with. Stop being a controlling asshole."

Jake let out a chuckle but then silenced it as she rounded, her eyes narrowing as she lasered in on him. *Uh-oh.* He sat back and waited for the explosion.

"As for you, stop pushing his goddamned buttons. He just lost his father, his ranch, and now he's gotta reconcile to a new brother who can be a smarmy, citified, arrogant prick. Cut. Him. Some. Slack!" she shouted, jabbing her finger at him with each word, walking toward him. He caught her hand just before she jabbed it square into his chest.

"Message received," he said, ducking to look into her eyes, and let her hand go when she met them. She was right, about all of it. She blinked, expecting him to argue with her, he assumed. Her nostrils flared, and he braced for her to let loose another tongue-lashing because he was taking it.

"Lizzie, he's no good," Tanner growled and stepped over to them, hand on her arm again. "You're not—"

"Fuck. You," she hissed at Tanner and shook his hand off her. She turned, grabbed Jake by the fabric of his shirt, pulled him in, and kissed him.

Jake grabbed for her before she pulled him off-balance and sent them both tumbling, and once his feet were planted, kissed her back, all the sense in his head sliding south. Sure, his blood was up from being a big damned idiot and fist fighting in the driveway, but Liz did something to him that blew his normal composure to smithereens. It was arousing as hell, so he went with it.

Her lips were soft, and he bent her over slightly in his arms while she tugged on his shirt more, twisting it in her fists as he tightened his grip on her. Except for the sting from his split lip, which he ignored, it was as fiery as their kiss in the office.

But this was not a kiss from being turned on. She was mad and trying to prove a point. He knew that but wasn't about to stop her. That might get him slapped, and he'd had enough of that for one evening.

He half heard Tanner mutter something and stalk away, and Liz released him, a satisfied smirk on her face as she ran a thumb along her lower lip, pleased with herself. The smirk slid away as they watched Tanner climb into his truck, gun the engine, and take off down the driveway in a spray of gravel.

"A bit much, maybe?" Jake said quietly as they watched Tanner's taillights disappear around the corner. "He's pretty upset, Liz."

"Well, so am I," she retorted, and stalked back to the house, leaving just as quickly as Tanner had.

"Oh my god, this family," Jake said into the evening air, and winced as he lowered himself to the bottom step of the veranda. Brady, standing off to the side, retrieved the ice pack and handed it to him as he sat down beside him. Jake placed it on his jaw and groaned.

"Fuck," he added, for good measure. "Now what?"

"Give him a bit. He's protective of Liz. Has been since she showed up here with her mom all those years ago. She's not blood, but she's part of our family, you get?" Brady said quietly. "He'll come back with his steam all let out and then we're all gonna get along."

Jake nodded at that and grunted his agreement, making Brady chuckle and lean forward on his legs, looking out into the darkening evening. Jake caught him smiling, but his eyes were serious, scanning the horizon for something, maybe working out what to say next. He let the quiet settle him back down, his heartbeat slowing while he shifted the ice pack around on his face.

Brady glanced at him. "Look. I know we aren't perfect, New York. Tanner's got a chip on his shoulder a mile wide, and we're all trying to reconcile how our dad fucked us over, Tan more than anyone else, maybe. But, in the middle of all that, we've gotta get along out here. When we fight, shit gets complicated, and that can be a big problem."

Brady patted Jake on the shoulder and stood up, sighing. "You're making things difficult by poking the bear with Liz, so tread careful. If she wants to do, well, whatever that was, with you, then I'm not going to get in your way. But I'm not going to get between you and Tan either. Not again, at least."

"I'm sorry, Brady," Jake mumbled, slumping. "For all of this."

"Not entirely your fault, New York. But don't make it your fault by stirring it up, yeah? Besides, I like your cookin'. Would hate to see those hands too hurt," Brady added, a hint of humor in his voice, as he vaulted back up the steps.

Jake waved him off, and sat, watching the sunset dip behind the trees. It dawned on him as he moved the ice pack to his knuckles, that for the first time in his life, he'd just had a dustup with someone other than a random dude in a boxing ring, or at whatever bar he was bouncing for as a twenty-something idiot.

He'd been fighting with his brother. *Family*. Something he'd never experienced before. Growing up, all his friends with brothers would constantly fight, and he used to get jealous of that, the idea that there was somebody in life you could argue with who would still be there for you no matter what. That despite pounding on each other, all would be right the next day.

He leaned over on his knees, letting out a big breath, the only other sound some crickets in the flower bushes.

Even though he was positive Tanner hated him six ways to breakfast, Tanner was his brother, and that counted for something. He'd been mad as hell when Tanner had burst in, but it had given way to something else when they had finally come to blows. For the first time since arriving, sitting on the front step of what was the West homestead, nursing his wounds, he realized he cared about that son of a bitch, and what happened to him. He cared about all of them.

They had a legacy in this sprawling piece of land in the middle of nowhere. A legacy he was responsible for keeping, for his family.

Odd and awkward, and maybe not exactly accepting, but it was, he realized, *his* family. Family didn't give up or let go when it was important. They fought for one another and stood up to each other. Which had happened tonight. Each one of them, including Peony with her damned pot.

"Oh my god, this family," he repeated, and laughed, because for the first time since he arrived, he felt like he belonged.

CHAPTER EIGHTEEN

Liz was sitting in the tiny kiosk area for the rental cars, impatiently waiting for Jake to finish up. At this rate, they'd be getting back well after dark, so she texted Trevor to arrange night check with Brady. Her mother had already texted her not to worry about getting back for dinner; she was eating in town with a friend, and the boys could fend for themselves for once.

That they could. Might be better to put some distance between Jake and the boys for a night.

She sighed and shifted on the hard plastic seat, tiredness from restless overthinking taking hold as she took a calming breath. Waiting was not her strong suit.

She'd spent a large part of the previous night staring at her ceiling, and she'd come to a decision to follow this thing she'd started with Jake. The consequences wouldn't be too bad if they were open about it, right? Rules, and definitely no romance. As she watched him interact with the rental booth guy, she hoped that today, as she spent time with him on the drive back, she could spell it out and draw the black and white back into the equation.

She needed black and white after the shitstorm from last night.

The immediate, sober second-guessing about kissing him in front of everyone had circled in her head until she had gone to bed, and then her anger over Tanner being so overprotective left and the overthinking had started.

Tanner was just trying to take care of her, even if it was annoying as hell and she hated it. It took two to tango, and instead of being an adult and just owning her actions, she had reacted like a child with both him and Jake, and she knew it had backfired. In her defense, she had reasoned to herself, Jake was sexy as hell all tousled and bleeding, and that was partly why she had spontaneously kissed him.

It seemed testosterone got to her too. Heck, it was getting to her right now, him leaning on the counter, his deep laugh distracting her from the silly game she was playing on her phone. Despite trying hard to stay objective and keep her hands to herself today, it was damned hard when he wore jeans that fit him perfectly and a crisp collared shirt with the sleeves rolled up.

Jake walked back outside with the rental car guy to watch him do his walkaround of the little car, and her mind wandered from Jake to the ranch, Tanner and Brady, and from there to Brett. The predicament they were in was directly Brett's fault, and she somewhat understood Tanner's feeling of being out of control. He had no context, or tools to handle the intense emotions that losing so much, so quickly, had given him.

It boiled down to the fact that Brett hadn't exactly been a shining example of emotional health. Brady had inherited his mother's demeanor and was the peacemaker most of the time, which sometimes meant he backed down and didn't stand up for himself when he should. Tanner, on the other hand, didn't know how to do empathy or express himself. He was stoic, uptight, and overly harsh most of the time because that was who he had been told he needed to be by his father. That was the kind of man who ran ranches. That was the kind of man who got shit done. Was respected. Didn't show emotion. God forbid cried.

All that utter bullshit.

Tanner meant well, but he was shit at showing it. She forgave him; she always would.

This morning when he'd strode past to the cattle pens, she'd run to catch him. They'd walked in silence the rest of the way, standing at the fence while ponderous heifers had inspected their boots resting on the bottom rung, moving off to the feeders once they'd satisfied their curiosity. Brady had joined them not long after, wiping his hands on a rag, his overalls already covered in bright-red wheel-bearing grease.

"Good morning, sunshine," he had said brightly, throwing an arm over his brother's shoulder. Tanner had tolerated it with a huff. They leaned on the fence as a trio, a picture of peace compared to the night before. No one needed to say anything else. All three of them together without yelling meant it was done.

"I'm sorry." Liz had apologized after a moment more, wanting to clear the air. "Last night got a little out of control."

"Yeah, it did. Me too," Tanner had replied, rubbing his jaw where a bruise was forming under his three-day-old stubble. It was as good as she would get, and she accepted it.

Brady hadn't taken his arm off his brother, and he shook him slightly, making Tanner wince and split his scabbed lip farther.

"Being the boss doesn't always mean bein' the rule maker, Tan," Brady had offered, humor in his voice. "It means being the bigger man, taking a step back when it ain't your concern."

Tanner had hung his head at that, shrugged off Brady's arm, given him a pat on his shoulder, and strode towards the tractor parked nearby. The universal Tanner signal of message received, but the touchy-feely stuff was over and it was time to work.

It was the way it was with those two, and she knew things would get back to normal now.

"We're good to go."

Liz blinked out of her thoughts and palmed her keys in her hand as Jake joined her.

Finally. All the waiting was giving her time to be in her head. She'd had enough of that for the past twenty-four hours. She needed a distraction.

Jake had a small bruise across one cheekbone, his lip split but not swollen. His knuckles were red, but he was in better shape than Tanner. However, paired with her bruised nose and fading black eyes, they must've looked like a modern-day Bonnie and Clyde, because the rental guy was giving them side-eye. She threw him a pissed-off look, and Jake caught it, trying desperately to keep a straight face as he put his hand on the small of her back, ushering her forward.

"Yeah, you should see the other guy," she muttered under her breath when they ducked through the door, which cracked Jake's resolve, and he let out a deep laugh.

Back out in the fresh air, she took in a lungful and rolled her shoulders. The concrete around her was grating. She hated being in the city, and the airport was always so busy—people rushing everywhere, the noise almost unbearable. The sooner she was out of here the better.

They hopped into her truck, and as Liz maneuvered out of the parking garage, she let out a huff of tense breath. They were alone, together, in her truck. The entire way in as she had followed him in that tiny rental car, she'd debated what she would say after what had happened last night. They hadn't had a chance to talk since then, her hurrying to finish her chores before they left just after lunch.

Now that he was here, she had no clue how to start.

"So," he said, as he cleared his throat.

"Yeah?"

Silence. She glanced at him, and he was staring out the window, one foot up on the side of the door, leaned back and resting on his arm, a picture of relaxation. He looked fucking marvelous, and she dragged her gaze away from him back to the road before she crashed the truck.

Damn it. This attraction was running at full freaking gallop. She'd been with guys before, felt that rush of attraction, so why did it feel different this time? She tried to remember if she'd ever had this exact feeling with Darren, and she couldn't. That might be a good thing, but the squeeze of her stomach and the hyperawareness of Jake beside her felt risky and enticing, which had never entered the equation when she started dating Darren. But that wasn't why she'd started dating him. Risk was the furthest thing from it.

Shaking her head slightly to get her asshole ex out of her mind, she focused on being present with Jake. Jake, who was beside her, and wanted her, and was currently so damned sexy it was unfair.

"Everything good?" Jake asked, and she nodded, maybe a bit too fervently, because he raised one eyebrow.

"Yeah. Hate driving in the city," she lied.

"Want me to drive?" he asked.

"No way am I letting you drive my truck," she said, and winced when she realized she'd blurted it harshly. "Sorry, no. No one drives my truck but me. It's a thing."

"No apologies needed. We're not in a hurry, are we?" he said, and turned his eyes back out the window. His voice had gone a bit flat, a sign she'd shut him down again.

They both needed a distraction, not just her. The rapport they'd had in the days leading up to that kiss was nonexistent. She had no way to read him; he'd closed up despite his relaxed pose.

"I was going to pick up some books for Mom. Do you need to stop anywhere?" she finally asked.

"A bookstore sounds nice," he replied, his voice quiet. "And a chance to get a proper coffee with you. No more crossed signals."

She turned the truck toward the shopping area where she knew a big bookstore with a coffee shop attached to it would be, resting her right hand on the shifter when she merged into the fast lane. "Up here. Coffee and books in the same place."

He smiled at her and reached over, putting his hand on hers. Warmth, and something else, flooded her. She flicked a glance at their hands. His thumb caressed her knuckles.

"Jake," she said hesitantly. "I'm—"

"Liz," he replied in the same tone. "Let's take it one day at a time, see where we end up, yeah?"

She nodded silently, focusing on the pressure of his hand, and even though her heart raced the moment he touched her, the pressure also calmed her thoughts.

His words were the right ones. Just take it one day at a time. She could handle that.

* * *

Liz stared blankly at the wall of romance-novel spines staring back at her, perplexed at what to choose. She sipped her coffee and slid her gaze over to Jake, who was picking up books, reading the covers, raising his eyebrows, and then gingerly putting them back, as if something sticky was on them.

"No wonder we can never do anything right," he said, his tone light. "Every single dude is a billionaire with perfect abs, royalty, or a special ops military guy who can kill you with his pinkie but won't because he's a good guy."

"My mom reads them, says she likes the happy endings. It's not reality, though. Love isn't like that. It isn't happily ever after," she replied bitterly.

"Easy there, Sister Mary," Jake murmured as he stepped close to her, his arm rubbing hers as he ran his finger over the spines. "Why else does your mom like them?"

Thankful for his deflection, Liz shook off the irritation his question had raised. She'd asked her mom that question many times, after hearing about the latest bodice ripper her mom was glued to. Her mom consumed at least two books a week, if not more. Liz had always wanted to buy her an e-reader, but they were expensive, and she wasn't sure her mom would like the experience as opposed to holding a real book and turning the pages. Liz thought it was more than just reading for her mom; it looked more like a form of meditation when she'd catch her mother curled up with a book.

"She says she likes the fact that the stories are about women being in charge of their destinies, they have agency, that sort of thing," she said. "I think truthfully she likes the sex in them. Some of them are really spicy."

"Spicy, huh? Like lots of sex?" Jake asked.

"Yeah. I don't know, though, sometimes the scenes in older books she picks up at garage sales feel wrong. Like the woman is forced to do things against her will, and stuff."

Jake *hmm*ed and picked a book off the shelf, examining the cover. "What about this one? The dude on the front looks constipated. Says here he's a 'shifter.' What in the hell is a shifter?"

Liz held in a laugh and shook her head. "Beats me. Maybe a fictional race-car driver type? Who knows. I'll just get her some of these, the historical ones. She likes them best."

She quickly swept up three of the New Regency Releases on the end of the aisle, with women in flowing dresses and frilly parasols gracing the covers, and tucked them into the crook of her arm. The fact that she was shopping for romance novels with Jake of all people felt oddly good, yet nerve-racking. His hand brushing her hip as they browsed made making decisions about which books to get her mother difficult. The entire time they'd been in the bookstore her body and her mind had been fritzing from the simple contact.

"It can be, you know," he said suddenly.

"What can?"

"Love. It can be happily ever after," he said, eyes roving the books in front of them and crinkling as he smiled.

"I wouldn't think you'd believe that," Liz countered. "I mean, you're divorced and all that, aren't you?"

"Yeah, but I still think it can happen. Love doesn't necessarily have to be this passionate adventure. It can be slow and gentle, strong and resilient," he said, surprising her.

"Why, Mr. West, I do believe you're a romantic!" Liz mock gasped, eliciting chuckles from him as he caught her eye.

"Nah. Maybe," he said, smiling sadly. "I met my ex at a restaurant we both worked at, and we just clicked. It wasn't passionate really, but it was mutual respect, and we thought it was enough, until it wasn't. Doesn't make it any less true, though. Love is different for each person, you have to learn their love language."

Liz thought about her mom, and how she'd had a very different take on her marriage to Brett compared to what everyone else thought was true. Perspectives Liz hadn't ever considered.

Black and white were more her speed. She was either in love or not in love. There were no semantics or variations on that. But it wasn't a switch you could turn on and off, and she had never really been good at being "in love" with Darren. He'd made that clear.

"What do you believe? I already know the happily ever after part isn't it," Jake asked suddenly.

They turned down another aisle, this one with a sign that screamed EROTICA in bold red letters. They browsed the books, most of them with suggestive names and oddly placed objects that were euphemisms for sex or something more. Apples, a whip lying casually on a tile floor, ripples of sensual silk across a bed with a hand clutching the folds.

Liz pursed her lips, thinking. *What did she believe?*

Darren had broken her heart. After she had dumped him in a very public way, he'd made stupid excuses, claiming that it was her pushing him away that had led to him cheating, not his own lack of respect and control. He went so far as to say he didn't think she really loved him.

She thought she had, she just didn't know how to show it the way he needed, and even though he'd asked her to marry him, she'd never felt head over heels for him. Showing love, or being intimate wasn't her strong suit. He'd tried to change her, but maybe she was too stubborn.

Because of all that, Liz decided that perhaps love wasn't enough, but that wasn't what Jake was asking.

"I don't know anymore," she offered, and shrugged. "I—"

"What happened between you and Doctor McFancypants, anyway?"

He'd caught on better than she'd expected and she laughed, making him chuckle too.

"Darren? He—" She stopped and inhaled through her nose, wincing at the pain of it, and touched the bridge with her finger.

Jake's hands were suddenly on her waist, and he drew her in close to him. He smelled damned good, like fresh soap and some sort of cedary cologne, the planes of his chest smooth and hard, and it was making her want to forget that they were talking about something she hated thinking about, which was her one failed serious relationship. He pulled her into a hug, nestling her head on his shoulder. They were somewhat shielded by the bookshelf, and he let out a deep, frustrated sigh.

"You don't have to tell me if you don't want to," he murmured in her ear.

"He cheated on me with one of the nurses he works with. It didn't last long, but it was enough. He blamed me. Obviously, my idea of love wasn't his, working on your theory."

Jake's grip on her tightened, and his arms flexed. "Jerk," he muttered.

"It was probably for the best," she replied lamely, and pushed away from him, the intimate contact a bit much. She looked up at him, and his eyes were serious, his face set the same way Tanner got when he was about to be a big, tough man about something.

"No one should ever be disrespected that way," he said. "He had no idea what he was letting go."

Her heart skipped a beat, and she wanted to lean into him again. He said things guys had never said to her before and it made her feel special in the moment, like she mattered. She studied his face, and he flushed slightly, maybe because she'd caught him being sweet.

He cleared his throat. "Right. You have what you need? You sure you don't want to buy your mom some of these? You did say she liked the sexy parts."

"I am not buying my mother erotica. I think that crosses some sort of hard line in mom-daughter relationships." Liz laughed, thankful he was being playful despite her surly mood and heavy topic. She hadn't laughed a lot lately, and it was nice to flirt with him like this.

"Suit yourself. Might buy myself one . . . for pointers, you know."

He'd said that as she was taking a sip of her coffee, and she nearly sprayed it back out everywhere. *Oh hell*, that was pure invitation. How was she supposed to answer that?

He ran his finger across a few spines and then chuckled, knowing he'd shocked her. Time to keep moving or she'd jump him behind the bookshelf, and that would get them kicked out of the store.

"Come on," Liz replied, and quickly turned toward the cash register with her armload of books before he could see her cheeks turn bright pink.

* * *

There were absolutely no streetlights on country roads, and it was unnerving for Jake as he sat in the truck, feeling every bump. More so because he couldn't see them coming.

The headlights on the truck wavered over the rough road as Liz drove, a study in concentration. She seemed unfazed by the inky blackness.

"It gets dark out here quick," he remarked, and Liz *hmm*ed.

"You tired? I got a high spot I should take you to. Stars are out tonight," she replied, and hit a turn he hadn't even seen coming, heading up a climbing gravel road before he could answer.

"Stars," he deadpanned, and raised his eyebrows at her as she smiled.

"S'beautiful," she replied, and pulled off suddenly into what appeared to be a parking lot. They were alone except for another car with fogged-up windows at the other end of the lot.

She turned the truck off and undid her seat belt, her body straight and tense, uncertain, like it had been all afternoon. Was she regretting her bold move the night before? Was this attraction all it was, and she was about to squash it because of his overprotective brother? He hoped not. He wanted Liz. He wanted her to give in to the attraction churning between them, see where it would go, because she was holding herself back from it. He couldn't read her right now; her anxiousness was a direct contradiction to her normally decisive, blunt personality.

He looked into the inky blackness, spotting the odd winking light from a house, and let out a big breath, trying not to take on the tension he felt radiating across the cab of the truck at him.

"Look. I'm no good at relationships," she blurted, and he turned in his seat to look at her. She was staring out the windshield, hands twisting nervously on the wheel.

"Okay," he answered, and waited. He had figured out last night that this was a woman you did *not* push. He wanted to, though, because that was when her natural feistiness came out, and he liked that.

"So if we're gonna do this"—she gestured between them and then turned to look at him—"I want some rules."

"No strings, no expectations when I go home, you mean?" he ventured. He hoped he was right that she wanted no room for any ambiguity. He liked that about her too. Her directness was refreshing, even if it was also maddening. It meant she jumped to conclusions, but she also didn't play games with your head.

He could give her direct, if that was what she needed.

"Yeah," she said, her shoulders dropping. "Yeah, that. I like you, Jake. You're really different from any of the men here. But I'm not wanting—"

"Serious stuff. Keep it casual," he finished for her. "I'm not looking for serious either. Hell, I don't even know what this is yet, so—"

She let out another breath, nodding silently. He had read her right, and felt satisfaction at that.

All afternoon they had skirted around the conversation they were having now, and Jake had somewhat enjoyed just getting to know her. They had browsed the bookstore clutching massive coffees, and she'd told him about her ex. He wondered how they met, her a horse trainer, him a doctor. Maybe when she was more comfortable talking about it, she'd tell him. He'd also found out where her head was when it came to romance, which was a dark place. That made him sad for her, but he understood why. Being cheated on could make anyone feel inadequate. So to figure out she wasn't ready for anything but friends with benefits was a relief. It meant they were on the same page.

"No overnights, no romantic gestures," she added a moment later. "I don't do that."

He undid his seat belt and slid toward her, swallowing the joke about sweeping her off her feet with flowers and chocolate and tickets to the opera. She was being utterly serious.

He threaded his fingers through her hair, combing it back behind her ear. She'd worn it down today and it looked temptingly soft, all wavy and flowing over her shoulders. It was longer than he'd thought, now that it wasn't in a ponytail or a braid or stuffed under her hat. She leaned slightly into his touch, and he desperately wanted to see it spread out over his lap if she—

"Whatever you need, Liz," he murmured, putting a pin in that thought, and forced her to look into his eyes. "I'm game."

He could tell that those words had gone a long way because the rest of her relaxed and she leaned into his hand fully, sighing. That sigh moved her entire body, and he watched her back arch into it, stretching.

It was enough to make him close his hand around the nape of her neck and pull her over, fitting his lips to hers, kissing her.

She opened to him immediately, her tongue darting out to his, her hands on his arms squeezing him, asking him for more. If she had a Go button, this was it, because she was fully responsive to him the moment they connected.

They'd been zero to full speed every time they had kissed. He'd never had a woman respond like this before. It kicked him straight in the ego.

"Outside," she breathed, and pushed him away as she opened her door, sliding into the darkness. He followed, slamming his door, his shoes crunching on the gravel as he joined her at the low retaining wall that bordered the lookout. His eyes adjusted quickly, and he could see her leaning against the wall, biting her lip, watching him walk toward her, her eyes flicking up and down his body.

"I come up here to think," she remarked as he pulled her into him, running his hand up her back, needing to touch her again, enjoying how solid and strong she felt. She was fit because of what she did, of course, but in a different way than women he'd dated in the city. She was all functional muscle, not yoga-toned and smooth. She had definition and athletic curves that fit into his large hands perfectly.

"Just think?" he drawled, as she nestled closer to him. "I hear all the country folk come up to lookouts for something other than 'thinking.'"

She chuckled and swatted at his chest, tilting back to look at him, humor in her eyes, the tension and reservations gone. *Thank god.*

He moved her hair away from her neck and kissed her pulse point, her rapid heartbeat on his lips exactly what he wanted. Her hand went into his hair as his lips made their way down her neck to her collarbone, and she let out a soft moan as he moved back up and grazed her jugular with his teeth.

"I could seriously strip you right here, right now," she murmured, and all the blood drained from his head to his dick. Then she looked him square in the eye and ran her hand over the bulge in his jeans.

"Is that a dare?" he growled, and dug his fingers into her ass, pulling her up and into him the moment she moved her hand. She laughed at that, a deep, throaty, turned-on laugh, and her fingers slid between them and unbuckled his belt.

"Yes," she replied, hefting herself up to sit on the wall, pulling him to her with the end of his belt. "Now."

If he needed further invitation, he was fooling himself. His fingers found the top of her jeans and popped the button, and hers hurriedly pulled at his as she bit her lip and threw him a look that was pure heat.

"Condom. Wallet," he wheezed as her fingers dove in and sheathed him. They were cold but warmed immediately as they circled and squeezed. He had to slap a hand onto the wall for balance, because she was making him lightheaded.

Headlights lit everything up behind them, tires crunched on gravel, and she squinted, pulling up her other hand to shield her eyes. He sighed and reluctantly tucked himself back in as the headlights passed. She let out a snort of laughter as a truck pulled into a spot a few down from them, and two men got out with cigarettes already glowing, talking quietly to themselves.

One of the men nodded to him, a knowing look thrown between them, and he was temporarily subdued as it hit him.

He'd nearly fucked Liz out in the open, on the side of a stone wall at a local lookout.

He normally had more control over himself. How she could take that away was somewhat scary to contemplate in the moment afterward.

"Well, fuck, fun spoiled," she muttered, and pushed his chest, a mischievous look stealing over her face. "Home? Bed. You, me?"

She was tucking her shirt back into her jeans, and even though his heart was hammering in his chest from the interrupted moment, he wanted to end tonight buried deep inside her.

"Home," he rasped, agreeing with her. He watched her sway back to the truck, flipping her hair over her shoulder as she went, her ass perfectly cupped by her jeans. She looked back at him, eyebrow quirked, and he pushed off the wall to follow her. She looked like trouble and heaven in the same package, and he almost tripped when she licked her lips and hoisted herself up on the running board, a sexy slow smile on her face.

"Come on, City Boy, move that fantastic ass," she said, and hopped into the driver's seat.

Was he in trouble? He thought, right then, that he might be.

CHAPTER NINETEEN

Liz pulled him through the door of her bunkhouse, fumbling for the light switch in the hallway, other hand firmly gripping his jacket. He was trying to lever off his shoes while also attempting to grab her, and she smacked at his hand, laughing so hard she could barely speak.

She squealed as he finally caught her and picked her up, striding farther into the house, stopping as he hit the doorway between the kitchen and the living room.

"Which way?" he growled, and smacked her ass lightly as she squirmed.

"Down the hall. Left!" she managed as she wriggled, trying to free herself, but also enjoying the caveman routine and playfulness that had stolen over him when they had pulled into the parking spot in front of her house.

They had driven the rest of the way with his hand on the back of her neck, playing with her hair, the heat from his palm bringing home the relief she'd felt when they'd said were on the same page with this thing they were about to do. Him agreeing to casual meant she could fully relax and let herself have fun.

That fun had ramped up pretty quickly, and she'd almost let him do her right on the lookout wall. On the drive, it sank in that she was wound up to bursting if she was willing to be out in the open, half naked with a guy she barely knew. What it was about him that undid her ability to keep herself in check, she had no idea. Well, other than he was ridiculously hot and was nothing like anything she'd ever put her hands on before. She didn't even want to compare him to Darren, because Darren was miles away from the sheer male presence this man had when he walked into a room.

Jake toed open her door and deposited her on her bed, which, she discovered, as she hit it, was neatly made. There were no piles of clothes on one side, clean but jumbled because she never put them away. The comforter was smooth and not a massive lump thrown open each morning.

"What the—" she managed as she looked around her in confusion. Her bed was never made.

Mom.

She must have popped in today, unable to help herself. It bugged Liz sometimes that her mother invaded her space, but it was also comforting that she still wanted to take care of her. Without Brett, Peony needed something to do, someone to take care of.

"I never took you for a neat freak, Liz," Jake teased as he crawled up the bed until they were nose to nose, his arms braced on either side of her head. "You are so not a tidy kind of girl."

She ran her hands up his chest, effectively trapped by his body, thrilled as his shoulders flexed under her touch. Sliding a knee under her thigh he nudged her legs apart, lowering himself against her with a rumbled groan. His eyes took her in, eyelids lazy and hooded, his intentions clear as he dipped down and grazed his lips over her jaw.

"I'm not," she replied. "I like it dirty."

With that, he pressed himself against her, his mouth finding hers. She unfolded around him, nestling him farther into her core, conscious of how delicious it was to have his weight solidly on top of her.

Jake's hand moved under her shirt and she arched into him, the smooth slide of his hand rippling across her nerve endings. As she tugged her shirt over her head, another soft growl met her ears as he lowered his lips to her chest, leaving hot trails wherever he kissed. He moved over her skin slowly, kissing and touching, pulling goose bumps and anticipation into the air.

He was teasing her. She wanted him now, hard and fast. The wait on the drive home had been bad enough, and the slow and soft was going to make her lose her mind. She didn't like waiting.

"Are all city boys so slow on the draw?" she teased. A soft laugh was the only response she got as he pushed the cup of her bra down and worked a nipple loose, his tongue circling it.

"Yes, that," she breathed, and reached behind her, unhooking the clasp of her bra, wishing she'd worn a nicer one. Comfort had dictated her underwear choices since her breakup, and her slightly frayed T-shirt bra felt a bit embarrassing.

Not that he noticed, since he'd zeroed in on other things.

"A good meal should be lingered over," he murmured as he looked up at her. She laughed at that and pulled on his shirt, which he yanked over his head. She immediately palmed the solid planes of his shoulders, happy to finally see them and touch them. Yes, they were definitely her favorite. Well, depending on how the rest of him looked naked, of course.

He kissed his way down her body, sucking along her stomach, hands caressing her legs, pulling them up and around him, gentle squeezes as his fingers dug into her thigh muscles. It was maddening, this slowness, and she wondered why he wasn't just getting on with it. Most guys would have her naked and bent over by now, and she squirmed impatiently.

"Jake, Jesus!" She hissed as he hit a ticklish spot, and his lips curved in a smile against her skin. He paused when she spoke, then kept right on going.

He popped the button on her jeans and yanked them clean off, underwear, socks, and all in one fluid motion. All thoughts left her head with the slight pinch of his teeth grazing over the point of her hip, his tongue soothing right after.

He deftly lifted one leg out and up, exhaled over her center, and looked up at her.

"You still good?" he asked, his voice rough.

"Yes," she managed, her entire body sparking with the need for his touch, her hand sliding down to his hair, threading in as his cheek rasped against her inner thigh.

She wanted him to touch her, but before she could urge him on, his mouth traveled downward, stilling her breath in her throat. His tongue circled her center, and he dove in, mouth and fingers sliding over her exactly the way she wanted.

Oh my god, that felt amazing.

"Does that feel good?" he asked, and she lifted herself to him as a response, greedy for more, his mouth against her erasing all angst about how much time he was taking. His fingers filled her, stretching her, and she shook from the quick buildup as he curled them inside of her, his tongue still circling on her clit.

She was going to come, and come hard, which was straining every nerve in her body. It had been too long.

"Yes!" she breathed, bucking into his hand. "Fuck, yes, more."

A *hmm* rumbled from him and he licked back up her stomach to her chest, then all the way up her neck with maddening slowness, denying her the release, frustrating her. Finally, he kissed her and forced her to look him in the eye.

"Not yet," he growled defiantly, taking her hand and guiding it down to his fingers still pumping in and out of her, sliding their joined fingers over her clit. She moaned and arched, the tension almost too much.

“I like making you wait, but I like watching you too. Such a dilemma,” he murmured, his tone teasing.

She needed him inside of her, she needed a release right fucking now. “Then let me solve it,” she said, shaking his hand off hers and reaching for his belt. She had waited long enough.

* * *

The more she wanted to speed things up, the more he wanted to slow down, enjoying her squirming in anticipation. He’d taken his time on purpose, because he knew the explosion was going to be incredible when she finally gave herself permission to let go. She was ready for him, wet and hot around his fingers, turning him on so much he could barely contain himself when he tasted her. But he wanted to enjoy every second, draw it out and learn her.

Her busy hands pushed his jeans off, and in short order she was stroking him, which felt so damned good he nearly let himself pump into her hand and finish right there. He reached for his jeans tossed to the other side of the bed and pulled his wallet out of the pocket.

“Wait. Condom,” he managed to gasp as she swirled her hand over him and fished it out. He hoped it was still okay; it had been in there a while. He’d put one in there when he and Ashley had finally split, to appease friends. Gordon had told him to “get back on the horse.”

Well, he certainly was now. He peered at it critically. The wrapper wasn’t bent or ripped, so he thanked himself for the foresight.

“Do you need to read the instructions, City Boy?” she teased, and he looked back to see her eyebrow lifted. He bent his head, unable to resist the tight, pink nipple nearest him, and sucked on it, eliciting a beautiful throaty moan from her as she arched her back, her hips meeting his, rubbing against his already rock-hard cock. God, she was responsive, and she had perfect breasts. Just enough to get his hand wrapped around but big enough that if she pushed them together, he could—

"Fuck. Now," she gasped, and his train of thought derailed completely. She wasn't used to foreplay or playing in bed. He'd had an odd thought when he first noticed her impatience that maybe she had never really, truly been given attention, been pleasured. He aimed to remedy that while he was here because there were so many things he could do to her that would have her vibrating off the damned bed if she let him, and the thought turned him on even more than he already was.

He opened the packet and slipped the condom on quickly, her roaming hands distracting him, her laughter as he gave her a dirty look light and sexy. He grabbed one hand to stop her, placing it firmly around the base of his cock, and leaned into her, his intent now very obvious.

"Show me what you want," he said, and she lifted to meet him.

The world narrowed in on her eyes, the piercing need in hers echoing into him as he sank into her, gritting his teeth to keep himself in check. She went stiff, trembling slightly, and he lost himself for a moment before he noticed. He stopped.

"Hey, you all right?" he murmured, and she nodded quickly.

"Uh-huh," she whispered. "I'm, uh, sorry. Been a while."

"It's okay," he murmured, and kissed her gently, waiting for her to be comfortable, slowly sliding in and out of her, each thrust a bit deeper. It was all he could do to be gentle; he wanted to just let go and dive into her fully, but her reaction told him slow was now more than just play; it was necessary. He wanted her to tell him when she was ready with her body, not just with her impatience and expectations. Her urgency had been nerves she was trying to hide, and he could understand that.

When he caught the impatient flare of her nostrils paired with a soft "oh," he sank into her completely.

"That's better," she breathed. She closed her eyes, her hips rolling into him, and he abandoned all restraint, roughly pulling out and thrusting back in, hard. Her resulting moan and grappling to hold him closer to her the exact response he had imagined.

"I want to fuck you. Hard. Do you want that?" he asked, and she gasped a *yes* in response, a moan following. It was intense, and he dared himself not to look away from her as he let go into her with all he had, sweat sprouting on his forehead from the effort.

The buildup over the past two days was obliterated by the pleasure in the moment, and he was blown away with how good she felt under him. It was fucking honest and real, and they fit together as if this wasn't their first time. They moved in sync, only the next thrust, her moans, her firm grasp on his body, the way she felt surrounding him mattering.

He wanted to fuck her all night just like this, if not for the fact he was holding himself back from coming because he wanted to watch her come first.

He was rewarded a moment later when her cries reached a level he'd never thought she could make, completely at odds with her normal whiskey-fire voice. He angled himself up to watch her, tightening his abs as her muscles clenched around him, her thighs shaking.

"Yes, oh Jesus! Jake, I'm—" she screamed as her hands went above her head, throwing her legs wide, gripping the headboard spindles hard, the entire bed creaking as she came undone underneath him.

He was so close, so damned close, and when she did that, screaming his name, he lost control and within the next three thrusts exploded, his vision blurry as pure pleasure rocketed through his entire body. He grabbed her waist roughly to hold her up and into him, to keep him deep inside her as he came.

"Liz. Fuck," he swore, closing his eyes to ward off the dizziness threatening him. They collapsed onto the bed together, breathless and sated.

Her hand floated out lazily, threading fingers through his damp hair, and she wrapped her leg around his waist, the other hand slapping him lightly on his ass.

"You good?" she murmured in his ear. "You gonna die on me now?"

He laughed at that and raised his head to look her in the eye, brushing hair off of her face to see her, utterly spent.

"You gonna let me go?" he countered, which made her giggle, and she released him so he could slide from her and flop to the bed beside her. They looked at one another. He couldn't believe that had just happened. His chest hurt and his hips and knees were complaining, but the rest of his body felt fucking amazing, pulsing with the aftershock of one of the best orgasms he'd had in a long, long time.

"Well. That was something," she quipped, a half-cocked smile on her face as well. "I may like that more than your cooking."

"I haven't even gotten started yet. That was just an amuse-bouche, darlin'," he drawled in a ridiculous fake Texan accent, trying to hide how overwhelmed he was in the moment.

Her deep, throaty laugh filled the bedroom. He took a steadying breath, pulled her into him, and kissed her.

CHAPTER TWENTY

"Goddamn it. Bright!"

Liz groaned as the piercing rays of dawn hit her sleep-itchy eyes. Her curtains were open, and the light had risen just enough to be annoying. She flopped onto her back, pressing her palms to her face.

Today was going to be another long day. She'd have to buck up in spite of the lack of sleep so Trev wouldn't tease her about what she'd been up to all night. That would go over like a lead balloon with the boys if they put two and two together. Not that she needed to be ashamed, she just didn't want to share yet. It was still new and heady, this arrangement she and Jake had made.

Jake had snuck out as she was falling asleep, and his quick rumble of *Good night* and kiss on her cheek as she drifted off had barely registered. But there'd been a pang of disappointment when he left, even though she was the one with the rule of no overnights.

"Prob'ly should clean up," she muttered to herself, peeling a foil condom wrapper off one butt cheek, and glancing at her clothes from yesterday thrown across the room. Thank god for her own stash of condoms under the sink in her bathroom, or it wouldn't have been such an adventurous night.

Jake hadn't disappointed her. With his big, tall frame, he muscled her over any way he wanted, fitting into her with an ease she hadn't expected. She'd tried to hide that she'd been nervous, and realized after the fact that he'd gone slow because he'd seen it, even though she'd been impatient with him.

A delicious sting from Jake's stubble burned as her thighs touched, and she stretched when she stood, hissing. If she got in the saddle today, that was going to be sore.

It was paired with other thoughts as she rubbed in some of the antichafe cream one of the barrel-racing boarders had given her to try. She paused, rolling the tube between her fingers. Jake had paid more attention to her than she'd expected, always making sure she came first, asking her if it felt good, if it was what she wanted. She palmed one breast, remembering how much time he had spent with his hands and mouth on them, how he had told her they were perfect as he had stroked and caressed her skin. Looking down, she noticed some whisker burn there too.

No man had ever complimented them before. She was called Barn Board in high school for a reason, and even now, years later, she assumed her small chest wasn't exactly what a man looked for.

Not that it mattered, there were benefits to not having to strap herself down in a sports bra that cost more than her groceries for a week just to get on a horse.

As she rummaged in her drawers for clean clothes—which her mother had rearranged so she couldn't find anything—she realized it did matter. His compliment made her feel good. Darren had never even so much as spared a glance at her tits, preferring to just go for the main act as quickly as possible, often not even waiting for her to remove her shirt, just a passing caress before he pushed her back onto the couch with a *Want you* mumbled in her ear.

"Fuck," she swore quietly. That was a shitty thing to be thinking about right now.

Liz waved a hand in front of her face, her nipples pebbling

automatically at the thought of all the ways last night had felt, Jake's arms around her, encouraging her, their bodies moving in sync. They'd fit together, and that meant good things would happen while he was here.

However long that may be, she thought next, and pushed that line of questioning away, just like the memories of her stupid ex, which had tried to wiggle in.

After she pulled on her tightest pair of riding jeans to prevent more chafing, braided her hair, and disposed of the night's wrapper evidence in the bathroom trash can, she made it into her kitchen to wolf down something and make instant coffee sludge to see her through the morning before she could go up to the main house for a real cup.

An old blue Thermos with a curled pink sticky note stuck to the top was sitting in the middle of her kitchen table. Liz recognized it as one of Brett's, dents scattered over the surface, the big handle wrapped in bandage tape.

When she opened it, the aroma of coffee made her involuntarily moan in appreciation. She assumed it was her mother who had brought it over, unable to resist using Jake's new coffee maker.

She eyeballed the note that had fluttered to the table when she'd opened the Thermos. It wasn't her mom's handwriting, so she squinted at the chicken scratching. It was as bad as Tan's when he made lists for the feed store run.

Thought you could use this. Made extra this morning.
-J

"Well, shit," she said into the empty room, and then laughed.

The ancient, rusty filing cabinet had exploded.

Jake started organizing papers slowly late in the morning, clearing off his dad's desk to make piles, and then one of the drawers wouldn't open. Blanking on ideas of how to fix the thing, he had yanked the offending drawer in frustration, and now he was sifting through a small tsunami of file folders spilled all over the floor. The drawer was now even more bent than before, and no longer in the cabinet.

"This looks like fun. Need a hand?"

Jake looked up to see Brady, his head poking through the door of the office. He hung his head, some old feed invoices in his hand, and let out the breath he'd been holding so he wouldn't swear and throw them, creating further chaos.

"I . . . yes," he replied, and stood up, wincing as his back twinged. He hadn't gotten much sleep and definitely hadn't used his back like he had last night for quite some time.

Brady stooped over to pick up a file folder, crumpled pink papers poking out of it at all angles, and tilted his head to read the label. "Auction records," he muttered, and set it on the desk on top of another folder with identical pink papers. In fact, so many of the folders had pink papers, Jake wasn't sure what was what; they all looked the same, even in the flurry of the moment as everything slid onto the cement floor. As Jake slapped a few more folders onto the growing—and only—pile he'd designated To Sort, it was plain on Brady's face he thought this was funny.

"Go ahead. Get it out of your system," Jake said peevishly. This was going to take hours to clean up, and was far less appealing than when he started into it.

"All right, all right, New York. It won't take long to fix. Trying to make sense of Dad's organization will drive you to drink, though. What were you trying to achieve? His method wasn't clear to anyone, except maybe Tan, but even he hated looking through these," Brady replied amiably, and bent down to pick up more paper.

Jake joined him, not sure how to answer that specifically, so he didn't. Achieve? He was trying to stay on top of the ways all this inheritance bullshit was making his head spin. He was trying to be useful, and maybe help out in the long run, after the upheaval of his existence had long become a footnote in the history of this ranch.

He'd do anything not to feel useless in the never-ending reminders of how out of his depth he was. Lunchtime conversations about machinery that he'd never heard of, or crop or cattle terms that sounded like a foreign language, meant he often stuck to the kitchen cleaning when everyone tromped in. The odd time he'd seen any of the crew working, he'd realized that the idea that he could run an operation like this was ludicrous.

So sticking to what he knew was a good thing. The kitchen, and here, the paperwork end of things. But not even that was helping.

The other side of it was that he was desperate to understand a man he had never met, whose blood ran through his veins, and maybe it might help him figure all this out, too, because the confusion in his head about who he really was was getting louder every day he was here.

Brady held a bunch of blue and white papers that all said *Ford* at the top and waved them in the air, grinning as he did. "Don't answer that. I'm just glad it isn't me tackling this."

"Well, if I can't wrestle cattle, like Tanner mentioned, I can at least do this for the ranch before I go," Jake said. "I can distract myself by getting this all figured out while we wait for news from the lawyer."

"Distraction? Hah, this is a full-time job for someone, honestly. Paperwork is never finished, and even when it's organized, more just keeps showing up," Brady said, and they both laughed.

Jake was telling the truth about that, though. He needed something to get his brain out of his pants as well, because all morning in the kitchen he'd been foggy headed and half aroused thinking about what he and Liz had done the night before, and wondering if he could give a repeat performance tonight. He wanted to, but he was dog-tired. He wasn't used to late nights anymore now that his clock had set itself to early mornings.

The cattle-barn office was the eventual go-to because cooking this morning had done nothing to quell the thoughts rolling around in his head, the sting of the fingernail welts on his back rubbing against his shirt, reminding him every time he bent over.

Diving into this mess was an act of desperation to focus on anything else.

It sort of worked, but it was sending his head in another direction he wasn't sure how to handle, just like Brady's question.

After only an hour of sifting, he recognized his dad's handwriting from the scrawled signatures on every invoice, but as for understanding anything more, he was lost. As he had attempted to create categories to sort, he quickly realized that he, Mr. City Slicker, had absolutely no idea what it took to run a ranch, despite his earlier thought of it being just like any other business. There were invoices for the oddest things—when he'd opened a folder called *Vet*, the first invoice he looked at had fees for castration services.

He'd closed that one quickly and set it aside. All thoughts of the softness of Liz's inner thigh were gone in an instant the minute he thought about what that bill meant.

"I was hoping to get it all into my laptop. At least put a few years of the financials in so you guys could see the business better. I have accounting software licenses from the restaurant, which I never canceled, so—"

"That's really great of you," Brady replied. "We could use some of that know-how around here until we get settled. Dad shoveled it onto the accountant and just seemed to have an instinct when it came to what was needed."

Jake nodded at him, and their eyes met. "Thanks. Bigger job than I thought, but a couple of days of this will keep me busy, right?"

"Well, you got in late last night from taking your car back. I'd say something, or perhaps someone, kept you busy?" Brady said, a lighter tone to his voice.

"Um, yeah. Something like that. Late . . . yeah," Jake replied. He didn't want to spill about Liz yet, although coming into the house at 3 a.m. carrying his shoes and his door hinges creaking likely woke Brady up. His guest room was just down the hall from Brady's.

"No judgment from here, New York. I already said my piece," Brady replied, and winked at him.

A bit of the worry about how his brothers—and Peony, for that matter—would react when they figured out he and Liz were sleeping together left. He cracked his neck and let Brady's comment lie, and changed the conversation over to safer topics, which turned into Jake asking questions and Brady plopping himself into a chair and very patiently humoring him, like he had before on the porch. Jake's natural curiosity took over, wanting to understand the real parts of all the invoices and receipts he was piling up. He quizzed Brady on the crops they grew and the cows, trying to get a sense for the revenue streams the ranch relied on each year, piecing together bits of information he'd pulled from the paperwork he had already sifted through.

Brady answered him candidly and seemed happy he wanted to know, and Jake appreciated that more than he'd ever let on. Jake hated being treated like an idiot, and it irritated him at the best of times. In the past, he'd been the expert, and he briefly wondered if he'd always treated his new hires with the respect Brady was showing.

It was humbling, feeling what so many young cooks might've felt like as they got their footing.

As Brady moved a stack of folders to his desk to sort, he began talking about some of his ideas for the ranch, and Jake started enjoying himself. Brady was a great storyteller, and learning more about him away from the dinner table meant he got to see another side to his brother. The rancher, the working man; not just the funny, kind guy who tried to please everybody.

"I've got this crazy idea to grow peanuts. The ranch has this area we call Sandstone Ridge, we bought it a while ago, and it has a south facing slope, plus the perfect conditions," Brady said.

"Peanuts?" Jake asked, intrigued. "Would they grow here?"

"The soil composition along the slope down from the ridge is really sandy. Not ideal, but we can amend it with nutrients that would suit a strain that's hardy in our zone. No idea on yield first year, but it'd definitely be fun to try."

"What else could you grow there?" Jake asked. If peanuts didn't work, there had to be something profitable.

"Potatoes or carrots, maybe. Not sure the ridge has enough acreage for sugar beets. The amount we'd have to grow to meet minimum supply quota for the sugar plant in Taber is a lot."

"What does Tanner say about all this?" Jake asked carefully, wondering if Brady had any sway with his older brother. "Or have you told him any of this?"

Brady shook his head. "Haven't. I talked to Dad about it a few weeks before he died. He was adamantly against any of it. Said peanuts weren't worth ... um ... peanuts when it came to cash crops. He said stick to soybeans and corn and leave the ridge to pasture. I've always wanted to try new things, given the sheltered nature of the ridge, but Dad never did anything with it except put cattle on it. He said, 'Corn sells. Experiments don't,' and that was that."

"Well, why not do it next year, then? The place is yours now," Jake offered.

"That would pop the top of Tanner's head clean off!" Brady laughed. "Now is not the time to experiment, with all of this up in the air. We'd have to start planning crops real soon, secure seed, that sort of thing. I'd need to buy a new type of planter and harvester. That all takes money he won't want to part with until West Line is back in our hands."

Jake sighed, and figured Brady knew what he was talking about, understanding his brother—and the nature of ranching business—better than Jake could. The entrepreneur in him wanted to dive into it, because it seemed like an interesting experiment. Peanuts. Huh.

"Well, maybe soon, then," he offered, wanting to give Brady a boost.

"Yeah. Listen. Let's finish this up. I originally came in here to offer you a chance to ride today, show you some of the land this afternoon. Weather's good, breeze knocks the bugs back, and it isn't fry-your-balls hot."

"I'd like that," Jake replied, meaning it.

"Okay, well, then. Start shoveling this sh—er, paper—and we'll get our asses out of the office," Brady drawled, and they both laughed.

Brady was fixing the warped side of the drawer of the cabinet by hitting it repeatedly with the bootjack from the corner when Tanner appeared in the doorway. Between each loud metallic whack Brady was full-on belly laughing at a story Jake was regaling him with about receiving a full truckload of tomatoes instead of potatoes at a restaurant when an assistant had filled out the order sheet wrong and they'd had to think fast to use them all up. Everyone had been stained red up to their shoulders from processing it all so it wouldn't go bad. The smell they'd contended with meant Jake still, to this day, couldn't make Bolognese sauce from scratch without feeling queasy.

"Brady," Tanner deadpanned, flicking a glance at Jake but not acknowledging him.

"Hey, Tan. What's up?" Brady answered, setting the bootjack down and examining his handiwork, then sliding the drawer very slowly in along the tracks, the metal-on-metal screech making Jake wince and Tanner swear under his breath. Jake looked back at Brady when he did. Brady was smirking from ear to ear.

Tanner's black eye was slowly fading, his jaw still slightly swollen along the left side. He hadn't shaved, and the haggard expression was deeper than normal, which meant he hadn't been sleeping.

"You got a minute? I need some advice on the big rotary combine. Bobby says the drum is off-balance and we can't get the screen bolted back on. He's trying to get it ready for the soybean test field."

"Yeah, sure. Listen, I'm taking Jake out for a ride this afternoon. You haven't swung a leg over all week. Come with us? That drum's always been off-kilter, and I think the axle on the cylinder is bent. We don't need it yet. Test field's a month out from being ready. The combine can wait."

Tanner stood still, eyes on the floor, his lips pinched together. Jake was expecting a flat-out refusal, asshole remark, or him simply storming out, but then his brother let out a heavy breath and nodded.

"Sure. Okay. Put City Boy on somethin' safe. Hell, put him on Dolly for all I care."

"Dolly?" Brady asked. "Come on, Tan, she's not sound enough to—"

"Then Sandy, or Casper. One of the cow ponies. Until he proves he recognizes the front end of a horse from the arse, I am not willing to take chances with him gettin' himself hurt," Tanner blurted, glaring at Jake, before, as expected, storming out.

Brady whistled and set the screwdriver down. "I expected him to—"

"Say no?" Jake finished for him. "Same. Who's Dolly?"

"Our forty-something-year-old blind cow pony," Brady said, a hint of humor in his voice. "I think he expects to lead you around on a rope, New York."

Jake blinked at that and then laughed. He'd give Tanner credit for that one. Inside joke, but one that was thinly veiled as an insult.

But he hadn't refused, and he'd said he didn't want Jake to get hurt. He hoped that could be a start to them figuring each other out, because they were both acting like horse's asses.

That he could recognize, no help from anyone needed.

CHAPTER TWENTY-ONE

"Liz! Liz?"

Liz poked her head out of the tack room as Brady strode down the aisle, his chaps slung over his shoulder, a huge grin on his face.

"Don't yell in my stable, Brady West!" she scolded, then noticed the sparkle in his eyes. He was practically vibrating. "Why are you so damned happy?"

"I convinced Tan to go for a ride," Brady replied as he reached her.

"Sourpuss could do with a gallop. So?" she replied.

"Jake's comin' too."

"Are you trying to kill one or both of them?" Liz asked, but grinned as well. Brady's mischievous joy was hard to ignore as he followed Liz back into the tack room and beelined for one of the far tack trunks that held Brett's personal gear, and began rummaging through it. He came up with an old pair of dark-brown chaps, the leather polished to a shine from years of use. He laid them on the bench, then went back in and found a beat-up old pair of Brett's gloves, still bent and darkened in spots from use. He examined them critically, and threw them on top of the chaps.

"Jake wanted to go out on a ride with Tan?" Liz asked, wondering if using his dad's old gear would be difficult for Jake, if he found out. She wasn't sure if the gloves would fit him; Brett's hands in the past couple of years had gotten gnarly with arthritis and he'd needed a wider size. The chaps should since he and Jake were really similar in height, and the belt was generously studded with extra holes to cinch it in.

The thought of Jake in chaps made her flush with heat, and she turned from her brother in case she gave away what she was thinking about. They'd frame Jake's ass perfectly.

"Nope. Taking Jake out to show him the place. Tan came into the office while we were talkin'. I asked him on impulse and he, well, he said yes."

Liz whistled.

"A ride could be just what we all need," she said quietly. She pulled a hatbox off the high shelf over the bridle rack and retrieved one of Brett's old felt cattleman hats from the stack inside. It was a dark tan with a black band, had only seen a few wears, and wasn't stained with sweat like some of the others. The hats were just sitting up here, not being worn, and Liz thought maybe it was time to go through all of it and figure out what to do with it. Reminders of Brett were more complex now, with everything that had happened, and what Jake had talked about with her.

She looked at it, thumbing a bit of dust off one part of the crown, reminding herself that it was just a hat, nothing more.

"He'll need this or he'll burn to a crisp," she remarked, setting it beside the chaps and gloves. "Who should we put him on?"

"Tan said to take Dolly," Brady quipped, and they looked at one another.

"Oh, hell no. He didn't."

The two of them were still laughing when Tanner strode in, his chaps already zipped, beat-up felt hat identical to the one she'd picked for Jake in his hand, a scowl on his face.

"I'm taking Chip," he muttered, and hefted a saddle up by the horn. "Brady, you taking Zane?"

"Yeah," Brady replied, the levity gone like a vacuum had sucked all the air out of the room, and turned to gather his tack. Liz pulled Chip's bridle off the wall and wordlessly handed it to Tanner, watching him for any sign that this was not a good idea. His temper was so razor-thin right now that any bobble might just do him in, and even though he'd never hurt a horse, he'd certainly fight with one if his hackles were up. Chip was as solid as they came, and knew his rider well, but lately nobody could put a guess on the stress levels bombing around inside Tanner. She had to try and poke through the storm he was carrying around before he got on a horse, especially if he and Jake pushed each other's buttons again.

"Tan," she said quietly as he turned to leave.

"What?" he growled curtly, his jaw flexing, his eyes snapping.

"Just stop for a hot second. You're like a bear with a burr up its butt. What's going on?"

Brady slid past them with his saddle and bridle, meeting Liz's eyes. She nodded at him, and he quirked an eyebrow but left them alone. She'd see if Tanner would tell her what he was pissed about now, maybe it would lessen the bowstring-tight tension she could see in his shoulders.

"Nothin."

"Bullshit."

He sighed and turned to her. She saw it then. The exhaustion, the hurt, the absolute rock bottom he was facing. The gut twist of helplessness hit her, because she didn't know what to do with that.

He'd dusted it up with Jake, and they weren't even talking to one another now. There had been no word from Frank. He was hating every moment of this exile imposed on him by a dead man he'd worshipped his whole life, and his hands were tied behind his back, his control gone.

"You gotta figure out how to be good with all this, Tan. It's eating you alive," was what she finally decided to say, hoping it wouldn't blow his fuse.

"It's not that, I was in town and saw—"

A horse kicked a stall and squealed just outside the tack room, and he stopped talking, instinct taking over to listen in case they needed to deal with it. When there was no resulting ruckus, Tanner frowned, not finishing his sentence.

"And saw what, Tan? Is everything okay?" Liz prodded.

He didn't answer her, just stood there, bridle in his hands, eyes focused out the tiny window in the tack room that faced the sand ring. His jaw flexed, his face went hard with what Liz assumed was the grief that was consuming him, and she braced for impact. The clock on the wall ticked into the silence of the room.

"You comin' on this ride too?" he finally replied, deflecting her question, his jaw clenched tightly. "The more eyes we have on City Boy, the less likely we'll be pickin' him out of the dirt."

"I'll set him on Sandy. She can keep up to our horses, and she's as safe as they come."

"Good. Who are you taking?"

"Finnegan. I haven't gotten on him in a few days. He could use it."

A sound of agreement came from Tanner before he stalked out of the room and she moved off to heft her own saddle, laying Finnegan's bridle over the seat. Her mind was already on the task of tacking up two horses quickly, deciding which saddle would be best for Jake. Brett had an old working saddle he used to ride the fence lines, and after depositing her saddle on the rack in front of Finnegan's stall, she went back and pulled the dust cover from it, eyeing the leather critically. It was still in great shape and would fit Sandy's long back perfectly.

A hand touched her, and she turned back to see Tanner, an apologetic look on his face, his saddle hefted up on one shoulder.

"I . . . damn it, Lizzie. I'm sorry. I shouldn't take my shit out on you.

I—" he started, and swallowed hard, his eyes leaving her to look at the ground, then closing. She put her hand on his.

"You don't have to answer my question, Tan. I'm just worried about you."

He let his hand slip away from her. There. She'd said enough to make his gears turn, maybe. She yanked her chaps off her peg near the door, and as she was zipping them up, prayed it would be a nudge in the right direction.

* * *

"I feel ridiculous in these!" Jake hissed at her as he stood on one side of Sandy, tugging on the edges of the chaps she had handed him when he'd walked into the barn. She eyed him critically and did up the buckle another hole at the back.

"That should help," she said.

"Thanks," he said. "They're heavy across my hip bones."

"You'll get used to them, and they're less heavy once you're in the saddle. Better than your jeans riding up and rubbing a blister on your shin," Liz replied.

"Still feel ridiculous," he muttered, and picked up a brush, sliding it over Sandy, who was in the cross-ties beside them.

Jake didn't look ridiculous, because the chaps fit him like they were his, the leather hitting him in just the right spot on the back of his thighs. She had been right, his ass—which was already superb—looked even better this way. With a long sleeve Henley shirt and his long legs covered in the polished brown leather, he looked every inch like his brothers, even though he'd never ranched a day in his life. She'd been right that first day on the porch. He looked the part easy, given his genes.

Moving around the horse, Liz met his eyes over its back, and she winked at him. "I think you look hot."

He let out a quiet rumbling *hmmm*, and continued to brush Sandy down, his big hands expertly flicking the dirt off her coat, like he'd done it a thousand times.

He stopped suddenly, leaned over Sandy's rump, and caught her eye again, his own sparkling with mischief. Her stomach fluttered, because he truly was devastatingly handsome when he was relaxed and happy, the way he was now.

"So I should wear them later? Maybe without the jeans?" he quipped, and then went back to brushing.

"Jake! Jesus," she hissed back, heat flaming over her cheeks, which were now likely the color of a tomato. "Not now."

He stepped around Sandy, dropping the brush back into the box on the wall, and as he passed her, he pulled her over to him, their bodies fitting against each other perfectly. His hand sliding dangerously up her back made her want to forget about the ride and just take him home, and his breath on her neck made her wish he'd pin her to the wall and—

"Yes, now," he said, and his lips found her pulse point, slowly sliding over her skin.

She fisted his shirt. "If you keep this up, we won't get on the horses." It was going to be hard to concentrate if he didn't let her go.

"I keep thinkin' about last night," he murmured in her ear, his other hand now pulling her hips in closer to him, their belt buckles clinking. Then he abruptly let go and walked over to the saddle rack, pulling up the saddle blanket resting on top of the saddle.

She was going to lose her mind with this man. He could rev her up and then set her on idle, all the while knowing exactly what it was doing to her. She growled at him and took the blanket from him wordlessly, mock glaring at him for good measure.

"Enough of that for now, Mr. West. You need to learn how to tack up."

He held his hands up in placation and dutifully listened as she showed him how to set the saddle blanket and place the saddle, how to do up the cinch.

He'd said he was familiar with English tack, so she showed him the differences, then stood back and let him do it himself. Sandy, as always, was the perfect teacher, sound asleep even when Jake pulled the cinch tight. Once he'd done that, he moved around to Sandy's front legs, and picked each one up, pulling it out.

Sandy woke up at that and obliged the odd behavior, wiggling her upper lip through Jake's hair as Jake bent over to pick up the leg.

"Get in line, sweetie, I've already got a girl," Jake murmured to the horse, then laughed and scratched the old mare's jaw, which promptly put her back to sleep.

Liz stopped, registering that Jake had just called her his girl. *Oh*. It probably meant nothing. She refused to put more meaning behind a simple silly statement to a horse.

But it flipped her stomach.

"What the hell is he doing?" Tanner asked. He was standing in front of Chip's stall. The horse's head hung out the open stall door, ears forward toward him, but Tanner's head was turned, and he was eyeballing Jake like he was a madman.

"Ask him yourself." Liz stood back. No way she was getting between them.

"I'm pulling the skin tight under the girth, er, cinch. Smooths the hair out, prevents girth sores, from what I remember. I dated a show jumper, she did this with all her horses," Jake replied directly.

Liz's eyebrows shot up. "Well, okay, then," she said. "We don't do that, but all the same, fill your boots, cowboy."

"We gonna offer them a mint and tuck them into bed with lullabies after?" Tanner muttered under his breath, and went back to buckling Chip's bridle. Jake didn't reply.

"Don't push his buttons today, you big friggin' idiot," Liz hissed at him.

Jake held the reins in his hands and fiddled with them as one side of his mouth lifted. "I'm not. If anything, I want to figure this shit out so we can maybe start over. Prove I'm not a useless citified idiot."

She heard the frustration in Jake's statement. Both these men needed to figure this shit out, but at least Jake was willing to try, it seemed. She didn't answer him, choosing to let it lie. It was time to get a leg up and get into the fresh air. They all needed it

They finished tacking up, Jake proving efficient at bridling as well. Maybe this wouldn't be so bad after all. She held up a hand to Trevor, who was pulling Finnegan out of his stall for her, having offered to tack him up so she could help with Jake's horse.

"All ready?" Trevor asked as he handed the reins to Liz. She slid her eyes over her horse and, satisfied, nodded.

"Thanks, Trev. We won't be out long. A couple of hours at most," she said.

"All good. Go have some fun with this bunch. Or referee, maybe," he replied, and winked before striding back into the stable.

Jake settled his father's Stetson on his head. As she had expected, it fit perfectly, and he tipped it back and posed. "How do I look?"

She let out a snort of laughter, causing both Brady and Tanner to turn, and pulled the front down, settling it more over his forehead.

"Like a country music star ready to go on stage," she joked, then patted him on the chest. "Seriously, though. Suits you."

Which was the truth. He looked exactly like that picture of Brett standing in the middle of a sand ring, clipped from the paper after he won a roping contest. It hung on the wall of the back den in the big house with the ribbon. She wondered if Jake had seen it yet.

"Maybe I'll wear this later too," he said quietly, and grabbed her waist before she could step away, leaning in. "Would you like that?"

“Is that a promise?” she teased back, trying her best to hide how flustered the thought made her.

His eyes roved hers, the heat blazing out to her. Her breath caught in her throat. He was sexy as hell right now, almost as much as when he was in the kitchen cooking. It was attractive how capable he could look no matter what he was doing, and with his arm around her, her pulse rocketed in her ears.

“Anything for my girl,” he said, and then let her go to unhook Sandy from the cross-ties.

A weird sensation of fullness hit her like a hoof to her chest. He’d done it again, called her his girl. She shoved the odd feeling deep down and slammed the door in her mind, because that kind of hope and connection was not what she wanted at all, even if her body was responding to it. She cleared her throat and pointed behind her.

“I’m gonna go get on my, um, horse now,” she stuttered, and walked down the aisle before she gave her thoughts away, Finnegan hurrying to keep up with her.

CHAPTER TWENTY-TWO

Jake had the reins in both hands, monumentally failing to sit the trot they had broken into, evidence that his horse was not exactly a smooth ride. He attempted a posting trot, remembering how he'd been taught to lift himself out of the saddle, up and down like a pogo stick, and his comfort grew. It was harder in the big saddle, but not impossible. Tanner gave him a strange look.

He heard Liz behind him, laughing at something Brady had said, and sighed inwardly. Tanner was barely moving in the saddle, the exact opposite of how he must look. He continued with his feeble efforts for comfort, his toes in the slightly too big boots he'd borrowed from the mudroom sliding in the stirrups. He lost his balance, cursing under his breath.

Tanner cleared his throat awkwardly and flicked a glance in his direction.

"Relax your back and open your hips. It's easier to balance when you settle onto your seat bones. Dad's old trail saddle is meant for sitting," Tanner said.

Had he just talked to him directly? Jake nodded, deferring to his brother, tucking the other tidbit that he was riding in one of his father's saddles away. He didn't need to dwell on that right now or it would consume him, and he wouldn't enjoy the ride.

He was determined to make the most of this, to understand the life he would've had if his mother had never taken him away. He felt out of place more often than not, but there was this hum of recognition in the background that wouldn't go away. That where he was right now was important to be present for. Maybe it was opening locked memories, or he was connecting with his genetic heritage? It certainly wasn't midtown Manhattan, the daily rhythm of the city fading each time he thought about it, and that stark difference made everything new he discovered about this ranch magnified.

"Thanks. A bit rusty," Jake replied. He sat, gave it his best try, and as he relaxed his spine and sat deeper into the back of the saddle, it helped somewhat.

"Sandy's got a long back, it makes her jog terrible. Can you gallop?" Tanner asked. "We'll lope for a bit first, so you can feel it out."

Jake took Tanner in as he spoke, envious of his brother's effortless ease. He had one hand on his thigh, the other holding the reins loosely, the leather looped. The only sign of the tension Tanner carried with him everywhere was his scowl and shoulders so tense they were halfway to his ears. Jake wondered if Brett had been like that too.

Their eyes met, Tanner waiting for his yes or no. It was something, at least. He'd take this back and forth over shouting and insults.

"Sure," Jake replied. His horse's lope, which he seemed to recall was the same as a canter, had to be better than the teeth-cracking trot they had settled into.

Tanner whistled twice, and then he and his horse surged forward. Jake clucked at Sandy, and she followed suit, picking up a rocking cadence that he easily sank into. Much better. He looked quickly behind him, and Liz and Brady were close on their tails. Brady had a huge grin on his face, and he spurred his horse up beside Jake as Tanner's pulled ahead, Chip tossing his head and squealing while Tanner muttered, "Hey, shithead, can it," and tightened his reins.

"This is better," Brady quipped as they loped along the gravel road. The sun was shining, there were a few birds out, and the breeze swishing through the long grass at the side of the road sounded soft and inviting.

"Definitely. I think my spine may be compressed," Jake replied, and winced. "This saddle will take some getting used to."

Brady chuckled and gestured at Sandy. "She's a good, safe girl. She's built like a barn, but she's never been lame in her entire life. Not sure how, since she's got the conformation of a camel, but we don't mind. Liz would breed her, if we weren't so sure the foal would come out looking like more of a camel than her mama."

Jake only understood about half of what Brady had spewed out, but he nodded all the same. "I don't mind. Safe is good. I haven't ridden in a long time."

"You're gonna hurt tomorrow, New York," was all Brady said, still smiling. "But I'm glad you rose to the challenge. Maybe that West blood will kick in, and we'll make a cowboy out of you yet."

That made Jake laugh, and Brady joined him, earning a peevish look back from Tanner.

"Coming around," Liz called, and spurred ahead of them, catching up to Tanner and pulling abreast. Jake watched her as she gestured to the west, and Tanner nodded, pointing in the same direction. Regret and want for a life he could have lived stole over him. His brothers and Liz were comfortable and easy in the saddle, proving they belonged here.

Liz held up a hand, and he was prevented from diving into that train of thought as they eased into a walk, the horses snorting and jostling. Jake barely had to do anything, Sandy automatically slowing down as soon as Brady's horse did.

"We'll skirt up over there, check the fence lines on the south pasture while we're here. I have fifty head of yearling cattle in that field that haven't had eyes on 'em yet this week," Tanner called back. "Up for it?"

"Sure thing," Jake lied, and shifted in his saddle. Brady echoed with a "Yep!" and gathered his reins in.

Tanner whistled and they took off, this time at a gallop. Jake grappled for the horn and held on until Sandy picked her pace, and then he let go and enjoyed the speed. Liz was leaned over in her saddle, churning up dirt behind her as her horse and Tanner's bumped each other, Liz's laughter echoing back to him, the two of them obviously racing. Brady was still smiling ear to ear but keeping pace with him. They followed along, and Jake leaned forward like his brother beside him, shortening his reins as Sandy tossed her head, her mane bouncing over her neck. She was also happy to get moving.

As they rounded a bend in the road, dirt flying everywhere, hoofbeats rattling on the packed dirt of the road, Jake's breath caught in the wind whipping into his face. The adrenaline rush stole over him, along with a hum of recognition in his body that whispered, *You are where you are supposed to be.* He liked it, because the only other time he ever felt like this was when he was in the kitchen, cooking.

"Doin' okay?" Liz asked him later on.

"Yes. I may need to be carried back to my room when we get back, might need a full-body massage," he murmured, hoping it would make Liz blush. He loved making her blush. Something about that, in complete odds with the unflappable woman, was so intriguing, and he wanted to explore that as much as possible. Plus, when she got flustered, he knew he was affecting her, which gave his ego a kick.

"Fat chance, City Boy," she sassed back, one eyebrow raised, but then laughed, her cheeks pink.

They had stopped by a gate, and Tanner, having dismounted, was opening the lock. He was scanning the field, squinting into the sun.

"Don't see 'em. Do you, Brady?"

"No. Could be over the rise," Brady replied, fishing something out of his saddlebag. He uttered a, "Heads up," and threw a granola bar at Tanner, who caught it without looking, stuffing it back in the pocket with his keys, and then levering the gate open, the hinges squealing.

"In we go," Tanner said as he led his horse through.

Brady made to throw a granola bar at Jake, but Jake shook his head. "I'm good, thanks."

"I'll take one," Liz said, and kicked her horse over to Brady, grabbed the bar, and tore into it. Her cheek full of food like a chipmunk, she muttered something to her horse and filed through the gate behind Brady.

Jake followed Liz through and pulled up beside her as they waited for Tanner to mount back up.

"You three work well together," Jake remarked, thinking that the camaraderie they had was so easy.

"We've worked together a long time," Liz answered. "Soon as I arrived, Brett gave me a job for the summer. Kept me out of mischief, I suppose. I followed Tan around on the cattle side until he got tired of me and gave me over to Keith, who used to run the stables. Worked alongside Brady for a few years, he was more interested in the horses as a kid, then later on he picked up a wrench and that was that."

"Brady was into horses?" Jake asked. "Huh. He's the mechanic and manages the crops end of things now. What happened?"

"He lost a horse he loved more than anything. It devastated him," she answered quietly. The sadness in her voice made Jake turn his head to look over at the ever-smiling Brady, not believing anything could get him down.

"Ah," he replied.

Liz *uh-huh*ed and shrugged. "He stopped riding for a while and fell into fixin' the machinery. He was good at that too. Brady is good at anything he picks up, really—he's ridiculously smart, like Mensa level. Brett noticed he could do math calculations in his head and could estimate seed and yield like it was breathing, so he put him to work on the crops as well. He liked it, and things ran well so he stayed put. Still rides and competes at the local rodeo, but for fun now."

Tanner walked past towing Chip behind him, eyeballing the ground, looking at the patches of clipped-down grass, kicking at the round plops of cow manure, his face a mask of concentration.

"What is he doing?" Jake asked.

"Checking the pasture quality. We'll move the cows if it's too eaten down. They need fattening, and this is a great way to do it. We're lucky to have pasture. Most operations use feedlots exclusively, but we have the acreage to feed summer beef without having to maintain so many pens."

"Is it better?" Jake asked.

"Some think so, the cows exercise more and you have a leaner, more marbled product, less overhead, but it's labor intensive according to the big outfits, having to move the herd the old-fashioned way."

"Old fashioned?" He had always assumed cows were in a big field and ranchers herded them. He had so much to learn.

"With horses and punchers, you know? Not through a chute into a big truck." Liz smiled as she slouched in the saddle, her eyes roaming the horizon in front of them. "Honestly? The beef is so much better when it hits market, and we get a heftier price per pound on the hoof when we advertise as grass-fed."

Jake brightened because this was he knew something about. The food industry had latched onto the niche of organic and free range, and if you served grass-fed beef and dairy products, customers flocked in. People assumed it was healthier for them, tasted better, had fewer chemicals and hormones, all that bullshit that the media said to stay away from.

"So these are all grass-fed? Costs restaurants an arm and a leg to serve premium ingredients like that," he remarked. Liz looked at him, tilting her head, and he knew he'd caught her off guard.

"Yeah. Truthfully, not on purpose," she replied. "It's cheaper this way for us, don't have to buy as much haylage and corn. Tan noticed a couple of years ago that people were bidding up lots at auction for beef that was pasture-raised, and he went with it. He calls it his 'hippie beef.'"

"Smart," Jake remarked, and a new picture of his brothers formed in his mind. They were tied to this place not only by their ancestry, but by their passions, and their life-long learning with their feet planted firmly on the ground that gave them their livelihood. From Brady's know-how of ranch operations to Tanner's understanding of trends in the market, they had a history and knowledge of the ranch that was more than he could ever have. Jake mentally measured his own footprint in the restaurant industry as he sat quietly on Sandy, her head dropped to crop at the grass, her tail swishing the odd bug away.

His career as a chef wasn't small, but his influence in the restaurant industry felt transient and temporary, easily forgotten in the constant change New York seemed to nurture. There wasn't permanence in it like the longevity this ranch held for his brothers, giving them the impetus to make it work no matter what.

He wanted to live up to his West name and ensure that the next generation could sit here on a horse and look out over the land the way he was. The thought hit him like a punch in the gut. Was it his legacy too? Was he overthinking it again? It was a confusing mess.

What was crystal clear was that this was home for his brothers, for Peony, Liz, the crew too. They'd known nothing else. His father had, in the oddest of ways, given him the chance to see and understand it all, and he was finally getting it. Tanner's anger made sense.

This was as heavy as learning that his dad had looked for him, and Jake added it to the tally of baggage he would have to deal with at some point.

"Shit," he muttered to himself, and Liz looked at him questioningly.

"You okay?"

"Yeah. Just getting stiff," he lied, and stretched his back.

Tanner had remounted while they were chatting and had disappeared from view over a small dip in the land. Fast hoofbeats made Liz stand up in the stirrups, her body tense, a squawk of alarm coming from her. Tanner and Chip reappeared, galloping up the hill. His face said it all. Something was wrong.

"What is it?" Brady asked.

"The cattle. They've broken through the far side fence. Looks fresh. We have to go before they make the soybean fields across the creek," Tanner barked, turning his horse and galloping back the way he came. Brady spurred after him immediately.

Liz turned to Jake, her face grim as her horse fidgeted to leave and catch up to them. "You up for this? We can send you back. Gonna be a lot of new thrown at you all at once, Jake. It's—"

"You can probably use me. Just show me what to do—if nothing else I can put Sandy in there, and she'll take care of me, right?" Jake interrupted, and hoped Liz would agree. If he wanted to learn, this was the way to do it. Trial by fire, so to speak.

Liz examined him a moment, obviously debating whether he should be there, then nodded curtly.

They turned their horses together, and Jake grabbed for his saddle horn again as they took off at a gallop to follow Tanner and Brady back down the hill.

CHAPTER TWENTY-THREE

Liz caught up to Tanner as he reached the fence line. It had been trampled into the mud, the lines of the wire snapped in two. There were no cows here now, but the manure was still fresh, so they couldn't have gotten far.

"Was the water hole dry?" she asked, looking back at the small marshy slough they'd dug out to water the cattle.

"Nope. Coulda been somethin' spooked them," Brady called as he loped back from checking just that. Jake was close to the fence, looking down at the end of the page-wire panel still attached to the post, his forehead furrowed.

"When a fence breaks does the wire break in the same place all the way down?" he asked suddenly.

"What do you mean?" Tanner snapped, and legged Chip over to see.

"The squares in this fence are broken in the same place all the way down, right in the middle, the ends are sticking out, right? If the cows pushed the fence, wouldn't it look more random, like it, uh, tore? Wouldn't the posts be all bent over from the cows pushing on it?"

Liz's heart skipped a beat in fear. Jake was 100 percent right. It should look like the fence broke under pressure, near the joins in the wire, and it would have been a mess, not neatly broken down the middle, in a perfect vertical line. Tanner jumped down and hauled up the broken side, examining it. Her stomach clenched along with her heart as he swore and ran a hand down his face, turning his back to the fence and stomping back over to Chip.

"It was cut," she murmured to herself, understanding his reaction. "Jesus."

She nudged Finnegan over to the other side, and looked at the crumpled panel of fencing, laid flat into the mud by the cows stepping on it as they left. The ends were cut in a neat line. Too neat.

She pulled her cell out of her pocket and texted Trevor to tell the staff the east pasture cattle were loose, and to stand by. She got a ten-four back from him, and shoved her phone away again so she could be alert. Looking around, she couldn't see or hear the cattle, so they must have booked it down the embankment beside the fence line and through the rough to the access road. If they hit the small creek beside the road and crossed it, they'd be into the soybeans, and that could be dangerous. Grazing on too much raw soybean would kill them.

This was not good, so very not good. Dread filled her as she continued to scan the horizon.

"What in the hell. This is fresh, they can't have gotten far." Brady echoed her thoughts as he jumped down as well. "Where's the nearest access road from here? Likely the dumb things will head straight for that."

He and Tanner both pulled out their maps, and Jake nudged Sandy over to Liz again. He looked worried. He should be. If these cows were lost, it was a huge hit to their revenue.

"What happens now?" he asked quietly.

"We go look. If this was cut, it could just be some asshole thinking it was funny, and the herd should be close by. Worse, it could be theft, but people who steal cattle wouldn't do it in broad daylight unless they were stupid. So likely just kids being idiots."

"Okay," he said, his voice quiet and serious. "Does this happen a lot?"

"No," she said. "Let's move out. We may need to bring in the rest of the crew if we can't find them easily. Gotta do it while we have light."

Tanner and Brady remounted after quickly picking up the downed fence and rolling it up to the next post. They filed through the gap, everyone on alert, heads on a swivel, and made a sharp left, heading down a hill where the scrub brush was beaten flat. They reached the gravel access road lined with birch and ash trees, and Liz craned her neck one way, then the other, looking for hoof marks, anything to tell them which way the cows had gone.

"There! Tracks!" Jake shouted, and turned his horse, kicking her forward and heading toward what he saw.

They rode down the road, following the distinct marks of a herd of cows on the move. Flattened grass, kicked-up gravel, the odd plop of manure. After a few minutes, Liz thought she saw something shiny glint through the trees farther down on a bend, but lost it when she reverted to scanning the side of the road. If any cattle were in the ditches or had veered off to the crop fields that were on their right or through the stands of trees on either side of the road, they needed to act fast.

Nothing appeared as they rode carefully at a walk. The cattle had stayed on the road, and were moving, from the looks of it, quickly. Odd. Normally cattle that were loose and looking for food would meander, and they would crop the grass along the side of the road as they went.

"What is that noise?" Jake exclaimed, breaking the relative silence as they all listened and craned their necks to see around a bend in the road. Everyone's heads snapped up, and Liz squinted to where Jake was pointing. More of the flashing metal, this time with the distinct sound of a diesel engine.

"I see it! A cattle hauler! What the—" Zane sprayed gravel as Brady immediately kicked him forward, Jake following right behind with Sandy.

Liz held Finnegan, about to shout for them to stop, but Tanner was already shooting past on Chip, uncoiling his rope as he kicked his horse into a gallop. Finnegan reared, the others leaving too much for him to handle. She let him go, coming in behind them as they rounded the corner. As they got closer, the sounds of cows bawling and the rumbling idle of a semitruck filled the air.

Dear god, was someone actually stealing their cattle in broad daylight? She'd just told Jake how stupid that would be, how unlikely it was, but now she had to eat her damned words, because there was a full-on commercial cattle hauler in the middle of the road.

She kicked Finnegan forward, hoping to catch up. This could get messy if they had guns. These assholes could be dangerous, and a herd of cattle was not worth any of their lives.

"Come on, Finny." Fear took hold, and she couldn't breathe as she bent over her horse's neck.

The semitruck was hidden behind a band of thick trees at a narrow spot on the road with fencing on either side. The back was blocked by beat-up plywood chute panels, and the cows were milling about in front of it, being funneled forward by three men, all with rigged-together cattle prods in their hands. Liz made a mental count, and figured they had half of the livestock already loaded.

"HEY!" Tanner bellowed. All three thieves turn in unison, startling the cows.

They scattered, but with nowhere to go on the fenced access road, and horses rapidly approaching, they stopped in a big, seething lump of mooing animals. Dust rose in the air, and the danger of the situation lodged in Liz's throat. This was not good. Not good at all.

"Steady, Finny. Steady!" she crooned as her horse tensed. He was still getting used to cattle, and the entire herd left outside the truck at risk of stampeding through them was not going to help. He reared as she thought it, and she kicked him, clucking and grabbing his mane with her hands to stay in the saddle. He landed on his front feet, but stood stock still, shaking like a leaf. He was ready to turn and run, his back humped, his neck arched as big, loud fearful snorts blew his belly in and out.

"Easy, easy!" she breathed at him. If she got off now, he'd be gone, and that was not a good idea. Her hands full of Finnegan's mane and both reins, her cell phone was a useless lump in her pocket. So much for calling 911.

Liz was mentally preparing to let Finnegan's head loose to ride for help when everything went into slow motion. Tanner and Brady were riding right for it all, like fucking idiots, Brady at the rear looking for a way through the side.

"Stop! Stopstopstop!" she shouted, but it was no use.

Tanner and Brady swung down from their saddles, Chip and Zane skidded to a halt the moment they did, and stood firm, staring down the cattle as they had done hundreds of times before, well-trained cow horses.

Then she saw Jake, already dismounted and running, Sandy a few feet behind him, her ears back as she stared down a cow of her own. Liz wanted to shout again, but it died on her lips when he reached the mass of animals. He ducked between two cows like he'd done it a thousand times, slapping one on the ass to get it to move, sending it bucking forward into another cow.

"Oh my god, Jake, look out!" she screamed in futility, knowing that it was unlikely he could hear her. His intent was obvious—he was headed for the two closest men, both of whom were still holding the long prods equipped with what looked to be automotive batteries with handles. If the prod didn't shock him, the battery swung at his head would certainly knock him out. Or worse.

She didn't want to watch, but she couldn't look away, swiveling her head to keep him in view as Finnegan spun in circles, sweating and shaking. He wouldn't go any closer to the mess in front of her.

Jake grabbed the first man by the collar of his shirt, and with a speed she'd never expected from him, punched him. In rapid fire, like he'd been born to it, he punched him again, twice, then the man went slack in his grasp, dropping his prod. Jake let him go as he crumpled to the ground, obviously out cold.

The other man was coming at him from behind, and Jake couldn't see him.

"Jake, behind you!" she screamed as loudly as she could. "Oh my god, he's—"

Jake had turned, but not in time, and let out a yell as the prod stabbed him square in the back. He arched away, spun, and cold-cocked the man square in the nose on reflex, dropping him like a bag of bricks. She couldn't hear Jake, but could see his mouth moving, and it was obviously swear words as he held his back and then dove behind the seething mass of cows.

How had that jolt of electricity from the prod not leveled him? Was he hurt? Liz attempted to get Finnegan to move closer to the cows again, but the horse stopped dead and wouldn't even consider it, so she gave up. She craned her neck to see where Tanner and Brady had gotten to, flashes of Jake's body in motion between the legs of the cows proof enough he was still conscious and fighting.

Tanner had pulled the third guy down and was kicking him, the man curled up in a ball, arms covering his head. She couldn't see Brady, but then the engine of the truck abruptly cut off. He must've gone for the cab of the rig, to make sure there wasn't a driver.

The cows were kicking up more and more dust, the lowing was getting more and more frantic, and the rig was rocking back and forth with the cows already loaded sensing the chaos outside. All three of the other horses were still in front of the mess, holding the herd back, but she couldn't see anything past them. With trying to prevent Finnegan from bolting again, and keeping her eye on the horses and cows, she was panicking.

"Jesus! Guys?" she yelled. "GUYS!"

Then Jake stood, his hair a mess, covered in dust, his chest heaving. As he wiped his mouth with the back of his hand, relief ran through her like a cold drink of water.

"Fuck," she breathed. "Thank fucking god."

Tanner reappeared then, too, blood trickling from his mouth. He strode over to Jake, and stopped, looking at what was obviously two downed cattle thieves. Tanner said something to Jake, and Jake grinned like a cat who'd caught the damned canary, then patted Tanner on the shoulder.

"Well, shit," Liz added as she whoa-ed Finnegan again, his agitation finally slowing now that he'd had a few moments to assess the situation. "Maybe there's hope for them after all."

CHAPTER TWENTY-FOUR

Brady was on his phone, and waved at Liz, who waved back and then urged her horse forward to keep the cows in line, Finnegan snorting and dancing but at least listening to her this time. She gathered up Sandy's reins, and the old mare put her nose on Finnegan and nickered. Finnegan relaxed immediately, and Liz slacked her reins, letting them stand close to the herd. She should have just done that to start with.

"You big dumb horse," she muttered, but patted him anyway. Truthfully, had she not been panicked, it would have been her first instinct. Grab the senior horse and couple up to calm the young one. She'd been too focused on Jake wading into certain harm to think straight.

Anger bubbled up to the surface, and she tried hard to let it go because it wouldn't solve anything. Her horse needed calm, and to be honest, they had to figure out how to get the damned herd back up the road and into that field.

The cattle were settling well with the rig off, curiously looking back at the horses, some of them attempting to graze on the dust-covered grass along the side.

Making his way back to his horse, Tanner glanced over each cow as he passed through the herd, holding a half-cocked smile. They'd gotten really fucking lucky, and her anger dissipated. She let out a breath, expelling some of her panic with it.

"You okay?" she asked when he'd gathered Chip's reins and moved toward her. He was still out of breath, licking at his once-again split lip, and he nodded, patting her on the leg.

"Yeah. You?"

"Finny wasn't easy," she answered lamely. "I wasn't much help."

Tanner looked straight at her and shook his head, patting her one more time before he took a big breath and stretched his neck. His brain was likely already going a mile a minute on how to deal with it all. They turned as Brady released a panel in the back, and about twenty cows clattered down the ramp back to their herd mates. Jake had Tanner's uncoiled rope and was dragging the unconscious men over to tie them to the back bumper of the trailer.

She'd have to ask Jake later how he knew how to wade in and fight like that. That was definitely not something someone learned in chef school. It was impressive, no matter how he'd learned, and now that she'd had a moment to calm down, she mused further that it was kind of attractive, the sheer strength and grit he'd displayed.

"It's all good, Lizzie. You're safe, and that's important."

"I should've ridden for help," she countered.

"I need you to help get these damned cattle back up the road," he shot back.

"I know, I just—" Liz felt the helplessness. She hated being helpless.

"They were burly assholes, all three of 'em. Jake took two of them on. I—" Tanner interrupted, then stopped talking, looking over at his brother, an oddly perplexed look crossing his face before he masked it.

"He's not useless, after all, you were going to say?" she teased. Tanner snorted out a chuckle at that.

"Maybe," he replied drily.

The knowledge that they were all okay, that there was perhaps a change in the war between the brothers, and that they'd found the cattle before they were gone all hit her at once. Tears welled up in her eyes again, and considering she was not a crier, she growled and looked away to hide them.

"Let's get these cows rounded up. I need to do a head count, and we gotta get some fencing from the ranch. Can your horse handle that?" Tanner called back to her, already throwing his leg up and over Chip.

"He'll manage," she replied. Movement beside her caught her eye, and Jake was vaulting back into the saddle as well, a smile on his face, his clothing dirty, his hat plopped back on his head carelessly, one side dented. Sandy shuffled closer to Finnegan, and Jake's knee touched hers as he leaned over to pull the stirrup fully onto his right foot.

She wordlessly handed his reins back to him, her insides unclenching as he settled into the saddle. He was making her think about things she shouldn't be in the middle of their situation. But mixed in with those dirty thoughts was also the sheer relief that he was okay, in one piece, and the urge to grab him and hold him close to her pushed more tears close to the surface.

Damn it, she was going soft because shit like this was not normal for her. She cleared her throat, looking at her hands, trying to think of something to say.

"Can't say I've ever done anything like that before," he said, raising an eyebrow, his voice light but careful. "I feel like a Western movie stunt double."

"Wading in like a damned fool, you mean? You could have gotten hurt or—" she chided, trying her best to hide the emotion still whirling inside her. She was interrupted as Jake leaned over, grasped the back of her head with one hand, pulled her toward him, and kissed her as if his life depended on it.

She let him because his bravado was too much to ignore in the moment, and grabbed at the horn of her saddle with one hand to keep him from yanking her out of the tack. His kiss was needy and possessive, and it curled her toes, heat flashing across her body.

The horses jostled and he let go of her, leaning back, obviously pleased with himself. She laughed as he puffed his chest out, brushing dust off his shoulders as he let out another heart-stopping smile.

Liz rolled her eyes at him but laughed. "Feeling good about yourself, cowboy?" she drawled. "We still gotta herd all these damned cows back up the road. Don't get too cocky on me yet."

With that, he pierced her with a smoldering look that stopped her laugh in her throat, replacing it with a shot of pure want. An irrational thought about pulling him off his horse and having her way with him up against a tree entered her head and she had to swallow it down, because it was ridiculous. They were in the middle of a herd of escaped cattle with three unconscious cattle thieves tied to the bumper of a semitruck.

"Jumped off a moving horse. Stopped some cattle thieves. Got a cattle prod to the back. I'd say I deserve a minute to revel in it."

"What do you want? Adoration? Praise? Hero worship?" she sassed back.

"You," he rumbled. "Because in this scenario, I get the girl."

Despite the insanity around them of bawling cattle, Tanner and Brady whistling, yipping and slapping their legs as they moved the cows into the safety of the fenced roadway, Liz's focus narrowed in on him. She met his intense stare, all thoughts of teasing gone from her head.

He held her eyes a moment more before grinning and kicking Sandy forward, and Liz let out a shaky breath. He did have her, damn it.

She let out another tense breath, stowed the thought, and moved Finnegan forward to catch up to Sandy so her horse would stay calm as sirens pierced the background.

* * *

Jake couldn't shake the adrenaline rush as they started back up the road, his hands trembling on the reins, his back aching from the cattle prod hit, his knuckles cracking from the abuse. It was a wonder he wasn't toppling out of the saddle.

"Stick back here, you've got the easy job," Brady said, grinning. "Sandy will show you what to do."

Jake doubted that but quickly let Sandy do just what Brady said she would to keep the cows moving with her laid-back ears, shaking her head if one of them stopped or turned around. All he had to do was keep himself upright, whistle, slap his legs, and point the horse in the same direction as the ponderous mass slowly ambling back up the road.

All the way back, Tanner took charge, grousing that they had to wait for the police to give them the all clear before they could herd their cattle. He kept looking at the sun, obviously worried they wouldn't get done before dark.

Tanner knew exactly where to be to keep the cows in line, shuttling his horse back and forth along the herd, pointing and barking orders. Brady and Liz wove in and out without needing to shout at one another, just hand signals and the odd "Yep!" Liz's horse reared a few times, and tried to run away once, and each time she handled it and then just kept pushing the cattle, a determined look on her face.

Jake was in awe of her, his eyes darting to her as he grew more comfortable riding behind the herd. He'd been the big damned idiot, wading into a herd of cows that could have kicked him in the head, toward men who might've had guns. She was the capable one, buckling down to work when not so long ago they were all in a stressful, dangerous situation. For that matter, all three of them seemed unfazed, apart from Tanner's mood, as they worked.

Jake still felt like a tagalong, even if he'd had a moment of fake bravado with Liz. He'd taken one look at her terrified face, the tears threatening to spill, and reacted to distract her.

The crew met them at the gap in the fence a lot quicker than he anticipated. Jake finally relaxed and let the tired in as they rolled the fence back over to repair it, offering to hold all the horses while everyone else finished up the job. Sandy stood still while he leaned on her, rooting at him with her nose then resting her muzzle on his neck and nibbling at the collar of his shirt. The other three horses dozed off, back legs cocked, tails swishing.

Tanner waved off help fixing the fence to the posts, grunting as he twisted wire to hold the new page wire that Bobby and Rowan were holding taut with a winch, his shoulders bunched as he strained to get it tight. He looked angry the entire time, but the crew moved around him like it was nothing new, accepting his clipped responses and orders with a smile, and a fatherly pat on his back from Harry when he straightened, the last twisted wire end hammered into the post.

At that, they mounted and followed the dust from the crew truck as it barreled back up the road, the horses tired, everyone slumped in the saddle. Tanner led the way, silently stewing. Jake didn't mind; he was too tired to carry a conversation with a rock, let alone his brothers or Liz. The sun was just dipping behind the mountains as the stables came into view, and the horses picked up the pace, as eager to be home as their riders.

Liz catapulted into Jake's arms once they dismounted in the stable yard. "Oh my god, that was insane," she murmured. "I am fucking done."

Jake circled his arms around her tightly, sensing she needed the contact, happy to oblige, and needing a moment to collect his thoughts before the circus of police descended for more statements. He buried his nose in her neck, grounding himself in the scent of her, the comfort of her in his arms. Even though they were all exhausted, dusty, and sweaty, she smelled good, and felt right, in his arms.

Brady lifted Sandy's reins out of Jake's hand and gathered up Finnegan's while whistling the theme to *Rocky*. Liz laughed, her face buried in Jake's chest.

"Thanks, Brady," Jake said.

"You get to untack 'em. I'll just put them into their stalls," Brady called as he walked away flanked by both horses.

Tanner stormed past next, silently glaring straight ahead as Chip jogged to keep up with him, nose pressing to Tanner's back, his ears trained on his rider.

"He's going to explode," Jake murmured. "Should we do something?"

"Nah. That's Tan. He looks madder than he is. He stews while he's sorting it all out in his head, makes him look like he's chewing rocks."

"It's more than that," Jake said. "He's got a reason to be mad, right now, and I don't blame him."

Jake's eyes followed his brother as he disappeared through the wide stable door, understanding his anger, wishing his brother wasn't so closed off. If things were different, he'd string up a punching bag in the cattle office and offer to teach him to box out his frustrations. It was certainly healthier than holding it all in.

A constable's car was already turning up the driveway as he reluctantly let Liz go, and he groaned. They wouldn't get to rest just yet.

"Let's get inside and take care of the horses, we've got that to deal with before we can collapse for the night," Liz prodded, pointing at the two officers getting out of their car, and he followed her into the stable.

* * *

"And then, he just turned and decked him! I saw it all from the side of the truck! I have no idea how that prod didn't take him to his knees."

Brady was gesturing wildly, his chair tipped back, his cheeks pink from the wine that Jake had pulled up from the cellar to celebrate their adventure. It was also doing a good job of relaxing everyone's nerves. Jake was leaning on the table beside Liz, her hand on his thigh warm and heavy. It felt good having her there beside him, celebrating their win, such as it was.

By the time they'd shuffled back into the house close to dark, Peony had a meal ready for them. She'd shooed them all off to have showers, and when Jake reappeared, Tanner had been sitting at the table, stopping Jake short. They'd looked at one another, and Jake had sat down across from him and passed him the bowl of salad silently. Tanner had taken it with a nod, and they'd all dug in.

Tanner's silence wasn't unusual, and Jake didn't go out of his way to engage him in conversation. Brady, with his natural flair, filled the room as he retold the story.

"I can't imagine the bruise you are going to have, Jake," Peony said. "You should get some arnica or muscle rub on that."

Jake *hmm*ed at that and ran a hand over Liz's. A massage, maybe mutual? The thought of her hands sliding over his skin was more than enough to make him adjust himself in his seat, and he cleared his throat while Peony side-eyed him, indicating she was onto him.

"Might be a good idea. I'm already sore from being in a saddle for so long. I'm not a seasoned rider like my brothers and Liz, here."

"You did fine."

Everyone turned as Tanner looked up at all of them, his fork stalled midway to his mouth. Jake caught his brother's eyes.

"Thanks," Jake replied, feeling the need for a bit of levity in the silence that followed. "Was quite an introduction, I think. Maybe next time I can try wrestling a cougar? Ride down a cliffside chasing wild buffalo?"

Everyone chuckled at that, and Jake jerked to his feet, restless from the compliment that Tanner had just given him. Liz leaned back and gave him a curious look, so he wiggled his eyebrows at her to convey it was fine. She rolled her eyes and swatted his arm, and turned back to ask Brady to pass the potatoes. Jake picked up a few empty dishes, and Tanner scraped back his own chair and grabbed his and Peony's plates. Jake headed to the kitchen, Tanner following him.

"So," Tanner said once they were alone, his back to Jake, his hands splayed on the counter. "I'll likely need you to pitch in tomorrow so I can get this shit sorted out. Harry can show you where we're short, but you won't need to do anything like—"

"This ranch is important to me too," Jake interrupted, wanting to get something out before Tanner tried to put him in his place again. At some point, his brother would get it through his stubborn head that Jake gave a shit. So if Tanner was open to sharing tonight, he'd give him both barrels.

"This was my dad's world. One I never got to see, never knew a thing about until a couple of weeks ago. But being here brings a whole new perspective. I have brothers. I have a family I never knew about. One that I intend to take care of, no matter what. *We* will sort this shit out tomorrow, Tanner. Not you. Us."

His brother was struggling with something, twisting his lips back and forth, maybe absorbing Jake's blunt statement, trying to find a response. Jake waited, hoping he would blurt it out, but when Tanner just sighed and looked away again, Jake bit back the frustration and realized that it would be a while before they were good. Even taking down cattle thieves together wouldn't erase the hurt that was grinding away at the man, because it wasn't Jake he was mad at. Jake was the proverbial messenger.

"Listen, enough for tonight. Let's regroup in the morning. We're all fucking exhausted," Jake said.

"Okay," and a raised eyebrow was the response from Tanner.

"Helluva thing we did . . . together," Jake added for good measure.

Tanner nodded, a tired hand running up over his head, through his hair. "Thanks for what you did today, Jake."

Jake blinked, because Tanner had just called him by his name. Not City Boy, not asshole, but his name. Another small victory, another crack in the wall Tanner had built between them the day Jake had arrived.

Tanner slowly pushed off the counter and headed to the back-door mud porch. He stopped and turned again, defeat in the droop of his shoulders. Jake again waited for him to blurt out whatever was circling in his head. He was using every ounce of patience he had to make sure he could keep the fragile peace dental flossed between them.

"I'll do night check with Bobby. Tell Liz not to worry. Think she'd rather spend time with you anyway, after today. She was pretty scared out there, though she won't admit it. Could likely use some reassuring, or somethin'," he finally mumbled, and then exited through the door quickly before Jake could answer.

"Okay, then," Jake replied to the now empty kitchen. That was the most that Tanner had said to him without shouting, and Jake absorbed the moment.

"Well, that was nice," Peony said, and Jake turned.

"Yeah, it was. Maybe we've figured something out," Jake replied. The front door slammed. "Did Liz leave?"

"She said something about night check, and Brady said he'd help her." Peony started moving dishes over to the dishwasher.

They spent a few moments cleaning up, Jake's shoulders aching, and he hissed as he stood back up from sliding the pans back into their slot in the low cabinet.

"I am going to hurt tomorrow. I'd like a quiet day, please," he said.

"It's been nothing but drama here since Brett died," Peony added, leaning against the counter. "Today takes the cake."

Jake just hummed an *uh-huh* under his breath. That might be an understatement.

"I'd like a day to just catch my breath too. There's been a lot of unease since Brett died. I trust things will settle eventually, but I never anticipated all this, and what it means for us," Peony added. Jake caught the tiredness, and maybe a bit of sadness in her tone.

"I won't let anything happen to you or Liz. Your home is here," Jake said quickly. Peony had as much right to stay here on the ranch as anyone, even if the will had left her out entirely.

Peony nodded her understanding, a brief moment of emotion showing before she smiled and took a big breath, shoving her shoulders back.

"It has been home for a long time. I wouldn't know where we'd go from here," she replied quietly. "But no sense in dwelling on that now. It's been a day, and we all need to wind down without stressful conversations."

"What would Brett do after a big day like this? I watched Tanner today after we got the cattle back into the field. He was so tight and silent, was our dad like that too?" Jake asked impulsively, his thoughts turning to his father, and how he would have let off steam, handled the situation had he been the one to ride up on it.

Would he have been proud of Jake for wading in? The thought snuck in that his father never got to see him ride a horse or learn to herd cattle. More things he might've known if his life had been different. It was a stupid place to go, but he was tired, and the darker side of his reason for being here invaded the moment he started thinking about it too much.

Peony stilled, studying him, her head tilted. He wondered if he'd asked the wrong question when she didn't answer right away.

"I want to show you something. Follow me," Peony said, pointing to the back of the house.

Jake followed her down the long hallway that led to the back den and laundry room, to a door he'd never noticed at the very end. Peony stopped, her hand on the doorknob.

"There's a key hidden above the door frame. I can't reach it." She pointed above her head, a rueful smile sliding across her face.

Jake ran his fingers along the molding and a key slid into his palm. He blew the dust off carefully and held it out to Peony.

"You open it, my dear, I think you should," she said.

He slid the key into the knob. "What is this room?" he asked gently, already suspecting it held his father's private business. "Was this Brett's study?"

"We called it The War Room. I've been inside once—the night Veronica died, when I checked in with him before I went home. Not even when we were married did I go in. It was his. He never explicitly said anything, but I just had this feeling he didn't want others in here, even me. He would disappear inside when he'd had a hard day or was struggling with something. That was his way. The last couple of years, those nights were more often."

"Do you want to go in now, or will this be hard?" Jake asked. "I can only imagine the emotions that come with going into a space that will remind you of him."

"I'm fine. It's time I went in and faced this last hurdle, and maybe there's something in there about his intentions with his will, but I doubt he kept anything like that in here, it all would've gone to the lawyer. Even if it's empty except for Brett's things, you should see it. Might help you answer that question you asked me in the kitchen."

Jake nodded and, with a breath, turned the key and opened the door.

The room was dark, with a window at one end, a desk facing the door. The air was stale, and Jake turned to look for a light switch along the wall, flicking it when found the hard plastic shell of the switch plate.

The smell of cigars and dust met his nostrils, and the lamps attached to the switch glowed yellow, splashing dull light over the '70s paneled walls and revealing a recliner, pictures hung on the walls, and a space heater in one corner. An antique crystal scotch set sat on a bar cart near the recliner, the tumblers dusty, cobwebs between them and the top of the stopper on the decanter.

They both stood just inside the door, and Jake let his eyes adjust to the semidarkness, taking it all in. It was sparse, the chair was threadbare, the drapes at least thirty years old, the carpet an odd color of yellow. The TV across from the recliner was ancient, with one of those remotes with a cord snaking all the way back to the arm of the chair. A VCR with several tapes stacked on top blinked 12:00.

What caught his eye finally was the large wood desk, with not much on top but an old, thick telephone book, a set of bull's horns, a blotter, and a chipped mug bristling with pens off to one side.

Then he saw the chair. It was tall backed with a crocheted throw across it, a riot of pink colors in a spiral pattern.

Jake walked toward it, not believing his eyes. He ran his hand over the throw, the lumpy stitches bumping under his fingertips. He let out the breath he had unconsciously been holding.

"Holy shit," he murmured.

His mother, when he was younger, before addiction took full hold, had crocheted like a madwoman. He would often sit with her on the front steps of wherever they were living at the moment and listen to her counting rows and stitches out loud as he lay back and watched the clouds go by. They would drink lemonade in the summer, Ovaltine when it got colder. She would give the blankets to neighbors in exchange for having them watch him when she had to work or needed food. In Washington Heights, those blankets meant you stayed warm when the heat cut out. All the neighbors had them, in whatever color yarn she could scrounge up on her meager paycheck.

Those were good days, and he swallowed the emotion that rose up the moment he saw that it was the exact same pattern.

The only one she knew how to do.

"My mom made this. I'm sure of it," Jake said, removing his hand from it.

"Made what?" Peony asked as she picked up an old newspaper folded into the storage pocket on the arm of the recliner and set it down on the seat, stepping over to Jake and eyeing him critically, probably because he was staring at a blanket like an idiot.

"This blanket," he said.

"Veronica brought a number of those over to me the day we moved into the bunkhouse. I didn't know they were Heather's. Makes sense that she wouldn't want them in the house. I've never seen this one before."

"I'm just going to leave that there," he muttered. That was a memory best left for right now. He wasn't sure of how much more he could manage tonight.

Jake pushed the chair back and turned to look at the desk. The blotter was dented and stained with coffee rings and random math calculations written in fading ink. But then he saw an address and phone numbers, and he peered closer, running his finger over the indentations that the lettering had made in the green paper.

"That was my address when I was still living with Ashley."

"Your ex-wife," Peony said. "Interesting."

He looked over the blotter, seeing other addresses, names of restaurants he'd owned, including the one he'd just sold—Amüs—in Greenpoint.

It was obviously the leavings of a man searching for his son, writing down the information on whatever he had on hand. Emotion rose in him again, and he lowered himself into the chair, the leather soft, the springs squeaking slightly as he did.

His dad had sat here. Jake tried to picture him staring out the window to one side, leaning forward with his elbows on the desk, scowling like a ranch man would. He couldn't, so he examined the desk in front of him, trying the drawers on the desk while Peony eyeballed the bookshelf.

The first drawer had a ball of elastic bands, a stapler, a crumbly old eraser, and an Altoids tin. The rest had random slips of paper, business cards, and pens, but no files or anything that looked official.

"Nothing in his desk. Maybe his bookshelf?"

"I don't see anything," Peony replied. "Perhaps he kept it in his files out in the cattle barn office?"

"I haven't found anything yet but ranch stuff. I'll keep looking, though."

Peony moved into the middle of the room, her fingers pressed to her mouth, her eyes misted over. Jake stepped to her, his arm automatically circling her shoulders.

"Hey, it's obvious there's nothing here, and you don't have to take care of this room until you're ready, yeah?"

Peony leaned into him. "This room still smells like him. I never thought I'd feel him with me when—"

She sniffled, and Jake held her tightly, a lump in his own throat. This was the closest he'd been to "seeing" his father since driving the Lincoln with Liz into the medical clinic. There were hints elsewhere, of course, but this was his dad at his most personal, not Brett West the cattleman everyone else had known. The space was inherently male, the indent in the recliner seat made by one person, the fingerprints on the scotch decanter and glasses left by a man Jake could only know by the memories of those who loved him, the spiky handwriting on the blotter a match to all the records in the barn office.

The scent in here, stale and dissipating now that they had opened the door, was the most visceral connection of all, but it had less meaning for him than it did for Peony.

He didn't want to be in the room anymore. He felt like he was intruding.

"Let's go," he said gently. "It's late and we're both drained."

She nodded and he ushered her out, turning off the lights then taking one more look at the space before locking the door and depositing the key back on the door frame.

"If you want, I can help clear it out once I have the books all organized," he added as Peony stood nearby, her eyes trained on the door.

"You're a sweet, sweet man, Jake. I'll think about it. Now off you go and spend some time with my daughter. I think she needs you after today's scare."

"Good night, Peony," he said.

"Thank you for defending our family today, Jake," Peony said softly before he could turn away. "I think Brett would've been very proud of all his boys today."

Jake swallowed and looked away from her. That was something he'd always wanted. A father to be proud of him. To tell him he was good enough.

With a final squeeze of her shoulder, he strode down the hall and away from the memories.

CHAPTER TWENTY-FIVE

Liz let him in, and he pushed the door closed, leaning on it a moment, eyes closed as she turned back to her living room.

"Glasses are in the top cupboard on the right of the sink if you want some of that now," she called as she sat down and turned off the TV.

He'd brought the remainder of the wine. He needed a drink, and he needed Liz in his arms so he could let go of the lingering emotion from being in his father's study.

He looked in Liz's kitchen for wine glasses, but the only thing he found were mason jars stacked haphazardly on the shelf she said they were on. He poured a measure into two of them and handed her one as he joined her.

"You don't have wine glasses."

"Never needed 'em," she replied, shrugging. "Mason jars are better. If you drop one, it's twenty-five cents to replace it."

"Makes sense," he replied, taking a big gulp of his wine. He expected it to taste different being in a jar, the nose funneling differently in the straight sides. Thankfully, he found no difference, and he drained his glass then set it on the coffee table.

She lived so simply, and he compared it to the list of expensive stemware and dishes he had tucked away in the boxes in the garage.

Such a difference in their perceived needs brought him up short, and he sat, thinking about that, staring at the jar.

"You okay? You want to just head back and sleep?" she asked, side-eying him.

"You're so different from anyone I have ever been with, you know that?" he said impulsively.

She wrinkled her nose, blinking at him.

"Not a bad thing, I just realized that I have glasses that are worth hundreds of dollars apiece, and here you are, happy with twenty-five cent mason jars. Just—"

"I'm pretty simple in my tastes, yeah. Don't need much to live. My world is pretty small, compared to yours, Jake. I'm sorry if that—" She bristled.

Jake reached out and pulled her hand to him, holding it firmly as she looked back at him suspiciously. *Damn it.* He didn't want to step in it now that they had achieved a better communication rhythm.

"No, no. Not what I meant. At all. I just, I think the past couple of weeks have given me some perspective on what is important. It isn't fancy wine glasses or expensive dishes. Today especially gave me a big jolt of reality."

"It certainly did, for all of us," she said and set her own wine down, then folded herself into him. He let out a breath as they relaxed into one another, and shook off the heavy from this evening. He'd tell her about Brett's office later; right now he wanted to forget it all and just drift on the comfort invading his bones. She played with the collar of his shirt and nestled farther into the crook of his shoulder.

Her soothing warmth felt right, like this, tucked in beside him. Like they were meant to be side by side. He ran a hand over her hair, smoothing it back behind her, and then impulsively kissed her forehead.

"What was that for?" she asked.

He looked down at her, her eyes questioning what was obviously too intimate a gesture for her. He caught the uncertainty.

"Just, this is nice, Liz," he rumbled. "Comforting."

"Mm-hm. Comfort. I can think of something comforting as well," she hummed, deflecting the intimacy, the suggestion in her voice unmistakable.

"You have energy for that?" He quirked an eyebrow at her as she slid over, straddling him on the couch and running her hands through his hair as he leaned back, letting her play.

Her fingers scraping his scalp immediately erased the noise from his mind, replacing it with the need to have her touch him elsewhere; comfort replaced by arousal. He liked the way her strong hands slid over him, her intention firm in the pressure she used. He'd always preferred intentional touch to featherlight caresses; it was a massive turn-on.

"You bet," she replied.

"Tell me what you want, then," he murmured, hands sliding down her back and coming to rest on her hips. He wanted her to suggest it tonight, to see where she would take them, find out where she was willing to go. Her eyes widened and she took a sharp breath in, very slowly grinding over him.

She leaned over, nose to nose with him, her hair a curtain around them. "I want to f—"

He didn't let her finish the thought and kissed her, his blood up the moment she had pressed into him, rotating her hips. He kissed her hard to show her he wanted her, too, but let her lead where that kiss went. Which she did, teasing him with her tongue, biting his lower lip with quick, soft nips.

"Here. Now," she gasped, her shirt flying, leaning back to let him yank his off over his head as well. The cold air pebbled his skin, and she ran her palms up his chest, over his shoulders, then down his arms, lifting his hands to her breasts, leaving warmth in the wake. He obliged her by palming her chest, the heat from her through the material of her sports bra more than he could handle.

"Off. I want it off," he growled, and she carefully unzipped it then tossed it backward.

He looked back into her eyes, his fingers lazily drawing circles around her breasts as a pink flush bloomed across her cheeks.

"You like that?" he asked, and pinched one nipple then the other, the tiny buds stiffening. *God, yes, that was perfect.*

She nodded, her hands coming to join his, her hips rolling against him as her fingers covered his. As he pinched again, she arched her back, letting out a raspy moan.

He loved how responsive she was to a simple touch. It made it hard to hold back, but he did, enjoying the anticipation sparking up and down his body.

"What next?" he asked, and her hands trailed down his chest, over his stomach, and hooked into his jeans. She was looking down between them, biting her lip.

Well, that was obvious.

She undid the snap, and he lifted his hips as she slid off him, taking his jeans and boxer briefs with her to the floor. She let out a sound of appreciation as his cock immediately hardened in front of her.

That was erotic as fuck. She was kneeling between his legs, eyes traveling up his body. He wanted her mouth around him, the perfection of her tongue sliding up his shaft would make everything better, but he held back. It had to be her idea.

"You look so fucking hot down there on your knees," he blurted anyway.

She slid her hands over his thighs, and licked her lips with a sensual slowness that made him groan in frustration. She flicked her eyes up to him.

"Do you want me to?" she asked, inferring exactly what he wanted, flicking her glance down, then back to him.

"Whatever you want to do to me, I want it," he replied.

She gently slid her palm and closed her fingers around him, and his cock twitched at her touch.

"This?" she asked.

"Yes," he breathed, unable to look away as she leaned forward, feathering a breath over him, eyes swiveling up, meeting his.

Compared to the night before, this Liz was obliterating his ability to think straight as she teased him. She had to know she was driving him wild.

"Say it," she murmured.

Jake was not one to talk dirty to a woman; he often found it sounded more crass than he intended, and he worried about being disrespectful when he was with someone new, before they were truly comfortable with one another. Ashley hadn't liked it at all.

But right now, as Liz stroked his cock agonizingly slowly and pressed kisses against his thigh, he couldn't help himself.

"I want to fuck your mouth," he gasped, his cheeks flaring with heat as he said it.

She dove in and licked his cock from the base to the tip, then slid her lips over in one quick motion, taking all of him, sucking in to hold him tightly in her mouth.

"Fuck!" he gasped, and bucked up into her, the sensation of her surrounding him like this more than he could have imagined. Her hair tumbled around her, and he gathered it up with one hand, holding it up so he could see her lips as she slid up, then back down, the wet from her mouth coating him.

He bucked up into her again, and she moaned, her tongue pressing against his cock, swirling. He didn't want to hurt her, but when she didn't protest, he slowly rocked in and out of her mouth. Each thrust in flared heat through him, the sensation rolling up his back in a wave of pleasure.

"Fuck, yes. Your mouth is so hot, it feels incredible," he managed, and she increased the pressure, a hand snaking under his balls to hold them. Hot, wet sucking noises combined with their gasping pants as she lifted and sucked on just the head, then licked it before diving back down. The sound alone was going to kill him, never mind the heat from her tongue sliding across.

"Touch yourself," he growled. Her free hand disappeared down, and she moaned, pressing forward into his spread legs. *Hot, so fucking hot.*

His balls tightened, and he held still, knowing full well the next thrust would have him shooting his load down her throat. He didn't want to come yet, because if he did it might knock him senseless, and that would be it for the night. He wanted to be inside her, to feel her come around him, to hold her in his arms while she screamed his name.

"I'm going to come if you don't stop."

She eased off his cock, her hands replacing mouth the moment her lips left him, sliding wetness up and down his length. She looked up at him, a small smile on her face.

"Really? That good, huh?" she said, and he caressed her cheek with his fingers, nodding, gentle pressure on her chin to bring her to him.

"Fuck, yes, that is incredible. Now take your pants off."

She shimmied out of her jeans the moment she stood. She was naked, standing in front of him, and all he could think about was touching her.

"Come here," he demanded as he stood and pulled her to him, kissing her, his hands trailing down her body, hungry to feel her against him. She was perfect in his hands, soft and curvy. What they were doing felt too damned good after the long day, and he lost himself exploring her body, kissing her shoulder, her neck, back up to her lips, the tension he'd built slowly easing, giving him more time to just enjoy her without having to hold back his own orgasm.

Her hand hit his cattle prod bruise as she did the same, and he flinched, pulling him from the moment. That hurt. He was lucky it hadn't hit his kidneys.

"Oh! Sorry!" she exclaimed and removed her hand. "That still hurts?"

He didn't want this moment to be over, but nodded, and she made a comforting sound.

"It's okay. Just sore. I'll survive," he murmured as he pushed her hair over her other shoulder and kissed her neck again.

"I'll kiss it better later," she said.

"I want to fuck you right here on this couch, that will make it better," he rasped. Her hands currently roaming over his ass was quickly bringing him back to the brink again.

She pushed him and he backed up, pretending to fall as he sat, his legs splayed. She followed, climbing back on top of him, her hand flying down between them. She curled her hand around his cock again, closing her fingers and sliding up and down.

"Let's not waste time, then," she murmured.

"Condom," he rasped. She reached over him to the side of the couch with her other hand, a flash of foil and a naughty look.

"Prepared, were we?" he said, and she *hmm*ed back at him as she opened the packet with her teeth.

He hissed as she touched the cold rubber to the tip, sliding the condom down, reveling in the constriction of it squeezing his dick, twitching as it made him so hard it was almost painful. She shifted, and as he opened his eyes, she was watching him with a mixture of arousal and curiosity as she lifted over top of him and slid him in all the way, all at once.

"This is what I wanted," she growled, her whiskey-fire voice wavering.

He held her eyes as she began to move, the flush on her cheeks now all the way down her neck, onto her chest. He put his hands back on her breasts, the feel of her tight around him, pulsing and hot. He held back from grabbing hold of her and taking over, because he was enjoying her like this, on top of him, taking charge, needy in the moment.

"Don't stop. I want you to come," he murmured, encouraging her. She bit her lip, and closed her eyes, moving faster.

"You feel so fucking good inside me," she gasped, her head tilted up, her hair dangling behind her. Her eyes fluttered closed as her mouth opened. He ran a hand over her neck, grasping it gently to feel the cords straining, swallowing against his palm.

"Look at me," he ordered, and her eyes flew open. He didn't want her to look away. It was intense, it was erotic, and he wanted to watch her shatter.

She was close, and he moved with her, opening her hips, sinking her farther onto him as they met thrust for thrust, his hand still on her neck. He circled her waist with his other arm, pulling her flush against him. He wanted her entire body on him when she came, and he couldn't help but let out a moan as she gripped his hair in her fingers, a small shiver erupting from her core that vibrated between them.

"Jake," she gasped and let out that wild, animal cry that drove him nuts, as her entire body shook, thrusting hard, her knees dipping into the couch with her effort. Her wide eyes were locked to his, and he knew he was going to leap over the edge with her, he couldn't hold it back if he tried.

"Fucking let go," he gasped as he lifted his hips one more time, emptying himself as he held her close. Her body shook as her orgasm ebbed and all the knots in his muscles melted to nothing as he, too, slid down the other side of his own.

She hadn't looked away and neither had he, and he steeled himself not to. He wanted to understand her, wanted to break down her barriers, wanted to prolong the connection with her, her pulse, her scent, her heat. His heartbeat thudded against his chest as they stayed locked into one another. She was out of breath, her chest rising and falling, and emotions swirled in her eyes before she finally, carefully, hid them.

He could lose himself to her so easily, especially after the intensity of what they had just shared. His hand came up and smoothed her hair back behind a pink-tipped ear, wanting to memorize this moment before it was gone.

"You are so beautiful when you come," he murmured, and with that, she closed her eyes and leaned forward, tucking her head. He circled his arms around her, kissing her shoulder as her arms went around him.

"You say the sweetest things," she muffled into his neck. "But I'm cold now. Bed."

They separated, and he lifted her up before she could walk away, carrying her down the hall to her bedroom, sliding her onto the bed and chucking the used condom at the wastebasket before climbing in beside her. He didn't want to go yet, even though the exhaustion in his bones was almost rendering him useless.

It had been a long, wild, impossible day. But being here, with her, was making it all seem like a dream. He pulled the covers up as she let out a sigh and stretched, fitting herself in beside him.

"Was that good?" he asked quietly, and she nodded into his chest, an almost catlike purr rumbling out of her.

"Totally a great way to end today," she replied. "Makes up for all the chaos."

"Today was nuts," he supplied. She tensed briefly, then relaxed again, running her hand up his chest, stopping over his heart.

"I was scared. I never—" she blurted, and he shifted so he could look at her.

He saw it again, the emotion she battled with, the vulnerability she was trying to hide. He didn't want to rock the boat, so he pulled her back down to lie against him, sliding down onto the pillow beside her. They had opened up to one another tonight, comfortable with each other's bodies. Maybe now she'd open up to him this way too.

"It's okay to be scared. I was terrified. I've faced muggers and drunk assholes in bars that were less dangerous than what I waded into today," he offered, looking up at the ceiling. It was true. He'd been held at gunpoint, knifepoint, all kinds of shit. But it had been a different kind of feeling when he'd launched himself off his horse today toward the men who were stealing the West Line cattle.

His family's cattle.

"I wondered—how in hell did you learn to punch like that?" she asked. "It was wild to watch. You dropped that first guy like he was a bag of feathers."

"I started boxing about ten years ago, maybe more, I can't remember when exactly," he replied. "I needed an outlet when shit got real."

"What does that even mean?" she asked, her body shaking with a suppressed giggle. "How does 'shit' get real in New York City?"

He caught that she would find it funny, taking the saying literally, and he smiled, enjoying the moment.

"We lived in some crappy places when I was younger, which meant I had to learn to throw a punch to stay on the good side of people. I didn't do that very well. Got my ass handed to me a lot."

"*Oof.* But you were likely a big kid. Tanner was. I imagine when you got bigger it stopped?"

"You'd think. But I was a scrawny kid with a short fuse, and I had a huge target on my back until I was a bit older. There were good people in all the places we lived, New York has some great communities, but some of them could be pretty rough," he said, wishing he could soften the image of the city. Truthfully, it *had* been rough. He had a brief thought as he lay there, that he would love to take her to New York and show her everything he loved about it, show her who he was away from here.

Which would send her screaming in the other direction. She'd been so tense in Calgary; he'd seen the distaste for the busy traffic and people everywhere.

He missed New York and his friends for a brief moment but let it go. He could wallow later.

"So boxing kept you safe," she said, her thumb moving over his skin. She was making it easy to talk about his past tonight, and he let out a big breath, trying to shake off the twist in his chest that remembering his childhood raised.

"I started when I was in my late teens, maybe nineteen? I had a lot of attitude I didn't know what to do with. I was a bouncer while I paid for school, and working both at a bar and as a prep cook meant I got used to shady shit happening at the back door every night no matter where I was. I picked up boxing at a local place to give myself an edge to handle what it threw at me. Byproduct was it made me less angry."

"Shady. Like drugs and stuff?" she asked, sitting up a bit. "Did you do that stuff?"

"No. My mom was, no, *is* an alcoholic and a drug addict. I've never touched any drugs. Saw what it did to people," he replied as lightly as possible, even though his chest was tight as he said it. He hadn't talked much about his mother to anyone here; it had felt disrespectful to Peony. It had only come up tonight in the study when he saw her blanket.

"Oh," Liz breathed, and settled back down. Her hand wrapped

over his neck, and she shifted to kiss him softly on the cheek, her fingers digging into the hair at his nape.

The gesture undid him, and he turned toward her, giving in to the moment to just feel. Intimacy was one thing she didn't want, but here they were, instinctively comforting each other as he threaded his arms around her.

He didn't want tonight to be heavy; he wanted to lose himself in her body and let today's stress go. But here she was filling a need for more. More connection. More healing. This was more than just sex with a willing woman, and he felt powerless to stop what he was feeling as they locked eyes in the semidarkness.

Liz gently slid her hand over his cheek, running her thumb over his cheekbone. The emotion was back in her eyes, and he swallowed the lump forming in his throat as he knew that she was seeing the same damned thing in his.

CHAPTER TWENTY-SIX

Liz stretched her back out and stood at the doorway to the stable, watching the constable's car leave a trail of dust down the driveway. Tanner and Jake both raised their hands in farewell, standing side by side in the middle of the barnyard.

It had been a morning of more police statements, driving out to the access road to look at the rig that was still parked there, and calling in someone with a Class 1 driver's license to drive it to the precinct impound once the officers were done processing the scene. The boys had gone and checked the fixed fence; the cattle were safely back in their pasture, none the worse for wear after their escapade. Brady was currently pacing in the office, pricing electric fencing and locks for all the gates on the ranch.

All in all, they were fucking lucky it had worked out how it did. Anxiety still crawled up Liz's back when she thought about how dangerous it could have been, and how it could've ended up if the thieves had been carrying the loaded shotguns the police had found in the cab of the truck.

She kept watching Jake and Tanner, who were now deep in conversation, likely talking about what had to be done today. Tanner in his work overalls, fidgeting with his hat, Jake in jeans and a tight T-shirt, arms crossed, nodding, his eyes hidden behind his Ray-Bans, looking too damned sexy for his own good.

He was so different from Tanner, but when she took them both in together, she saw the mark of their dad so clearly it was like Brett had used a damned stamp.

She bit her lip, focusing back on the man who had let her have her way with him on the couch last night, remembering how good it had felt to let herself go, the sheer physical need that she had let out. That was good sex. Best sex she'd ever had, if she thought about it honestly, both of them relieving the stress of the day, melting tense muscles. He'd opened up to her as well; his sexy talk had really kicked her up a notch.

Jake put a hand on his own back, gingerly stretching, and she muffled a laugh. They were both paying for it today.

He had dozed off after she'd put some of her muscle gel on his legs, shoulders, and lower back, carefully avoiding the spreading bloom of the bruise from the cattle prod. She woke up to him gone, the faint menthol scent on his side of the bed a reminder that he'd stayed long enough for her to fall asleep before he'd let himself out. She hadn't heard him go.

Part of her wanted his warm body beside her in the morning, not just a dented pillow. Last night they had talked about a lot of things. She'd learned about his mom and gotten a sense he hadn't had a great childhood. She didn't press. She knew what it was like to grow up with only a mom. Those wounds ran deep, and his mom hadn't been there for him like hers had been, so he'd had to grow up fast.

There was this current of something more after they'd had sex, too, and she didn't want to think about what that meant, so she turned away from him before her thoughts ran away with her. It meant she was feeling things she didn't want to feel, and that wasn't part of the plan.

The mail van was bouncing up the driveway as she turned, and she wondered why it was here instead of just stuffing parcels in the mailbox at the end of the road. Hopefully it meant they had some of her packages today. She'd been waiting a week for feed supplements, and those wouldn't fit in the parcel cubby.

She reached the van as it stopped, and Herb smiled out at her from the window.

"Hello, Liz!" he exclaimed and leaned on the door. "Heard the news about the dustup here yesterday. Everyone okay?"

Ah. He was coming out to be nosy, and Tessa, the gossipy clerk, didn't drive the van. The two of them were a pair. Liz smiled as sweetly as possible, mentally gritting her teeth.

"We're all fine, Herb, thanks for asking! You got packages for us today?" she replied, hoping to keep the conversation on the mail, not cattle thieves. She'd already rehashed yesterday over and over for the police when she gave her statement.

"Tessa said it was a thing, the boys catching them in mid-load! Must've been quite a dustup," he added, opening the door and stepping out. Herb prattled on as Liz stayed silent, and opened the back and pulled out a few boxes.

"Some for you, and one for your new brother, I think," he added, handing them over to her.

Jake was definitely not her brother, but she held her tongue, not correcting him. The less she reacted to Herb, the less the rumor mill would spin when he reported back to Tessa. She set the two big boxes down and looked at the thinner rectangular one. It was marked with an official AHS emblem, and she hefted it. It wasn't heavy. New health benefit certificates for the ranch crew, most likely.

Herb was casting a curious eye over it, and she quickly stuffed it under one arm as he set up the machine for her to scrawl on with her finger. It never looked like her signature, but it was good enough.

"They never look right, don't worry about it." Herb chuckled when she finished. He tucked the machine back in the van, his grin widening as Tanner joined them.

"Tanner! Glad to see you none the worse for yesterday's excitement. Quite the thing!" Herb exclaimed again, and Tanner grimaced and caught Liz's eye with a distinct look of suffering. She wordlessly handed him the box and picked up her supplements.

"Well, Herb, I'm glad to see you, but duty calls. I'll pop in next week." She breathed out quickly and strode away, a resigned sigh from Tanner echoing in her ears as she left.

The cool of the stable enveloped her as she deposited the boxes in the feed room, opening them quickly and stowing the bottles on the shelf above the table. The morning was busy around her, the young boys trundling past, the wheels of their wheelbarrows scraping against the concrete of the aisleway. She took in a deep breath, letting the scent of grain invade her mind and settle it. There was work to be done, and she needed to set the tension aside and keep moving. Trevor poked his head in just as she lowered her shoulders.

"Next ride's ready if you have time. I'll take that gray for you today, if you'd rather?"

"Sounds good. I can get on that bay Julie just bought from the Nichols. They've asked me to ride him in a bit before the next competition."

"Ten-four," Trevor replied happily and whistled as he walked away from the feed room and up the aisle.

They had three youngsters to work and seven boarder horses to exercise, their own horses already ridden early this morning while it was cool, the four that had gone out yesterday already turned out for the day, making the ride list light.

With another breath, she thought about crawling into one of the bins in the room, burrowing under the sweet-smelling feed, and turning off the world for a while. She cracked her neck and headed for the tack room to suit up, her back twinging.

Keeping busy would work the knots in her muscles and keep her mind occupied.

* * *

"Mom?"

"In here, dear."

Liz poked her head into the kitchen to see her mom happily humming to some music playing out of Jake's speaker and Jake setting sandwiches and what looked to be spinach salads studded with strawberries into the lidded tray that bolted to the ATV.

"I can take the lunch to the crew if you want, they're out checking the high pasture," she offered.

"You stay here, my dear, and have lunch with me. Jake is just getting it ready for Harry to drive out to them. He says he has to get into the office, right, Jake?"

"Your mom is saying she wants to talk to you, I think," he stage-whispered as he passed by her, muscling the tray up by the handles. He winked at her, and her body betrayed her by flushing with heat when his arm brushed hers.

"Okay, then. I'll come by later, distract you?" she asked, hopeful. Anything to get her hands back on that big sexy body of his.

"Please do," he replied, let out a heart-stopping smile and disappeared through the door.

Liz turned back to find her mother giving her that look she had when she was waiting for Liz to spill the story. Liz ignored it, willed herself to stop blushing, and instead headed to the cupboard to grab a mug for coffee.

"That's quite a grin on your face, young lady. I have to say, Jake is doing wonders for your demeanor," her mother remarked, and poured from the carafe as Liz held out her mug.

"What grin?" Liz replied after she'd plopped some milk into the mug, sipping and studiously avoiding her mother's gaze. "I'm just relieved everything is back to normal after yesterday, and we're all safe."

"Bullshit, young lady. You have the look of a well and truly laid woman," her mother said, and Liz choked on her coffee, spraying it everywhere.

"MOM!" she sputtered. "What in the hell?"

Her mother was laughing, and Liz glared at her, gripping her mug tightly as she wiped at her mouth. What had gotten into her? Her mother wasn't a prude, but that was a little bit of a . . . a what Liz didn't know, but her mother had never talked to her that way before.

"Come sit with me in the back den, we can chat," her mom offered. They grabbed two wrapped sandwiches from the fridge and made their way to the back of the house. The den was a safe space for Liz, comfortable and less decorated than the rest of the house. Liz preferred it here, the lumpy leather sofa and mismatched throw pillows, the piled-up DVDs on the side shelves, and the myriad of framed winner photos a reminder that this was home just as much as the bunkhouse.

The sun was streaming in through the window, and Liz lifted her face to it for a moment, breathing in. Despite her mother's odd mood, she felt good after the morning of riding. Her back was loose, all her tight muscles gently complaining but not stiff. An improvement on the start of the day, for sure.

Her mother sat down and leveled a look at her that made her sit up. *Uh-oh.*

She'd come in to steal a bit of lunch before it got sent out so she wouldn't have to eat with the crew today, just maybe deliver it and leave before she would have to rehash the story once again. Now she wasn't so sure she should have. She was about to get the third degree from her mother. *Wonderful.*

"I want to ask you, Liz, and I'll be blunt. Are you sure you know what you're doing with him?" her mother said the moment Liz met her look. Liz glanced at her sandwich, the cling wrap rustling as she fiddled with it.

"Yeah, I think so," she replied, not knowing how to answer.

"Wanting a man and caring for a man are two different things, Elizabeth," her mother said, reading her mind. "I understand the want part. I look at him and I see Brett in his prime. Lord that man was hotter than the sun and burned just as bright wherever he went. But caring for him was a whole other kettle of fish. That care burned me to a crisp in the beginning."

Liz hummed and bit into her sandwich. "But you married him."

"I wanted to be burned, because I thought the two things were one and the same," Peony replied, a tone in her voice that Liz wasn't sure what to make of. Was this her mother talking about desire? Attraction? She'd already said that marrying Brett was for convenience, companionship . . . it didn't make sense.

"I don't get it. I knew you were doing something with him, I wasn't a stupid kid, but then all of a sudden, you were engaged. No one even knew you were together, and BAM! You couldn't have been that burned if—"

"And what are your plans with Jake?" her mother interrupted with an irritated sigh, changing the subject. "Because, honey, I see you. You care about him, and I am dreading what it will do to you if he leaves. You might think—"

"If? What do you mean by that?" Liz asked. There was no *if*.

"You never know what could happen," her mother said.

"I don't think there is a forever. This is a just-right-now!" Liz blurted back. "We're filling a need for each other, period. When he goes back to New York? I'll be fine because we're not, you know, together."

Her mother shook her head and sighed. "You will not be fine, Elizabeth Jaqueline Baker. I know you don't see it that way. I watched you two last night and just now. That man is mad about you, and you are mad about him, even though you're fighting it with every ounce of stupid in your body. If he sews it up here and jets back to New York, it will hurt, for both of you. I guarantee it."

Liz glared at her mom. Pink in Peony's cheeks and a sparkle in her eye that hadn't been there in a long time appeared, even though her mother's frown was an indication she was talking about serious things. Liz looked back down at her sandwich, the lone bite now a lump in her stomach. Her mother might be a little bit right, but Liz wasn't ready to admit that to her, or to herself, for that matter.

"Why would I complicate things now? We've set the ground rules. We were both pretty clear on those," Liz grumped. She sounded petulant, and frustrated.

Her mother *tsk*ed and waved a hand. "Fiddlesticks. There are no rules when it comes to love."

"Why are you meddling?" Liz asked. It was one thing to ask Liz what she was doing, but another to mess with her head when she'd already explained it wasn't going anywhere and using *that* word.

"I'm not meddling, dear," her mom said as she got up and moved to sit beside her, patting her on the arm. "I want you to be happy, and to be honest, if you give that man out there a reason to stay, then that will be icing on the damned cake. I like him. I think he fits and he's good for you. If you let him lo—"

"He's got a life all the way across the fucking country, and . . . and . . ." Liz interrupted, not wanting her mother to utter that damned *L* word again. That word meant something she didn't even want to contemplate.

Liz jumped to her feet. She didn't want to talk about this right now, and she definitely could not talk about it with her mother. Her hackles were up, and she didn't want to yell at Peony or get mad, because she knew her mother was just being her mother but—

"I have to get back to work. Thanks for the chat," she snapped icily, and left the room before she said anything else she might regret.

She banged out the back door, took an angry bite from her sandwich, and chewed, stewing. Her temper was razor-thin, and the confusion that had shoved in with what her mother said had cracked that firmly held control she had exerted over her arrangement with Jake.

Damn it, why did her mother have to say it like that? That stupid *L* word flashed in her brain, and she growled. She rubbed at her eyes, more tired now than angry, and realized that she was indeed on her way to being burned, if what her mother said was getting to her as much as it did, so quickly. Could she be going down that path again?

No. She couldn't even contemplate it. It was not a good idea, and her stomach flipped and her chest tightened at the thought.

"Fuck—" she muttered and walked back to the stable. "Goddamn it, Mother, fu—"

She stopped in the path, the swearing not even helping her loosen the ball of unease, and leaned over, willing her stomach to settle. She had to figure this shit out. The mere mention of something more serious was tying her in knots. Obviously that meant she wasn't ready by a country mile.

But last night there had been something else, and maybe that was why she was so wound up about it. If they were just casually banging, she wouldn't have reacted the way she did. Right?

Fuck. Black and white was quickly blurring into a whole lot of gray.

CHAPTER TWENTY-SEVEN

The still-warped filing cabinet drawer closed with a screech, and Jake dusted his hands, heaving a sigh of relief. He adjusted the ancient feed-store magnet straight, and quirked a smile at the ridiculousness of keeping a calendar from the 1970s. Even if it was useless, he couldn't throw it away.

A magnet was one thing, the filing cabinet was another. Once this mess was settled, he was going to buy a new one for his brothers as a parting gift. The rust, barely openable drawers, and flaking paint had to go.

He'd make sure the magnet transferred over, though.

It had taken him most of the afternoon, but all the files were sorted and entered, and he officially had a working set of books. The older stuff he'd just refiled. When—or if—he had time, he'd enter more.

He'd looked up Canada Revenue Agency rules, unfamiliar with how to submit taxes in this country when he realized he didn't even have a clue about how to set them up either. The rules he'd skimmed said seven years of records were required if a business was audited. That was a lot of shuffling through papers and tearing his hair out, so he banked on three to save him some time down the road if it ever happened.

His laptop was humming away, the accounting software importing all of the spreadsheets he'd hammered out, and the ranch was about twenty minutes away from a set of financial statements ready for the accountant.

"Box for you," Tanner said as he strode into the office, interrupting Jake's thoughts as he stared at the progress bar on his laptop. "Came this morning in the mail delivery."

Jake caught the thin parcel box that Tanner tossed to him, and peered at the label.

"It's the paternity test thing," Tanner added as he sat down in his chair at his desk.

Cheek swab results were back. The tests were a formality, and he wasn't keen on opening it up, especially with all they had to deal with today, but he figured he might as well; no sense in delaying it.

Jake wondered why Frank had mailed them instead of calling him. *Huh.*

He'd talked to Frank this morning, catching him up on where they were, poking him for progress on their much-needed loophole to get out from under Brett's will.

Frank was still elbow-deep in inheritance law and was no further ahead. However, Jake wasn't suffering due to the delay, his thoughts turning to Liz as he drummed his fingers on the box. He wasn't where he should be, even if right now he was where he wanted to be. New York was home. Restaurants and new ventures were where his head should be.

Instead, he was thinking about whether Liz would want to go into town for dinner tonight, if the reports that were generating on his laptop would be enough to give him a picture of the ranch financials and maybe help prove the viability of Brady's peanut idea.

It felt strange not to be hustling like mad, always thinking and moving and working on the next big thing. The pace out here was changing the hurry inside him, the quiet at night urging him to let go of the ever-expanding to-do list in his head and just listen.

"Let's have a look, shall we?" Jake pulled the tab to open the box, and a fat envelope fell onto the desk. He lifted the flap and unfolded the papers. Four pages, one with a summary of the tests done, and a bill that showed PAID IN FULL. *Odd.* He'd assumed there would be more to it, like a manual on how to read the damned results or something.

Instead, there was just a page for each test subject, with a bunch of letters and numbers dotted in a column down each one. He shuffled them and squinted. He had no idea what he was looking at.

"Let me see. These can't be much different than cattle genome indexing," Tanner said gruffly, and Jake handed them over to him wordlessly. Tanner shuffled them as well, squinting much like Jake had, but then stopped when he got to the third page.

"What is it?" Jake asked. He knew Tanner well enough to know that the wrinkles on his forehead and his mouth forming that thin, angry frown said he was about to get mad.

Much like his own face, really.

"I think we need to find Brady. Now."

"Okay," Jake said, his brother's tone indicating it was something serious. He looked at the paper that Tanner was holding as he texted Brady. Tanner pointed to the line at the bottom, which had two results. Only one mattered.

Probability of paternity: 0%.

A chill stole over Jake and he looked up at Tanner, who was trying his best, surprisingly, not to explode. He handed the papers to Jake and slouched in his seat.

Jake scanned the rest of the paper and then looked at the top of the sheet.

It was Brady's name at the top.

"Fuck." This was serious. He glanced at Tanner, who was now worriedly rubbing at his forehead, eyes closed.

"How do I tell him this? What do I say?" Tanner muttered.

Jake didn't know what to say, either, right now or to Brady. Brady, who was as much a part of this place as Tanner, who had poured himself into it to please his father.

Who wasn't actually his father.

Jake set the papers down on his father's desk and blew out a big breath, closing his own eyes for a moment, counting to ten. A wastepaper basket flew across the room, crashing into the wall opposite them. Jake followed the trail of empty potato chip bags and crumpled paper across the floor then back to his brother, where Tanner had his face buried in his hands.

"This can't get much worse." His voice was muffled. "I—"

Jake needed to handle this situation for Tanner, who had just been dealt yet another blow in the never-ending drama that seemed to be unfolding around them. He sent a quick text to Liz to come over to the cattle barn as soon as possible.

If you were going to rip off an adhesive bandage, it was better to do it quickly. Liz being here would help, because he had no idea how Brady was going to take the news, and she could run interference. Brady was always the happy one, the one who made everyone calm down, made jokes, kept the peace. But this? This changed things.

Brady stuck his head around the corner a minute later, then picked up the very dented basket, looking at it curiously before setting it down under his own desk. He didn't remark on it, which meant that it was likely not the first time Tanner had abused it.

"Liz is on her way. She was on a horse when you texted. What's up?"

Tanner hadn't moved since he had sent the basket into orbit, but he looked up now. Pain and anger radiated out of him, and Brady immediately went over to his brother and put a hand on his shoulder.

"What's happened?" he asked gently, looking over at Jake. "What do you need?"

"I don't know how else to do this, so here."

Jake handed him the papers. Brady side-eyed him curiously, but took them and scanned them. He looked each one over, then stopped when he got to his.

"Well, shit," he said, and sat on the edge of Tanner's desk, his hand on his mouth, blinking rapidly.

"You're still a West," Tanner growled quietly, steel cutting through the emotion in his voice. "That doesn't change."

Brady nodded, eyes scanning the rows of numbers, and Jake put his hands in his pockets, waiting it out. This was not something he could comment on, nor would he want to intrude until they'd said what they needed to say to one another, if that was going to happen now. These two men had been brothers since birth, were still brothers by their mother, of course, but there was a deeper bond that no one could break that had formed during a lifetime together.

A bond Jake could never fully understand.

He watched Brady process, and then Brady sighed, put the papers down, and leveled Tanner with a look.

"Hoo, boy. More than ever, I wish Mom was here to explain this one," he said.

"You think?" Tanner muttered, raising an eyebrow.

Silence followed. The two men looked at one another, not saying a thing, but you could tell there was a conversation happening. Jake cleared his throat, and Brady snapped out of whatever he was thinking and looked between Jake and Tanner, sighing heavily.

"I don't know what to say to this, you know?"

"Nothing. There is nothing to say. You are *still* a West," Tanner cut in, and stood. His temper had finally won, and he was mad. He flexed his hands, glared at the papers, then grabbed his hat and shoved it onto his head.

"Got shit to do," he muttered, and strode out of the room.

Brady watched him go and let out another deep sigh. He slouched, leaning against the desk and leveled Jake a tired look.

"So I guess this explains why I'm not a tall, dark-haired tornado like you two," he said, a smile flicking across his face before it fell, his eyes darting out the window. Jake followed his gaze, watching Tanner angrily jump onto a tractor with a hay-bale spike on the front and ram it into gear, heading toward the hay shed, dirt from the big knobbly tires churning up behind him.

"You okay?" Jake asked.

"I will be, yeah. Truth? I always wondered," Brady replied, and stepped around the corner to his brother's recently evacuated chair, sinking into it.

Liz walked in just as he did and looked between them. She put her hands on her hips.

"Who pissed off Tanner this time? He's currently spiking round bales and moving them from one side of the storage shed to the other for no apparent reason. He only does that when he's really mad," she said, humor in her voice. The smile on her face vanished the moment her eyes met Jake's.

Jake shook his head at her and handed her the papers. "This."

She raised her eyebrow at him, looked down at the page, and gasped, her eyes then flying to Brady.

"Brady. Is this—"

"Yep. Brett isn't my dad. Got any theories on who it might be?" Brady interrupted, raising his eyebrows at her and sticking his tongue out over his bottom lip.

"You're taking this awfully well," Liz shot back, and tilted her head. "You knew, didn't you."

"No, not one hundred percent. But I've suspected for years. I mean, look at me!" he said, and gestured at himself. "I'm not a slightly less weathered copy of my dad, like these two meatheads. Me? I'm the weird one."

"You aren't weird," Liz muttered, and set the papers down, coming over to Brady and leaning over him from behind, circling her arms around him. "You're my adopted baby West brother, no matter what some stupid piece of paper says. You're also still the smart one."

At that, he chuckled and patted her joined hands. "Yup. I'll agree to that."

Jake, thankful for Liz right then, nodded at that statement and picked up the test results. He opened the bottom drawer of the file cabinet and dropped them into the file marked *Inheritance Mess*. He'd deal with what this meant later.

He was wondering how much more his brothers could take. This was yet another straw on the proverbial camel, which Brady considered the horse he'd ridden—Sandy—to be, and he shifted, stiffness invading his legs. Yesterday's insanity seemed far away and inconsequential now.

How did you deal with finding out your dad isn't your dad? Jake had always known who his father was, proven now by the testing. Brady had been lied to his whole life. Maybe Brett had been lied to as well? If Brady had always wondered, did others?

This family was one big mess. Him included.

"All right, then. Moving on. If I'm not a true West, then when paperwork gets signed back over, it will be under Tan only, right?" Brady said, and stood, snapping Jake back to the problem at hand.

"No. This place is as much yours, man. Listen, I'm going to call Frank and ask why he didn't give us a heads-up about this. I'm surprised, unless he never bothered to look, assuming the tests would be the results we expected. But who knows. We'll work it out." Jake was grasping at things to say to make it sound like it was okay. It wasn't, not by a long shot.

Brady nodded and put a hand on Jake's shoulder as he passed him, heading toward the door. "You're a good man, New York. Thanks," he said quietly, and then left the office.

Jake pulled Liz into him and circled his arms around her. She put hers around his waist, chin on his chest, and looked up at him. He looked down, into her eyes. She looked worried.

"This is . . . I don't even know what to think or say about this," Liz said.

"I wasn't expecting so much excitement when I first got here, you know," Jake said, trying to keep his voice light. "It was so quiet I thought I'd go mad from boredom. You all had me fooled."

Liz snorted a laugh and squeezed him. "You okay?" she asked.

"I will be after this," he murmured, and kissed her gently. She lifted herself up to him, returning the kiss, then stepped away from him just as quickly, biting her lip.

"Work first, City Boy, then play," she teased, waving her index finger at him, chastising him.

"All right, all right." He laughed and turned back to his desk, waving her away. He jumped as a hand dug into his back jeans pocket and pinched his butt, and before he could turn around and grab her, she was already running out the door, laughing.

She was taking it quite well too. Likely catching up to Brady to make sure he really was okay. That had been nice. Natural. Normal. He had a brief thought that this could be every day, that small moment of comfort that would erase any amount of tension. To come home to her laugh and touch.

He stowed the thought and picked up his phone. He needed to deal with the paternity results first. Then he could figure out just what Liz was starting to mean to him. Which was something more than just a casual fling. Last night had proven that, because the look in her eyes when he was deep inside her and the tenderness afterward was anything but casual.

As he was dialing Frank's number, he spied the blue lettered DAD sign Brady had made, and ran his fingers along the edge of the lettering, the paint smooth, the edge of the wood rough. It had an entirely different meaning now, not just for Brady, but for all of them. More secrets to unlock from a man who'd seemed straight and narrow. More twists and turns in this entirely messed up situation.

Frank's receptionist picked up, and Jake adjusted his eyes out to where Tanner was still angrily ramming round bales with a tractor, and sighed.

This news might affect Tanner more than Brady, and he wasn't quite sure how much more his brother could take.

CHAPTER TWENTY-EIGHT

Liz jumped off her last horse and looked at her watch as her feet hit the sand. It was well past six, but with all the interruptions she'd had today, she was still riding when she normally would've been in her office finishing up. Her stomach growled in response. Looping the reins over her horse's neck, she headed back into the stable from the sand ring, the clip of hooves on the shiny paved floor the only sound save the rustling of hay from all the horses that had been brought in for the night. It was a soothing sound, one she enjoyed sitting and listening to when she needed a moment to think, or not think, as the case dictated.

The arena lights buzzed as they winked on, and as she made her way down the aisle she nodded at one of the clients who had arrived to ride their horse. It would be busy here in no time, full of lesson kids and social boarders.

This was why she usually hid in her office if she was still working. Trevor was the evening man, running the show and ensuring chaos didn't descend. A couple of coaches would drive in on weekends to teach, so thankfully Liz didn't have to anymore. She didn't like the people side of the business, never had. Give her the horses and the quiet of the stables during the day. The snorts and rustles, the chirping from the barn swallows in the spring, the call of the crows on foggy early summer mornings. The ease of simply getting on with your day, no interruptions. It was why she'd fallen in love with this place the summer she had arrived with her mother. It was solid and peaceful.

But today, none of those things were working the way they should after she'd left the office, and Jake. She'd checked in with Brady once more. He'd been about to head out and check some of the bean fields. He'd told her he was fine, but the worry on his face was right there to see. She hoped he could reconcile this without internalizing too much. This would confuse anyone.

She pulled her horse into a stall, and as she took the bridle off, she stood a moment, watching a dad and daughter across the aisle tack up a school horse for a lesson Trevor was about to teach. The dad was pretending not to know what anything was, the young girl laughing and correcting him every time. The dad winked at her, holding up her helmet and asking her where this went on the horse, to peals of laughter and an, "Oh, *Dad*!" from the girl.

Liz turned, not wanting to be caught staring, and finished untacking her horse, tiredness settling into her arms as she hoisted her saddle off the horse's back. She needed to go home and collapse, eat something, and not have to deal with the world until tomorrow.

"Earth to Liz?" Trevor said a moment later, and she blinked, startled by his presence in front of her. She was still standing in the door of the stall, the saddle over her arms. She'd zoned out completely.

"Hey!" she replied brightly, stepping out. Trevor took the saddle from her and set it on the rack and peered at her.

"All right?"

"Yeah. Fine. You headed in for your seven o'clock?" she deflected.

He nodded, greeting a boarder as they went past. He turned his eyes back to her. "You aren't. You're exhausted."

"You should know better than to tell a woman she looks tired Trev," she teased. "But I am," she admitted right after.

"You know I think all that is horseshit. A spade is a spade in my world. Besides, Liz, you know very well you'd say the same to me."

"I would. Sorry, been a wild couple of days. You talk to Brady at all?" she replied, changing the subject again.

"I talked to him, yeah. Holy Hannah, you guys have had a time of it."

That was an understatement.

"You need a day off to recuperate? You should take one, Liz, if you need it," he added.

She appreciated his concern but shook her head. "No, I'm okay. Need to have the normal of a day on the horses. It helps."

"That it can," he agreed. "Especially with today's news, right?"

"Yeah. I just don't know what to make of this whole business. Who in the hell would Veronica have hooked up with?" Liz said. "I mean, she and Brett, everyone always said they were close, had a happy marriage. But what people see and what really happens . . ."

"I have some ideas," Trevor cut in offhandedly, a hint of humor in his voice.

"Oh, you do, do you?" Liz replied, equally amused. *This ought to be good*, she thought.

"Well, Veronica loved her horses. She'd spend all day out here, from what folks have told me, before she got sick. We all figured Brady got his horse sense from her. But—"

"Oh, spit it out. I need to get finished here," Liz interrupted, shoving him playfully. Trevor could gab on, which was why he was good with the boarders.

"Well, Keith had auburn hair, too, could fix pretty much anything that broke around here, and wasn't he always so frickin' happy you could kill him for it?"

"No. Couldn't have been," she said.

"Ah, just a guess. We might never know, really." With that, Trevor winked at her, a grin as wide as the world on his face, and stepped across the aisle to talk to his seven o'clock lesson, who was now saddled and ready to go, helmet firmly fastened in the right place.

Keith had talked about Veronica all the time after she'd died, remembering stories with surprising clarity. Liz had always found it sweet and humored him, because he was her boss and she had to. Thankfully, he never did that around her mom. But, in the same vein that he was so good with everyone, he and Brett had never seen eye to eye. Brett kept him around for some reason, despite the heated arguments they'd have. They were barn clearers, sometimes.

Had Brett known?

She pondered that as she put her tack away and gave the horse a quick brush. A memory hit her as she closed the stall door, of Keith, the day he retired, telling Liz to *Look after my boys, will you?* while patting Baron, Brady's horse.

She'd assumed he meant Brady and Tanner, but nothing more than the fact that they were close. Brady had looked up to Keith more so than Tanner, and Brady and Keith had both worked hard to bring Baron along.

Baron, Brady's horse. He'd had to be put down not long after Keith left, and Liz had taken over the stable management when Brady needed time away, his grief overwhelming. Brett put him to work elsewhere immediately, his brain proving too useful to "waste it on horses," as Brett had muttered at dinner many nights.

"Holy freaking shit," she muttered. "How the hell am I gonna bring that up later?"

* * *

Liz's ancient laptop sounded like a jet engine sitting on the kitchen table, and she clicked back and forth between an email about the upcoming Brightside Rodeo and the article she was reading about new equine vaccinations aimlessly, not really reading either. Her mind was not where it should be, the mixed-up day sending it places she hadn't gone in a long, long time.

The little girl and her father across the aisle from earlier kept replaying in her mind, the warmth and devotion the dad had for his daughter, the connection they shared. She'd never had what that dad and daughter shared. A dad who would tease and play but who would show up for her and protect her.

Her father had never taken her to anything other than the liquor store, and left her in the car when he went to the racetrack to gamble. It was a relief when they'd left him and never looked back.

She rarely thought about her father or played the what-if game anymore. He hadn't been the kind of man to give her memories to hold on to. Brett hadn't been much more of a father to her, either, but then again, she'd never expected him to be. Too many bad memories meant she'd been hesitant to open herself up to another man as a father figure by the time they'd landed at West Line.

Maybe Jake talking about his own childhood and the thoughts of Brady having to navigate this horrifying news had dredged up the understanding of how much it could hurt, and now she was wallowing in self-pity and memories she'd rather keep buried.

But why was it affecting her so much? She'd long ago made peace with her father being who he was, and how she'd never gotten close to Brett. It was annoying having it whirling around in her head, analyzing everything, and she wiped at her eyes as an overwhelming need to lay her head down on the table and cry or get up and rage around the house swearing battled inside her.

"Get your shit together," she hissed at herself, closing the lid of her laptop, the frustration winning. She blinked back the tears forming behind her eyes and decided an early bedtime was the best course of action to ward off more of her navel-gazing. Or maybe something to eat.

As if he'd read her mind, the hinges on her screen door squeaked and Jake stepped through, a foil-covered plate in his hand. As much as she wanted time to herself, the sight of him was a rush of comfort, and she smiled as he spied her through the door.

"I got your text that you were working late. So, room service!" he announced, and she snorted a laugh as he stepped in and flourished the plate in front of her, looking very much like a high-dining waiter as he bent at the waist, the plate perfectly balanced on his fingertips.

"Oh my god, thank you," she said as he sat on the chair opposite her.

She lifted the foil and breathed in the aromas of Caesar salad, roasted pork loin, and a perfectly square piece of cornbread. Her stomach rumbled. Dinner, up until this moment, had been a handful of jelly beans and a glass of milk, with the idea of cooking anything too much of an effort, despite how hungry she'd been.

"How did you have time to cook all this?" she asked as she jumped up and fished in the mess of her cutlery drawer for a fork. Realizing she lived like a pig, she slammed it shut, the tangle of silverware jangling angrily at her as she did.

Jake hadn't said anything more, was just sitting, watching her, his eyes following her as she moved around the kitchen. His gaze was possessive, and she must have blushed because the corner of his mouth quirked and he raised an eyebrow at her. She grabbed a mason jar and filled it with water, and gestured to him with it.

"You want a drink?" she asked.

"I'm good, thanks," he replied, and leaned back, hooking his elbows on the back of the chair. "I'm just the delivery boy. But I was hoping for a tip."

"If you're lost, moss grows on the north side of trees," she quipped back, earning a chuckle from him.

She stopped beside him, looking down into his eyes, and he reached up and took her free hand.

"You okay?" she asked. The dark circles under his eyes made him look as tired as she felt. No wonder. It had been a long day for him, too, and with so much extra to do because of the cattle thieves, his brain was most likely mush. She ran her hand through his hair, smoothing it back into place. Not that she minded it rumpled, but it meant he was thinking too hard. Tanner did the same thing.

"I am beyond exhausted, Liz. Today, yesterday . . ." he replied, and stopped mid-sentence, his eyelids fluttering closed, groaning as she massaged his scalp with her fingertips.

"A lot to take in," she finished for him, and lifted her hands before that got any more intimate, her mother's words echoing in her head. He smiled tiredly at her and gestured at her food.

"Eat before it gets cold," he said, and went to stand, but she pushed him back into his seat. Despite her whirling brain and the questions hanging over her head about him, she took a big breath and ran her hand over his jaw, leaned down, and kissed him gently on the lips. She wanted him to stay. For what, she wasn't sure, but her body hummed as their lips met.

"Stay. Just for a bit. I'll eat, and you can tell me about your call with Frank."

He leaned into her hand, a sigh coming from what seemed his toes sagging his whole body. She took her hand away, the intimacy again a bit more than she wanted, but what she seemed to find whenever she stopped thinking about it. She sat down in her chair, picked up the cornbread, and bit into it.

It was buttery soft, and so good she let out a moan and looked down at it, her eyes crossing. She'd never liked Rosy's cornbread—it was always bone dry—but this was like biting into a piece of heaven. A chuckle from Jake lifted her eyes back to him.

"You make that same noise when you're about to come," he remarked huskily, and leaned on the table, chin in his hand. "I think I like watching you eat."

"Jake!" she choked out. "I'm eating, not—"

He put his hands up in surrender, a stupid, shit-eating grin on his face, then stood up and headed for the sink, where he rolled up his sleeves, preparing to wash the dishes she hadn't gotten to yet.

"You don't have to do that," she said, but he waved a hand at her.

"Gives me something to do while you wolf that down. I'm tired but I'm restless as well, a lot of shit to deal with gets me like that."

She understood that. She'd been feeling the same way not even five minutes before he'd arrived.

"Anyway, Frank hadn't looked at the results yet, his assistant had mailed our copy the same time they came in to him. He was up to his eyeballs in another client's mess, apparently," Jake said, launching into it as he turned on the tap and squirted dish soap into the sink.

"Normal, everyday lawyer stuff, I'm sure," Liz remarked, enjoying the view of Jake's shoulders as he moved. She could watch him do that all day. She took another bite of the cornbread and then dug into the pork. She let out another soft moan. It was so good, it wasn't possible.

"Liz, I'm going to be hard in a minute if you don't stop making love to your food," he chastised, turning his head to look at her, grin still firmly in place. She rolled her eyes at him, making him chuckle, and he turned back to the sink.

"But had he seen them by the time you talked to him?" she asked between mouthfuls of food. She was shoveling it in now, her appetite restored by the absolute perfection of every bite.

"They were on his pile. I told him he might want to look at them. He dropped the damned phone, after he swore. He had no idea," he continued. He set a glass on her drip tray and paused, looking out the window.

"What do we do now?" she prompted around another mouthful.

Jake shrugged, the material on his long-sleeved shirt bunching across his back as he did. "Not sure. It doesn't change things from my end, and since none of this was in any of Brett's paperwork, it's kind of moot."

"We'll just have to wait and see, I suppose," she added lamely, and Jake made a sound of agreement as he set another glass on the tray.

Liz pondered that, the two of them lapsing into a comfortable silence. She finished eating and pushed back from the table, her stomach full, her thoughts fuller.

Jake turned and took her plate, setting it in the sink, and she muttered a thanks then turned to watch him. He was here, with her, in this strange domestic moment, and it was as if they had always been like this. Her mother's words popped back into her head once more, pestering her. Was she about to be burned? When she wasn't with Jake, it was easy to say she was fine, she was in control.

But when he was with her? All bets were off. She couldn't think straight, her heart and her head at war.

He caught her watching him, and she must have looked very serious because he looked concerned for a moment, studying her, their eyes meeting. Then, very carefully, he dunked a hand into the sink, swirling it. He winked flirtatiously at her, and slowly raised his hand, covered in soap suds. He quirked an eyebrow.

"Are you quite finished, Ms. Baker?"

"Oh my god, no . . . Jake! NO!" she squealed as she launched out of her chair, anticipating what was about to happen as he lunged at her playfully. They went twice around the table before he caught up to her.

They were both laughing as he slowly ran his hand down her face, leaving bubbles all over her, and then ducked away from her as she went to grab him, coming around behind her and snagging her around her waist. He dragged her over to the sink, and she was completely unable to resist, laughing hysterically. He picked up another handful of bubbles and covered her chest with them, soaking her shirt.

"Oh no, look what happened. Better take those wet things off," he drawled theatrically, and both of them went breathless from laughing, his arm circling her waist, hers wound around his neck. He stilled, his arm tightening, head dropping into the crook of her neck.

"Come on, City Boy. You can dry me off in bed," she teased, sensing the serious invading again, wanting to turn it off.

"A sound plan," he conceded, tiredness edging the humor, and she took his wet hand in hers, towing him toward the bedroom, deciding not to decide if she was stepping into the fire for at least another night.

CHAPTER TWENTY-NINE

Sunlight.

It was coming from the wrong side of the room and Jake blinked groggily, momentarily confused. He let out a frustrated groan when he realized he also couldn't move because a warm hand was flattened against his chest, and an equally warm leg was languidly hooked over his.

He was still in Liz's bed. *Shit.*

Nothing he could do about it now. He turned his head toward her. Her hair was spilling over the pillow and across her face, her other hand tucked up under her cheek. He settled back down to just look at her, not wanting to move and wake her up just yet.

Softness etched her features, her freckled, tanned skin glowing against the white pillowcase. She was fucking beautiful, and he couldn't take his eyes off her. His heart stilled in his chest as she shifted, adorable sleepy noises murmuring out. He held his breath, hoping that when she finally woke up, she wouldn't be angry.

They had collapsed into bed last night, both of them bone-tired. He was in his boxers, and she was in his T-shirt. They'd fallen asleep curled up with one another, neither of them initiating sex, because both of them were exhausted. At some point Liz must have woken up because the bedside lamp was off, and she hadn't been wearing his shirt when they'd gotten into bed.

He wasn't sure what this meant, and he wasn't sure about rocking the boat by prying into it. He just wanted to get out of the bed without her murdering him.

He took a chance and tucked her hair off her face, behind an ear, running his fingertips down over her cheek. She slowly opened her eyes and met his, confusion flickering in, quickly replaced by her lower lip disappearing between her teeth. She quirked an eyebrow at him, and he couldn't help but grin back at her. He knew that look. She was about to pounce. He didn't think he would mind that at all.

"Good morning. We seem to have broken the rule," he murmured as calmly as he could. She stretched herself down the bed, and let out a soft groan, sliding along his body, her leg sliding up over his hips, brushing against his already hard cock.

"I can see that," she replied, and scooted closer, laying her head on his shoulder.

Palming her hip, he ran his hand up and down her thigh, marveling that a woman who could physically master a fifteen-hundred-pound animal could, at the same time, be so delicately sensual and enticing. She was a cacophony of contrasts. Tough, yet caring. Strong and capable. He liked how she fit at his side like this, sleepy and soft, just as much as it turned him on to watch her work.

"You okay with this?" he ventured, and she nodded, her tongue coming out to slowly lick the nipple nearest her. It stiffened, and he hissed. He tightened his grip on her hip to her small growl of appreciation.

She took that invitation and ran her hand down his stomach, into his boxers, and circled his cock, sliding down and gently swirling back up. He lifted his hips into her hand, and then found her mouth, pulling her up to kiss, her tongue meeting his, the intention behind that dominant gesture quite clear. It jolted his core.

If this was the greeting he'd get from her in the morning, he'd spend every night here, damn it.

As quickly as she had revved him up, she hopped out of bed, throwing the covers back over him, and ran for the bathroom. He sat up, clawing them off his face, then fell back to the bed, laughing as she slammed the door.

"Tease!" he yelled at her through the door.

She laughed, then the toilet flushed. A moment later she emerged, peeled his shirt off, and threw a strip of shiny blue foil-wrapped condoms at him, hitting him squarely in the chest.

"Saddle up, buttercup. I'm a morning person," she drawled, and jumped onto the bed, sending the comforter flying, the springs squeaking ominously.

He laughed along with her as he set the condoms aside, grabbing her and rolling her over so she was underneath him. He looked down at her, and they both stilled.

"I know you said no overnights. I'm sorry."

She groaned and pushed at him, but he held her firm. He wanted to make sure this wasn't just her deflecting the intimacy they had back to something safer, not wanting to show any vulnerability. She did that so well, and he could see it as she let out a big breath and attempted more levity.

"It's fine, Jake. I'm not mad. I like morning sex, so let's break that rule today, okay?" she said, her eyes shooting fire at him as she lifted her leg over his hip and nudged him into her. He debated for a moment more before he pushed his boxers down, and kicked them off, fitting himself between her thighs, her smooth skin whispering across his as one of her heels dug into the back of his thigh.

She wanted sex, that was clear. But he was seeing something in the way she had responded to him that he hadn't seen before, and the daredevil in him decided to call her on it.

"What's the hurry?" he said, holding her gaze, his hands sliding over her. She let out a soft moan and wriggled underneath him.

"I want you. Now," she said, but she broke eye contact when she said it, and he stilled. She was desperately blocking anything other than keeping it casual, and with that, he knew it was bothering her that he was still here, had stayed the night.

"I don't want a quick fuck this morning, Liz. Let's—" he taunted, rotating his hips into her.

"Well, it will have to be, we've got jobs to do." She interrupted him, turning her head away from him to grope for the condoms on the bedspread beside them.

Damn it. Jake wanted her to tell him what was going through her head and admit that what they were doing together was more than just a casual fling, because it was preferable to her bottling up in front of him and making it impersonal.

He was going to rock the boat.

"I want to make love to you," he said quietly, turning her head so she had to look at him.

She let out an exasperated breath, flitting a glance at him and then tilting her head away from his hand. "Whatever. Slow, fast. Just—"

He was raised above her, his heart beating a mile a minute in his chest, looking down at her. She had stiffened the moment he said *make love*, and it took the wind out of his sails. He sat up and moved over to the side of the bed.

"Jake," she said, then stopped. "Come on, it's—"

"S'okay," he muttered, frustration slamming into his chest, utterly confusing him. He'd pushed, he'd wanted her to open up, and when she didn't, it reminded him of what they'd agreed to. He was only here for a short time, neither of them looking for anything serious, right? No connections. No romance. Definitely no "making love."

Complications were not something either of them should do, with all the other shit going on in their lives.

But there it was. Complication.

Looking down at her, he'd wanted this to mean something more than just getting their mutual rocks off. He wanted her to feel the same pull he felt every time he looked at her, to absorb her, never let her out of his sight. When she had looked away, he realized she likely didn't feel anything close to what his heart was careening toward. He couldn't ask that of her—she'd made that clear—and he just had.

"I need to get moving," he said quietly. "It's late, I think."

He didn't look back at her as she let out a frustrated sigh and then shifted to reach for her phone on the side table.

"It's six a.m., Jake. Sunrise. It isn't late."

He stooped to grab his jeans, and her hand touched his back. He stilled, the heat from her palm sinking into his skin. He almost turned and took her in his arms, wanting that heat to spread through both of them, to make it right.

"I'm sorry," she said. "What is it that you want?"

"Obviously not the same thing as you anymore. I—" His voice was gravelly.

"What does that even mean?" she asked. "Jake—"

"I think I just need to go. I can't be here right now." He stood, stepped into his jeans, and then threw on his sweater as he scanned the room for his socks. He swiped them from under the bed as she sat up, her hair everywhere, a sad, hurt look on her face, her hands braced behind her, throwing her chest up and out.

It was all he could do not to crawl back onto the bed and bury himself in her, tell her that this was more for him, laying her out and dragging the connection he knew she felt out of her by sheer sexual force. The idea of slowly rocking in and out of her was making him ache, to tell her anything he could to make her see, to feel the way his heart was hammering in his chest because of how much he wanted her. Not sex. *Her.*

But he didn't.

If he did, he knew he would fall over the fucking cliff and she would be the one who pushed him.

The barn office was empty except for the grumpy ginger tabby that haunted the front area of the barns, and Jake frowned. He needed to talk to Tanner; the morning meal prep was done and now he had to go through payroll with him, but he couldn't find him in all the usual places. Tanner's truck was still parked at the house, so he wasn't out inspecting any of the pastured cattle, and Jake counted all three tractors still in their parking spots, so Tanner wasn't out on one of them either.

Jake decided to check the main area of the cattle barn, catching the metallic bang of tools coming from that direction, hoping Tanner would be there. He followed the aisleway around the corner, the pitted, cracked cement wet from the humidity in the air today, and stuck his head through the door. The big space was empty save for Rowan and Kevin, who were stringing out a faded red hose along the concrete, country music blaring from a dusty old radio in the corner, big push brooms leaning against a wall beside a stack of metal pen panels. Kevin saw Jake and waved.

"You seen Tanner?" Jake asked as he reached them. "I need to go over some accounting, but he's vanished."

"Haven't seen 'im since this mornin' when we went over the schedule," Kevin said, and stopped feeding hose out from the roller. "Come to think it, he said he was headed to town, maybe?"

"His truck's still here," Jake replied. "I'll check with Brady. Thanks, Kevin."

Kevin nodded curtly, and he and Rowan went back to it. Jake had no idea what they were doing, but then, what did he know about cattle, really? All he knew about the cattle barn was that was where the calving happened in spring and the weaning tagging happened in early fall.

He should offer to help at some point and get an idea of what a day of work was really like here. He saw how tired everyone was every evening. Sometimes guilt snuck in, and he wondered if they thought he really was a pampered city slicker, only spending time in the kitchen and the office.

He squinted over at the machine shed as he exited the door of the barns and frowned, frustrated. Where was Tanner? He never took any truck but his own to go out and check other parts of the ranch, and as far as Jake knew, he wasn't fond of riding the ATVs Rowan loved buzzing around on.

Brady's truck was parked in front of the shop, indicating he was probably inside tinkering away on something. There was always some piece of machinery and equipment that needed fixing.

Jake's boots crunched on the gravel as he made his way across the main farmyard, the stable down in front of the yard, the small forest that separated the cattle barn from the main house and lawn to his right. The machine shed bordered the left side of the yard, and beyond that were fields and the foothills that rolled up to the mountains lurking in the distance. He stopped, casting his eyes around him.

This was a beautiful place, and he absorbed that thought, maybe for the first time. So much had happened since he'd arrived, he hadn't really seen the place properly or appreciated the peacefulness of it. Peace that in the beginning had been an irritant because it was too quiet, too slow, louder with the absence of the crush of people than the city ever was. Now, he looked forward to the nights when the only sounds were the crickets in the bushes, the hoot of an owl, the nighttime breeze ruffling the big pines along the driveway.

Brady had his head stuck in the side of a big green hulk of a machine, Bach filling the space. It brought Jake up short. He hadn't taken Brady for a classical music kind of guy, and another piece of the puzzle slotted into place.

If Brett wasn't his brother's dad, who the heck was? He'd have to ask Liz if she had any ideas. So far even Peony had been mum on the subject, not wanting to talk about it, simply shaking her head and stating *Let's let it settle a bit first* when it had come up at dinner, much to Brady's obvious relief. He didn't want to talk about it either.

Jake looked over at the bench, a riot of wrenches and tools piled on top of one another, none of them hung back on the pegboard wall. A big rolling tool chest had half the drawers open, rags spilling out of one. Jake wondered how Brady could keep his office desk so neat but his shop so messy.

Brady was humming along to the music, random mutters punctuating the hums. He pulled a wrench from a side pocket and reached in, twisted something, muttered some more. He grabbed for a rubber belt hanging off a lever on the machine, and after a few moments of grunting and a large *thunk*, a "Got you, fucker" echoed into the garage from the belly of the machine. Brady hadn't stepped back yet, and Jake hesitated, loathe to speak and startle him.

"Jake, stop lurking. Come hold this socket for me," Brady called from inside the machine, without turning.

Jake stepped over to him and reached in where Brady was gesturing, Brady smirking at him. Jake shook his head, chuckling.

"Just hold that socket solid while I tighten it from this side."

Brady slotted another wrench on the other side of the bolt and ratcheted it twice before he stepped back, wiping the sweat from his forehead with his sleeve, his hands covered in grease and black from the rubber belt.

"Thanks. Easier with an extra hand," Brady said, his grin wide as he tossed the wrench in the general direction of the workbench.

"Anytime."

Jake handed him the socket that had been attached to the bolt. Brady tossed it into a plastic clamshell toolbox, then pulled his phone from the back pocket of his overalls and turned the volume down on the speaker sitting above the garage door.

"What's up?" he asked. "Come to learn how to fix a baler?"

"I'm looking for Tanner," Jake said, shoving his much less work-worn hands into his pockets, conscious he knew nothing about what Brady, as the main mechanic for the ranch, actually did in here. As for what a baler did, which he guessed was the thing in front of them, Jake had no clue.

"I figured you were hidin' from Liz. She's in a foul mood this morning. She stormed over to the stable, and I haven't seen her on a horse yet, which means she's stewing on something. She won't swing a leg over if she's mad."

That was a whole thing he didn't want to get into with anyone else; it was personal. But, with that description, he was going to steer clear of her until she'd let go of some of that steam. He hadn't handled this morning very well, so she had every right to be pissed at him.

"Well, maybe I should," he replied with a grin, deflecting a possible needling by Brady. "That good, huh?"

Brady raised his eyebrows but didn't respond, and reached for a grease-stained ball cap hanging on the end of the machine, pulling it into place. He looked at his phone and furrowed his brow.

"Tan didn't check in with me for lunch. He's not in town still?"

"Nope. Truck's in the driveway. Would he go out on a horse?" Jake asked. "He was dead silent this morning coming through the kitchen, looked like he hadn't slept. He was carrying a bag of some sort, took a Thermos but didn't grab a coffee."

"Doubtful, if there was work to be done," Brady replied, and they both walked back out into the sun. Brady leaned on the side of his truck and looked out over the back into the yard, obviously thinking.

He tapped the side of his truck after a moment. "Well, I think we don't have a choice but to poke the grumpy bear. See if Liz knows."

Jake swallowed a groan and nodded. That was the last thing he wanted to do, but he followed his brother, hopeful it wouldn't be too explosive. Maybe after he could pull her aside and talk to her.

He was still frustrated with her, but the more he thought about how he'd run out of her room this morning, the more he realized he had to tell her how he felt so she could let him down and make it easier for him to leave when it came time.

* * *

The brown paper cube burst open, spilling stall bedding everywhere in the hallway before Liz could catch it.

"Fuck," she swore, and grabbed a fork to shove the resulting pile of loose woodchips into the stall she had been carrying it to.

One of the young boys who cleaned stalls hadn't shown up today, but the work still needed to be done, so she was on shoveling duty. Given how Jake had left this morning, it was fuel to the miserable mood she was brewing, and an excuse not to get on a horse when her patience was so thin it would do no good. The last thing she needed was to lose her temper and mess up months of training.

So, as she worked, her mind took what had happened this morning and ran full tilt, analyzing his reaction to her reaction, playing it over and over, mad at herself. He'd shut down completely when she'd deflected his attempt to be sweet and loving.

He'd said the *L* word. Maybe not in the context of what her mother had meant, but it had spooked her, and her reaction had shoved him in the opposite direction of what she wanted.

He'd thrown a curveball at her, and she'd panicked.

After he left, she knew she'd fucked up, reacting how she had, wishing she wasn't so messed up about letting someone into her heart again. All the reasons she had misgivings pushed to the surface. Trusting a man to mean what he said when it came to his heart. Trusting that how she was with him would be enough. Letting herself open up just to get hurt again because the big elephant in the room of Jake leaving when the ranch ownership was reverted still yawned in front of them.

Despite all that nonsense floating around in her brain, Liz knew she was falling for him. She just didn't know how to go about actually telling him she was feeling more for him than she'd expected, and it was scaring the fuck out of her. And now? She'd likely given him the hint that it wasn't possible.

She was stupid. So stupid.

Her eyes caught Jake and Brady walking down the aisle and she set the fork along the wall. They met up in the middle and Jake looked away, his shoulders hunching, his hands in his jeans pockets. Brady was watching both of them, eyebrows in his hairline. Likely she'd get a question or two from him later. Brady never missed anything, damn it.

"You seen Tan?" Brady asked, breaking the awkwardness.

"Yeah, no. Haven't seen him, but Trevor said he went out on Chip mid-morning. I assumed he wanted a day to clear his head, what with those test results coming in and everything."

"Not like him to bugger off like that," Brady replied quickly. "Jake's a little worried."

She knew the look on Brady's face. He was worried, too, but trying not to show it. Tanner sulked, but it never impacted the ranch. If anything, it meant he doubled down and took on more of the daily work, running himself to exhaustion so he wouldn't have to think.

Liz pulled her phone out of her back pocket and called Tanner. It went straight to voicemail. Frowning, she texted him.

"Well, I can go look for him, you're both busy," Jake offered.

"And you'll get lost. I'll come with you. We can take my truck,"

Brady said, slapping Jake on the shoulder. "I'll go get it, you and Liz iron out this shit, okay?"

Brady gestured between them as he backed up, then turned and strode out of the stable. Liz closed her eyes and sighed, moving to lean against a stall wall. Of course he would stir that up and skedaddle. She opened her eyes and found Jake leaning against the opposite wall. He looked up at her, his face unreadable, his arms crossed.

He looked pissed off.

There was no one else around them, so she stood up and crossed to him, and looked up. "Hey."

"Hey," he said. His voice was tight.

"You're still upset," she said.

"A little worried about my brother," he replied sharply.

"He's a big boy, he'll be fine. He makes good decisions," she replied.

"We all are, Liz. But we're always supposed to be fine, not make mistakes, not fuck it up, and that's hard," he growled, looking away from her, his jaw working.

It wasn't about Tanner anymore. He was still mad about this morning, even if he couldn't say it directly to her. She swallowed her pride and put a hand on his arm, making him look back at her.

"We don't have time to really talk right now. But . . ." she said, unsure of what to say.

"I'm sorry about this morning," he interrupted. "It won't happen again."

"Okay, then," Liz responded, abandoning her original thought to invite him over tonight to get it all out. What was that all about? Apologizing for what? Staying over, or his about-face exit?

He sighed at her response and scrubbed a hand over his head. He was weighing something in his mind, and it was heavy, so she waited, removing her hand from him, worried that was pissing him off more. Was he going to tell her he had made a mistake? That this thing between them wasn't a good idea anymore? Sure, he'd stayed the night, but that wasn't that big a deal, was it? She'd already decided it wasn't, if they could figure whatever this was out.

"Okay, I'm just going to say it. I know you said you don't want serious. Casual, right? No strings."

He reached for her, turning her against the wall, leaning in over her, their hips touching. A rumbling groan left his body as her hands flattened against his chest, and he closed his eyes for a moment, his jaw ticking. She ached to reach up and smooth her palm over the tense muscles, to calm him, but she resisted because right now he was trying to get something out and it might derail his thoughts. Thoughts she wanted to hear.

He opened his eyes and emotion stared back at her. She held her breath, caught in the intensity.

"I can't stop thinking about you . . . us. Thinking about how you make me feel when we're together. Right from the start, I think I knew this couldn't be casual, and I fucking tried. I can't do it anymore. I'd be lying to both of us."

She didn't know what to say to that. He was telling her what, exactly? She said nothing as his eyes studied hers. He leaned in, lips hovering over hers, heat ratcheting up between them as her hands slid over his shoulders. He kissed her gently and then leaned back, eyes fixed on hers again.

"Liz. I'm f—"

A horn honked, Brady yelled, and Jake straightened, pushing away from her.

"Finish your sentence, Jake," she said. He frowned, looking away from her.

"Later, once we find Tan. You and I will talk more then," he said as Brady beeped again, hanging out the driver's side window, looking down the aisle to where they stood. "This isn't how I want—"

Liz nodded silently, sensing he was desperately trying to control himself in the moment. Jake growled out a frustrated breath and then strode away, leaving her reeling, her hands braced behind her as she attempted to get her stupid heart to stop beating out of her chest. She took careful, deep breaths, the quiet in the stable yawning out after his heavy footsteps faded and the truck sprayed gravel as Brady peeled out toward the road.

"Well, shit." She swore into the empty stable and picked up her fork to keep working. Her mother was right.

Burned. To a crisp.

CHAPTER THIRTY

Brady took Jake on an unofficial tour of the ranch land as they looked for Tanner. They drove down access roads leading to the main pastures, over to the edge of several fields of corn and soybeans, up to an open pasture near a tree-covered rise in the land that Brady referred to as Sandstone Ridge.

Jake took it all in as they bounced past, wondering where his brother would have gone, wondering if it was futile to search for him in the thousands of acres of the ranch, if they should just wait it out. It seemed like needle-in-haystack odds of finding a man on a horse in all this open land.

When they were headed up the road toward the east pasture where they'd found the cattle thieves, both of them silently scanned the area. They hadn't found a trace of Tanner or spotted him in any of the expected places. Jake could sense Brady was becoming agitated.

"Where the fuck are you, Tan?" Brady muttered as he slowed the truck down to ease over the uneven potholes in the gravel road, his eyes roving over the area ahead of them.

Jake was getting an inkling that Tanner didn't want to be found.

"Would he have gone up to the family cemetery?" he asked, suddenly thinking of Brady's offer to take him. He had no idea if his brother would be that kind of man, to wallow in a place like a graveyard when he was at rock bottom. Jake knew himself, and he would do just that, likely with a bottle of scotch to keep him company, similar to when he'd lost his restaurant. So, given they seemed to think the same way sometimes, it was worth a shot to at least check.

Brady stopped the truck and looked over at Jake. "I hadn't thought of it. Worth a look."

Brady turned the truck around and they bounced back over the potholes toward the main road a little faster, Jake holding on to the handle on the door to keep in his seat. Brady didn't seem to notice how rough it was, but Jake's teeth rattled until they reached the smooth asphalt of the main road.

The truck creaked as they swung onto the main road, and Jake relaxed the death grip he'd had on the handle. That road should be regraveled. They all should. Driving through ruts and potholes the size of a small pond couldn't be good for the trucks, and he found himself wondering how much it would cost to bring in a dump truck of gravel to fill them, what roads were the most important to do first, and if they had one of those tractors that smoothed out dirt with a big blade.

He was about to ask Brady about it when it struck him that there was no reason on earth he needed to worry about that, since this wasn't his ranch and he'd be gone soon. What did he care about potholes?

But a voice inside him said he did, and it was important, and like he'd been doing since he got here, he added it to the giant bag of issues he'd unpack when he was back in New York and he didn't need to worry about anyone other than himself. Which was a world away from where he was right now, staring at fields his family owned, looking for his brother and a horse, and falling in love with a woman who would never follow him home.

He'd gotten in deep, and he didn't know how to climb out.

"It's just up here," Brady said, and turned down another gravel road, this one a little smoother, with grass growing between the wheel ruts. An iron gate with the word WEST arched over it stood a little way up a hill, and Jake's chest prickled, his heart kicking at his rib cage.

His family was buried here. His father, his grandfather, aunts, uncles . . . an entire side of his family. A legacy he had squarely sitting on his shoulders to make whatever his father had done right again.

Brady stopped the truck at the end of the lane and they looked up. Chip was quietly grazing around an old headstone just inside the gate, his mane and tail wafting in the breeze, a picture of peace.

"Son of a bitch. Looks like you have some sense," Brady muttered, flicking a glance at Jake. "He's here all right. He hasn't visited once since Dad, I mean Brett—"

"He's still your father," Jake interrupted. "He raised you. He's more your father than he could ever be mine."

Brady *hmph*ed at that and stepped out of the truck, the squeak of the hinges loud compared to the quiet where they were. Jake did the same, apprehensive to walk under the metal bars with his name on it. But if Tanner was here, it was more important to suck it up and make sure his brother was okay. He could deal with his own emotions later. As Brady had indicated without saying, this was not normal grumpy-asshole Tanner behavior.

They climbed the slight rise to the middle of the small cemetery. Jake noticed faded names on the headstones, most of them West, but some names he didn't recognize. Right in the middle was a large, black marble obelisk-shaped monument, with WEST across the top tier of the base. Underneath that were names, his father's most recently chiseled into the polished rock.

"Dad—he was cremated. He and his family are buried around the base of this one." Brady murmured, gesturing at it. "There's a spot for Tan and me, too, apparently. I've never looked."

Jake nodded, reading the name over again, tracing the curve of the *B* with his eyes, seeing the dates, the rock uncovered by the chisel still milky white, waiting for rain and winter to weather it to the darker patina the others already had. He glanced over the other names, and there was Veronica beside it, her birth and death dates. Underneath that was Tanner and Brady, their birth dates but no death date. Peony was not, which irked him a bit. She had as much right to be buried as a West as anyone.

As Jake scanned the rest of the granite, over to the other side, in not quite as fresh but nonetheless newly chiseled letters, was his name, the same way.

"Fuck," he whispered, and pointed. "He put me on here too."

Brady crouched and ran fingers over the lettering, then looked back at Jake with raised eyebrows. "Well, look at that. We never noticed at the interment. Dirt was heaped up, maybe it was hidden by some of the flowers."

It hit Jake squarely in the chest as he stood there, and he couldn't breathe, narrowing in on his own name, the hair on the back of his neck rising as his unease took hold.

His dad was in the ground in front of him, and someday he would be too. He'd never dealt with death like this before, at least not so directly and visibly. It was fucking scary to contemplate, and he hadn't even known the man. He had actively hated him for most of his life.

Did he still hate him? It was a huge question, and it added pressure to the weight sitting on his chest as he stood there. He let out another big breath, looking away, the tension cording across his shoulders. They were here for Tanner, not this, and he forced himself look for him instead of focusing on the mild panic creeping across his body.

They heard a cough, and Jake stepped around the monument to find Tanner sprawled out, his back propped against the stone, the bottle of Crown Royal in his hand almost empty. The view of the Rockies from this side was spectacular, and obviously why this hill had been sectioned off. Jake looked at the hazy peaks in the distance before squatting beside his brother. Brady had done the same on the other side, a hand already on his shoulder, which Tanner shook off.

Bloodshot eyes turned Jake's way, then back to the horizon. Tanner had been crying, or he was already completely drunk, Jake wasn't sure. Brady hung his head but Jake caught the look on his youngest brother's face that said he was in uncharted territory, just as much as Jake was. Jake immediately steeled himself like he did when he had to talk his mother into a cab or help her in the door of his apartment.

He stuffed all the worry and unanswered questions deep down inside and went calm.

"Come to rub some salt in?" Tanner rasped, and took a long pull from the bottle.

The liquid sloshing against the glass was such a familiar sound, Jake swore he'd been transported to a back kitchen somewhere in the city. A gentle breeze and the smell of fresh-cut hay were the only reminders that it was a different time, a different family member.

He reached out and took the bottle from Tanner, who let it go without a fight, fingers slack, hand falling to his lap. Jake gave him a gentle nudge.

"Move over."

Tanner shuffled sideways, and Jake lowered himself down beside his brother. Brady sat down cross-legged where he was, and the three of them went silent, looking across the fields toward the mountains. The breeze lifted Jake's hair off his forehead, and he took in yet another deep, cleansing breath, filling his lungs.

From this vantage point, he allowed himself to find calmness in the fresh vibrancy around him. There was no dirty concrete, no skyscrapers blotting out the sun, no smog that could make you choke, no sirens that made your ears bleed.

Right now, there was only peaceful, centering, open space.

"You know, Dad used to tell me *One day this will all be yours, son.*" Tanner's voice was slurred, and he flailed his hand out in front of him. "Bullshit, all of it."

"Not bullshit. It is yours," Jake replied, catching Brady's eye.

Brady nodded but thinned his lips, squinting back out at the mountains in the distance.

"It is bullshit. He never told us 'bout you, or that my own brother isn't—"

Tanner hiccupped and stopped talking, squeezing his eyes shut. He was beyond drunk, but not to the point where he was going to toss his cookies back up. At least Jake hoped not. The truck ride home would suck if Tanner did.

"I don't know what's right anymore," Tanner added finally, which was the heart of the issue. His father, whom he had looked up to his whole life, had lied and kept the truth from him. Jake understood that now more than ever.

"I get it. Peony told me on one of the first nights I was here that Brett looked for me after my mom left, apparently never stopped, even long after he had you two. My mom always said that we were kicked out, that my father was a good-for-nothing asshole who didn't want me. That we were better off without him."

"Really?" Brady said, finally speaking. "That had to be really tough to swallow as a kid."

"Well, apparently he . . . he was an asshole," Tanner spit out, and sniffed, running the back of his flannel shirt cuff under his nose. "He knew you weren't his, Brady. He had to."

"Maybe. But here's the thing, Tan. It doesn't matter anymore," Brady said, and stood up quickly, looking over his shoulder.

Jake followed Brady's gaze, and Chip's brown muzzle popped around the corner, his ears forward, nosing Brady, who grabbed his reins. Chip dragged him forward toward Tanner, seeing his human on the ground.

Jake sensed that Brady was really uncomfortable, unsure of what to say or do, and the distraction was a welcome one as Brady busied himself with looking the horse over.

Liz had told Jake that Brady was usually the one who could smooth out Tanner if he was stewing, and if not him, then it was Brett.

Jake guessed that Brady didn't know what to do or say this time, his own messed up feelings about their father coming into play. How did you defend a man you were angry with for lying to you your whole life? How do you reconcile the confusion when you're already confused? Jake had been there so many times he couldn't count. His brothers hadn't, until recently.

Jake stood up, dusted off his jeans, and stepped over to Brady, who was checking the saddle cinch.

"I got this. Why don't you ride back to the ranch, I'll get Sloppy over there into your truck and get him home, at some point," he said quietly.

"You sure? You two aren't exactly buddies," Brady said, leaning on the horse. Chip nudged at Jake's arm, and Jake ran his hand over the horse's forehead. Tanner hiccupped behind him, and Chip's ears went forward, toward the sound, and he stretched his neck until he was touching Tanner's shoulder. He lipped at Tanner's shirt and nickered. Tanner reached up and ran his hand lazily down Chip's muzzle. It was good enough for the horse, who then straightened back up and looked at both of them expectantly, as if to say *Aren't you going to help him?*

"He's fine," Jake murmured, and tweaked the horse's ear. Brady chuckled at that and grabbed the horn of the saddle.

"And here you are talkin' to horses like you've been country this whole time," he joked, then hooked his foot into the stirrup and lunged up and over into the saddle. He met Jake's eyes and frowned as he gathered up the reins.

"Thanks. I don't know what to do to make this better."

"You can't," Jake supplied, and shrugged. "He has to do the heavy lifting."

Brady looked over at his brother, who was now watching them both, blinking like an owl. "Look. Tan, you're drunk as a skunk. You gotta go home, you can't stay here. New York can drive my truck. I'll get Chip back to the stable and tell Liz that we found you."

Tanner waved him off, and Brady turned Chip and with one more nod to Jake, kicked the horse into a jog back down through the headstones.

"I can't do it anymore," Tanner blurted as soon as Brady was gone. Jake sank back down beside him, propping his arms on his bent knees and relaxing into as comfortable a position as he could get leaning on cold stone. They could be here a while, and if Tanner was opening up to him, he'd sit here all damned day if he had to.

"Do what?" he probed carefully.

"Keep all this shit together," Tanner stated, and waved his hand in the direction of the ranch, the defeat plain on his face.

"Why do you think you have to?" Jake asked bluntly. "You have Brady, Liz, and me. Peony. Heck, the crew too."

"I know that," he replied, "It's not about— More like I'm pissin' off the one man who isn't here to piss off anymore, and bein' pissed off at him at the same time. Don't wanna go back on what he needed from me, but angry at him for doin' the same."

"And you don't want to be mad anymore," Jake added.

Tanner nodded. "It's fuckin' with my head."

"Ah." Jake didn't understand exactly what that would feel like, but he got the point. The expectations that took root in the child of a parent who had molded his children to take over for him. Those were not easy boots to fill when said parent had secrets that threw it all into the rough.

"You know, I think it's eating you alive that you can't tell him off for what he did to us, and tell him to make it right," Jake said, hoping it wasn't too forward of him to suggest.

Tanner looked at Jake like he was certifiable, then bowed his head and let out a sigh that came from somewhere deep. He shifted a bit and picked at his fingernails.

"Maybe."

The silence enveloped them once more, and a few birds in some nearby trees started chirping. It was restful, if not for the cloud of doubt and sadness covering both of them as they wrestled with what Jake had just said. Jake wished he could talk to his father.

Just once.

To ask him what in the hell he had been thinking and to hear what his voice sounded like. Did Jake sound as much like Brett as everyone said he did?

He would never truly know.

Darker clouds were moving in from the west and north, and Jake wondered if that meant rain. Not able to read the skies like everyone else could out here, he scanned the horizon.

"Rain coming?" he asked.

"Yeah," Tanner mumbled, pointing the way Jake had been looking. "Likely some, over there."

"All right then, up you get," Jake said, rising to his feet. It was time to get going, even if he needed to be patient. This was better handled at home with some strong coffee in a nice, dry kitchen. He held out a hand to Tanner, hoping he would take it and follow Jake's lead.

Tanner grabbed it and Jake hefted him up, Tanner's other hand going out to steady himself as he found his feet, swaying a bit. He blinked a few times and then planted himself against the stone pillar, obviously dizzy.

Jake gave him a once-over just in case, the habit long ingrained in him from his mom, because she usually had some sort of cut or torn clothing, and he stopped his hand halfway toward his brother. This was not his mom, and Tanner was not in need of coddling. He frowned and stepped back, looking away from him, stuffing his hands in his pockets. When Jake looked back at Tanner, he blinked in surprise, because tears were spilling down Tanner's face.

Shit.

That was not something Tanner would want him to see, so he reached forward and pulled him into a hug, bracing for a punch or a shove.

Surprisingly, Tanner didn't push him away, but instead leaned into him and put his arms around him. Jake held him up, letting him get it out of his system, and cleared his throat because he didn't want to cry either. But, as he held Tanner, a strange unplaceable emotion overtook him. This man, his brother, the one who had hated him on sight, needed him.

Tanner let go after a few moments, shrugging up his shoulders and wiping at his face, not meeting Jake's eye. It was really significant what had just happened, and Jake patted him on the back, wanting to maintain the contact for a moment more, to reassure himself that this wasn't some anomaly. Maybe he'd needed that hug as much as Tanner had.

Jake glanced at the big headstone, then reached down to pick up the mostly empty bottle of booze, the familiar feel of the cold neck grasped in his fingers a reminder of how many times he'd held an almost empty bottle wrestled from his mother in his hands before herding her into bed to sleep it off. The scent of the whiskey reached his nose, and he looked up and around at the beautiful view, the silent, stoic gravestones, feeling at odds with the serenity, inside him a chaotic mess. Maybe he would bury his mother here, when she passed. Maybe then she would finally be at peace.

Maybe he would be too.

It clenched his heart, and he took a deep breath in, then out, trying to push the resentment and regret away from his body. He didn't want to feel this way anymore, and he certainly didn't need to feel it right now.

"Listen. I resented this man my whole damned life. You resent him now. I think that's enough resentment for an entire lifetime," Jake blurted as he turned the bottle in his hand and looked back at his brother.

"You gettin' head-shrinky on me now?" Tanner mumbled, cocking his head. "This snowflake bullshit ain't gonna—"

"No. Just want to be done. How's about we let this shit go, right here?" Jake interrupted him impatiently. With a flourish of the bottle, he paced around to the front of the headstone, looking for his father's name. Tanner followed him, a confused look on his face.

"What're you doin'?" he mumbled, still not steady on his feet, his voice slurred.

Holding the bottle up, Jake slowly poured out the remainder of the amber liquid on the stone. It splashed over the freshly carved words then flowed along the edge and into the bright green square of new grass where his father's remains were placed. He waited until the last drop was done and then pierced his brother with a look that hopefully conveyed what he was trying to do.

Jake wanted to bury that resentment here. Release it so he could move on. He had to; it was holding him hostage, preventing him from truly letting himself be present, no looming deadline of what would happen when he could leave people and a home he had come to truly give a damn about.

No holding back on being with a woman who could very possibly be the one.

"No matter what happened in the past, or what happens now, he was our dad. This place is his legacy, no matter which one of us is on the deed. *Nothing changes that*. This place is your home. He may have dragged me into this mess to appease his own failure, but—"

Jake stopped as Tanner went wide-eyed and then looked away. *Yep*. This was getting emotionally uncomfortable, but it needed to be said. He needed to have Tanner understand what it meant for him to have been brought here, the change that was happening in him.

"And I'm glad for it, because I found a family that—even if some of them are assholes—cares about each other."

Tanner snorted a chuckle and leaned his shoulder on the smooth stone obelisk, leveling one of his patented *you're an idiot* looks at him.

"I've never truly had that before," Jake added, which wiped the look right off Tanner's face as quickly as it had appeared.

Jake waited for the smartass quip, but none came. It was tacit approval of what he'd said, so Jake clenched his jaw and set the bottle down beside the wet patch of ground, like a symbol of finality, leaving it here to make a point that it was done.

"I'll go wait at the truck. You say your piece and meet me there, if you can walk a straight line."

"Don't need to. You said it," Tanner said, and started weaving his way down the hill toward the truck.

Jake fell into step with him. As he did, Tanner put his arm up and around Jake's shoulders.

"You're a good man, Jake," he slurred quietly. "I'm sorry."

Jake couldn't respond, the heaviness of what he'd done balancing out the weight of the bond he'd just forged with his brother, making him feel oddly centered yet newly burdened. So he put his arm up over Tanner's shoulders as well, and they walked down to the truck together.

CHAPTER THIRTY-ONE

Peony strode into the living room with a cup of steaming coffee and handed it silently to Tanner, who was slumped over on the couch. He took it wordlessly and held it in his hands, turning it slowly. Liz crossed her arms, tapping her foot and glaring at him, waiting for an explanation she wasn't sure she was going to get, just yet.

Jake and Brady were on the other side of the room near the entryway. Jake's arms were crossed as well, and he looked as angry and tense as she was, his jaw tight, his eyes snapping.

She was stuck between two men she was angry at. Both throwing curveballs at her. One she was worried about, and one she was pretty sure she was falling for and might have blown a chance with.

She caught Peony's eye, and her mother raised her eyebrows in a gesture of *What now?*, sitting down in her favorite chair with folded hands, waiting. Liz let out a huff and sat down herself, unsure how to reconcile what had her more riled up: Tanner losing his shit or Jake's statement in the stable.

She desperately wanted to punch something, she needed a hug, and the only person she wanted one from was Jake, which was fucking with her. Confusion sucked, especially when it came to . . . well, all of it.

Tanner took another sip from the mug then set it over on a side table, flopping against the back of the couch, his eyes closed. He'd sobered up some, having upchucked out the window of Brady's truck on the way home.

"Tanner," Peony said, finally breaking the awkward silence. "You gave us a worry today."

He grunted and flicked a glance toward her. "I know."

"Well, I'm glad you know, because Lord above knows we don't. Fighting in my house, getting so drunk you can't even stand? This isn't you."

Tanner gestured with his hands, then let them fall, his entire posture admitting defeat. Peony *tsk*ed and moved over beside him on the couch, her hand brushing his hair away from his forehead, like she would when Liz was sad about something. His composure crumpled when she did, and he leaned forward to hide it, head falling into his hands. Her mother slipped an arm over his shoulders.

"Maybe it is who I am now. I don't know anymore," he said quietly.

"I'm sorry it's been so hard," Peony said, her voice gentle. "You should have come to me, my dear."

Liz was intruding. She stood up, deciding to wait until he was completely sober and less upset to talk to Tanner. Cranky, stoic Tanner was sometimes easier to deal with, and with her restlessness, she was liable to snap at him, which wouldn't help. She got up and headed to the other two men.

"I'll see to it he gets a meal into him, and we'll make him rest," Jake was relaying to Brady, as she reached them.

"I'll check that his list is covered for today. I've not much left to do on my end but some paperwork, which can wait," Brady replied.

With that, the two men nodded and parted, leaving her standing, mouth open to ask what she could do. Obviously both of them were too deep in their own heads to even acknowledge her presence. She debated following Brady to discuss spreading the rest of the day out among the men, but let it go. He had it well in hand. He always did.

She stood a moment in the front hallway and let her anger at being snubbed fade away. She listened for another moment to her mother's murmurings from the living room, followed by the low rumble of Tanner's voice, quiet as he answered. A slice of worry slid through her when it was followed by a soft, gut-wrenching sob from him.

Everyone was already on edge, and it would do no good to get indignant about not being included or listen in on a conversation her mother was having with a man who never showed emotion outwardly.

She had more important things to confront, so she slid farther away from the living room into the house. There was still one West brother in the house she could talk to, and this particular conversation couldn't wait. If it did, it might not happen.

She knew Jake would be where he'd always gone since he was forced into this ridiculous situation and needed to clear his head.

He was washing his hands, and she observed him from the door as he leaned on the counter in front of the kitchen sink. Hands braced on the rim, he bowed his head, his shoulders rising tightly, the tension in them radiating over to where she stood. He took a loud breath in through his nose and let it out through his mouth in a watery huff.

He was hurting.

She hesitated, wondering if her timing could wait, but when his knuckles went white on the sink and his biceps bulged out in an obvious attempt to keep his emotion in, she reacted.

Without thinking, she strode over to him and put her hand between his shoulder blades, like she'd done before, the tension rock hard against her touch, the heat of him echoing through her. She gave in to the worry she had been battling since they had left to go find Tanner, and leaned into it.

He turned his head and looked at her, his hair a mess over his forehead, his mouth closed and stiff.

"Today, with Tanner, was hard," he murmured, his voice gravelly and low. "Brought me right back to Mom."

She wondered what he'd had to endure, dealing with a parent who was an addict, which, as she thought about it, she understood all too well. That was another story for another time, because right now, he obviously needed not to be reminded of his past. Visiting the cemetery was plenty for one day.

"You know my dad put my name on the West monument?" he added.

"No." She raised her eyebrows. How strange was it that Brett had secretly done all this reconciliation without telling another soul? It was so at odds with his normal outgoing gruffness. He was never secretive, or at least they had never known him to be. Brett was all out front; he told it like it was.

Boy, did they have him wrong. Secrets upon secrets were unfolding around them now that he was gone. He'd hidden everything so well no one would have even guessed at them. How many more were they going to uncover as time went on?

"We didn't see it at the interment. Must've been hidden," she said. "Secretive old fox."

He nodded and slid an arm out, circling her, pulling her into his side. They stood by the sink hip to hip, and he dropped his forehead to the top of her head.

"Today has been an absolute mindfuck," he stated. "I'm sorry about earlier, in the stable. We need to talk but I need to get my head screwed back on straight, and that idiot out there needs some carbs and protein or he's gonna faint if he tries to get up."

"I get it," Liz replied. "I'm not going anywhere. It can wait."

"Liz," he groaned. "It can't. I don't—"

"It can wait," she interrupted, restlessness vibrating just under her skin. Being in his arms was making it really hard to focus, confusion and comfort swirling. She needed space to get her head on straight, too, before they talked, and he obviously needed to process. She unfolded herself from him and made sure she met his eye when he faced her. He was worn out, and she could see the thoughts he was trying to sort out in his head. About them, about his brothers, his father . . . all of it.

"Get through this first." She gestured at the house around them. "Then we can talk."

"All right," he said after a moment of studying her, worry lacing his eyes. "Later?"

"Later," she said back, and with a squeeze on his arm, forced herself to leave as he turned back to the sink.

She met her mom, who was bringing Tanner's empty coffee cup back to the kitchen, as she was walking to the front door. Peony stopped her with a hand on her arm.

"Honey, are you all right?"

"I am, Mom. Just frustrated," Liz replied. "I'm worried about Tan, and all this shit happening at once for him could—"

Her mother *hmm*ed at that but didn't let her go. "Not about that, sweetie, about the other one. You two have a tiff?"

Liz hung her head. It seemed everyone could read her like a book these days. Was it that obvious they'd gotten out of sync?

"No, Mom, believe me, that isn't the problem. What Jake and I do is—"

"Important," her mother said, interrupting her. "What you have with him is worth fighting for."

"This is my problem, Mom. Not yours. I don't need you to tell me that."

Peony sighed and waved a hand at her daughter in resignation. "No, you don't. But just in case you needed someone else to say it, I will. You and Jake need to figure out what you mean to one another, because once you do, you can move forward, and we can all stop walking on eggshells around each other. Black and white, Elizabeth."

Black and white. There it was again. Yes, that was a necessary thing. Trouble was, Liz didn't know what that looked like anymore.

Jake looked up from the book he was reading, having picked up one of the romances Liz had bought Peony in Calgary the day he'd returned his rental. Surprisingly, he was enjoying it, and hadn't noticed it was now late afternoon.

Peony was reading as well, curled up in her chair, and Tanner was sound asleep on the couch across from them.

Jake was loathe to get up and go start any dinner, but as he set the book down, restlessness twitched inside him. Sitting here, listening to his brother snore, the clock tick, and the odd truck pass by out on the main road was about as laid back and quiet as he'd been since he'd gotten here. He hadn't thought about financials, or menus, or inheritance law. But as he acknowledged it, the noise came back into his head. He must've let out an audible sigh, because Peony looked up from her book.

"Let's order pizza," she blurted, and Jake raised an eyebrow. *Pizza. All the way out here?*

"There's good pizza here?"

"Brightside has a pizzeria, called The Minute Man. I love their special. Has mushrooms and olives on it and it isn't greasy like the other place in town."

"Okay, then. Want me to go get it? I can't imagine they deliver," he asked, and Peony waved him back to his seat as she got up.

"They'll deliver. The owner is an old friend of mine. He'll bring it out himself if I ask. I'll go order it now, so we can eat at a reasonable time."

"It would be nice not to have to make dinner," Jake admitted. "I'm so mentally worn out my body isn't quite sure what to do with itself."

Peony laughed quietly and glanced over at Tanner. "Him too. He's been running on empty for days. Thank you for what you did today. I don't know if I should even utter the what-if's, but the two of you, if you'd met under other circumstances—" She pressed her lips together and looked at Jake for a moment then back at Tanner, who let out a small snore.

"I want to say that we're good now, but jury's still out on that one," Jake said.

"I think you two could be friends," Peony added, a look almost like relief as she said it.

"We're a lot alike," Jake replied. "It would be anyone's guess if we killed each other fir—"

"Tan needs someone who can go toe to toe with him, and you need someone to remind you that you're a West, and push come to shove, you can do anything you set your mind to. I think the two of you would be a powerhouse for this ranch," she said quickly, before he could finish his own thought.

Jake blinked at that statement. If anything, Tanner had reminded him he wasn't a true West time and time again, and he was well aware he hadn't grown up here with the experiences and honing of ranch life to give him the hardness and skills a spread like this needed.

"I don't know about that," he said. "I'm pretty sure he thinks I'm too soft to make it out here."

Peony smiled. "It isn't about what he thinks, it's about how he pushes you, and what you can be for each other. You're not alone anymore. You've got someone to remind you of what you're capable of who shares more than just a last name. You've got family here to guide you, no matter what you decide to do in the end."

Jake looked over at his sleeping brother. Maybe Peony was right.

"Point taken. It would be nice to be on good terms when all this is figured out."

"I think so too. Now, you should go find Liz. She loves Minute Man pizza, and she'll be ticked if we don't share."

Jake caught Peony's eyes sparkling with mischief as she stood.

He'd been around her long enough to know she'd seen their tension and was meddling, as any good mother should. He chuckled and they smiled at one another.

"All right, all right. Message received. When should we be expected back for dinner?"

"Pizza reheats, dear. Take as much time as you need," she replied as she headed to the back den. "I don't doubt you have some things to talk about."

Jake set his book down and looked over at Tanner, who was sprawled out like he hadn't slept in weeks. Completely relaxed, his legs half on, half off the sofa, his arms flopped out, his mouth wide open. He was out cold and hadn't even woken up as they were talking. This might be the first real sleep he'd gotten in a while.

Jake carefully laid a tartan lap blanket over his torso, which Tanner, in his sleep, grabbed and gathered up under his chin, muttering something about rotating fields.

"Get some sleep, cowboy," Jake muttered, and paced out of the room to the back mud porch. He pulled on his boots and headed to where he thought Liz might be, deep in thought about what he would say to her when he found her.

He was out of his element with her, how he felt, what he wanted very different from what he was supposed to want. Between this afternoon's drama with Tanner and everything else that had been thrown his way the moment he stepped onto West Line Ranch land, he was completely and utterly lost when it came to understanding how Liz fit into the picture other than the fact that he was falling for her despite himself. He had to figure out how this could work, given that he wasn't a permanent fixture here.

The stable was full of laughter and happy conversations among the boarders as they tacked up, horses and equipment everywhere he looked. He ducked into Liz's office, but she wasn't there. He looked into the arena, but none of the women on horses were her.

He wandered down the aisle and spied Trevor, in the middle of tacking up a horse. Trevor waved him over.

"She's up in the loft, doing a bale count," he said and pointed to the steep stairs off to one side. He winked at Jake before he turned away to grab the bridle he'd set down, and Jake suppressed a groan.

Small towns and families. They always knew your business. This place was no exception. It didn't bother him as much as it had when he'd first arrived. At least Trevor knew why he was going up there and wouldn't bother them.

He stepped onto the loft floor, closing the door behind him and locking it for good measure. He'd never been up in the hayloft, and the high walls of square bales and the scent of sweet, drying grass wasn't unpleasant. It was cozy and quiet, the sounds from downstairs muffled and distant.

He found her sitting in the tiny loft window, legs hanging over the edge. She turned as his boots clunked on the wood floor, and she tilted her head beside her, inviting him to sit.

"Bale count?" he asked as he sat.

"Excuse to get away from the crowd," she replied with a small smile. "I can't think when there are a lot of people around."

"Lot to think about," he said, trying not to be too obvious.

She hummed an *uh-huh* and shouldered him gently. "You too. Can't imagine what was going through your head being in that cemetery."

"I'll deal with that later. I want to talk about what happened this morning," he said, gesturing between them. They needed to clear the air, and if he didn't do it now, it wouldn't happen.

She sighed heavily and looked back out the window, scanning the landscape. He waited, the tension in her shoulders stiff and high. He wanted her to open up to him. He wanted more from her, and it was the same feeling he'd had this morning when he had to back away from overloading her and himself with the feelings that took hold when he so much as even looked at her. He wanted their easy intimacy to mean more than just friends with benefits.

Every rational thought in his head was telling him it would lead to nowhere because he was leaving. But his heart would have none of it.

Even when he'd proposed to Ashley, his heart hadn't contradicted him like this. His head had made that decision. Right now, his heart was screaming at him to not throw away this opportunity at something amazing. Right here was a woman who could stand up to him, for him, with him.

"When Darren cheated on me, I retreated into myself, not wanting to put myself out there just to be hurt again," she blurted before he could say anything else.

"You said as much at the bookstore," he replied. She was talking, so he waited to explain why he'd reacted to her the way he had.

She let out a heavy breath and her shoulders settled. "I think I don't trust others easily, in general. Like, I trust Tanner and Brady, right, but that's different. Or at least I tell myself it is."

"Right. They're family," he said.

"Yeah, they are, but my dad . . . he . . . well, he wasn't a good dad. Mom packed us up into her station wagon and we left in the middle of the night. I was eleven."

"That must've been hard leaving like that, as a kid," he said.

"Easier than staying," she said, and glanced at him. "He was an alcoholic. You know what that can be like. My dad was an angry drunk, and he had a gambling addiction, which meant he could get—"

Jake hadn't known anything about Liz's father; it had never come up with either her or Peony. However, he did know what it could be like to live with someone who suffered from addiction. He and Liz had more in common than he'd even realized.

"Anyway, yesterday, there was this kid with her dad in the stable. He was making her laugh and helping her tack up. It got me thinking about Brady's situation, about Brett and all his damned secrets, and then I started thinking about my dad, which made me think about—"

She waved her hands in the air in a big circle and let out a breath.

"About what?" he prompted quietly.

"I think, in some stupid, fucked up way, I don't trust my gut or my heart when it comes to love of any kind and it's because of my dad, somehow. Not being what I needed, disappointing me over and over. If I don't trust people, I can't be disappointed. If I don't fall in love, I can't have my heart broken. Case in point, Darren telling me I was emotionally unavailable."

"Doesn't excuse his cheating," Jake groused, and she nodded, a soft, "Uh-huh," echoing out of her. Jake watched her face as she wrinkled her nose and looked out the loft window. He wasn't sure what else to say to that. She was digging deep into herself right now. He touched her arm, and she let out a huff, focusing back on him.

"Some next-level daddy issues, right?" she said.

"You and everyone else living here right now," Jake replied dryly.

That made her snort and push at his shoulder. He chuckled, happy that some of the tension was broken. They sat quietly, Jake's eyes following some swallows diving up and down from a tree nearby, little trills and warbles echoing into the evening air.

He was waiting for her to put her walls back up or lash out when he pushed the idea of them being more. The heaviness of her admission wasn't what they needed to say to one another, but if it was part of her process to explain why she'd pushed him away this morning, he'd sit here all night if he had to. Just like he'd been prepared to with Tanner earlier.

Liz turned in her seat and caught his eye after a few minutes. "You know, I think I wanted no strings because it meant I wouldn't have to expose myself to emotions and shit that would mean I'd have to let someone in. I deluded myself it would be easy to turn all that off."

"It isn't, is it," Jake murmured.

"No, if fucking isn't. It was a decision I didn't want to make, that I still don't know if I can make. This morning, you put it right in front of me and I didn't handle it very well."

"I didn't either," he admitted.

"The stupid part was I wanted what you were offering, even if I wasn't sure what it was," she said.

"Something has changed between us, and I should have been more up front about how I was feeling," he replied.

"You kinda were, but—" She huffed a breath, annoyed as she obviously searched for words. "Whatever this has become? I don't know what to do about it, and I still don't know exactly what is happening, despite what you said downstairs earlier."

"What is happening is that this hasn't been casual for a while, Liz. We're more," Jake said, and held his breath. That was the statement that would send her spinning, and he expected this was where she would push him away.

She turned to look at him, her forehead wrinkled, her eyes questioning. "Why, though? It's easy. Just sex, and when you're gone, a great memory. Seriously, you're from New York, I'm from butt-fuck nowhere. How in the hell would that work?"

Her voice had risen, and her shoulders were back up around her ears. He steadied himself. He had to get this out before she rejected him outright.

"I don't know, but I'm willing to find out," he said.

"Why?" she repeated, her voice small and quiet.

His heart skipped a beat, hearing the uncertainty in her voice. *Fuck it.* He'd lay it out and if she ran, he'd chase her, even if it killed him in the end.

"You're worth it," he offered.

She stilled and looked like she might start crying, which wasn't what he wanted. But with that reaction, he knew she was feeling things for him too—she just couldn't get out of her own way to trust him or herself to let it in.

"I don't want it to be just a memory, Liz, and I know you don't either. I can see it when you look at me, when we touch," he ventured, and moved closer to her. He put his forehead against hers, daring her to lean into him, to open herself. She took in a breath, and her hands flew to his chest, her eyes turning up to his.

"We can't. You're leaving."

He leaned in and kissed her gently and tenderly, sensing he could. "I'm not leaving yet. We'll cross that bridge when we get to it."

She snorted and pushed at him, separating them. "Are you saying you'd stay and give up your career and big-city lifestyle? Is that all it would take? Well, bring it on, then. That sounds perfectly rational and simple, doesn't it?" She jerked herself out of the window, further distancing herself from him, and folded her arms around her body as she stood away from him.

There it was. He watched her warring with herself, her words a defense against what he'd just said, trying desperately to push away the connection to how she refused to let herself feel. She said she didn't want to get hurt again, but when emotion like this entered the equation, he knew it was inevitable. She was already hurting with her reminder that he was leaving.

"It doesn't have to be safe, you're allowed to feel what you feel," he said.

"You don't get to tell me what I feel," she snapped. "Seriously, Jake, what exactly do you want out of this?"

He knew what he wanted as they stared at each other. It crystallized in the slowly fading light of day, as she stood in the loft, dust motes surrounding her, jeans stained with god knew what, her hair coming out of its hasty braid. Her proud upraised chin and stubborn stance anchored it as his chest constricted, squeezing all the air out of his lungs.

He wasn't just falling for her. He loved her.

He'd fallen off the damned cliff. It was too late. But she needed to want it, too, or it wouldn't work, which might tear him to pieces, the way he was feeling. A way he'd never fucking felt before right now.

Jake vaulted up and turned to her, intent on making her understand. She backed up against a wall of hay bales, her eyes darting between him and the door, so he followed, leaning into her, hands on either side of her head. She twisted her lips and looked up at him, her eyes defiant. It riled him, and even though they were talking about heavy things, the need to feel her body against his muddied his thoughts. He forced a breath through his nose and willed himself not to go hard as they argued.

"What I want is you. I can't stop thinking about you, and I'm in awe of your strength, your depth, your capacity to give. I've never been with a woman who makes me think so damned much, and I want more. I want it all."

Liz was staring at him, her eyes wide. He leaned in farther, his nose just touching hers.

"I don't have all the answers, but I want to find them. I can only do that with you," he said, trying his best not to come off as aggressive, adrenaline and need skipping up and down his body like a Ping-Pong ball.

"What if I don't want all that?" she spat back.

"You do," he said softly. She was wrestling her emotions with all she had, and he needed to break through. He'd figured out how to push her, it seemed, and he wanted her to explode, to push through the fear.

If she just let him in, she'd see what he saw.

"Well . . . well—" she stuttered, then growled, rubbing her hands up and down her face. "You are so frustrating, Jake West!"

"I am?" he said, grinning at her.

"Damn it, yes. Because I do want all that . . . to trust myself. For days I've been thinking I should just let this happen and—"

Finally. He licked his lips, determined to stay even. "It's fucking scary," Jake answered. She nodded and lowered her hands to her side, vulnerability and emotion on full display. He groaned and reached for her, fitting her body to his as her arms wrapped around his waist. She buried her head into his chest.

"Let me in, Liz," he whispered into her ear. "Let someone love you. Let it be me."

He looked down into her face, and the tears he'd seen gathering were now tracking down her cheeks. She looked up, blinked, and then kissed him, hands coming up to hold his head steady. He held her tightly as she did, arching into the need in her, the aggressive pull of her mouth all he could handle without pressing her back against the hay and peeling her out of her clothes.

She pushed him away suddenly, angrily wiping at the tears on her face, and he braced for the defensiveness to kick in again, or for her to run. She was grappling for control, and it was eluding her.

"Fuck you and damn you to hell for making me want," she swore, then grabbed his shirt, pulled him into her again, nose to nose as she glared at him.

"Liz," he murmured as she shook him slightly, her hand fisted in the fabric.

"Jake," she snapped back at him, but her body softened, the fight leaving her.

"It's okay to want," he murmured as she let go of his shirt and smoothed the wrinkles out with her palm. "And it's okay to be afraid too."

He'd said that as much for himself as for her. His heart was hammering and his mouth was dry, but he'd do anything to help her get over this last hurdle, to show her how good it could be.

"I want to want you," she whispered. "I want to stop being afraid."

"Then let me in and we'll figure it out together," he stated, his heart in his mouth as he leaned in and kissed her again, hoping it was enough.

CHAPTER THIRTY-TWO

The tumult of emotions ripping Liz apart ebbed away as Jake kissed her, giving way to a crushing amount of need. She went with it, because this was preferable to the indecision she'd been fighting.

He'd pushed all her fucking buttons tonight after she'd said what she said, him saying the things she had dreaded but needed him to say all at the same time. But he also understood her fear and hadn't tried to tell her she was stupid for being hesitant.

He was scared, too, and willing to face it with her.

She wanted this, with him, and the idea made her heart hammer like a galloping horse as his lips moved over her, heat sparking through her body, incinerating her to a husk of coal on the floor, because his admission that he wanted more had melted her.

He wanted her. Not her body, not the distraction she could give him. But *her*.

She'd compared him to Darren as she had stared at him, before he'd come over and neatly trapped her against the haystack. Or, more precisely, she'd catalogued the ways Jake was redefining what she thought love was supposed to look like. She'd told him happily ever after didn't exist, she'd shown her bitter and sad side, she'd shown him her anger, her attitude, and her stubbornness, and still here he was, asking for her to open her heart to him instead of telling her she was being unreasonable.

Darren had never made her feel so utterly bewildered. He'd never bared himself the way Jake just had. Darren had never expressed himself other than to say he adored her, shushing her if she fumbled about, trying to say the same back. Maybe that was why she thought he'd been a safe choice, because he hadn't challenged her. Darren had never said he loved her. Not once. That had suited her fine when they were together, but now? She suddenly craved that from Jake, and he'd said as much, the words foreign and shocking.

To Darren, she was a novelty until it got serious and she couldn't give him what he wanted anymore, so he found another. It was all take with him, and she realized she hadn't demanded anything else, hesitant to let him in. Their communication had been one-sided and broken from the start. That had been both their faults. His impatience and her unavailability. Even though she'd stayed because he was stable and accomplished, she hadn't trusted him.

Jake didn't want to possess her the way it had sometimes felt with Darren; Jake wanted her to let him in. He didn't want to take from her, he wanted to give to her, to face what they felt together. That was different, or at least it felt different when he asked her to let him love her, dropping her stomach into her toes. He wanted her to feel the reckless emotion currently rocketing around inside her but, even though he'd been pretty persuasive, was letting it be her choice.

Darren also never once asked what she wanted until he screamed it at her while they were fighting, and she hadn't been able to answer because that had been about him, not her.

Jake had cracked her last defense wide open, so she threw Darren away when Jake kissed her, and let the memory of him go. He could rot for all the shit he'd put her through, the walls he'd helped her reinforce in herself. That little voice inside her head telling her she shouldn't do this was gone.

It had been silenced with Jake's words.

They had backed up against the hay again, the mix of the fresh timothy and Jake's scent delicious. She ran her hands up and down his chest, his muscles tense as he held her. He deepened his kiss, pressing into her, their bodies flush against one another, both of them now fully on fire with need.

She bit his lower lip and he let out a growl, his hands moving all over her body, squeezing her waist, her thigh, back up to her rib cage, hungry for her.

A horse nickered downstairs, and she wondered if they could get away with making love upstairs in the hayloft while boarders and clients were just below their feet. It was completely unprofessional.

"We really can't, not here," she gasped, but he shook his head and nipped at her ear. She tilted her head and he slowly kissed down her neck, his hands now firmly gripping her hips. She gestured at the loft door, words unable to form as his teeth grazed her skin.

"Door's locked," he murmured into her neck. "Didn't need interruption while we talked. No one can get up here right now."

All excuses gone, she grabbed the hem of his shirt and pulled it out of his jeans, hastily fumbling with his belt. She wanted him inside her, *now*. No foreplay, no slow and sensual; she was desperate for the connection, wanting him with a fierceness she recognized had been there from the beginning.

He helped her push his jeans down his thighs, and he grasped for the buttons on hers, while she sent her boots flying with quick tugs, kicking them away. His fingers hooked into the waist of her jeans and underwear, stripping them down her legs. Cold pebbled the skin on her thighs as the denim bunched under her feet, the hay prickling her ass, but she didn't care. Her sole focus was on him, in front of her, the heat from his skin against hers all that mattered.

She reached for him and wrapped a hand around his cock, stroking quickly up and down, the feel of him hard in her hand a thrill. That was for *her*. His deep groan of relief as he hardened more at her touch threaded arousal up through her stomach, and her core throbbed in response.

"Now. Please. I need you," she begged, and his eyes opened to her, the fire in them pouring back. He pushed her other hand toward her, entwining their fingers, his eyes widening as they slid inside her together.

"You are so wet for me already, oh my god," he groaned, as their fingers slid in and out, his curling over hers and sending shocks of pleasure up through her. She thought her eyes might roll into the back of her head as his thumb reached up and pressed on her clit at the same time.

"I don't have a—" he stuttered as she moaned and squeezed his cock. She shook her head, and somehow managed to hook one heel around his waist, leaning back, balancing on her tiptoes and grinding her hips against their joined hands.

"Don't. Care. I want you. Just you. No more . . . barriers," she panted, the familiar swirl of imminent climax catching her breath. She wanted him, and only him, the perfection of him erasing any doubt.

The moment she said it, he pulled their hands from her and reached to lift her hips to meet his, holding her with a ferocity that she *really* liked. His mouth covered hers as he braced her against the edge of a bale sticking out from the stack. She wrapped her arms around his neck, her legs wound around his waist, and cried out into his mouth as he thrust into her to the hilt. Undone, she moved against him, wanting him to fill her over and over. She wondered if it would always feel like this, this sense of completion when he was inside her. She acknowledged it and let herself feel it, feel *him*.

"Liz," he breathed as he held her still, sweat sprouting on his forehead. "You are so fucking hot and tight right now. I won't last. I—"

"Let go, Jake," she growled. "Show me how it feels."

He pulled out almost all the way, and his eyes met hers as he drove into her over and over, his muscles rock hard with the effort. He was so deep, so utterly entwined with her, and she grappled for his shoulders to hold on, his efforts moving the entire stack of hay bales behind them. She briefly wondered if it would topple, her back rubbing against the spiked ends of the bales, her shirt rucked up.

"I can feel you, Liz. You're so close, and you feel so fucking good. Come for me," he gasped, his breath hot against her ear.

She stopped caring about the haystack or if her skin was getting scratched to heck, as an orgasm took over her entire body with his words and his next thrust into her. Ripples of pleasure flew over her skin when she exploded, his knowing smile into her neck replaced by teeth as she shook.

He was going to come too. She could sense it, the tightening of his hands, the uplift in his thrust, the guttural, deep moans as he took his pleasure. He slowed down, gritting his teeth.

"Don't stop. I want you to come like this," she whispered, digging her fingernails into his shoulders.

"Oh god, Liz. I'm going to . . . I need to pull out," he gasped.

"I want to feel you come. Damn the consequences. Come inside me."

He leaned back enough to look into her eyes, and she met them, completely and utterly certain about her impulsive decision. Damn the consequences indeed, because she wasn't ready to let him go, wanted to feel how he felt, breathe with him, shake with him.

"Are you sure?" he asked, attempting control as she squeezed him from inside. "Goddamn it, Liz I'm going to fucking explode right now if you say yes because, damn it, I—"

"Yes. Fuck, yes, Jake. Fill me," she begged, and he pushed her back, holding her tight, nose to nose with her, eyes boring into hers as he emptied himself into her, his back muscles rippling, his hips tight against her as he came.

"You are so perfect, I fucking need you," he growled as he thrust into her once more, rendering her boneless as another orgasm took hold of her, stronger than the last one, this one fueled by the declaration between them.

She collapsed against the hay, utterly defenseless as he gently set her down, sliding out of her, the result of their lovemaking wet against her inner thighs. He leaned along her length, kissing her gently, hands stroking her hair, and she held his face in her hands as more tears made their way down her cheeks.

She was in love, and she wasn't scared. Letting go, letting him in, had released some sort of seal. The emotional response was overwhelming her.

"What is it?" he asked, concerned, peering into her face. "What?"

"I fucking need you too. Which is insane and—" She sniffled, unsure of how to explain what was bouncing around in her body.

He blinked, taken off guard, and wrapped her in his arms, effectively silencing her. Their heads bent into each other's necks, wrapping all the emotion into an embrace that would hold them together in the face of what they had said. As their breathing settled and the heat of what they'd just done slowly dissipated into the breeze coming from the open window, she checked in with herself.

He had said he needed her, and it was okay. Where it went from here, she didn't know. As he'd said, they'd cross that bridge when they got to it. Together.

He released her from his arms and stooped to pick up his jeans, still wrapped around his ankles. She smiled at him as she hopped back into her pants and wiggled a little as she did up the buttons. He side-eyed her as she did, and ran a hand over her butt, smacking it. "I like these jeans on you, they're tight," he said.

She laughed, which felt damned good, easing the pressure in her chest and giving her a shot of energy as she tiptoed over the floor to find her boots, which were halfway across the loft where they'd been thrown. The heavy was over. Now they could move on and just go with whatever this ended up being. Which was pretty fucking serious, almost as if they'd said that *L* word.

Which they had, indirectly, maybe. *Holy shit.*

"Your mom ordered pizza. Wanna go eat?" he asked, holding out a hand when she finished pulling her boots back on. She nodded and took it, picking hay out of her hair as they walked to the door.

CHAPTER THIRTY-THREE

A week later

"Hang on, Frank, I can barely hear you," Jake yelled into his phone. He was managing to hold the phone to his ear in one hand, the reins of the horse he was on in the other. He made a face at Liz, who was laughing as she moved her horse back over to him. Wordlessly, she gestured, and he handed his reins over so she could hold his horse for him.

"I said I have some ideas I want to run past you," Frank repeated into the phone. "Where the heck are you?"

Where was he? In the middle of fucking nowhere, on a horse, the wind whipping around them, the sun out in full force. He and Liz had decided to play hooky today, get on some horses, and ride into the foothills at the very back of the ranch.

That, and have hot, loud, uninhibited sex under a massive old tree overlooking the path down to a valley. Perks of being the boss, he supposed.

Jake winked, throwing a grin at Liz. "I'm on a horse, Frank, if you can believe it. Out for a ride with a beautiful woman," he replied, and Liz rolled her eyes at him, catching the innuendo.

"Well, then, I won't keep you. Call me when you have your own two feet firmly planted again." Frank laughed and ended the call before Jake could say another word.

Jake stuffed his phone into his jacket pocket and took the reins back from Liz, who was now giving him that look that said if he didn't spill, she'd kill him. Her mother had much the same look.

"Frank. Has some news, I think," Jake said. "I'll call him when we're back at the stable."

"So we need to get back, then?" she replied.

"Yeah. Should maybe have the guys in on the call if it's good news."

He sobered at that, and so did Liz. She clucked at her horse and started back. There was the rub; they were both now thinking. If it was a way out of this mess, then it meant he might be able to go home.

Which was no longer an easy decision.

The past week had been some of the best days of his life, and as they started back down the trail between two fields, he sank back into the saddle and looked around him at the open field, the swaying pine trees, and the dotted shadows of clouds as they floated east.

The biggest change was with Tanner. Jake had finally connected with his brother, the resentment easing now that they'd figured one another out. Tanner was still on edge, but it was a good start toward them becoming friends. Jake had even bought and strung up a punching bag in an unused corner of the cattle barn and was showing Tanner how to actually throw a punch.

Tanner had invited him to the local auction out of the blue two days before, introducing him to some of the other ranchers in the area, including him without reservation when they'd sat in the stands beside Harry and watched the lots go through. Tanner had patiently explained to Jake what they looked for, what was necessary to put cattle through a sale. Jake only caught about half of it, taking in the noise of the mooing cattle, the shouting from the spotters when a bid was raised, the auctioneer droning on in a nasal, rapid singsong that he couldn't even begin to understand. Harry had explained more of it when Tanner had left to see to the lot they'd put through.

He'd understood even less of it after that.

And just last night, Tanner had been laughing his head off when Liz had sassed back at Jake about something. Tanner. Laughing so hard he had to hold his stomach.

Jake didn't think it was possible.

Tanner was slowly coming out of the fog he'd wrapped around himself when his father had died, and it was easing everyone's minds and stress levels. No more walking on eggshells, even if he was still a temperamental grumpy ass more often than not.

The relief of his relationship with his brother meant he had dived headfirst into learning, and he was googling and reading, often falling asleep on Liz's couch, laptop open to articles about something ranch related, like cattle feed requirements or birthweight ratios.

All the fresh air, the space, the quiet, was becoming more and more normal. Life was simpler here, easier, more about what truly mattered. It was getting harder to remember the noise of the city, the horns and people everywhere you turned. The stink of overflowing dumpsters in back alleys emanating onto the streets; the rude, loud, harried strangers brushing past you without a care.

Country life was growing on him.

He hadn't missed the late nights and stress of a dinner rush either. Gordon was enjoying his new job in Manhattan, and his other former staffers were all working again. The urge to hustle and put a team together wasn't there as he got up in the mornings and made coffee while the sun came up and the rest of the ranch woke up around him. The need to stay relevant and in the know wasn't pressing on him as he picked fresh vegetables from the garden for that night's meal.

Running a restaurant for strangers was less appealing every day the crew thanked him for the food when he delivered it to the main barns and dug in like they were starving. Here, he was feeding people who mattered and truly appreciated simplicity. He certainly wasn't flourishing perfectly plated meals out to critics, but the validation he got from one of the men closing their eyes and sighing as they bit into a from-scratch panini? That resonated in him much more than any starred review ever would.

Who he was had changed.

He looked over at Liz, who was quiet and serious, her smile gone. *Damn it.* He wished Frank hadn't called at all.

She was the other side of the equation.

Time with her had solidified how he felt, which meant this news could be . . . Well, he didn't want to think about that right now and ruin the afternoon they had just spent. One where he'd laid her down in some long grass on a blanket and made slow love, the cicadas singing in their ears, the sun hot on their skin, abandoning restraint in the novelty of sex outside, where they were completely alone.

The scent of her was still on him, and he adjusted himself in the saddle as he thought about how erotic it was to have her laid back and spread before him, his head buried between her legs. He had nearly lost himself when she had threaded her fingers into his hair and screamed, the birds in the tree taking off squawking, indignant at the noise disturbing their peace.

He urged Sandy up beside her. "Hey, we'll cross that bridge, right?" he said to get her attention.

"Right. Let's shake a leg, then," she replied, and clucked to her horse, picking up a lope, avoiding the elephant in the room, which had now joined them. He did the same, and they headed off, the stables just in view across the pasture.

* * *

They were all in the dining room, Jake's phone on speaker as he dialed Frank.

"Frank here. Jake, back on the ground?"

"Sure am. Got Tanner and Brady, Liz and Peony in here with me. What's your news?"

Brady was sipping a steaming cup of tea, Peony sitting across from him, her hands wrapped around hers. She was watching Liz, who was chewing her fingernails and pacing.

Tanner was leaning on a wall, arms crossed as usual, not wanting to sit when there was serious business to deal with.

"I have been through every inheritance and property lawyer here in Calgary and that will is ironclad, folks. But I did some thinking on some of those clauses," Frank said, and they heard the rustling of paper on the other end of the line.

"Remember that loophole you mentioned about makin' someone an animal charity so they could buy the place, which was the stipulation if you tried to sell it? Why not do that?"

"That would change the business to a nonprofit, wouldn't it? This place runs incorporated right now, Frank. Not sure how we'd be able to make a living and have staff the way we do if we can't make money," Jake answered automatically.

"Uh-huh," Tanner grunted. "Be a might difficult to untangle the business the way it runs now."

"Now, hold on, not done here," Frank interjected. "We could set Tanner up as the nonprofit, and he buys it back, runs as that for a bit and then folds, renewing the business. It's been done before. As long as you report up and up to the government, it should be fine."

Jake tensed, sensing everyone else in the room doing the same. That would be a huge change, one his brother would likely veto outright. He cleared his throat, and Peony interjected before he could say anything.

"Let's think about it. That line from that damned will stated that if one of the boys did try to buy it, it would go on the market for charity, for a buck. There's nothing in there that says they can't buy it then, is there?" Peony said, immediately picking up on Frank's idea, surprising Jake. She must have been looking into things on her own, because she winked at Jake and took a sip of her tea.

"No, ma'am," Frank said curtly.

"So they do that, and Tanner can buy it for that loonie, providing he's set up as an animal rescue, not a nonprofit. Seems simple enough," she added.

"Right," Frank replied. "That's a whole different thing—"

"I know you can make that work. Tanner could revert to a full-on business after a certain amount of time, or not, depending on how the rescue is set up," Peony interrupted, her eyes sharpening, leaning forward toward the phone.

"What do you mean, or not?" Jake asked curiously. He and Liz shared a look, but she shrugged, obviously not in on what her mother had been looking into.

"I was thinking this. There is nothing saying that the charity has to be a nonprofit. You can run charities as a corporation. Look at all those racehorse rescues. They make a killing bringing in stock and reselling as riding horses. As long as you can prove you're doing the work and can show capital expenditures, it's all above board," Peony stated, her eyes roving to each of them in turn.

"Peony, you've been busy! I hadn't thought of that." Frank chuckled. "I knew Brett married a smart woman. I'll look into that, too, see what I can dig up."

Peony laughed, leaning back into her chair, her eyes sparkling, and Jake unclenched his jaw. It wouldn't be easy—the paperwork alone would bury them—and it seemed a little harebrained, but it might just work.

If everyone agreed to it.

"All right then. An interesting idea. Might just be the ticket to solve this mess and revert it back to Tanner, and Brady, too, of course?" Jake asked.

Brady sighed and leaned back, furrowing his forehead as his name was spoken.

No one had brought up who they thought his father was, but Jake had an inkling Peony and Liz knew and were staying mum. Eventually they would have to figure that dilemma out, but he was in no hurry to add new drama when things were just starting to settle.

Brady had sworn up and down that he didn't want to be on the paperwork when the ranch was handed back over. He and Tanner had yelled at one another for a while about that one. But in the end, Brady had backed down from Tanner's stubborn refusal to consider him any less of a West than before the paternity tests.

"Unless Brett had some other paperwork stashed away in his files or personal belongings, it would be more of a headache than it was worth. Has anyone looked?"

"We checked his personal study and found nothing. Maybe we'll do another pass through the house just in case, but we've already been at this for weeks, it probably isn't anything that would help even if we did find something," Jake replied, and Frank *hmm*ed on the other end of the phone.

"Fair enough. Let me know if you find anything, I can vet it to see, like life insurance policies or deeds. Otherwise, this is it. If this idea of Peony's doesn't work, there would have to be lawsuits brought against you and the ranch if you wanted to contest it, and that could get expensive. You've all had enough stress, especially with the mess of those thieves you caught on top of all this. I would advise against it. Could mire the ranch in liens and such for years," Frank added.

"What do I have to do to do all this rescue bullshit?" Tanner blurted suddenly.

"Not sure. I'll investigate that, of course," Frank replied. "Don't worry about it on your end yet. Decide first if this is in the best interest of the family, then we'll dive into the details."

Jake could sense his brother was struggling with that the entire notion. It would shutter the generational business, but it would keep the ranch in the hands of who was supposed to run it, which was Tanner. That Tanner had asked meant he was considering it despite his reluctance.

"We'll figure it out, but let's decide if that is the best thing first," Jake replied, catching Tanner's eye as he looked up. "We'll make sure the ranch transfers back into the hands of a West."

Tanner let out a big huff, shook his head and glared at Jake. "It already is," he growled, and then paced out of the room, shoving his hat back on his head.

"Tan, hold on, you—" Brady shouted at his brother's retreating back and then let out a resigned sigh. "He's so fucking stubborn."

"I take it you folks need some time to think this through," Frank interrupted. "I'll send you some of the reading I've done, Jake. Peony, can you share what you've found with me?"

"Of course, dear. You should come for a visit next time, you hear?" she replied.

Jake half heard the end of the conversation, turning away to look out the window at the back gardens. Late summer flowers were in full bloom. He could just see the heads of the tall dill plant starting to bud in bright yellow, and he sighed, running a hand over his head.

Liz handed him his phone and put her arms around his waist, looking out with him.

"Think he'll do it?" she asked.

"Tanner deserves to be on the title, but he needs to want to change the way we operate on a fundamental level, so he's gotta decide." Jake sighed. "That is what all this is about, right? Making sure Brett's legacy stays with his sons."

Liz went quiet, and he turned as she detached herself from him and fiddled with the drape beside the window. She was frowning, her thinking face on, and he touched her shoulder on impulse. She looked upset. He could guess why.

"The thing is, Jake, Brett's legacy is intact the way things are now," she murmured as she pushed at the fabric impatiently.

"How? With me? It isn't supposed to be me!" Jake replied. "I'm not—"

"Not what, Jake? A West? You damned well are! Not entitled to one blade of grass on this property? Bullshit. I . . . I—"

Liz exploded, her hands flying, tears filling her eyes, and she stomped past him in a flurry of mad, out the same way Tanner had gone a few minutes before. He stared after her, not quite sure what to say.

Peony put her hand on his arm as she passed him on her way to the kitchen and he looked at her imploringly. "Now what do I do?"

"She's right, you know," Peony remarked, and hummed at him, her eyebrows raised. "You fit here, young man. You fit with her too. It wouldn't be the end of the world if this all stayed the way it was. But it's your choice Jake, just as much as it is Tanner's."

Peony patted him gently on the arm and made her way past him, leaving him alone by the window.

"Oh my god, this family," he muttered under his breath, before stretching his tense shoulders and following her in.

CHAPTER THIRTY-FOUR

Tanner was sitting on the open tailgate of Liz's truck when she left the house, wiping at her eyes. She stopped in front of him, and he patted the metal beside him.

"Up you get, Lizzie."

She hefted herself onto the tailgate beside him and slouched against the side of the truck box.

"So?" she asked simply, focusing on him rather than the giant question of Jake staying or going. "You gonna become a tree hugger and rescue cougar kittens so you can get this place back?"

He snorted a laugh and leaned back, looking at her from under the brim of his hat. He didn't look mad, which she was glad to see, but he did look like he'd been thinking. Hard.

"I don't know. It's a lot to try to understand. You know I have no head for the numbers side of this place," he replied.

"No, you don't, but it doesn't mean you can't learn, you know," she teased. He frowned.

Tanner liked being the hands-on guy. Spreadsheets, paperwork, accountants—it made him break into a cold sweat whenever he had to buckle into that chair in his office and fire up the old computer. He could organize the work, keep schedules, and knew the cattle inside and out, but balance sheets, bills, and banking? He avoided it whenever possible or wheedled her and Brady into helping.

"We could always hire a business manager," Liz hinted. Tanner would squirm at the mention of adding staff, and they already had one with Jake. But if he didn't stay, they'd have to think about it. Liz had no idea if they were solvent; Jake hadn't mentioned anything about financials being dire. All the same, securing a salary for a full-time office person would put a dent in their operating costs, she at least knew that.

"Not the right time, not with all this up in the air," he confirmed, and sighed. "But you're right. I do hate it. Not like Jake. He's a natural at keeping up with the books."

"He's run a few restaurants, I think," she replied dryly, trying not to think about Jake running a restaurant, and not here.

"What if he stayed?"

Liz blinked in shock as she gaped at Tanner. He was looking out at the main road, squinting, the corners of his eyes wrinkled up. He glanced over at her and huffed out a laugh.

"What?" he asked.

Liz let out a strangled noise of exasperation. "Damn it, Tan, you just about made me fall over. Stay? *You* want him to stay?"

Tanner adjusted his hat on his head and hopped off the back of the truck. He turned, hands in his pockets and leveled her a look that was pure West grit.

"I mean it, Liz, what if he stays? What if he's the West who's supposed to run this damned place and Dad knew it? Lets us keep our hands in the dirt. Do what we're good at."

With that, he turned and walked away. Trademark Tanner-last-word antics. He was whistling as he made his way to the barns, his hands still in his pockets. Almost like a weight had been lifted.

"Tanner, wait—" she called after him, but he just waved and disappeared down the path.

Of all people to suggest it, that it was him and not Brady was a small miracle. Liz sat back and closed her eyes for a moment, still processing his statement when the truck jostled. Brady hoisted himself up beside her, right on cue.

"Tanner looks happy. What'd you say to him?" he asked, his tone light.

"He, well—" she stuttered, gesturing, not sure what to say. "He suggested that Jake stay on, even said that he should be the one running this place. If I didn't know better, I'd say he was drunk again, but—"

Brady burst out laughing, his head back, his eyes shut tight. It got Liz going, and in moments the two of them were howling, holding their stomachs.

Brady put his arm around Liz once he'd gotten himself back under control. She leaned into him, thankful once again for these men who had adopted her as one of their own all those years ago. Tanner for his no-nonsense work ethic and decision-making, Brady for his spirit and sense of humor. Both of them buffers from Brett, there when she needed a hand. If not for them, she'd have thrown in the towel long ago.

Jake had remarked that they made a good team when they had gone out for that ride. They did. Jake was part of that now, too, whether he wanted to be or not. She had already considered him so, and apparently now Tanner did too.

"Of all people," he said through his laughter, then sobered a bit. "But he's right, you know. It could work. Jake has to want it, though. He's not from here, not a rancher. He's a chef. A damned good one. Shouldn't he be doing that?"

Liz hung her head, all the levity from a moment ago sucked out of her in that statement, like air escaping a balloon. Brady was right, damn him. Jake needed to be where his career was. Which was not running a ranch in Alberta. It was running fancy restaurants in New York City, cooking for millionaires and celebrities.

Brady squeezed her and then let her go as he stood. "I know. If he stays? Holy hell, that would be awesome. But if he goes, we gotta be okay with that too."

"No. I don't," Liz grumbled, and jumped down, slamming the tailgate closed, her eyes filling with tears yet again. "I don't gotta be okay with it, Brady. Because, damn it—"

She let out a sob and his arms were around her again, this time comforting her as she attempted to get control over herself. She was entirely too emotional for her own good right now, bouncing in and out of moods like a damned tennis ball thrown from the roof.

"Fuck," she warbled, through tears. "Mom warned me about this. I—"

"Mmmm, ya think? She does have some experience with West men, maybe?" he replied, and gave her a squeeze. "I'm sorry, Liz. I shouldn't have said anything."

Liz wiped at her eyes and stepped away from Brady. "No, it's okay. Shitty as it is, it's reality, and I walked into it with my eyes wide open, right?"

"And your heart too. You love him," Brady stated, eyeballing her.

She nodded and he grinned widely, gesturing out with his hands. "Then tell him and see what happens, you big stupid marshmallow!" he exclaimed, and pulled her under his arm while they walked toward the stables.

Would it be enough to make Jake stay? She didn't want to put him in that position. What if he did? Would he resent her over time? All her doubts and worries crept in as she and Brady walked.

She had no doubts about how Jake felt—they'd said as much in the hayloft, he'd shown her in the following days. But was it enough to make him change his entire world for her, and this place? Feelings were one thing, but life was more than just feelings and desires. It had to be more than just love to make it all work.

"Stop thinking so hard," Brady admonished as they reached the stable door. "Just take it one day at a time right now. Nothing's been decided. I think Tan needs to have a sit-down with New York and see where his head's at."

"And you. You're part of this as well."

Brady frowned and stopped, leaning against the bars of a stall. He looked away from her and she reached out to touch him, to reassure him. This was another wrinkle in the entire drama that they'd been living through.

"Brett wasn't my father. I have no claim to this place," he said tiredly.

"Brady," Liz intoned. "You do, and that is ridiculous. You grew up here, Brett gave you his name, you were his son, even if he knew—"

"Knew what?" Brady blurted, his voice tight.

Liz met his eyes, unsure of what she should say or not say. He needed to process this on his own schedule, but should she say something? It might make things more complicated if she was wrong.

"Even if he knew you weren't his, or knew whose you were," she replied finally. "He raised you anyway."

Brady let out a frustrated sigh. "You know what? I don't care."

She shook his shoulder, and he looked back to her once more. "You do care," she murmured quietly. "And you'll figure it out."

Brady thinned his lips, his face betraying his normal happy attitude, and adjusted the beat-up ball cap on his head. She waited for him to say something, but when he stayed silent, she quickly leaned in and impulsively pecked him on the cheek.

"Let's get back to work," she said. Maybe now was not the right time to send him off by himself to tinker. The look in his eye all but gave away that his gears were turning. She handed him a fork and tilted her head toward a stall.

"Need a hand in the stable?" he said, catching on.

"Anytime," she replied. They all had some heavy decisions to make, and she did some of her best thinking while cleaning a stall.

And she had a *lot* of thinking to do.

Jake and Tanner were on their own for dinner.

Liz had stayed at the barn late to catch up on month-end invoicing, and Peony had gone into town to eat with friends. The house was strangely quiet, which Jake decided wasn't unwelcome.

He and his brother had slapped together sandwiches standing side by side at the kitchen counter, unceremoniously eating them over scrounged-up Christmas napkins to catch the crumbs.

Jake learned that he and Tanner both had an aversion to sliced tomatoes on sandwiches. When Tanner had made a particularly awful face at Jake handing him a tomato to slice, they had laughed at the similarity, and the tomato had gone back into the fridge.

Brady had texted Tanner to eat without him, and Jake wondered if today had reignited the hurt Brady felt about not being a true West.

"He okay, you think?" Jake asked as he fired his balled-up napkin at the paper garbage bin at the side of the kitchen. Tanner had poured them each a beer, and Jake picked his up, watching the light bounce off the glass onto the counter like a reverse shadow, wavering across the polished stone.

"Dunno. He said he needed some space. When Brady needs space, I give it to him; he doesn't ask for it often," Tanner replied, and leaned back against the island.

Jake worried the glass a bit, then took a large pull. It tasted good after the day they had had, which had started out with making love to Liz in a field and ended with him and his family wrestling with a solution to what had brought him here in the first place.

The decisions he and Tanner were going to have to make were

clouding his brain. It was hard to think about what to do when he was so confused about what it was he truly wanted.

"So I'm thinkin' about what Frank offered," Tanner said. Jake looked up at him and set his glass down.

"All right," Jake said slowly. "And?"

"I don't know if I've got what it takes to run this place like some animal rescue. I mean, it's been a cattle and horse ranch for as long as it's been owned by a West. If we gotta fold that to run some sort of foundation just so I can own it—"

Tanner stopped speaking and leveled his gaze at Jake, unwavering. That was one of the longest speeches he'd heard from Tanner without a swear word thrown in. It seemed he was having doubts about Peony's idea.

No matter what, they needed to talk it out. Jake had wondered how to broach the subject with him all evening, considering Tanner wasn't the most talkative man on the planet. One-word answers and a razor-thin temper were not ideal for discussing big things like this, and tonight had been relatively easy, just the two of them.

Tanner was calm and seemed in control of what he was thinking and saying, so Jake tilted his head and made some assumptions about what Tanner had indicated with that statement, furrowed brow and all.

"Are you saying you don't want to do that?" he asked carefully.

Tanner gestured at him and sighed. "I'm sayin' that you are doin' a good job learnin' and runnin' the business end. With a bit of experience, getting through this fall's weaning, and Brady to help through next spring's plant, you'd be fine to run this place for the year Dad put in the will."

"You think so?" Jake asked, honestly shocked at his brother's compliment. That had been hard won, and he wondered if it was his resistance to change and worry for the simple survival of the ranch that was pushing Tanner to keep things the same, or if indeed that was a genuine compliment on Jake's ability to muddle through an entirely new industry.

That fear of change had put them on the wrong foot at the beginning. Now that they had figured each other out, and the world hadn't imploded without his name on the deed, maybe Tanner was having a change of heart?

"I do," Tanner added and took a sip of his own beer, then tipped the glass in Jake's direction. "You've got a head for this. You're—"

Tanner swallowed the last of his beer instead of finishing the sentence. He looked away from Jake, thinned his lips as if trying to decide what to say, and then blurted, "Dad would have liked you."

Jake bowed his head, absorbing the impact of that statement. Tanner had no idea what those words meant to him. It was profound, at least from this side of the conversation. Since Tanner didn't do platitudes, he took it at face value.

All this time Jake's identity had been the one given to him by his mother, his environment, his upbringing. He'd fashioned a view of who he was from the knowledge that he wasn't wanted by his father. That bit of his personality, the awkwardness of becoming a man without that influence? It was a huge part of him.

Now, coming here, finding his roots, learning that his father had searched, getting a taste for another way to live . . . it had shattered that perception of himself into a thousand pieces.

Maybe he was afloat and looking for that connection so he could reimagine who he was now that his father was gone and reconciliation wasn't possible. But Jake already knew he wasn't afloat anymore.

With everything that had happened, Tanner's words weren't validation for him to find himself, they were confirmation of who he had become in the short time he'd been here.

This place, Liz, his brothers, these were the missing pieces that had dogged him. Tanner's certainty that Jake fit into this world was not a reinvention, it was filling in the gaps.

"I don't know what to say to that," Jake answered finally.

Tanner *hmm*ed as he crossed the kitchen and rummaged across the key rack at the door to the mudroom. It held dozens and dozens of keys, mostly for farm vehicles and buildings; some looked like they hadn't moved in years. Tanner came up with one on an amber-colored polished rock fob, palmed it, and gestured to the back of the house.

"This is for Dad's war room. Peony told me you looked in it for paperwork. Let's go take another look. I keep feeling like we're missin' something."

CHAPTER THIRTY-FIVE

Jake drained his beer and followed Tanner as he strode through the house to the back. Tanner stopped in front of the door and examined the key. Jake resisted the urge to pull the key from over the door and be a smartass. Tanner obviously didn't know about it, and Jake sensed he needed to let his brother have this moment to process what they were doing without him trying to lighten the mood.

"Dad would never let us go in here. I remember once he left the door cracked and I peeked in. I think I was what, seven? He was sittin' at the desk, writing in a book, papers piled up on the desk, *Jeopardy!* blaring on the TV. He yelled at me to get the hell out."

"You never went in, even if he wasn't in here?"

"He was that kind of mad you don't mess with. It scared me so I never did it again. If me or Brady even thought about tryin' to go in, the threat of what he'd do kept us honest."

Tanner inserted the key into the doorknob. He turned it with a *click* that echoed through the quiet house, and both men looked at one another at the sound. Tanner gestured in the doorway to him.

"He can't yell now, can he?" he said, and Jake chuckled. No indeed, he couldn't.

Tanner fumbled for the light switch as they entered the tiny room, and the lamps lit the interior. It was just as imposing as it was when he'd been in here with Peony, the stale cigar smell, the old furniture, the presence of his father looming in the air.

"I didn't know what to expect," Tanner said as he stepped in, and his eyebrows rose. "Thirty years ago, time stopped in this room."

"Maybe he liked it this way. It was familiar, comfortable. The rest of the house is a showpiece, you know," Jake said.

Tanner *hmph*ed and gave Jake a look. "You're not wrong. Dad renovated the entire place after Mom died, but I guess he didn't want them touching his space. He didn't like change much."

No kidding. Like father, like son, Jake thought.

They stood just inside the door, neither of them moving into the room. Tanner obviously needed a moment, turning in place, eyes moving from one thing to another.

"We didn't find anything in the desk, but I didn't look too closely at the bookshelf. Maybe there's something there?" Jake said finally, restless. "Peony looked a bit, but I think it overwhelmed her when we were in here."

"Hard for her maybe, being where he wouldn't let anyone else in, not even his wife," Tanner said, looking around, and his eyes landed on the throw across the back of the desk chair. "Hey, we had tons of those when I was a kid, all packed away in the back of the big linen closet in the hall. Mom gave 'em all to Peony and Liz the day they moved into the bunkhouse. Said they were ugly and needed gone. Must've missed one."

"My mother made those," Jake said. "I recognized the pattern when I saw it before. Maybe Dad rescued it as a reminder of her?"

"He was never sentimental like that, but who knows anymore." Tanner grunted and turned to the bookshelf, cracking his knuckles. "There's some binders on the end, let's check those."

He and Jake pulled each of the dozen or so hard-backed blue binders off the shelf one by one, leafing through random pages. Jake found invoices from private detectives, neatly ordered and stamped PAID. Brett's ranch paperwork was a mess, but in here everything was filed neatly, in order, years and years of fees and expenses, reports typed out, carbon copies of missing person reports slowly fading purple. It was like two different men had inhabited the same place.

"Is this all from him looking for you?" Tanner asked, thumbing through grainy photocopies of pictures, notes and lists of what looked to be names in an old phone book.

"Maybe? I have no idea. Peony told me he did. Found me two years or so ago, from what he told her."

Tanner closed the binder in his hands with a thump. "There's nothing in here," he snapped, obviously frustrated, and shoved it back onto the shelf. It wouldn't go in all the way, and frowning, he gave it another push. "Come on," he hissed.

"Hang on, there's something blocking it," Jake said, and fished in behind it.

A small notebook appeared, the black cover scratched and worn on the corner, a crumbling blue Tropicana banana elastic holding it closed.

Jake opened it to a list of what looked to be number codes running down the first page. They were in date format but truncated with dashes, almost like combinations.

"What the hell is that?" Tanner muttered.

"Safe combinations," Jake muttered, and his head shot up to the painting on the exterior wall opposite the bookshelf. It was a print of the famous *Cowboy* painting by Frederic Remington. Very appropriate for the décor of the room.

He strode over to it and carefully lifted it off the wall.

Nothing behind it but some cobwebs and a rusty hook. "No safe," he muttered.

"Mom bought that print for him. It used to hang in our living room," Tanner remarked. "Maybe the safe isn't in this room? I have no idea where it would be, though. Back den?"

"I bet it's here, we just haven't seen it yet." Jake scanned the room again, hoping they'd find something to validate his hunch. His brother was right. More fucking secrets that his father had been hiding. Like a scavenger hunt but with no clues.

Tanner started tapping the exterior walls, and Jake tapped his foot along the floor. Nothing echoed back to them, and after a few minutes, Tanner gave up, his hands on his hips, frowning.

"Would there be a safe in the master bedroom maybe?" Jake asked, his own frustration growing. This was a wild goose chase. He looked down at the book in his hands, the numbers scrawled in faded pen, the pages yellowing.

"Peony would know about it if so. She's cleaned every inch of this house for years. It wouldn't have gone unnoticed."

Tanner turned, eyes roving over the bookshelves, and strode over behind the desk. "There, maybe?" he said and pointed to the middle of the bookshelf nearest the desk.

A piece of stained paneling that matched the color of the shelves covered an entire section. A cover in plain sight. Jake joined him and grasped it with his fingertips, and with some wiggling managed to loosen the panel. Sure enough, underneath it was a black iron safe with a combination dial.

"What's the last line on that list?" Tanner asked, and Jake thumbed a few pages in to find it.

"07-15-96."

"Brady's birthday, huh," Tanner remarked. He spun the dial and then stepped through the numbers Jake read out, one ear cocked to it, turning it slowly as it clicked.

The door sprang open slightly, and they both stood back, looking at one another.

"Here goes nothing," Jake said, and opened the door all the way. A pile of envelopes and various file folders were stacked neatly inside, along with a couple of beaten-up cigar boxes. On top of that, a 5 x 7 photo in a polished wooden frame was perched sideways. Jake pulled the photo out first and dusted it off. It showed a young child on a palomino, reins lifted in his hands, too-big cowboy hat on his head. The child looked like he was laughing, and the man whose hand was clamped around his waist was grinning, a cigar clenched on one side of his mouth.

Jake studied the picture. That looked like his dad, but he couldn't be sure.

"Who is that?" Jake asked, and tilted the picture so Tanner could see it.

"It's not me or Brady, but that's Dolly and Dad, I'm certain of it. Brady 'n me learned to ride on her, so did Liz when she got here," Tanner said.

"Dolly, the ancient blind pony in the shaded pen at the front of the stable?"

"Yep. I've never known this place without her," he replied. "She's earned her retirement and then some."

"How old is that horse?" Jake muttered, and looked at the picture again. A sudden hope that it was him, the one remembrance his father had hung on to before his mother had left, flitted through, but the picture looked too old, and he would've remembered that, wouldn't he?

"Maybe there's something written on the back. Dad used to do that to all the pictures we'd put up from rodeo wins and stuff."

Jake pried off the backing, and Brett's spiky handwriting appeared in faded black ink.

"'Henry on Dolly, Spring 1993,'" Tanner read.

"Who's Henry?" Jake asked, disappointed. It wasn't him, but it was really odd that *this* was the photo his father had decided to keep in a safe.

"No fucking idea," Tanner muttered.

Jake set the picture aside and reached in again, pulling out all the off-white file folders. Several envelopes slid out, and on each, in Brett's trademark spiky cursive, were names. One for each of them. Tanner, Brady, and Jake.

A smaller one, more the size of a greeting card, slid out between them, and had Liz's full name on it. Tanner peered back into the safe, and then fished farther back, producing two more. One for Peony and one for Jake's mother, Heather, which was wrinkled and slightly yellow with age.

"What have we found?" Tanner murmured, looking at them.

They were standing in silence, staring down at the envelopes, when the square of light at the door darkened. Jake looked up over the top of the desk to see Peony was standing there, her hands firmly planted on her hips.

"So you found it. What was that old fox hiding?"

* * *

Liz looked at the letters sitting on the kitchen island counter, lined up in a row. No one had opened them yet. Jake stood, hands in his pockets. Tanner was in the dining room on the phone to Brady.

"You went into Brett's yelling room?" she said, watching Jake as he shifted the letters with his fingers then stuffed his hand back into his pocket. He looked lost, unsure, a bit haunted.

"Yelling room?" Jake asked.

"S'what I called it when I was younger," Liz answered. "Brett would go in there in the evenings, and I'd hear him yelling sometimes. The window faces the side of the house, where our bunkhouse was. I always wondered if he watched sports in there or something so as not to disturb Veronica. Had no idea it was—"

She stopped, realizing it was likely where he'd kept all the information about finding Jake and his mother. Or whatever else he didn't want anyone finding out about. Lord knew what that was, the number of secrets they had uncovered in the past few weeks.

Her mother bustled back in, an armload of something that she dumped onto the counter. It was motley shades of pink, with red splashed in random places. Jake picked it up, thumbing over the stitching.

"Something about a handmade thing gives it value, you know? Even if you don't know who made it right away," she said.

"My mother's sense of style was practical. Didn't matter what it looked like, as long as it did the job," Jake replied, and set it down again. He must have sensed that Liz was confused because he looked up at her and the side of his mouth quirked up.

"My mother made this."

"Ah," Liz replied, and touched the blanket. "This is just like the ones we have out at my place. They're really great in the winter, but I always thought they were, ah—"

"Ugly as fuck? Yes," Jake supplied, and they giggled together.

Peony gave Jake a reprimanding eye for his language, then smiled. "Take it. Yours. It shouldn't be just left to get dustier than it already is. Not everything about Heather's memory is bad, my dear."

Jake nodded and slid it over to one side, the lost look sliding across his face again. Tanner strode back in a moment later, his phone in his hand. He pinched the bridge of his nose and bowed his head.

"Brady okay?" Liz asked.

"He's headed back. Be a half hour or so, he said."

"Where'd he go?" she asked.

"Didn't say. I saw him right before he took off. Stalked out of the stables like he was bein' chased before I caught up to him," Tanner added, leveling his eyes at her, raising one eyebrow.

"Okay, well, I'll go first ,then," Liz exclaimed, hoping to derail that conversation, because she didn't want Tanner to ask if Brady's mood had anything to do with her conversation with him. She was still thinking about what Trevor had said about Brady's real father.

"No point in waiting," she added for good measure.

She picked up the envelope for her, reading her name looped on the front. Her full name. Elizabeth Jaqueline Baker. The one her mother used when she needed to get Liz's attention.

"These are private, Liz, if you want to look at it later, that's okay," Jake said, coming over to her and ducking down to catch her eye. "There's no rush."

Part of her wanted to hurl the damned thing into the garbage unseen. Brett wasn't her father. There had been a small part of her, when her mother had married him, that thought maybe he could become that for her, but it had never really happened, and perhaps that was partly on her for not fully trusting him.

But Brett had always been gruff, like he didn't know what to say or do with a girl, kept her at arm's length. He could reprimand her fine, but there was never any softness sent her way as a kid, and definitely not when she got old enough to argue with.

She didn't hold a grudge against him for that, but it had stung a bit when she'd turned eighteen and he'd given her the keys to the bunkhouse she and her mom had originally lived in. He'd unceremoniously barked that it was time she took care of herself, and that was that. She'd moved out of the spare room that Jake now stayed in, no longer a part of whatever it was they had settled into as a family of five.

"I don't care. Not like he was my dad or anything. Barely put up with me," she muttered, and decided she did want to see what was inside after all, to confirm it. She lifted the flap with her index finger and ripped the envelope open.

A nondescript card with a galloping palomino horse remarkably like Dolly fell onto the counter, and she picked it up, curious. A card?

He must have been well and truly fried when he wrote all these, because the quaintness of the card was unlike the no-nonsense man it was from. She opened it and a folded piece of paper fell out, but the card was blank.

"Want me to read it?" she asked. "I don't mind."

Everyone was silent as she flipped the paper, not unfolding it, just feeling the ominous silence from everyone. She looked at her mother, who was twisting the edge of the blanket she'd brought out for Jake, worriedly biting her lip.

"No," Jake said firmly, flicking his eyes over to her mother, closing his hand over hers holding the paper. "Read it to yourself."

Shit. She stuffed the card and letter back into the envelope, and then reached her hand out to her mother, who grasped it with a firmness she'd not felt from her in months. She pulled her mother into a hug, squeezing her gently. Jake had seen her mother's distress before she had, once again.

"I'm sorry, Mom. Let's sit down later and read them together, okay?"

"Of course, dear," her mother replied, her voice tired and strained. Peony quickly picked up her own letter and stuffed it into the pocket of her cardigan.

"Here. Tanner, can you give Brady his when he comes home? I think we all need to read them in private," Jake stated, and handed Tanner two of the envelopes. Jake had two in his hand—one looked older than the others—and Liz left her mother's side and went to his, sliding her arm around his waist. He immediately tucked her into his side and bent over to kiss the top of her head.

"I'm going to take some time now to read this alone, if that's okay?" he asked her quietly.

"Of course. If you need to talk, just come over, I'll leave the light on and the door unlocked," she replied, and he squeezed her in thanks.

Tanner tapped the letters against the counter and nodded. "Night check, Liz. Let's go."

Liz leaned into Jake a few moments more and kissed him. He held her close, the scent of him echoing into her, and she breathed in as he buried his head into her neck for a moment.

"You okay?" she asked.

"I'm good. If anything, this may answer some big questions for all of us, yeah?" he replied into her neck.

She leaned back a bit, and their eyes met. He smiled and smoothed some of her hair back behind her ear. "Don't worry too much. I'm sure whatever is in here doesn't change anything," he rumbled, and kissed her gently.

Her heart skipped a beat as he let her go. They were alone in the kitchen. Tanner impatiently cleared his throat from the back mud porch, so she reluctantly headed that way as Jake picked up the crocheted blanket and tucked it under his arm.

"Come over if you need me, Jake, I mean it," she said, and he stopped, eyes swiveling to her.

"You already know I do," he said, his voice rough, and then walked out of the room.

She stood a moment more, the words echoing in her head, the implied meaning of them clear.

"I need you too," she whispered, and moved to follow Tanner out the door.

CHAPTER THIRTY-SIX

Jake,

By now, hopefully you're on the ranch and know about your brothers, are owner of your birthright as the eldest of my sons, and have busted into my private study and found the safe. If not, then my wishes were not followed and whatever the situation is, I hope you are at least reading this on West Line soil.

I don't know what to say to you or write to you, but I'll try. For an old man, addled as I am in the head, it doesn't come easy now.

I've never known you as an adult, only held you in my arms as a baby, watched you waddle around in the garden as a tiny boy, and set you on your first horse when you were only as high as my knee. For days all you wanted was to climb back up on that mare, screaming "Dolly! Dolly!" whenever your mother would bring you down to the barn to see us. She never got on with horses despite my cajoling; it was a rare thing when she came to watch us men ride.

You were my pride and joy, my firstborn son, and I was never so full of hope for the future of our home.

But Heather took you from me before I could teach you to be a man. Before I could teach you right from wrong, to read the land, or master a rope. I looked for you for a long time, and I didn't find you until now. She hid you from everyone in our families, disappeared without a trace.

You weren't named Jake when you were born. We named you Henry, after my father, Henry Michael. But your mother registered your birth certificate without me knowing, and you were only ever Jacob Christopher West, hence why I couldn't find you easily, and even then, you never went by your full name. At least she kept your last name the same.

I'm sorry I was never there. I don't know what your life was like, what hardships you endured or didn't. My investigator says you have become a successful man, well-off, live in nice places, and are well liked. You are a businessman like me, and that is solace I can take with me when I go. I read the article in The New Yorker *about you, from a few years ago. My investigator forwarded it to me. It was how we found you, because you looked just like me.*

I would never have expected one of my sons to become a master chef. I'm proud of you nonetheless, because a West always does their best at whatever they do, no exceptions. I just hope you know how to properly cook beef.

I'll never forgive your mother for what she did, leaving like that. I loved her, more than I have ever admitted to, nor did I get the chance to make her an honest woman. Why she left, I can understand. I was a fool, young and stupid, taking her for granted, not understanding what she needed to live out here and be a rancher's wife. I shouldn't have stepped out on her, either. But I did, and I paid the ultimate price. I lost you.

I should have told your brothers about you long before, and I regret that too. I have many regrets as I face the end of my life. You are my biggest.

If you need to go back to the life you have, do it. The will was intended to bring you here, show you what you were meant to be. To apologize for not fighting harder to keep you here, where you should have grown up.

Give the place back to your brother Tanner. He loves this ranch as much as I do, and I know he's likely angry at me for the burden I forced on him when his mother died, then when I dismissed that loyalty by leaving the ranch to you. In the files in that safe is a legal document nullifying the will, if you choose to.

But I hope that you will love this place as I have and stay, be part of the family you should have had. I'd like to think you'll take after me and feel connected to the land as I do, because it is part of you. Always has been.

I didn't know you, son, but I loved you from the moment you were born and I held you in my arms. I only wish I'd had the guts to tell you in person.

Your father,

Brett

Jake wiped his wet cheeks and looked up from the letter in his hands. He was sitting in his father's chair, in the war room, the best place he could think of to read it, in the spot where it was likely written. He looked at the picture from the safe, which he'd put back together and propped on the desk earlier in the evening.

A picture of him, on Dolly, with his father, right before he turned three.

"Holy shit, Dad," he murmured into the empty room, and looked back down at the letter. A letter that answered so many questions but gave him just as many new ones.

He opened the file folder in front of him and carefully pulled out the papers. Sifting through them, he found the documents his father had mentioned immediately.

They reverted ownership, pending Jake and Tanner's signatures, with a space for a lawyer to notarize them. Not Brady, just Tanner. With that omission, it was obvious that Brett knew Brady wasn't his son, and Jake wondered if he could amend that after the fact, because there was no way he wasn't including Brady.

There was also a stipulation that Peony was to stay at the ranch as long as she was able and be cared for by whomever was running the place.

"Well, old man, I won't kick her out, if that's what you're worried about," he remarked, and scanned the document further in case there was anything else he needed to make note of. The corner of an insurance policy peeked out of a yellowed folder marked *Peony*, and he set that to one side. No mention of that in the legal documents at all, so he'd need to do some research. It was a lot to wade through, and he would need some help deciphering it all.

Frank was going to have kittens. All the work he'd done to find a way around the will, and the solution was right here all along.

"Damn it, Dad, why couldn't you just have been straightforward?" he said, and dropped his head into his hands, scanning the papers again. His eyes drooped after a few more minutes of scrutiny, and he looked at his phone. It was well past midnight. He needed sleep, and he needed to get his head straight because tomorrow was going to be a big day.

This letter and the paperwork was his ticket home. Back to New York, back to his old life. He could wash his hands of this place, and it would be an odd, strange tale to tell around the table at parties. But as he folded the files up and set them on the desk in a neat pile, it hit him.

This *was* home.

He sucked in a breath, the declaration in his mind crystal clear as he looked around the dusty office, the last refuge of a man he'd never met, who'd given him something priceless that Jake could never thank him for. If he could, he had absolutely no idea what he'd say, but maybe that didn't matter.

More internal debate on that felt like entirely too much effort, because right now, bed was calling, and he was too emotionally drained to think about it anymore.

He stood up, stretching, and dragged himself out of the study, down the hall, and into his room. The urge to fold himself up in bed with Liz was strong, but it was really late, and because she was up early for work, he didn't want to disrupt her sleep, even though she'd told him to. He also didn't want to end up talking all damned night and be wrecked for tomorrow.

He shucked his jeans and shirt onto the floor and climbed into bed without turning the light on, too tired to brush his teeth or do anything remotely domesticated.

Instead of the normal chilly sheets, his bed was warm, the bedding pushed onto his side. He reached under the piled up covers and found a soft, seminaked body curled up on the other side.

Liz. He reached back behind him and switched on the bedside lamp.

She was asleep, curled in a ball, his mother's crocheted blanket in her arms, her face buried in it, wearing nothing but one of his old New York boxing gym T-shirts and bright-blue underwear with a horseshoe on each butt cheek. She'd been crying, her nose red, her eyes puffy from it. He slid a hand over her hip, and she stiffened.

"Liz," he whispered, glad for her presence and worried all in the same breath. "Liz. It's okay."

She sleepily opened her eyes, and with a tiny whimper threw her arms around him. This was not the no-nonsense woman who could stare down anything in her path. Something in Brett's letter to her must have cracked her right open, otherwise she'd be at her place, asleep. He wrestled the blanket out from between them and pulled her closer, holding her as she curled into him.

"Hey," he whispered as gently as he could. "Sleep. We can talk in the morning."

She sniffled and raised her mouth to his, the need in her gesture shaky and frantic. He relented, kissing her back, trying his best to absorb her distress, sliding his hands over her to soothe her. She was hurting, and he hated the way it made him feel.

A need to be close to her, to take comfort in her as well kicked at him when she relaxed in his arms, her hands wrapping into his hair, her legs tangling with his. He was hard the moment one of those noises she made when she was turned on slipped out of her; that quiet, throaty hum that was a promise of pleasure. He hesitated. Could he take advantage of this, with both of them so emotional? Was it the right thing to do?

"Liz, we don't have to—" he tried, but she shushed him.

She pushed him onto his back, straddling his hips, and shucked her shirt. Circling her waist with his arms, he pulled her flush to him and kissed her, because she was damned near melting on top of him and he wanted to connect to that heat.

"Need this," she murmured, her hands roving low over his body.

"Then take," he murmured back. If she needed, he could give.

A flurry of hands removed their underwear, and he held her hips as she found him and sank slowly home, the feel of her surrounding him all he could handle as he slid inside her, inch by inch. She rolled her hips and folded over, nose touching his, eyes focused on him. She let out a small cry and rolled her hips again, moving against his length, wet and tight.

He wanted at that moment for this to never end, for the world to fade away, be replaced by her body sliding with his, the complete and utter surrender to her shocks of pleasure as he watched her, held her close to him, absorbing her.

"Come for me, Liz. Let it out, sweetheart," he breathed.

She braced herself on his chest, her hair a wild halo around her head, her breath fast and hot, her cheeks flushed, her back arched as she moved. Nothing had ever come close to how possessed he felt by her right now, knowing she was his in the same way.

She let out another throaty moan, covered her mouth with one hand, and shattered hard and fast, her muscles shaking. He held her as she sagged against him, rolled her over, and thrust into her the moment she was on her back under him, pulling him down to her at the same time.

"I need this too," he gasped and let go of the control he'd held on to so she could take what she needed from him. Now it was his turn; the drive to lose himself to her felt all-consuming. He slammed into her and she took it, biting his shoulder, murmuring his name over and over.

He came as she hooked her heels together over the small of his back and dug her fingernails into his shoulders, branding him, mixing delicious pain with his release. His entire body exploded with pleasure, and he surrendered everything in him to her in that moment.

"Liz," he breathed, head buried into the pillow beside her, his body shaking. "I—" He was at a loss for what to say, the unbelievable sensation of completeness unlike any endorphin rush he'd ever experienced. He thought he'd been emotionally drained after reading his father's letter, but this was overwhelming.

It could be the culmination of a day that would shake anyone's composure, or it could be he was just bone-ass tired, but he realized he was crying when she wiped at a tear with her hand, slowly sliding out from under him to fold over his now prone, boneless body.

"It's okay," she whispered.

He lifted an arm and pulled her close, his pulse in his ear, the rubbery, shaky buzz of his release rendering him unable to move. More tears slipped out, but he wasn't upset. It was the oddest feeling in the world. He felt utterly fucking amazing, but here he was, tears slipping down his face. He huffed a watery laugh out and concentrated on slowing his breathing.

"You good?" she murmured a minute or so later when he let out a big breath, expanding his chest, most of the tears done, it seemed.

"Yeah. Today was a whole lot, and we've all got a lot to think about with these letters. Decisions and ideas are swirling in my head, and I feel like I'm in the spin cycle of a washing machine, but the last thing amazing sex should do is make me—"

"Happy cry?" she supplied.

"I don't know what's wrong with me," he said. "And what exactly is a happy cry?"

"I know what's right," she whispered, not answering his other question. She wiped the last spots of wet off his cheeks, a soft smile spreading across her face.

"You do?" he replied, shifting to his side. "Tell me."

She brushed his lower lip with her thumb, and scooted up, kissing him gently. "If I tell you, you can't tell me no because it's the truth, I can feel it," she said.

"And what is that?" he asked.

"You know what you want now."

"I do?" he said, wanting her to spell it out.

"You've figured out where you belong, and I hope—" she whispered.

"Yes," he interrupted, goose bumps rising along his arm. He looked back at her, this woman who in the matter of a few weeks had challenged his heart almost as much as his brothers and the ranch had challenged his head. Both had irrevocably altered his soul.

"I don't know how it'll work yet, but there's no way I could leave this ranch. Not now," he added when she smiled widely, her eyes dancing over his with his admission.

"And why is that?" she asked.

"You are my home, Liz. I love you."

She blinked slowly, and then leaning into him, nose to nose, took a breath and held it. He hoped it wasn't the wrong thing to say. He prayed she was just absorbing it, figuring out what to say back. He knew those words weren't frivolous for her. They had been heavy in the past.

"I love you too," she blurted, and kissed him.

CHAPTER THIRTY-SEVEN

Liz sat cross-legged on the edge of Jake's bed, Jake sprawled in his underwear, asleep on top of the rumpled covers.

With the dawn peeking through the crack in the curtains, she'd finally given up the effort of sleeping any longer. She was jumbled and disoriented for a moment, then the night before came back to her and she was now thinking, putting all the pieces together so she could process.

What they had said last night was as black and white as it got. They had admitted to love, and it was still echoing in her head.

She fished Brett's letter from the back pocket of her jeans on the floor, the card bent, the letter wrinkled. It had been short and to the point. She worried the edge with her fingers, then set it on the bedside table. She'd read it once. It was enough.

He wrote that she had grown into a good woman. He instructed her to be patient with his sons, all three of them, and shepherd her mother, making sure Peony got whatever she needed.

He'd also said he loved her mother and hoped she knew that.

That was it.

It was an odd feeling, seeing his words, praise in them, purpose in their hastily scratched out lines. Odd in the sense that there was more admission of care in those words than he had ever said to her in life. She wasn't sure what to do with them.

Last night after she'd read the letter, alone at her house, she hadn't known what to do with herself either. She didn't want to be alone but was resolved to give everyone their space. Her mother had gone to bed, declining Liz's offer to read their letters together.

She'd paced her living room. She'd swept the floor in the kitchen. She'd checked her email, of which there was none. She'd flipped TV channels and contemplated going for a drive. All of it seemed trivial.

Knowing she was snooping where she shouldn't, she'd snuck into her mother's room after finally being fed up with the anxiety and nerves gnawing at her. Guiltily, she fished the letter out of her mother's sweater, which was hanging off her reading chair. It had been opened, and carefully folded back up, only slightly wrinkled.

Her mother had been sleeping, the rhythmic up and down of her breathing quiet in the massive space of the master suite. So Liz had tiptoed into the bathroom down the hall, closed the door, perched on the toilet, and opened the letter.

She hesitated, knowing she was committing some grave sin, but helpless to stop. The need to know if Brett really had cared for her mother as he said, or if it was as Peony said, indeed a business deal, had bothered her since the day her mother had mentioned it. After a moment's more hesitation, her curiosity won out over her morals.

So she dove in, deciding to ask for forgiveness afterward.

My darling Peony,

You are the strongest woman I know. When I am gone, I know you will pick up the reins and keep riding, no matter the cost. I hope you did not grieve overly much. It doesn't suit your practiced steel.

In my private study safe, which has been opened now, is a life insurance policy. You are named on it. It is set in a way to be a lump sum, but when you contact George, the man listed on the document, he can outline what options you have. I hope it will keep you well, instead of relying on the ranch to provide you an income. This is why you are not mentioned in the will. I wanted no contest for that policy if things do not pan out how I have set them up.

Jake has a letter as well, and in it I have instructed him that you are to stay here, on the ranch, under his—or Tanner's—care. I'm sure the boys have discovered all the documents in my study by now. If not, I trust it was you who finally dug through my mess and found it all.

With regards to our burial plot, I have instructed the funeral home that your stone is to be placed beside the West monument, with your own name on it and room for Elizabeth and whoever she ends up marrying, if she wants it. You are a West by marriage, but you and she deserve a spot of your own, near where I am, but not in shadow of those who came before you.

Jake. Is he the same as I described him to you? Is he strong, is he levelheaded? From what I was given as information, he is a good man, and I based my wishes from that. He took care of Heather for all those years, and I can only imagine what that meant for him. I want him to have the ranch—it is his by inheritance, but he is a West, and we are stubborn asses. If nothing else, I wish for you and the boys to know him and at least give him a picture of who I was.

I hope in all this subterfuge, he and his brothers can forgive my need for secrecy. I honestly don't know why I kept him from you all this time. I have so many failures when it comes to my sons, and I can only think the habit of keeping those failures hidden was spilling forward, I suppose. Forgive me. I asked too much of you, keeping my secrets until it was too late.

I know you are likely angry with me for not telling you about the cancer. I didn't want to endure the pleas to treat it, the long, drawn-out conversations around a sickness I could do nothing about. Better to live fully and die with dignity instead of in a hospital room, connected to machines, barely coherent from the drugs they would pump me full of. I wanted to die in my boots on the land that I loved, or at least in my own bed, asleep beside you.

I love you, Peony, more than I ever told you. I didn't know how to show you that it overwhelmed me the day I realized that your presence in my life was no longer negotiable. Your touch was soothing, your sweet smile a balm every day we were together. You understood me in ways no one else did, and were tolerant of who I was, without asking for anything in return.

What we had was comfortable and easy for me. I know I frustrated you at the best of times. I sometimes wondered why you were with me, what you saw in a grumpy, tired man who couldn't give you the romance and gentleness you deserved. I tried, in my way, to give you the security you needed instead.

This letter feels like a poor substitute, and I must find the courage to tell you in person, before I die, but I have the insurance of words on the page in case I run out of time.

You are the matriarch of this family now; take care of my sons. I know you will keep them in line.

Your husband,
~Brett

After that, Liz had snuck back in, carefully put the letter back, and, muffling the uncontrollable sobbing that had started the moment she began reading, made her way to Jake's room, slid into a T-shirt that smelled like him, and folded into his bed. She needed him; she needed to have someone hold her, touch her, tell her it would be okay. Brett had loved her mother, and all this time, her mother hadn't known.

She was angry with Brett for never telling her. She was angry with him for being a coward, a self-serving selfish prick and not facing them all with the secrets he so obviously regretted keeping. If he'd told them about his cancer, her mother could have said goodbye.

It hurt her heart to know that her mother could have felt with Brett what she was feeling for Jake, but it was denied to her. So she had let the tears out, and when Jake had finally come to bed, her need was so strong she'd just reached out to him. And he gave her what she needed.

Her mother deserved a love like that.

Jake stirred, and she turned as he rolled over, a sleepy smile on his face as he reached out and ran his hand up her arm.

"Mornin'," he said, gravel in his voice. "You need to get moving?"

She looked over at the dresser, where a small clock sat ticking away. It was almost five thirty. Soon. Horses waited for no man, nor drama.

"Not yet. Just—"

"You want to talk about it?"

She nodded and laid herself down, her head resting on his stomach as his hand went to her hair, combing it back. She closed her eyes, the comfort in that gesture swelling her heart, threatening tears. Would she ever get used to how good it would feel, these touches?

"You read your letter?" he asked quietly. "That good, huh?"

"I read Mom's too," she admitted. His hand stopped, and she opened her eyes. His eyebrows were raised, a quirked smile of amusement appearing as she did.

"She know that yet?"

He shifted and sat up against the headboard, so she did as well, and they looked at one another on the bed. He sighed and reached for her.

"You can't help yourself, can you? You have to know what's happening, know what to do." He chuckled, and kissed her forehead. "I get it. I would love to know what he wrote to Tanner and Brady. But, jeez, Liz, you couldn't have just waited and asked?"

She rested against him, and they folded in together, comfortable and easy. It was too much, and her eyes were wet with tears. She was in love, and it was overwhelmingly emotional, especially added to everything else that had happened.

"He said he loved her and—"

"Don't. That's for your mom, not me," he said. "Listen, this has been gut-wrenching for all of us, and now, with it all out in the open, we can move on. Your mom can heal, my brothers can do what they are meant to do, and I can—"

"Can what?" she asked, a nervous ping flitting through her stomach. If he went back on what he'd said last night, she was going to murder him and then fall apart.

"I can figure out where I fit in all of this," he finished.

"Right here." Liz sniffled and looked him square in the eye, deciding defiant was how she would defend any argument he came up with, damn it. "With me. With us. Here."

He was studying her again, his face serious, unreadable, that wrinkle in his forehead a copy of his brother when he was about to say something profound, or close down the conversation. She waited, anticipating some sort of noncommittal answer. Even now that they had pledged themselves to one another, she was expecting the disappointment.

"I meant what I said, Liz. I love you. There's no going back. This is it."

"It is," she echoed back, relief washing over her like a heavy stone had been lifted off her back. She barked out a laugh and rubbed at her face. "I have had enough crying for a lifetime. Shit, I'm a mess."

He laughed at that and got out of bed, stretching. When he turned to her, smiling, his hair rumpled and stubble over his jaw, she wondered how she'd gotten so damned lucky. He was hers, and he was beautiful.

"I'm hungry. Let's go make breakfast for everybody. The heavenly aroma of bacon should get 'em up, you think?" he said, and turned to head to the bathroom. Liz flopped back onto the bed, smiles replacing the tears, the worry gone.

Was this what true happiness felt like? It must be, because she couldn't describe it any other way.

CHAPTER THIRTY-EIGHT

"Pass the ketchup, please."

Jake handed it over, and Brady squirted a dollop over his eggs. Jake eyeballed his brother, wrinkling his nose. To each their own, but as he watched his perfectly fluffy, Cordon Bleu–perfected recipe utterly ruined, he held back the urge to gag.

Liz elbowed him and mouthed the word *snob* at him, and then very deliberately squirted some ketchup on hers as well when Brady passed her the bottle.

Jake raised his hands in defeat good-naturedly, seeing how ridiculous it was for him to fuss, and feigned absolute shock. "Me? A snob? If you want to ruin perfect eggs, far be it for me to—"

Tanner burst into a full-out belly laugh, and everyone joined in, including Jake. The old him would have said something and been offended. The new him? What did it matter? His family was enjoying food he had made for them, and that was enough.

"Get off your high horse, City Boy. Out here, we don't care about highfalutin recipes. We just want to eat good food," Tanner said as he picked up his fork. "This ain't steak and eggs from the Brightside Diner, but it comes close."

Peony, who was carefully buttering a piece of toast, shook her head at both of them. "You boys," she happily muttered under her breath.

Everyone was in a good mood this morning. Despite the somber letters and the heavy emotions they'd dragged up to the surface, it felt as if everyone had experienced some form of closure after what had been a month of drama, grief, and uncertainty.

Conversation eventually reverted to the day to come, and Jake got up and took his empty plate to the sink. He looked out the window, watching the flowers waving in the early morning breeze, the sky a light, hazy blue with puffy clouds in the distance. It would be warm and sunny today, but the breeze would make it less miserable. That would be good for the crew.

How interesting that he was now thinking of the weather as an important thing to keep track of. The idea of running a restaurant was so far gone, that life descending into a fog behind him.

He returned to lean on the door frame into the dining room, his family sitting around the big oak table, talking, teasing, laughing with one another. Waiting to tell everyone how he felt, and what he'd decided seemed ridiculous. Liz looked up at him and he nodded, and her eyes brightened.

"You gonna tell 'em?" she asked, and everyone turned to look at him.

"I should probably get this out in the open," he announced, raising his voice. Peony lifted her eyebrows and then smiled as she picked up her coffee cup. He caught her eyes, and she winked back at him, her smile spreading as he shook his head in mock chagrin. That woman could read him like a book.

"Okay, New York. Spill," Brady said, and tilted his chair back. "What's the plan? What'd you find in that study last night?"

"I have documents nullifying the will, pending signatures. We can have that done when I call Frank today, and the title goes back to you and Tanner by default. There's a lot of other paperwork for life insurance policies and then we'll have to revert the banking, but the solution is all in there."

"And if we don't want to change how it is right now?" Tanner replied. "Like I said last night—"

"I know what you said," Jake replied quickly, and paused, feeling the weight of his decision. "If that is what you want, Tanner, we can—"

"Are you staying to run this ranch with your brothers like your father wanted or not?" Peony asked point blank, interrupting him. She cocked her head to one side as he turned and raised his eyebrows at her. "Because, Lord above, if you don't—"

"I would like to do that, if you'll all have me."

Silence echoed through the room except for a garbled gasp from Liz, who scraped back her chair and beelined to him. She buried her head into his chest, her arms around his waist, squeezing. He dropped his arms around her.

"I don't think that's the only reason you're staying," Tanner said, and stood, walking his plate over to the sink and setting it in, before coming back to put a hand on Jake's shoulder. "You're meant to be here and run this place. With her."

Nods from Brady, and tears in Peony's eyes that she dabbed at with her napkin were all he needed to let the breath out he was holding. *There. Decision done.* It felt simple, easily made, even though it wasn't. It was a huge, fundamental change in his life, who he was, what he did for a living, but the click in his mind last night sitting in his dad's chair had been almost audible in the quiet. The admission to Liz after they had made love had acknowledged his heart and his head were both on the same page.

"I'll come see you later, after you've called Frank," Liz said, pecking Jake on his cheek as her phone buzzed and she fished it out of her jeans pocket, making a face at her screen. "I'm late out to the stable now."

Peony sat back, her coffee cradled into her chest, and watched it all, still silent. Brady was wolfing down a second helping of breakfast and finished the last bites as he too headed for the sink.

"S'good. Thanks, Jake," he mumbled as he finished chewing.

"Let's get goin'. Animals don't feed themselves," Tanner broke in, and Liz and Brady moved out to the back mudroom. The flurry of activity left the kitchen and suddenly Jake was alone with Peony.

He sat down beside her, and she leveled one of her Peony-looks that he now knew so well. He leaned on the table, fist against his cheek, propping himself up, and they appraised each other.

"Did she tell you she snuck into my room and read my letter last night?"

Jake chuckled. "Didn't tell me what was in it, but she did, yeah. How'd you know?"

"I heard her, sniffling and stomping. That girl cannot sneak anywhere, Lord love her. I put two and two together in the morning when the letter was stuffed sideways into my sweater pocket, and was slightly damp."

"She came to me last night in tears. I thought it was likely something in her own letter from Brett, but obviously it wasn't," he said, and Peony waved her hands.

"I don't mind. I figured she would've pestered me until I gave it to her anyway. Was quite a letter. Brett was never very verbose in life, but his flair for the written word was always a bit less restrained. He had a beautiful soul. I wish it hadn't been buried so deep inside him."

"He loved you, Peony," Jake replied, and she nodded, a frown flitting over her face, quickly masked, her steel back in place.

"Brett gave me a second chance at a decent life. He gave my daughter and me a place to call home, and a living. I can never repay him for that, other than to ensure his memory isn't lost."

"It won't be. I don't think it could be," Jake admitted, and sighed as he slouched, realizing that what Brett was to this place was now on his shoulders in a different way. Now it wasn't about solving a problem; it was about not letting the place fail. The work ahead of him was daunting. He hoped he could handle it.

"What is it?" Peony asked, and he smiled tiredly and shrugged.

"Just hope I can get it right, is all. This is going to be a huge change for me."

Peony leaned into him and patted his leg as she held his eye. "You have us, my dear. Besides, you're a West. It isn't in your nature to be wrong."

He let that sink in as she took a sip of coffee, then took another breath and finished her thought. "You have Liz too. And if I am not mistaken, I think that is for life."

Jake grinned then and bowed his head. "Yeah, I think so. Or as long as she'll put up with me. I'm not the easiest man out there, I can be a stubborn prick sometimes."

"As I said. You're a West, my dear. Comes with the territory," Peony quipped back. "Now, let's get moving on today's lunch, shall we? I think you have a lot of paperwork to get to."

* * *

Frank drove out just after lunch, canceling his entire afternoon to come and see for himself. As he and Jake sifted through all the documents, Frank muttered and cursed under his breath, shaking his head and groaning about how sneaky Brett had been. Ultimately, as he finished sorting it all, he looked relieved.

They decided to get the letters amended so all three brothers were equal partners. The will didn't need to be challenged with the new documents they'd found, so it was an easy fix from Frank's end.

"I wish you'd found this sooner or at least made this damned decision before now."

"You and me both, Frank. It would have solved a lot of headaches. But I also think, in some way, this entire episode was necessary, and Brett knew what it would do. It did bring me here, which was what he wanted. We'll never know why he just signed it all over to me but never once contacted me."

"Maybe he was afraid you wouldn't want anything to do with him and his plan would fail if he did," Frank mused. "As a parent, it's a constant fear of mine that I'm letting my children down. For Brett, he had regrets, and it colored everything he did, I think."

"I wish to hell we could ask him what happened with Brady," Jake said. "That's still a mystery, but we're not pushing him to talk about it. He needs time."

"That *is* a mess, isn't it? Any idea who his father is?" Frank asked, stretching his shoulders. There was nothing in any of the paperwork that indicated Brett knew. Other than the omission of Brady's name from the documents.

Peony appeared in the doorway with fresh coffee and set the steaming mugs down in front of them. She looked over the documents, which included her letter.

Frank had reluctantly asked for it because it was in Brett's writing and would prove the life insurance policy was to go to her without any further need to investigate. Peony had handed it over, and Frank had read it, wiping his eyes afterward.

"I know who it is. I've known for a long time," Peony answered as she sat across from them.

"Oh? Who?" Frank asked, leaning forward. "A dalliance with the rancher next door? Do we have any legal worries to come from it?"

"No. It's long settled, and unless Brady decides he wants it known, I've already told him I'll keep it to myself." Peony chided Frank, and then changed the subject. "Remind me to give you the stack of books I have for your wife before you go."

"We're just about done here, so why don't you grab them now?" Frank replied and *hmph*ed as she left. "She's a tease, that one."

Jake laughed as they finished the to-do list and gathered everything up. Frank had to file some forms and said he would be back out next week with the partnership documents to wrap up.

Jake walked him out to his car, and Frank stopped in the middle of the gravel driveway in front of the house, looking out around him, squinting into the bright sunlight.

"Brett was an interesting man. Known him a long time, and even I was blindsided by all this," he mused.

"I've gathered that," Jake replied. "I've come to know a little about who he was, being here, rummaging through his life. Learned more about myself than I expected too."

"It would have been a thing to see you two beside one another, standing man to man and making amends," Frank remarked.

Jake wanted that more than anything, but he had to let it go and move on. His father, in some way, had given all of them the ultimate push to set his offspring on their own path, a gift of forced independence. To have his sons make the leap instead of him and change the legacy of this place from Brett's to theirs.

He was thinking too hard, the lack of sleep catching up with him, and if he kept going he'd run himself in circles. He quirked a smile and gestured to the stables.

"In a way I've met him many times. He's in all parts of this place."

"True enough, son. True enough," Frank replied.

They walked the rest of the way to Frank's car and said their goodbyes. Jake stayed rooted in the middle of the driveway, watching the dust billow out from behind the big black Caddy, letting the breeze sighing through the pines lining the edge of the driveway and the chickadees in the nearby flower bush be the only noise in his head.

Liz appeared beside him, her hand on his back an instant calming touch, lowering the shoulders that he hadn't even realized were headed for his ears.

"I got five minutes. You done with all that paperwork?" she asked, her hand running up and down his spine. When she did that, it was always a grounding moment, the woman behind him connecting to him, understanding him. Ever since that first night in the kitchen, he'd sought it out. *Her*.

"Yeah," he said, sliding his arms around her. She leaned in, pressing her forehead to his temple, standing on her tiptoes, her chest pressing into him. That was nice, and he let out a hum of appreciation, sliding a hand down to cup her ass through her jeans.

"Whatcha wanna do?" she whispered in his ear, wiggling in his grasp.

It was too easy. All she had to do was touch him and he was putty in her hands. But two could play this game, and he growled, earning one of her throaty, whiskey-rich laughs.

He swept her up over his shoulder before she could move an inch from his grasp and strode toward her house on the other side of the turnaround, lumberjack carrying her with one arm curled around her. She squealed and kicked, shouting his name through deep belly laughs but not really trying to escape. She loved it as much as he did.

He set her down on her front porch, and she ran her hands over his chest, her eyes gleaming in happiness, her hair a mess. She was absolutely stunning, and all his, and there was nothing more he wanted to do than be with her.

"I've got more than five minutes, Liz. I've got the rest of my life," he replied, before opening the door and pulling her through.

EPILOGUE

December

Liz pushed the door closed on the stable and did up the top of her zipper on her canvas barn coat. The flurries were just starting, and it looked as if they might be snowed in by tomorrow morning, if the radar had any truth to it.

Thank god Jake had flown in yesterday. He'd gone back to New York to finally tie up loose ends there, then flown back through Ottawa where he could submit his application to "reactivate" his Canadian citizenship in person. It had been a mountain of forms and fees for that, and for the ranch.

By September, the entire place had come under joint ownership between Jake, Tanner, and Brady. The sign had been repainted to say WEST BROTHERS instead of WEST AND SONS, the paint shiny and new. They'd done a little unveiling, Peony planting early fall mums underneath in the flower box to replace the withered geraniums and petunias. Jake bought an expensive champagne to toast, that Tanner had, of course, hated, much to everyone else's amusement.

Liz had missed him when he'd flown back to New York. He'd offered to take her with him, but she'd declined. She could barely handle Calgary; the idea of being in such a big city made her hair stand on end. Maybe someday, but for now, she left that to him.

They had talked to each other every day. He'd bought her a new laptop before he'd left, and she'd learned how to use Zoom. She'd met Gordon and some of Jake's other friends via video, and they'd all been really happy for him, which made Liz feel better. She still worried he would regret his move when he went back, reminders of his life in New York more attractive than the Alberta foothills and a small town with only one coffee shop.

Jake had shown her some sights as he video-called her on his phone, giving her a tour of Manhattan and parts of Brooklyn. It had also made for some interesting conversations late at night. Liz discovered she enjoyed phone sex, as did Jake. The way he grew a bit bolder each time when he realized she was comfortable and wanted him to talk dirty made for several really intense and hot phone calls.

Her cheeks flushed thinking about it, and she kept walking up to the house along the forest pathway. The lights from the main house haloed in the falling snow, a beacon through the wintery forest, and she stopped for a moment to admire it. Every year, the first real snowfall made her think of Christmas, which was less than a month away.

Her first Christmas with Jake.

She was fretting about what to get him, unsure of what a man who had the best of everything would want. She still hadn't figured it out. Riding gear? Something more personal? It wasn't easy to decide.

"Hey, slowpoke!"

Brady jogged up beside her, Tanner just behind him, and she smiled as both of them stopped, looking in the same direction she was.

"We'll be plowing this by tomorrow morning," Tanner grumbled. "You got the salt buckets out at the stable?"

"Yeah. I sent one over to the machine shop, too, Brady," she replied, and Brady nodded silently.

Brady had changed in the past few months. He was less happy, more withdrawn, but put on a brave face whenever they asked him what was going on, hiding behind jokes and his affable nature. Ever since his paternity test had come back, he had spent more time in the stable, ridden more, but never once talked about it with either Tanner or Jake.

No one pressed him, and Liz wasn't sure that was the best idea. She'd tried several times to bring it up, but he'd shut her down and changed the subject. Her mother finally told her to leave it, because it wasn't an easy conversation for Brady right now. "Give him grace, he's hurting," she'd said.

"Dinner on?" Brady asked as they continued walking.

"Should be. I'm starving!" Liz said. "Must be the cold weather because lately I've been eating a lot more."

Tanner raised an eyebrow but didn't say anything. Brady just chuckled and slapped her arm. "Has nothin' to do with the weather, sis. I think it's all the sex. Burns calories better than ridin' I hear."

"Brady! Seriously?" she shouted, and he dodged out of her way as she went to smack him. She turned to Tanner who was trying, and failing, to hold in his own laughter, and shoved him as he clasped his hands to his chest in mock shock. "Don't blame me, he said it!" he said through his laughter.

"Screw you both." She giggled and chased them, scooping up some fresh snow and attempting to stuff it down Brady's collar, throwing the rest at Tanner. By the time they got to the house, they were all out of breath, covered in snow, and laughing like hyenas.

They clambered up the steps into the back mud porch, and as they filed into the kitchen, the aroma of beef wafted out at them. Liz's stomach rumbled on cue, and as she looked up she could see Jake was expertly sharpening a knife, his sleeves rolled up, shoulders moving in perfect unison.

She stopped, drinking him in, and he looked up, saw her, and smiled.

Life was perfect.

* * *

"We're all done," she said as she closed the dishwasher door. Jake threw the dishcloth into the sink and pulled her over to him by her hand, swinging her onto the counter and stepping between her legs.

"We are?" he drawled, raising an eyebrow and leaning in to kiss her neck. "I'm thinkin' I'd like to get started."

She laughed as he tickled her neck and put her arms around his, blocking his access. "Stop it, Jake."

"Never. You are too delicious," he countered, and tried to worm his way in. She blocked him again and laughed as he growled and burrowed in through her hair.

Leaning back, he caught her eye, all traces of play gone, his eyes studying hers. She tilted her head and looked back. "What?"

"You are so fucking beautiful when you laugh," he murmured.

"Um, thanks?" she replied, taking him in. He was thinking. "I know that look, Jake. What is going through that gorgeous head of yours?"

"Ah, fuck it," he muttered, and pulled her down from the counter.

"Fuck it? What—" she said, almost tripping to keep up with him as he towed her through the house. The giant Christmas tree was twinkling in the darkened living room, the scent of the enormous fir tree sharp and pleasant as they entered. Her mother had insisted on a big tree this year, and had decorated it herself, much to Liz's surprise, because normally that would have been too much up and down on the ladder stool for her joints.

Jake pulled her over by the tree and held her close to him, the multicolored bulbs casting festive oval blobs of light over the entire room.

"Listen, I know it isn't Christmas yet, but I want to give you something now."

"I don't have your present yet, Jake, I mean—" He stopped her with a kiss, and she let him, the feel of his lips on hers always the best way to make her lose her train of thought or stop her argument cold. It was also really nice, loosening her stomach, his big body close to hers, suggesting something else entirely. She wondered if it would be prudent to steal in later and make love under the tree, or if that would be a bit too much for Tanner and Brady to handle, because she had a very hard time being quiet when she and Jake made love.

It would be almost worth it to do it anyway, after Brady's earlier teasing.

"Give me a sec," Jake said.

He reached into the tree and pulled out a box, wrapped in fire-red paper, with a fluffy white bow on top. He held it between them, and she looked down at it, then back up at him.

It was small, balanced on the palm of his hand, and Liz stopped being able to breathe.

That was a jewelry box.

Her heart racing, she picked it up out of his hand and looked back at him, eyes searching his, hoping he would give away what was inside.

"Open it."

She slid the bow off, then pried the ends of the wrapping paper open. A black velvet box with a domed top slid out. She stared down, her brain taking a moment to catch up with what she knew she was holding.

This was it; he was going to ask her to marry him. She wanted to both run away and dive into his arms at the same time, the contents of that box and what he was about to say exciting and scary in the same breath. She'd been completely blindsided by Darren when he'd proposed to her very publicly at a hockey game in Calgary.

This felt ten times more profound, and personal.

What should she do, or say? Was she ready for this? She carefully flipped the lid, holding it between them. A set of silver bands winked at her. There was no diamond on the thinner one, no jewels. It was faceted, and brilliantly polished. Simple. Elegant.

Exactly something she would wear. She wasn't into fancy jewelry, because wearing a big ring on the job was asking for an accident. She'd never worn the solitaire Darren had given her. This would be perfect.

"What is—" she managed before he got down on one knee, holding a hand out to her.

"Liz, the day I met you, you jostled my world. I don't think I could have stayed away from you if I tried. This entire wild roller-coaster ride has not only given me a family, but a life I never imagined," he said, his voice wavering slightly, his hand shaking.

"Jake—" She froze, dumbfounded, the ring box and rings clenched in her hand.

"Not done," he interrupted. He gestured to her to hand him the box. She did, and he wiggled the smaller ring out of the holder.

"I know it's fast. I know you've done this part before, so have I. I don't want to wait any more, and life is too short to worry about making sure everything is in place. I want to break the rules."

"Me too," she murmured.

"I want to be yours," he said, and cleared his throat, his own nervousness showing. She put her hand to her mouth as he grabbed her left hand and looked up at her. "Let me love you, Liz. Forever."

Tears burst from her eyes as she nodded, unable to say anything in the torrent of feelings that his proposal had pulled from her. He loved her, she knew that, and she loved him just as much. More than she could have ever thought possible to love another person.

It was an easy thing to say yes to this man. She'd been saying yes to him since the day they had kissed in her office. He stood up and slid the ring on her left ring finger. It fit perfectly.

"I had it sized for you. It's—" He stopped, swallowing, obviously emotional.

"It's what?" she asked, holding it up to the light and then touching his chest. "Tell me."

"When we searched Brett's study I found cigar boxes full of buckles and jewelry in the safe. Inside one of them was this band set. This one and that thicker one, sized for a man. The stamp on the bottom of the ring box was a local jeweler in Brightside, so I went in with it, to find out more. The old jeweler was still alive and in the store, if you can believe it. He's got to be about a hundred years old now. When he saw it, he knew exactly who it was for, remembering Brett and the fuss he made about it being exactly to his specifications. The jeweler made several rings for him over the years, the last one your mother's. But this one, and the one I will put on—"

She looked at it again and gasped, interrupting him. "No . . . for your—"

"Yeah. This set was for him and my mother, apparently. In my letter, he said he'd never gotten around to asking her, and then apparently he cheated on her."

"Maybe he did ask, and she said no?" Liz offered, looking at her hand, the facets winking in the light from the tree. It was perfect, so much more valuable to her than one he would have bought from the store. It had history, a tie to this place, even if the story was sad.

"It doesn't matter, in the end. I decided it was too significant to be sold. Their story was cut short, but ours is just beginning. I knew what I wanted to use these for the moment the jeweler showed me my father's name on the copy of the bill of sale. To give them a better ending."

She reached and took the box out of his hand, yanking the larger band out of the folds, and grabbed his left hand, sliding it on carefully. It fit perfectly, like it was meant for him.

"There. Done," she murmured. "Like you said, why wait?"

"Was that a full-on yes, now?" he asked, flexing his hand, looking down at it. He smiled at her while he took the empty box back and tossed it under the tree, weaving his fingers between hers, pulling her closer to him.

Liz looked up at him, awestruck that this man would be hers, officially forever, and giddiness replaced the heavy emotion. That he would be willing to let the painful history of his mother and father go, to replace it with good memories, with her, melted her heart completely.

It also gave her ideas of how she could reciprocate such a romantic gesture. She quirked an eyebrow, pushing him back to the couch beside the Christmas tree, and they fell onto it together.

"What are you doing?" he murmured, his arms sliding around her, pulling her into him. "You aren't thinking—"

"Damn straight, Mr. West," she drawled, and kissed him.

ACKNOWLEDGMENTS

I think I have to begin the acknowledgments for this book with teenager me, who dreamed about making horses her first career because four-year-old her sat on a small fuzzy Shetland pony named Suzy and instantly felt whole. Horses were my world for a time, and this book is what it is because of that.

I need to acknowledge the people from where I grew up and with whom I worked over the years, who taught me what it is to love the land, to raise the animals who form the backbone of the tangible, physical world that is a working ranch. The dedication to the life and the skill of the calling is romantic and aspirational, but also very hard work. This book's inspiration comes from their passion.

My father was my copilot and business partner for years as we experienced running a stable together. I'm thankful for it all, and I hope I have woven that good, bad, and soul-rewarding essence into West Line Ranch. Our Locust Grove Farm was my oasis, and our legacy. Thank you for building a little barn and kickstarting an education for your daughter that has meant everything.

But it isn't all about horses.

As I said in my dedication, I found a home where I least expected it, just like Jake and Liz. Royce, you are the inspiration for Jake, your big shoulders and effortless grin the exact thing I pictured when he came alive in my mind. Thank you for being my muse, for the support, the encouragement, and above all, the love you have for your family, which eclipses everything. This book is for you, to remind you that amazing things happen when we do it together. I love you.

This book is also for William and Carrie. Every time we go to a bookstore, you look for my books and get excited when you find copies. You are my cheerleaders, and I do most everything in my life for you. The two of you changed me irrevocably for the better the day you were born.

This would not be acknowledgments without talking about the team at W by Wattpad Books. Fiona Simpson, you understood what I wanted to say in this story, you "got" the characters, and understood that the ranch is a character as well as a setting. You have given me an editing journey that has been an absolute dream and pushed me to dig deeper into my characters' brains. Also to Rebecca, who during the copyedit of this book was likely muttering the words *towards* and *clipped* well after she had finished. Thank you for your keen eye and patient editing.

Deanna McFadden—who is in the business of making writer's dreams come true—I simply bow.

There are so many other team members to thank I'll be concise by saying that over the years of working with the passionate people at Wattpad, I am grateful for the experiences and the enthusiasm from all of you.

Friends are the backbone for a writer to keep going. I must mention the WritersConnX and Ottawa Romance Writers communities—I know I've been absent, but I would be remiss in not mentioning your role in keeping me connected. Sabrina Blackburry and Tamara Lush, strong women with amazing author careers of their own who have been both sounding boards and a source of levity when I needed it—thank you. Becka, my talented and steadfast friend. I don't know if I have told you what your support has meant to me. From camping shenanigans to using your skills to make me look nice in pictures, I am grateful for you.

I'll end with a story about the first horse I ever owned.

She was wholly unsuitable, had terrible conformation, was wild and unbroken, and I loved her with a ferocity that I couldn't explain from the moment we met. Experts told me she was dangerous, too much for a new, inexperienced horse owner. She proved everyone wrong because once we understood each other, she became the best horse I have ever owned.

It was fate that we drove past Keith Sheil's place all those years ago and I pressed my nose to the window and shouted *Dad! Stop! She's beautiful!* when I spotted a cream and brown-spotted Appaloosa, her tricolored tail filled with burrs, standing ankle deep in the mud.

It was her solid dependability that eventually moved her on to teach so many other young riders. It was a joy when she came home to us to live the rest of her days, having earned her retirement a thousand times over.

Flash, thank you for everything. You are the inspiration for Dolly, even though you didn't like peppermints.

~Caro

ABOUT THE AUTHOR

Caroline Richardson sat on a pony for the first time at the age of four and never looked back. Years later, she turned her passion for horses into her first career. Now considered a "recovering horse girl," Caroline writes horses and the characters who love them into her books, relishing the chance to revisit the rural, hard-working way of life that has shaped who she is today.

She lives in Ottawa, Ontario, Canada with her husband, two teenage children, and an out of control monstera plant collection. Find her on social media as @carolinerichardsonauthor on popular platforms and @mustangsabby on Wattpad.

Ready for more from the West Line Ranch?

Read on for a sneak peak of

WESTERN CONNECTION

CHAPTER ONE

Muttered grumbling from the changing room in the menswear shop made Brady grin ear to ear; his brother was completely out of his element as he wrestled himself into a suit.

"This should be entertaining," Jake said, barely holding in a snort when a *thump* against the side of the wall shook the curtain, followed by a stream of swear words.

Brady couldn't help it, and burst into laughter as Tanner muttered a, "Goddamn stupid suit, where the fuck are the buttons?"

"You okay in there, Tan? Need some help with the big boy pants?" Jake managed through his own laughter.

"Fuck you, asshole," came the clipped reply.

The clerk currently circling Jake with a floppy tape measure raised a bushy gray eyebrow and looked over at them both.

"He doesn't wear suits often, I take it?" he said around the pins in his mouth.

"He lives in Carhartt overalls and Wranglers," Brady replied, tugging at the lapels of the dark-gray suit jacket he'd tried on, the tag scratching at the back of his neck, the sleeves dangling a bit too far over his fingers. None of them wore suits often, if at all.

He thumbed over a chalk mark that the clerk had made on where to pin the cuffs, anticipating taking it off once Tanner was done with the lone changing room. He'd never admit it, but he'd struggled with the different clasps and buttons on the pants too. But Brady would wear whatever the hell Liz wanted him to if it made her happy on her wedding day.

So really, he could put up with a nice suit, even if it was scratchy.

As Tanner emerged from the change room looking far better than he should in the same dark-blue suit that Jake had selected, Brady reflected that a lot had changed since Brett had died and chaos had descended over the ranch. This included Tanner's new tolerance for finicky tasks, even if they were pushing the envelope by forcing him to try on formalwear in the suit store at the Southcentre Mall, all the way in Calgary.

It felt like a lifetime ago, all that chaos.

Most of that change was because of Jake. A half brother they never knew about and an abrupt change in ownership at the ranch had upended their entire world last summer. It could have been a soap opera script, complete with fistfights, cattle thieves, and drunken tirades, the way it had all played out.

Tanner scowled and stuffed his hands in the pockets of the suit pants, testing the depth. Brady was thankful that Jake had bargained Peony down from fancy tuxedos. New suits were a far less expensive alternative to losing their deposit on rentals, because Brady could picture Tanner in a black tux with a bow tie driving a tractor, trying to get morning chores done before the ceremony, and Jake having to explain manure stains when they returned them.

Brady had conceded as they drove in that they needed new suits when Tanner had asked why he couldn't just wear the one he had. He and Tanner had last worn theirs at the arraignments and sentencing for the cattle thieves last fall, forced into them by Peony's chastising *Look professional, boys!* Brady's suit had been uncomfortably tight; Tanner's wasn't much better, and was possibly older than their oldest bull.

So here they were.

Jake was more at home in suits and ties, and was relaxed as he stood for measurements, casually adjusting the lapels on the jacket, critically glancing over his reflection in the mirrors. He'd mentioned—after he had bargained Peony down—that he wanted a new suit anyway. His jackets were all too tight across the shoulders and down his arms now.

Fresh Alberta foothills air and the past nine months learning the ropes on the ranch was good for him. They were slowly working the city out of him, as Brady had joked one too many times for his own good. But it was all in good fun, because Jake fit right into the ranch, and Brady couldn't picture them running the place without him now.

"Gonna have to bust out the custom sizes for those guns," he remarked as Jake hopped down from the platform in front of the mirror.

"Ha-ha," Jake replied.

"Liz is working you too hard in the stable," Brady teased. "You're not spending nearly enough time with the paperwork like you should."

"Well . . ." Jake wiggled his eyebrows as he shrugged off the jacket and handed it to the clerk, who slid a hanger inside it and set it on a coatrack. Jake grinned widely as he drawled "She's a taskmaster . . . and a mornin' person, if you know what I mean."

Brady groaned and covered his eyes. "I did *not* need to know that. She's like a sister to me, damn it!"

Tanner huffed, obviously not impressed with how long this was taking, and sent a peevish look to Jake and the clerk, who was waiting for him. As he tugged on his pants, the pissed-off look on his face spoke volumes about what he thought of the whole process.

"Get up there, Tan, let's get you measured, yeah?" Brady said, slapping Tanner on the back. "You look nice, brother."

"These pants ride up my ass, and I can't move in this jacket."

Brady grinned at him, which earned him a further disgruntled sigh and an eye roll. He pulled out the collar of Tanner's jacket, which had folded under, and smoothed it down, adjusting the shoulders while Tanner gritted his teeth.

"Stop fussing, it's not like you'll be driving a tractor in it," Brady said.

"It itches."

"You're fine, just need to get used to it. Maybe you'll find someone crazy enough to put up with you, and when you get married, you can wear it again!" Brady teased, deciding to poke the grumpy bear just a little. It was too easy, really.

The look of horror that crossed Tanner's face made it worthwhile, and Brady started to laugh again. The clerk was chuckling as well, looking between Tanner and Jake.

"Well, I'll tailor it so it's a bit roomier for comfort, son. Looks like you picked a different lapel style as well, which I think suits. Wouldn't want the bride confusing herself between twins, now, would we?"

Jake snorted a laugh and said, "If Liz can't tell us apart, we're all doomed!"

"They're not twins. Different moms," Brady explained when the clerk gave him a confused look. "The bride is their dad's widow's daughter from her first marriage. No blood relation."

The clerk hummed under his breath, the confusion even more evident as he tried to make sense of the family tree at that point, looking between them. He beckoned Tanner to the mirror to take his measurements and smiled politely at him as Tanner's forehead wrinkled as he eyeballed the platform like it might swallow him.

"You have to stand on that so he can check your pant length," Jake said, pointing. "Up you get, cowboy."

"Won't take long. Just need a few notes," the clerk said crisply, and Tanner nodded curtly as he stepped up.

"Sorry. Not used to this."

The clerk crouched to adjust and pin Tanner's pant leg without another word.

Brady sorted over some ties splayed in a circle on a nearby table as the room went quiet. He let his mind wander as he browsed, the reds and blues and greens all jumbled together in a pleasing mosaic of silk.

It was an honest mistake for the clerk to make thinking Jake and Tanner were twins, because if you looked at them side by side, they were spitting images of each other. Tall, wide shouldered, dark hair, dark eyes, and that ruggedness that made you think they could chop down trees with their bare hands.

Just like Brett.

But their temperaments were vastly different. Jake had grown up in New York City, away from his father's influence, while Tanner had taken after Brett lock, stock, and stoic barrel.

"And you're the friend?" the clerk glanced over at him after a few moments, obviously pointing out he was *not* a tall, dark-haired bulldozer. Brady topped out at six feet with light hazel eyes and rusty auburn hair instead. The hair he got from his mother, but the rest . . .

"He's our baby brother," Jake replied, nodding to Brady, then thumbing at Tanner. "He keeps this one and me from killin' each other."

Brady's body went taut at that statement, but he didn't correct Jake. He was no more Jake's brother than a pig could fly.

He wasn't a true West.

In all the mess of Brett dying and Jake coming into their lives, Brady had found out that Brett wasn't his father. Veronica, his mother—Tanner's as well—had had an affair after Tanner was born. In the paternity testing they'd all done last year to certify Jake was who he said he was, it had been a surprise when Brady's results came back as a zero chance of Brett being his biological dad.

Strangely, he'd always had a niggle of doubt that Brett was his father. They had been like oil and water as Brady had gotten older, never seeing eye to eye, Brett often coming down on him harder than Tanner or ignoring Brady's successes. It had been a tough pill to swallow that Brett had played favorites.

Now he knew why.

He'd thought about it a lot since the results had come in, and as he turned it over in his head, he concluded that Brett had known. He had known exactly who Brady's father had been but had raised him anyway, the entire thing a big secret in the family that had never once been spilled.

Peony had approached him the day they found out and bluntly asked him if he wanted to know who it was. He said he didn't, even though he had a very good idea and wanted to shout at her for it. It irked him that even Peony knew, had been privy to secrets about who he really was. He didn't let the anger through and abruptly walked away from her before he said something he'd regret and upset her. He stuffed his own shit down like he always did, because the ranch had bigger things to worry about.

A few days after that, he'd apologized to Peony—which she'd told him to stuff because there was nothing to apologize for—and then asked her if he was right in his notion.

She'd confirmed it, and now, here he was, still holding that information to himself, unsure what to do with it.

"Brady. You gonna go change?"

Brady looked up from the ties to Jake, back in his jeans and button-down shirt. He'd fallen down the damned hole thinking about all of it, zoning out like an empty-headed idiot. The entire problem was always there, just below the surface, popping up more and more often to pick at his anxiety. There wasn't a day that he didn't think about his real father, and what he should do about it.

"Yeah, yeah," he replied, and stepped into the change room. "We need to get Grumpy a beer for putting up with us."

Jake laughed at that and turned to talk to Tanner while Brady stepped behind the curtain.

He needed a drink too.

Ten minutes later, as they were leaving the store, Tanner slapped Brady on the arm. "Isn't that Keith?"

Brady looked to where Tanner was pointing. Sitting on one of the fancy mall benches not far from where they were was a stout gray-haired man, his equally as gray beard trimmed close to his jaw. The familiar set of his shoulders and the way one leg splayed out farther than the other was instantly recognizable.

"Yeah, it is," he said, his chest constricting. It was Keith all right. It had been nine years since he'd retired as their stable manager, and several since Brady had seen him at all.

A beautiful woman was beside him, her long, glossy dark hair shining in the mall lighting as she tossed it over her shoulder. She was holding a striped shopping bag and a purse, and she and Keith were obviously talking about something funny, because she was laughing while he spoke, his hands waving in the air like they always did when he told a story.

Then Brady noticed her scrubs top under her jacket. A care worker? His stomach dropped as he took in the shiny metal walker parked squarely in front of the older man. He'd missed it upon first seeing him.

Keith looked up as if sensing them, and Brady met his eye. The recognition was there, and for a moment, neither of them moved. Then the older man stood shakily and waved them over with a smile that went from ear to ear.

Brady hesitated as Tanner and Jake started over, both of them waving back. Tanner looked behind him with a questioning glance.

"You comin'?" he asked.

Of course, Tanner had no idea why Brady would hesitate. Brady needed to get his shit together and deal with everything that was swirling inside of him the moment he laid eyes upon the man.

"Yeah," Brady replied, steeled himself with a steady breath in and out, and made his way over to greet his father.

* * *

Caitlin nervously eyed the three imposingly handsome men standing in front of her. She rose to her feet with Keith, one hand automatically on his walker so it wouldn't slip as he balanced on it, her other hand out to his arm in case he needed help as he straightened. When she shifted her attention from Keith to them, her breath caught and the spiral of anxiety that had been her constant companion for the past year or so rose up.

"Caity, my dear, I'd like you to meet the West boys. This one over here, I'd hazard, is Heather's boy all grown up, and this is Tanner. The one beside him is—"

"Brady," the least tall of the trio interjected, hands in his pockets. His eyes had not left Keith since they'd walked up, but they flicked to Caitlin, and she caught the worry in them before he looked away.

"This is Caitlin, my home nurse," Keith added, and she nodded, trying to smile. *Be polite, don't let on that you are three seconds away from melting down for no apparent reason.*

"Hello," Jake said, nodding at her before turning his attention to Keith. "You're right, I'm Jake. You would've known me as Henry, I think? I'm Heather's." Jake stepped in and shook Keith's hand. "You're our former stable manager, right?"

"I am indeed, son. My god, it was like Brett used a photocopier. Look at you," he exclaimed, and if it was possible, beamed wider. He was almost animated with how happy he was to see these men, and she focused on that instead of the response she'd had to them. She turned her attention back to Keith and put her hand on his shoulder. "Keith, you should sit again."

"All right, all right," he said, and eased himself back to the bench, sighing as he did. Brady, whom she had decided was the least intimidating one of the bunch, smiled uneasily and sat down beside him.

"What did you do to yourself?" he asked.

"It's my hip. It wore out. They gave me a titanium one instead," Keith said, knocking on his hip gently with his fist.

Tanner's biceps bulged as he crossed his arms, and she tamped back on the anxiety that caught her breath when she noticed. She backed up beside Keith, and sat on his other side, her legs shaking slightly from the tension that was taking over her body.

These men are not him, she repeated over and over in her head. As silly as she felt with her reaction, little spikes of adrenaline across her skin tightening her chest were so familiar she couldn't remember what it was like not to experience it whenever she met unfamiliar men, especially ones who were as big as these three were. They were simply strangers, and she didn't have to be afraid of them. She wasn't in danger and hadn't been in danger for a while now.

She took a few cleansing breaths as silently as possible, the tightness easing as she reminded herself over and over in her head that she was fine.

"All those years getting thrown off horses caught up with you, didn't it?" Tanner replied, his smile quirked to one side, humor in his voice. "I remember when you busted your back. How's that doin'?"

"It healed up nice. Only twinges when we're about to get rain," Keith replied with a chuckle and smiled back. "Caity, I watched these two boys grow up, and I remember that one when he was still in his nappies."

Keith pointed to Jake, who blushed and ran a hand through his hair. It immediately disarmed him, as had Tanner smiling. She glanced over at Brady, who was still sitting beside Keith. He'd gone silent, his face serious, almost sad. Their eyes met again, and he smiled tightly. Something was bothering him. He was about as tense as she was.

It clicked a moment later, and she was able to calm herself further. *The West boys.* Right. These were good men.

She'd heard a few stories now from Keith about the West boys, how much trouble they'd gotten into, how they'd grown into strong, fine men. Stories that involved horses more often than not and invariably ended with someone getting into some sort of trouble. More stories about Brady, now that she thought about it, and none about Jake. Keith had been at the ranch there a long time. Obviously, they had lost touch with one another, since they were now catching up.

She forced herself to clasp her hands casually in her lap, trying her best to mirror their effortless ease. She needed to get better with these knee-jerk initial reactions that sent her into a very dark place in the moment and left her tired afterward. Her therapist said it was important to try pushing through them, even if it didn't work. Be present, take interest. Keep the conversation light, and it would get easier every time, the panic response less and less.

She took a deep breath and joined the conversation. "So, you didn't grow up on the ranch, then." She turned her attention to Jake, and his eyes swiveled to her. They were a gorgeous, warm brown. Kind and full of happiness.

"I left when I was around three, so I'm told, with my mom. We went to New York City. I came back last year when my dad died, and, well, liked it so much I stayed."

"I was sorry to hear he'd passed." Keith sighed. "How is Peony? It can't have been easy for her, losin' him like that."

"She's handled it well. Keeping us all in line." Brady spoke up and gestured at Jake. "She's neck-deep in wedding prep with Liz. This big lunk is marrying her."

Keith let out a happy laugh and clapped his hands to his legs. "Little Lizzie, gettin' married? Well, that is good news. I did hear she broke it off with that doctor. Never thought he was right for her, but then, you young folks will do what yer gonna," he mused. "No surprise. She's got the guts to take on a West man like her momma did."

They all laughed at that, and Brady shoved to his feet, his hands deep in his pockets as he did. Caitlin knew the look on his face, the nervous tic, the tense posture. She'd seen it on children of sick parents time and time again. Sons and daughters who needed to have that serious talk but didn't know where to start.

It was obvious he cared deeply about the older man and was perhaps regretful of their time apart.

"Listen, we need to get goin', Lord knows what waits for us when we get back," Tanner said, eyes darting to his brother. "Keith, you need to come visit us. It's been too long."

"I surely should. Once I'm on my feet better, I will. Peony can make some of her rhubarb cake to ease my pains. Harry still about?"

"You bet. His son joined us full time a bit back. He'd be happy to see you too," Tanner said.

"Lord, I haven't seen Rowan since he was just a boy. He was a hellion then," Keith said, with a chuckle.

More laughter and agreement from the men, and Keith stood again, this time without any shake, which Caitlin thought might be on account of the happiness practically beaming from him. Brady leaped to help him, and she blinked as she saw emotion cross both their faces when his hand gently grasped Keith's bicep. They both cleared their throats and Brady let go, Keith steadying on his walker.

There was more to the story of their relationship than just a former employee, and her heart twinged to think of what had caused that hurt. Her original anxiety at being faced with these men was gone, and she breathed easily as they all shook hands with her charge, promising to stay in touch.

She hurriedly rummaged in her purse for a pen and paper, an idea popping into her head. A chewed-up Bic in hand, she found an old receipt and scrawled Keith's phone number and address on the back, then picked up her shopping bag, screwed up her courage, and touched Brady on his arm.

You are okay, this is fine, she repeated in her head as she fought the instinct to pull away and run. Even though she wasn't exactly scared of him, it was a very big deal to touch another man, and her body knew it.

He halted, a curious look on his face. Her stomach did a small flip as she looked into his eyes.

"Hi." Her voice wavered, and she took a deep breath, holding out the receipt. "I have something for you."

"What's this?" Brady asked.

"He doesn't get many visitors. I can see how much you all mean to him. I thought maybe—"

"He's by himself?"

She nodded. "I think he's lonely."

Brady took the receipt, looking down at it and then back at her. There was that emotion again, and she patted his arm, surprising herself at the urge to reassure him.

"I think you care about him too?" she said.

"He was a big part of our lives. We lost track of him, and I regret that," he replied, carefully folding the scrap of paper into his jeans pocket, his eyes darting to his brothers and Keith ahead of them. "I . . . maybe I should come see him soon."

With that, she removed her hand from his arm. She might've just overstepped. Keith was her favorite patient at the moment, and she wanted to help him in any way she could. It was hard to see him alone the way he was; he was such a wonderfully warm and charismatic man.

Keith had no children, no wife. A few friends would drop by for coffee once in a while, he'd said when she'd asked, but that was about it. This was an opportunity to give him some social support she knew he needed.

They caught up to Keith and the other two men a moment later. Brady caught her eye as they all said their goodbyes. His eyes were intelligent, flecked hazel, and she rather liked the color; they reminded her of her mother's green and brown polished jasper pendant. His gaze lingered on her for a moment, and she knew her face had flushed from the scrutiny.

"Thanks," he said quietly to her, and she nodded.

She put her arm through Keith's as they left, processing the gamut of what she'd seen. There was a lot being unsaid. Not her place to pry, but it almost felt like a reunion of family, not randomly bumping into old friends.

"Ready to head home yourself?" she asked brightly. "You've already done had quite a bit of walking, we don't want to overdo it, and it's a bit of a drive back to Brightside."

Keith nodded, the same emotion she'd seen from Brady in him. She squeezed his arm, and he took a deep breath and plastered on his big smile, the one she liked most from him, because it meant he was happy.

"My dear, yes. I'm glad we came out today. But I'm mighty tired now."

They turned and headed for the opposite exit, where Caitlin had parked his truck. He turned once as they shuffled along, watching as the three men pushed through the glass doors back out into the sunshine.

"They mean a lot to you, don't they?" she said.

"More than you can imagine, my dear," he replied, and patted her hand resting on his forearm. "But it was a long time ago, and another life. They've done well. Proud of them. All three."

He smiled again, this one tinged with sadness, and she didn't press further, knowing he wanted to shake it off, as he did when he had something hard to do. She'd seen that many times when she pushed him through a new exercise or stretch, and she admired his tenacity to keep going, even when it hurt.

"Well, then let's go home and I'll make you some coffee before I go," she said brightly.

"A sound plan," he agreed. "I could use one."